Those Bones at Goliad

a Texas Revolution novel

sequel to *How Far Tomorrow*

Judith Austin Mills

Other books by Judith Austin Mills

How Far Tomorrow: remembering the Georgia Battalion in Texas (Plain View Press, 2011)

Accidental Joy: a streak of poetry (Plain View Press, 2014)

Those Bones at Goliad

a Texas Revolution novel

sequel to *How Far Tomorrow*

Judith Austin Mills

Plain View Press, LLC   www.plainviewpress.net
1101 W 34th Street, Suite 404 Austin, TX 78705

ISBN: 978-1-63210-013-9
Library of Congress Control Number: 2015945784

Cover art: *Sycamore in Goliad State Park* by Karen Boudreaux
Maps of Texas and Southern Region by Karen Boudreaux
Cover design by Pam Knight

Note: This book is a work of fiction. While people and events connected to the Texas Revolution were researched for reasonable accuracy, all characters are fleshed out according to the author's imagination. For authenticity, many names and dates included are those about which historians mostly agree. The author claims no special knowledge of any nineteenth-century individual's heart or everyday actions.

Monument to Joanna Troutman. Photo by author.

The Texas State Cemetery in Austin, Texas: Honoring the Georgia girl who first crafted the Lone Star flag, the Joanna Troutman monument is not far from the headstone of her friend, early Texas general Hugh McLeod. In the same neighborhood, the French Legation, built for the attaché in 1841, still stands. A few blocks downhill on Congress Avenue is a statue of Angelina Eberly firing a cannon to defend the republic's archives.

Contents

Truth in the Telling

March 27 of 1836 is still a lost day from the Texas fight for independence. Three hundred and forty-two American captives, who thought they were marching to deportation, were shot outside Goliad by order of Santa Anna. Their names, later etched onto one monument or another, are mostly forgotten. Only a few from the doomed army eventually made it home. No trauma counselors awaited them.

Their stories are rarely told: an older soldier returning at last to his three children in Georgia; a sixteen-year-old battalion volunteer who narrowly escaped; a less fortunate recruit among the first to die. Women rallied too at the heart of the new republic—the Southern girl crafting a lone-star banner; the bold Austin innkeeper defending the capital's honor.

Also imagined here is the peace-lover in cruel times—one man whose troubled childhood left him without thirst for battle, but whose quest for a mended heart drew him into the Texas wilderness.

Strangers Converge

Map of Southern U.S. Region, 1835

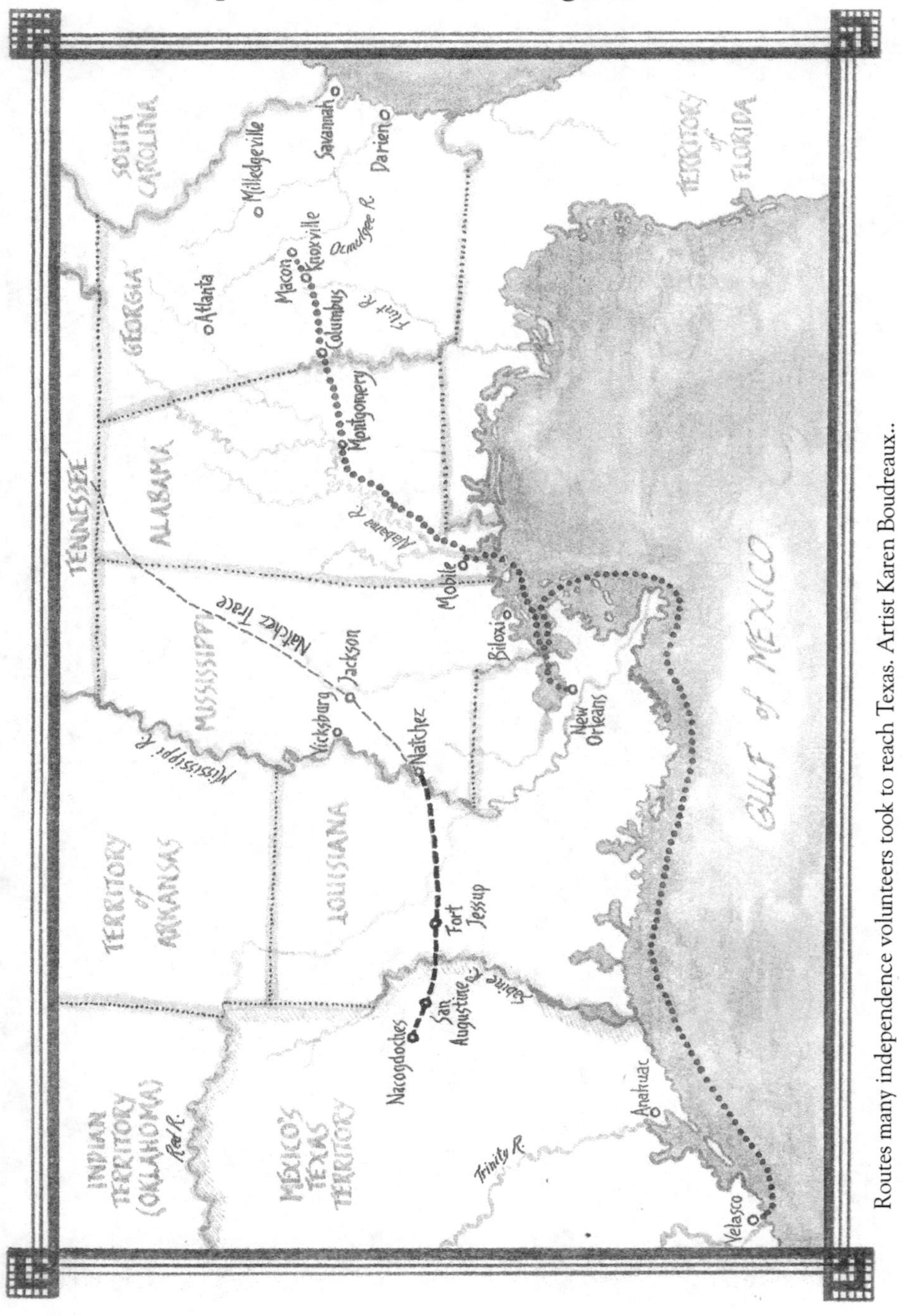

Routes many independence volunteers took to reach Texas. Artist Karen Boudreaux..

1821 Natchez, in the new state of Mississippi

1   Voices in the Dark

The innkeeper wound his way past trunks deposited on the porch. Shivering in damp sleeves, he stepped to the driftwood railing where he could lean and call out to his helper. A boy no more warmly dressed clung to the last pier post over darkening water. The youngster held his lookout piece aloft and watched for one bend in the Mississippi to yield a final flatboat of travelers.

"Head home, Shelby, or up to Mrs. Weeks' place!"

"I got a feelin'!"

"Hope you're wrong!" Mr. Todd didn't know how his wife was going to stretch supper for their lodge guests as it was. "We're full up!"

"If there's another boat, Mrs. Ann will take in some."

"The piano just started!" Music from the tavern was a regular evening alarm bell. The innkeeper worried about any young person outdoors after dark. A pistol went off over near Silver Street, Todd thought, or some drunk fool was pitching gunpowder into a fire. "Head in somewhere before your face freezes or gets shot off!" The man hollered something else to Shelby Whitmire, but the north wind swallowed his words. Daylight would be gone in an hour.

"Thomas will bring a blanket," Shelby said to himself, shuddering. It was rare for a December sundown in Natchez to turn this cold. His teeth were starting to chatter, but he didn't want to quit his lookout. He liked feeling the spyglass leather up around his eye, just one small circle of warmth. Thomas' mother had recognized that the hired boy was mature enough to borrow one of her late husband's effects.

Sometimes, just thinking about Mrs. Ann made the eleven-year-old shiver.

When a shadowy platform at the bend edged into view, Shelby waited with the viewing tool up close until he could count the huddled travelers. The porch at Todd Inn might accommodate more baggage. First overflow would go on to Knight House, a close neighbor and fair protection against the lawless paths under-the-hill. But Shelby thought the count went beyond what either lodge could take.

He set out at a run in the fading light and kept his feet well on the main path. Structures along the lower Natchez shore stood on pilings, and anyone wise enough to aim for the inland bluff stayed clear of ground-level shadows. Weather beaten shelters crowded one another on either side of the strand's rough thoroughfare. Underneath buildings, white men and sometimes Creek Indians threw dice or set roosters down to battle. Trap doors were common in the raised saloons, and no one born in Natchez would chalk up to mere rumor the stories of ambush and disappearance.

Since losing her husband to yellow fever, Ann Weeks regularly lent her cart at the bottom of the bluff for any civilized travelers that might be staying longer than a night in Natchez. The third street parallel to the river ended on an incline, a steep road leading straight up to the tamed sections of town where the mother and her children lived. Small commercial carts and wagons went up to and down from the top of the hill at all hours. Shelby was relieved to find the Indian worker Apokta at the reins of the widow's cart. His pay was half a fare. Shelby had never seen the driver throw away a dollar for a swig of Madeira, the way his own father once did. And any sober man would recognize the Creek Apokta as too alert and muscled to be worth challenging. Otherwise, Mrs. Ann wouldn't have trusted little Thomas Weeks to the man's protection.

She would be worrying now about the fading daylight. She had thought to give her son an extra gray blanket earlier in the day, and the child handed it to Shelby, who was too exhilarated to talk at first.

"How's your mama set for kitchen kindling? Did you collect eggs this morning? Is the floor in your daddy's study clear for bedding?"

Thomas was only five, but he sensed that the loss of his father was somewhat eased by his friendship with Shelby Whitmire.

"We just now brought the patchman back down. Mrs. Greenfield had him tar a place in her roof. We were fixin' to wait on you another ten minutes."

"Could be three or four on the late boat, looking to sleep safe for the night."

"Apokta and me, we were only waiting to see if you went on home." The driver nodded. "Or if you wanted to stay over with us and the babies again and…"

"Thomas, don't talk about babies when these travelers board." Shelby knew the boy could prattle to the exasperation of adults. The sky concerned him more. "Is there enough daylight left? To get to the river and back?" He was asking the grown man with the reins, who usually stayed at the bluff trail and transported only those making their own way safely through the wharf streets.

"Dark comes soon with just stars tonight. The river people will be tired. We must go quickly."

The two boys hopped into the bed of the cart, protected from the wind. Curious loiterers, watching the horse trot toward the riverbank, could see it was the formidable Indian in charge of passengers.

"Hope it's no company that can't abide a birthday," Thomas said. He clung to extra layers of woolen shirts from his father's boxed things. Sweat was making the older boy shiver, too, but he took time to smooth the blanket around his shoulders.

"Your mama didn't forget?"

"It's a sweet potato pie. Started boiling and mixing as soon as you headed down to the river. One dozen years tomorrow, she said!" A pistol shot hushed him for a moment. "She made me promise not to tell."

An hour later, in early darkness, Shelby and Thomas led an exhausted man and his wife from the top edge of the bluff where Apokta had let them off. Mrs. Ann and the driver had an agreement that there should never be tarrying with the cart after sundown. It was also arranged that he should regularly take the rig to his own stables off the edge of lower town. No one would plot a theft where so many Creeks lived, at least three families all related, and every adult efficient with a rifle.

Shelby held a small torch, shielding it as best he could from the wind. Thomas put the coins for half fare in his pocket. The Weeks house was just near the end of the first dirt road, but in the moonless evening, a misstep could break an ankle. Mr. Todd had recommended that the pair's domestic stay behind with the other help in a supply shed the two riverside inns shared. The man and his wife, however, almost too tired and stiff to walk upright, had chosen to leave only their trunk on the river's edge. The attendant they called Delilah trailed along behind, carrying a cloth bag. The three "from up north" followed the boys farther into the bitter night.

The lady traveler was somewhat taller than her husband, or at least it appeared so when the older pedestrians stopped in the cold to catch breath. The man stooped over to cough. His straight black hair fell limply over his brow. While he was bent, the wife gave him a pat and kissed his shoulder.

"Angelina, I'm sorry."

"Don't talk," she said. "There's kitchen smoke just on ahead. Windows are lit." Then she stood up straight as a pier post. She looked past the two boys and in all directions as if the deepening pools of darkness, even in the upper part of town, harbored some fearsome threat. Their servant squinted at the dark as well.

A Natchez host usually knew which guests were destined to stay only a night or two, but it took some instinct to guess which ones would rather plunge headlong into the wide river at midnight than speak a few words about where they had come from or what their business was downstream. As a welcome gesture, Shelby often asked those passing through if they planned to stay on the river all the way to New Orleans. But he could feel the tension that clamped down any conversation with this couple. Mrs. Ann's five-year-old did all the talking.

"Don't take ole Mrs. Greenfield as cross. She visits from next door every day. She'll be there, smiling mostly at the babies. She can look out of sorts. That's only because she won't wear pearl buttons or put pretty combs in her hair. She lives in a bigger house, but she doesn't put on any airs—you'll see. My daddy built ours from Boston birch. He learned how in New York. Mama says the King of Spain could set his head down where we live. Your own house, where's it at again?" The woman glanced at her husband.

"Tenne…" He coughed. "Ohio…a little place there."

"I'm their regular hired help," Shelby said, suddenly protective. They had reached a handsome house with green shutters and a varnished door. His hand was on the latch, and he knew it was Mrs. Ann's touch wiggling the bolt from the other side. "I can run and fetch anything you need."

"I was letting worry set in!" The slight woman in the doorway leaned down to wrap her arms around Thomas, and her thick red hair fell to her waist. Shelby thought he might turn faint if she threw an arm along his shoulder with the same abandon. "You all come on in. I don't know but what that hill will have ice by morning." She took one polite look at the travelers and went to pull out chairs from the dining table where an older woman sat with a baby. "I must look a sight with my cap off and half ready to turn in, but I expected only Thomas this late." The husband straightened up before speaking.

"We won't bother you for more than one night."

"Just warm up over here first," the young mother said. She was about to select another chair for Delilah, but Mrs. Greenfield rose and handed the baby to a dark-skinned girl not much taller than Thomas.

"Sit here, dear." There was nothing judgmental in the neighbor's gaze as it fell on the strangers. Her gray dress was as plain as the frock her servant girl wore. "Tomorrow will be soon enough to decide on more travel," she said before introducing herself. "We were just about to go on home. Elizabeth and I only stayed to help Mrs. Weeks fret a little longer, didn't we?" She shook her head in a sympathetic way at Thomas, whose mother was laughing about her own lapse of social grace.

"You folks must call me *Ann.*"

"It's *Jonathan* then…" The man sighed, wiped his chiseled face, and mumbled into a handkerchief. "Peyton…And this here is the missus… Angelina." All three visitors seemed to have melted into their chairs, but the wife nodded in the direction of their attendant.

"Delilah's been with my family since she was this girl's age."

"If she's like kin, it's no wonder you didn't leave her to stay somewhere under-the-hill," Mrs. Greenfield went on. "No Christian should have to choose between a beet shed and a slave pen for a place to bed down. If Master Whitmire here ends up setting his blankets down by Ann's hearth, there won't be sleeping space left in this house either." She lifted the baby from the girl's arms and handed the infant to its mother. "Miss Delilah, come stay over at my house with Elizabeth and me. Are you fond of singing?"

The mouths of all three travelers opened, but none could argue against the offer. In a few minutes, Mrs. Ann was setting a pan of biscuits to warm near the rekindled fire. A stove flame had grown under a pot, and Shelby brought a waxed cheese in from the cold box. Tea with cloves was beginning to steam on a back burner, and Thomas' mother poured a warm drink for the strangers. Soon, she ladled beans onto three china plates, so that one could be taken next door.

It was pride Shelby felt, with only a twinge of jealousy that all eyes were on Ann Weeks. She bustled from the stove to the stair landing to the long pine table, where her guests waited for numbness in their hands and faces to subside. When the baby Levi grasped at his mother's cascading hair, Shelby told himself it might be the late kitchen smoke stinging his eyes. How she could smile and talk in a friendly way while making progress with her chores was a mystery the hired boy was in no hurry to solve. By the time he had his own twentieth, he had figured lately, she would still be on the young side of thirty. He could wait.

"I don't doubt your daddy and Mrs. Whitmire are on the watch for you." The youth suddenly realized she was talking to him. Thomas and he were sorting through a pile of guest bedding by the stairs, and he first doubted his hearing. "Shelby?"

"You don't need me?"

"Your daddy will be wondering."

"He knows where I am," he rushed to explain. "My stepmother bars the door by sunset. She had me sleep on the beach stoop last time I was late."

"You'd freeze tonight, Lord knows."

"Even Mrs. Greenfield saw I could be of use by taking a pallet near your fireplace again. Your guests might have need of something during the night." Ann Weeks was smiling at him, and his face grew warm. "I can ask your sisters for eggs at daylight. Whatever you might need come morning." Shelby couldn't let himself say, *It's my birthday tomorrow and don't forget you've made me a pie!*

Mrs. Ann was still holding the baby Levi, and her other little one, Sara, had toddled up to hug her knee. The mother seemed pleased about the hired boy, as she reached to pat her daughter's curly hair.

"Your parents will likely conclude you latched onto more work up here than you could get away from."

There was noisy movement at the table, and Mr. Peyton was backing his chair away as he struggled to overcome a coughing fit. Both plates looked swabbed clean. Now, however, the couple seemed to need sleep even more than air. When a door to the late Mr. Weeks' study was finally closed, their lamp went out in minutes. The widow and the children went on up the stairs to the family bedrooms, and Shelby settled into the thick quilts and pillow that he had come to think of as his own. A slight draft from the north window enlivened the hearth coals occasionally. He turned, facing the wall where fresh air seeped in as wind hit the panes. Buildings this close to the water breathed, even those built by craftsmen like Thomas' father.

Rooms in the Weeks home went quiet, except for gurgling sounds from the baby upstairs and a sharp cough coming from the study.

In the middle of the night, Shelby pulled his knees up to fend off an urge to relieve himself. He wished he hadn't accepted a cup of tea so late. The downstairs chamber pot had been set inside the study being used as a guest room for the evening. Wondering how many steps he could tolerate outside in the cold, he was about to roll back over, but he froze all movement instead, listening. The sound of breathing was followed by subdued sighing. Someone not four feet away sat in darkness at the long dining table. Motionless, he listened again. It was one of the women, or there would have been coughing. The breaths went quick and shallow, and then it was clear that the person at the table was suppressing sobs.

It had to be the traveler Angelina Peyton. All Shelby could think was—like the sequence went at his house when the new Mrs. Whitmire began to cry—there would be shouting and accusations soon. All Shelby could conclude was that he had brought these strangers to Mrs. Ann's house, and if any harm should come to her and Thomas and the babies, it would be his fault for hanging onto the pier until the river became all shadows. If these strangers brought turmoil, he would have his own yearning and foolish dreams to blame.

Shelby was trying to think what he could say to reverse the scene. He struggled to recall if he had ever said anything to his stepmother that didn't provoke the worst, when he heard another soft sound that took a while to identify. Now someone was coming down the fine stairway Mr. Weeks had built. Thomas often boasted that there wasn't a single loose plank along it. Mrs. Ann was the only person who could be coming down the stairs to the dining table, and she hardly made a sound.

The lady of the house found her way to the stove and lit a candle. It must have been a short stub of paraffin that she put a match to, and the pewter colander that she set over the flame. She sat down near Mrs. Peyton. There was only the faintest glow and flicker. An unnatural quiet continued for so long, that Shelby wondered if women could speak to each other in silent ways men didn't know about. The uneven breathing calmed. Shelby kept still with his quilts around him, his knees drawn up, and his back to the two individuals sitting in the dark. He would have predicted Thomas' mother to break the silence first.

"My husband used to pour a glass of cognac from time to time. It's not been a year since his passing." It was quiet for longer than women would have tolerated in the daylight. "I miss him most at night."

"I'm sorry I woke you up," Angelina said.

"When we married…I was barely past girlhood. I never thought of pouring myself a glass, but I wouldn't mind sharing some with you."

They were whispering almost, so as not to wake the boy by the hearth. Mrs. Ann rose and went to the china cabinet. Next came the sound of a stopper being pulled out, a gurgle, and splashing at the bottom of each glass. Shelby had to wince at the sound of released liquid. Then he heard the swish of a woolen gown on the scrubbed floor.

"I might have poured too much."

"It won't take much to calm me down," Angelina admitted. "Or get me crying again." The boy detected a different noise from the stranger, and he realized that she had begun to laugh softly. "Shedding tears and drinkin'—neither one is my usual habit."

"Coming down the Mississippi at dusk is hard enough. It deserves one good cry."

Shelby didn't hear glasses clunk on the table, and he thought the women might be cradling their cognacs. He began to hope that this was a different kind of drinking from what he saw under-the-hill in his father's house most nights. He would have liked to sit up and take a chair at the head of the pine table, saying, *Pay me no mind. It's as good to listen as it is to talk sometimes.*

"When Jonathan gets over his last cough," the visitor went on, "I know he'll finally sleep steady. His nerves take a while to ease up. Like mine."

"Riverbank air doesn't do a cough any good."

"Won't be but another three days or so from here…"

"Then you all aim to settle in New Orleans?" Mrs. Ann had asked in a soft voice, and Shelby knew it to be a friendly question, but the silence was awkward, and he could imagine his friend's mother putting her hand out to Angelina's. "You don't have to tell me a thing about your plans."

"What's been sworn never to tell is not always easy…"

"I understand about secrets," the widow said, after another long silence. "Lord, what this river knows." She sighed in a way the boy had never heard before, and Shelby realized that his own breathing was becoming unsteady. "My Mr. Weeks came rushing downstream to Natchez when I was no more than an infant myself. From the way he told it, he spent every waking moment expecting to be jumped and strung up. Never fell asleep, he said, but what he half believed he'd get his throat cut while dreaming."

"Afraid of…somethin' catching up to him?"

"After one year here, then another and another, he was still waiting for the sound of an angry crowd." Ann's chair creaked and the noise stopped her line of thought, but then her chuckle surprised the boy. "I should toast ole Aaron Burr's plan to stamp this territory with his name. The treason he was accused of stole power from any other horror tale drifting into these parts." Shelby began to take in air through his mouth.

"Jonathan and I weren't but children when that trial came to pass," Mrs. Peyton said. A glass was set down on the table, and she cleared her throat. "To think a vice-president would plot to steal this entire part of the country. Mr. Burr's jury came out saying 'not guilty,' as I recall…"

"Not convicted," Ann said. "Still, his schemes stayed in the headlines a good while after. My Levi said he was grateful that from then on not one column paid mind to his own past troubles." It was quiet for so long that Shelby almost fell asleep again. He fought off the pang in his lower abdomen. He was about to drift off, and he was wondering if he had only dreamed about the women talking. Then his friend's mother started up in a whisper again, "I'd be ashamed to burden a stranger with details about my husband's woes. But he left our older boy some papers. He wanted Thomas to have the New York articles one day. In case he ever happened upon gossip in his own life, later. To brace for the crossing of a shadow, even in happiest times."

"I'm so sorry I woke you up." Shelby had never heard his friend's mother talk about such dark worries. He wished the Peyton woman would tell her there was no need to divulge more.

"Who his New York lawyers turned out to be is worth having a news page to prove," Mrs. Ann said more brightly. "The very same Aaron Burr—I suppose that's why I remember his name so easy—and the doomed Mr. Hamilton himself!"

"I am so sorry," Angelina said again. The stopper was being set back in the bottle and the boy at the hearth took in air more easily. "It's a wide world for forgetting troubles, if you ask me." The houseguest might well have been patting Mrs. Ann's arm now. "Jonathan says we're headed… into Mexico's Texas territory." Angelina's whisper had grown even more hushed. "They take settlers from anywhere. Texas, he says, is where we won't feel our hearts jump. Any place in America will likely call his action…*murder.*"

Mrs. Ann's voice had been sounding husky, but now he heard her make a gasp that stopped the lady guest from speaking further. All three listened for Mr. Peyton's cough. The study remained quiet. The boy wondered if he would be twelve or twenty before he took a turn at drink to calm nerves. He didn't want to douse every sorrow the way his father did.

"Guilty or not guilty," the widow finally said. "I have a news-clipping about a New York City crowd with no use for an acquittal."

The candlewick began to sputter and would succumb soon in a pool of paraffin. No moon cast any light, and it looked as if the stars had given up shining, too. For a while, the only other sounds were Shelby's own shallow breathing and wind worrying the pines. Then a single cough came from the study, and glasses clinked as they were slid along the table. He couldn't be sure if he had heard or imagined bare feet, a child's feet, padding away on the upstairs hallway.

Both women rose, and they stood without speaking, the way long-time friends find words of little use upon parting. The thread of their conversation would not be picked up again in daylight.

"I won't apologize again for waking you up, Mrs. Ann Weeks. I'm too happy we had this talk." The baby upstairs began to whimper. "I know I feel lucky the river brought us to this spot."

"Secrets from this house go downstream, Mrs. Peyton," the mother said again. "They all get lost at sea."

"Goodnight, then."

Shelby waited an hour before slipping his boots on and sliding into his jacket. Out in the cold, he couldn't bring himself to trot farther than behind the shed on the kitchen side to relieve himself. A violent shivering overcame him, and it was no use heading back to the house any faster than a walk. He couldn't stop trembling once he lay down again, no matter how tightly he wrapped himself in the quilt. His teeth clicking, he finally dozed off, imagining he was Aaron Burr or Levi Weeks at the moment a mob caught up.

In the morning, there was some concern about Mr. Peyton, who slept far past time to catch the same crowded flatboat that had brought them to Natchez. But the Weeks family said that was just as well. The notorious Captain Lovejoy had an appealing name, but Mrs. Ann said his reputation was grim, and that *Captain Capsize* was a more appropriate title. It was no laughing matter that two Lovejoy flatboats made of loosely strung logs had unraveled in the middle of the wide river. In just one calendar year, he had lost a dozen travelers to the deadly silt at the bottom. Their neighbor Mrs. Greenfield said it was a sign of God's love that Jonathan Peyton was still too exhausted to travel. It was a sure blessing the couple would have to wait until the day after for the remaining fare to New Orleans.

Shelby didn't mind hitching a ride down the bluff with Apokta later in the morning. He trusted no one better than Mr. Todd, as far as the Peytons' trunk was concerned, but riverbank inns were always scenes of frantic packing and shuffling of belongings. On the back of a soiled menu paper, the boy wrote, "Weeks property. Apokta will collect!" He set the sign down on the large trunk and weighted it with a driftwood burl. Returning, he congratulated himself for securing the couple's next-day flatboat passage. He had almost forgotten the significance of the frosty December date.

It was the first birthday Shelby wanted to etch into memory, a celebration on no one's behalf but his. Even Mr. Peyton had risen in time to join his wife, Mrs. Ann, and her children. The widow's younger sisters from a house two streets away joined the family greeting Shelby when the latch of the varnished door was opened. The small pianoforte in his friend's house was usually covered with folded laundry, but today it was cleared and the bench was out.

The family provided baked chicken and lima beans, and Mrs. Greenfield and Elizabeth carried over two loaves of yeast bread. Delilah held a jar of the neighbor's fig jam in each hand. There were two sweet potato pies in the widow's safe—not just one.

No Christmas or New Years, Shelby thought, could entail a more savory meal. After the pie, his friend's mother gave him a small package wrapped in Natchez newsprint. The spyglass that Mr. Levi Weeks had used to first gaze upon land suitable for construction was Shelby's to keep. And Thomas didn't look the least bit affronted by the nudge against his inheritance. The lookout piece would be Shelby's forever as would the memory of a performance that came next.

He had often heard singing as he passed Mrs. Greenfield's on a workday. But he was dumbstruck along with the others as the dark-skinned girl, plainly dressed like her mistress, began to sing. She was timid, at first, even among the Weeks family with whom she was well acquainted, but then her voice grew as clear as an ebony flute. It was a hymn their neighbor said the girl sang often, but only at home. Ann

Weeks had a hymnal open, and it was clear from her expression as she touched the pianoforte that she was reading the music for the first time. The older lady said she didn't want the child's pride to swell, but she had thought about Shelby's birthday, and she believed God might approve this sharing of talent.

> *He sends the snow in winter, the warmth to swell the grain,*
>
> *The breezes and the sunshine, and soft refreshing rain…*

The child servant looked at her hands while she sang, or glanced at Mrs. Greenfield. Across the room, Angelina Peyton leaned closer to her husband.

"I heard this in Tennessee…growing up."

> *All good gifts around us*
>
> *Are sent from heaven above,*
>
> *Then thank the Lord, O thank the Lord,*
>
> *For all his love.*

The girl's angelic voice and shy demeanor left the listeners without the vulgar impulse to clap. It was Ann's younger sisters who first took turns embracing the child. Next, the widow's toddling daughter approached Elizabeth and rested her hands on the singer's apron.

"We have more of a church right here, at this moment, than all the rich altars I ever read about," the graying lady said. "One day, I'll discover a spot on God's earth where divine love is the only language spoken. No fancy glass, just song."

"This child's singing could hold any congregation in awe, though I don't expect the Friends you credit so much in Pennsylvania would think much of public singing on any account." Ann Weeks had discussed religion often enough with her neighbor. She didn't want any differences of view to trouble the Peytons or skew Shelby's day, but she'd let herself make the good-humored observation.

"I would hate to choose between this gathering and salvation, Ann, dear. I know you don't want me moving out of your daily life."

"Don't you ever."

"If Apokta were to take me and Elizabeth down the hill," Mrs. Greenfield went on in a lively way, "and this beautiful child of Africa were to sing that same hymn…in front of the slave dealers' stockade— you might urge my relocation far north if *that* were to take place!"

"I do get confused thinking about…station in life," Ann admitted. She hoped to keep the word "abolition" from the conversation, and she had observed that Mr. Peyton appeared tired again.

"It crossed my mind, coming down the Mississippi," Angelina spoke up, "that Christmas festivities might be abandoned this year, with all our time spent traveling and settling in…somewhere." She nodded to Mrs. Weeks. "Now, after this perfect occasion, we won't feel we missed the season."

The next morning, Apokta came up the street to stop directly in front of Mrs. Weeks' house. They would just have to tell anyone expecting the same favor that their guests had been special this time. They just wouldn't hear of putting these travelers from *Ohio* out on the bluff or letting the couple find their way from the bottom of the hill to the riverbank. The familiar cart would take them to their departure point. The Peytons seemed like relatives. Feeling as if his birthday had stuffed him with more information and worry than he usually took on in a whole year, the Whitmire boy accompanied the couple to the dock. Joy was also tinging his perceptions, and colorless shacks packed in on the shore took on the hue of possibility in the morning sun.

Near the pier where Shelby had been on lookout two days before, a smaller but more seaworthy craft was moored and ready to make the trip to New Orleans. Mr. Jonathan Peyton looked a different man after sleep and peaceful company. Rested, he could be credited for appealing features. And Shelby thought that the wife Angelina, when she wasn't standing right next to Mrs. Ann, was as handsome a woman as any living in Natchez. She had been smiling almost the entire last day of their stopover, even when her cash offer for the overnight lodging was refused by the widowed mother.

"You find a time to slip this into her money tin, won't you?" she said later, putting two folded bills into the hired boy's hand.

"I never saw her take to someone new like she did you."

"Well, young man, hang onto this payment until the next time she counts out what's due for your help." Her expression had gone soft as if she still heard the African girl singing. "Tell her you won't be hanging onto any *good gifts* that aren't yours."

"It's good how she has the sturdy house Mr. Weeks built, but cash is mostly scarce."

"No mother on her own has an easy time."

"All right then," Shelby said. Mr. Peyton was busy with the captain, and the two men were securing the couple's trunk and directing Delilah to her spot. It was time for Angelina to find her seating and brace for the wintry ride. The boy couldn't keep himself from a wish that his own father had remarried a lady like Angelina Peyton. A finality in their parting made Shelby's emotions suddenly surface.

"You all take care in Texas!" he blurted out.

Angelina Peyton turned from where she had stepped into the flatboat. She looked startled, not angry, but not tuned to affection the way she had been a moment before.

"Who ever said…we were going to *Texas?*"

The Whitmire boy stood shaking his head. His mouth hung open slightly and Mrs. Peyton seemed to be weighing what she needed to say.

"Shelby…" In just a few moments, the captain would loosen the moorings. "Don't you ever tell young Thomas anything that would make him think less of his daddy."

"I never would…"

"Memories are as sacred as any *heavenly gift.*"

"I never—I take care of Thomas."

"And don't you ever tell…"

"I know what *sacred* means. Like remembering my real mama."

Angelina Peyton was blinking at the boy, and he realized that she was a stronger woman than she had seemed when first stepping ashore at Natchez. She was rested, and he could tell she had the natural strength and energy to leap from the edge of the boat if she wanted to. She could have pressed strong hands to Shelby's throat. She could have made him swear to maintain silence about whatever he had heard pass between the two women in private that first night. But the traveler appeared to conclude that the boy didn't need more telling. She looked to be contemplating only the long, long voyage ahead.

"If anyone asks, I never even had a thought you'd be going to Texas," Shelby whispered as the captain untied the ropes on the other side of the boat.

Angelina Peyton and her husband Jonathan settled in alongside a handful of other passengers and a collection of boxes and livestock. Shelby knew somehow that this somber parting at the shore would float a great distance in his thoughts.

His geography wasn't good. For two years during primary school, he had stayed home from lessons entirely, first taking care of his ill mother, then looking after his distraught father. He couldn't remember reading much about Mexico, except that a place called Santa Fe could be frozen white in every direction this time of year.

"He sends the snow in winter," Shelby recited to himself. He hummed the melody as he watched the boat disappear in shadows downstream from Mr. Todd's pier. He watched until he began to shiver and to wonder if he had the heart to drift on back toward his own home any time soon.

1827 in the village of Knoxville, Georgia

2 The Pull of Purpose

Hugh McLeod and his academy classmate kept their horses off the dirt road from Macon to Knoxville. They kept out of sight. Up ahead, though, was a meadow to cross before they reached a path to the swimming hole where they planned to spend most of that summer day.

"There's a rig coming down the cross trail," Hugh warned.

"Young'uns, it looks like…three. Could be the fellow is our age. No one waving a switch at us anyhow."

The two weren't close friends, but they had both been on the edge of a Macon group asked to pitch in on some whitewashing at the school building. Hugh and Charles had both stepped to the rear and found themselves hastening along together where their horses were tied several blocks away. The town's main headmaster would keep them strictly engaged come September, and that was soon enough, they decided. They avoided observation on their escape toward a swimming spot a few miles from town.

Hugh felt most like himself when taking such a gamble. His mother was visiting her daughter Isabella in Savannah. The visit with the newly married eighteen-year-old would be brief, just long enough to deliver land entitlement papers from the bride's McLeod inheritance. Acquaintances in Macon knew the daughter to be a comfort to her sole parent, as responsible as any churchgoing citizen could want grown offspring to be.

There was no such confidence about Hugh. Management of the youth without his mother's oversight was worrisome to the Lamars, longtime friends and unofficial protectors of Mrs. McLeod's family. Early in the morning, Hugh had come with the cotton dealer John Lamar down to the wharf where the businessman felt he could keep a watchful eye.

The sudden bell at the Bibb County Academy had sent a dozen youngsters running. No one with business at the docks would have time to check on the whereabouts of a fourteen-year-old until afternoon faded. The two boys weren't too worried about the open carriage they were about to encounter.

"Isn't that Colonel Troutman's little girl?"

"I don't recognize the others," Hugh said, nodding. "Guests at their inn, I suppose."

The Macon youths continued across a meadow where Indian blanket had already bloomed past its peak, and their horses trotted easily through the diminished foliage. On the dirt path ahead, the young man holding cart reins pulled up and brought a calm chestnut mare to a stop. Hugh smiled at the more petite passenger.

"Hey, Miss Joanna." The girl whose father ran the fine lodge at Knoxville looked different every time he saw her, and he thought she might be getting near the final level of primer school. "You all get a stagecoach today?"

"One from each direction!" She only let her eyes dart at the boy she didn't know, but she was comfortably acquainted with Hugh. The McLeod boy dropped in every few weeks at the hotel kitchen. He was keen on pastries. "We're going for a picnic. Jacob and Olivia are my cousins."

"We head back to Charleston day after tomorrow," the older girl said.

"Our parents had us see proper Georgia—as well as this wilderness— firsthand." The South Carolina youth scowled at the withering field as he spoke, and his tone irritated Hugh.

"I wouldn't say the Troutmans are living in the wild."

"Well," Olivia said, "Savannah had some charm. We were there a week before we took the Ocmulgee River."

"My family resided on the Georgia coast for a while. After New York City, Charleston and Savannah seemed barely towns. But then McLeods and Lamars struck out for these fierce western parts." Hugh enjoyed seeing Jacob shift on the rig seat. A smile passing Joanna's expression convinced him that she was willing to bid her city cousins farewell. "Anyone in South Carolina sophisticated enough to make use of a swimming hole?" He gestured at the road turnoff where locals sought cool, deep water.

"We're better dressed than what a muddy creek might invite. You boys go on," Jacob shrugged. "We'll dine somewhere upstream." The Troutman girl was reaching into a covered basket.

"Wait, Hugh! Here, take some scones. We brought more than enough."

"Scones?" Charles wasn't sure what they were.

"Our cook only makes them for company. Camille hasn't used the recipe since back when Lafayette and his people stayed over."

"Macon bakeries put them out on occasion," Hugh explained. "Let's have a taste of civilization!" He let his horse amble up to the rig where Joanna held out a small bundle. Then he bowed to the side. "Your generosity, Miss Troutman, is unrivaled." Jacob flicked the reins and the Macon boy gave him one last study. "If our wilderness assaults your nerves any today, write down a call for help and float a bottle in our direction."

Colonel Troutman's carriage rolled away, and the three cousins went on quickly toward a stream off the Flint River. Closer to the bank, the horse turned in a direction opposite the swimming spot. Hugh couldn't tell if Charles was laughing or sneering.

"*Unrivaled generosity?* When did you get a head for such dignified speech?"

"I can get inspired."

"Not in school."

"My mother passed her way with words on to me," Hugh admitted. "And I can reconcile myself to a book—even if our headmaster never opens one."

Two hours went by uneventfully. The creek just east from the village of Knoxville, and a mile from the banks of the Flint itself, took a winding turn every quarter mile. The broad eddy was deep and private enough that Hugh and Charles might have stripped off all their clothing in the summer heat, had they not been wary of the girls' proximity upstream. Both were tempted to show off at the sandy promontory used for diving, but they wanted to steer away from trouble. Keeping their linen under-trousers on, they floated on their backs and chatted as they seldom had occasion to do in a classroom.

"My grandpa was in the Revolution, like Colonel Troutman's father," Charles said, "a mere boy like the heroes that went in." Hugh's grandfather had come from Scotland just after America's first war with England, so there was no such legacy to claim.

"The blasted Indian depredations don't allow pure glory."

"My parents sometimes speak of revolution, like it almost happened again. I heard them saying Aaron Burr was set to carve himself a new country along the Mississippi."

"Over and done before we drew our first breath, like New Orleans and all that excitement. But the Lamars still discuss Burr, too. They speculate Jefferson started those treason rumors himself. Whatever it took to stop the aggravation." Hugh expelled a mouthful of water in an arc. "Can't maintain an interest in politics, myself," he shrugged. "But I'd gallop onto any battlefield."

"West is where all adventure crops up!"

"You have to cross the Mississippi," Hugh agreed. Charles rolled over in the water and stood for a while punching at the swirls in the creek. He swung harder and harder at the currents.

"I mean Mexico! Their Texas territory can't be corralled. Papa's cousin went as far as Texas years ago. Crossed the Sabine River into Spanish soil. As long as he tends his acres and keeps some fear in the Indians, the new Mexican rulers don't care what language is spoken."

Hugh was lost in his own thoughts. The glare where sunlight struck the water made him squint, but shadows nearer the shore intensified an odor of decay and made him reluctant to keep his eyes closed. He had been only three when his father died. Lately, he felt family pressure as the namesake McLeod to take first steps as a man.

"My mother is bent on my going into the military, if she can enlist a sponsor…and if I can stomach the academy another two years."

"A private school? Somewhere far off?"

"West Point. The Lamars know the right people who can—"

"Hush!"

"It's true. Maybe you don't know about officers."

"No! I hear some noise!" In the quiet, a girl's scream clearly came from upstream where the three cousins had directed the Troutman rig. The two Macon boys clambered out of the water, pulled on their breeches, and rushed to their horses. As they rode within sight, the school girl, Joanna Troutman, was on the bank waving her arms and shrieking. Her cousin Olivia was already kneeling in the water, next to her brother. His leg, it appeared, was pinned under a cypress trunk that must have dislodged.

"He was balancing! Just walking across—Olivia and I, we'd already passed to the other side and back!" Hugh had slid down quickly and was wading into the stream as the colonel's daughter called after him. "He was in easy balance. Then the current moved the log a little, and he fell—his leg is trapped! Can you move it?"

The sodden trunk had rolled over Jacob's right leg, and he couldn't get the other one in a position for leverage. Fortunately, the water was only up to his chest as he lay pinned. His sister, skirts soaked, bent alongside, giving him enough support that he wouldn't weaken and collapse into the flow. First, Hugh got down on his knees and leaned his shoulder against the stout log. When Charles made it to the middle of the stream, he added his weight to the effort, but the trunk still would not budge. The stream was beginning to muddy, but both boys could see that the trapped boy's leg was only getting more wedged.

"If we dig, more weight might edge over on you—"

"Hurts like the devil!" The face of the trapped youth twisted in fear.

"If we had sturdy rope, then the horses could—"

"Do something!" Olivia's strength was giving out, too. Charles took a turn at giving the pinioned boy a shoulder to lean on.

"John Spillers lives close by!" Joanna suddenly remembered. "His family has ropes and harnesses, stronger horses. I can go—you won't find it on your own—it's between here and town."

"Will your rig take a fast pace?" Hugh thought better about lifting the girl up behind him. At a gallop, his own horse might throw her. It appeared Charles and Olivia could keep the Charleston boy above water and calm until they returned.

Joanna sat on the driver's seat next to Hugh. As he raced the carriage back up the path toward Knoxville, she kept one hand gripped to the seat. She couldn't keep the other from making a fist on the wet knee of Hugh's trousers. When a rear wheel dipped into crevice, she wrapped both hands around his upper arm. She clung in controlled panic until she made out the Spillers homestead through the dense trees.

"There are two families…" She was breathless. "Two brothers…their wives are sisters. Someone will be within hearing!" A door on one of the cabins was open to the eastern view and Hugh guided the horse as close as the dense poplars would permit before leaping down and running. Into the doorway stepped a pregnant woman holding a little boy.

"Is that Miss Joanna yonder? You're in a mighty hurry, son." All Hugh had to say was that a boy was trapped in the creek. Matilda Spillers handed Hugh the child and ran off to the side of her cabin. "John T.

and my sister are gathering corn! Our bell can bring them in, but her husband is all the way out at the Flint!"

"We'll need a strong horse, if not two!" he called after her.

The tiny boy wriggled to be set down. When the child scurried into the two-room structure, Hugh followed him. Inside, a perfect calm clashed with the scene he knew was unfolding at the creek. The rooms were pristine as bluebird feather, and the pine floor glistened. A braided gray rug lay next to a bed, its coverlet tucked at each corner. On the mantel, polished boots sat next to a clock. The next rushing footsteps were Joanna's.

"Are they coming? Are they getting their strongest horse?"

The Spillers man hastened from the field. He and the other woman brought around two muscular animals. They threw coils of coarse rope into Joanna's rig, as well as hooks, each big enough to hoist a side of beef. Matilda urged her husband on, and her sister Martha held the child close.

"Don't tarry for any more tools!"

"Might be you two and the other Macon boy can shift the log without horses!"

"Go on, sweetheart," the pregnant wife said. "We can manage here."

The Troutman rig raced toward the stream, and the plow horses read their master's urgency. The one Mr. Spillers had mounted, as well as the tethered horse, fell into a canter.

"I always have some fear of leaving Matilda!" John shouted to Hugh.

"At least it's not the big river!" He felt Joanna's grasp tighten on his arm. "It shouldn't take us long to free him!"

At the creek, Charles and Olivia looked like statues as they knelt. They spoke to the exhausted victim until the passenger cart and horses drew up close along the bank. At first, Hugh and Mr. Spillers tried to roll the trunk against the current, but once it budged, it began to drift back in the dangerous direction. The Charleston boy's groan convinced them not to risk a half-effort again. Full force of the horses was needed. Once the log could be secured with ropes and hooks, Spillers would spur the horses upstream, while the two Macon friends dragged Jacob away.

The girls were instructed to wait at the bank, but neither was of a mind to hear orders. Joanna and her cousin stood ankle deep in the shallows. Olivia, whose skirt was already soaked, had loosened her sash, and both readied to join the watery struggle if the men's effort went amiss.

Mr. Spillers set the hooks and then secured the ropes to the harnesses. Gently, he walked them upstream until the tie-lines grew taught. He warned them all, in a voice almost too low for hearing, that they would need to get utterly clear of the fallen tree once it lifted.

"Do something!" Jacob's eyes had grown wide with alarm, and tears brimmed at the corners. In his struggle to steady his face above water, he was gradually sinking into the creek bed. The muddied water crept to his collar as Hugh and Charles both put their hands on the cypress bark. A foul smell bubbled up. "Fools!" the frantic boy sputtered as water rimmed his face. The girls grasped each other's hands.

"Fast, but sure," the man said gravely. "Even good horses can balk."

"The count of three, Mr. Spillers?"

"Lord help us," he nodded. "One, two, three!"

The mount horse pulled much harder than the other, and it was the bottom of the trunk, despite its heaviness, that inched upstream first. Jacob's head was pulled underwater, and for a few seconds Hugh could discern the youth's expression freeze in terror, his pursed lips allowing large bubbles to escape. Then mud and filth swirled over him.

It took both Macon youths to lift Joanna's cousin from the silt and drag him from danger before the fallen log turned chaotically at a new angle. The Troutman girl and Olivia waded in as the three fellows staggered to shore. Dislodged and floating a few yards away, the cypress trunk came to a hard stop in the next shallow eddy.

"You're all right, young man! You're all right. You're only going to suffer a bad bruise." John Spillers breathed hard but his voice was steady. "It doesn't look like a break." The Charleston youth gasped for air as he struggled on the bank to rise from his knees. Regaining some composure was harder.

"Well done…by any account," he managed to say. He didn't look down at his pant leg, and he avoided eye contact with Hugh. "My uncle will see to it that you have a proper reward."

The family man turned to attend to his horses, whose ropes now needed untying. He and the local youths felt Joanna's embarrassment at the well-meaning offer.

"Knoxville neighbors watch over each other," she explained to her cousins. "Anyone will come running when there's need."

"I'd best get myself and the horses home. With my brother out of earshot, our wives and the little one might…" Mr. Spillers rushed to get back in the saddle. "Will you Macon boys be all right seeing the rig on over to the colonel's?"

"I know how it handles." Hugh was sorry he had sparred verbally with Joanna's cousin. A ghastly outcome had been avoided, everyone knew. "Jacob ought to rest his leg in the back seat."

"I'd follow you all to the inn, but Matilda and her sister…"

"Colonel Troutman knows me. He'll let me stay over and head for home in the morning." Hugh wouldn't allow Spillers to apologize further. "If Charles will ride back to Macon and let the Lamars know where I am—what happened here—I'll take the rig. Don't worry."

"We're pretty peaceful with the Choctaws and Chickasaws up here around the Flint," the man went on anyway, "but I wouldn't want to picture either woman reaching for the child and a musket at the same time."

Returning to Knoxville, Joanna sat next to Hugh on the driver's seat. Olivia positioned herself so that Jacob could stretch out his bruised leg and rest it on the picnic blanket. The horse that the Macon boy had ridden in the morning was tethered to the rig, and there was no reason to speed along the trail. It was easiest on the injured youth to avoid any unnecessary jostling.

When they approached the Spillers homestead, Joanna waved toward the mostly obscured cabin. The little boy, whose uncle had just saved the day, sat on the stoop and put a finger in his mouth as the Troutman rig passed by. The girl waved again with both hands and the smiling child stood up.

"Both women come in to town and join the ladies for quilting sometimes," she said so softly that Hugh leaned over to better hear. "Their late father was in the Revolution, too." He was sure she too was thinking of the shiny boots displayed on the mantle.

"I wouldn't keep up any contest of words today." He turned to verify that Jacob and Olivia were managing the return trip comfortably enough. The close brush with tragedy had shaken them all. "But if anyone claimed Georgia people don't show proper civility…"

"They're somewhat homesick, I think. Their talk about wilderness wasn't meant to tread on rightful pride." The Troutman girl smiled, and Hugh decided he was enjoying the afternoon more than if he'd been in the company of Macon females his own age.

"I never saved a life before. I didn't know…when I left my house this morning that I'd end the day…" He felt odd telling a girl what he was thinking. "It's like I traveled a thousand miles…and discovered home for the first time."

The rig was coming up on the spot where the red dirt widened into a road fit for coaches that stopped at the inn just ahead. The Charleston cousins had nodded off, leaning against one another.

"I do wonder sometimes," Joanna spoke on, "what it might be like… to travel far from here." She was shaking her head, and her dark curls hung loose around her bonnet. "I expect I wouldn't like it much."

"Mr. Spillers couldn't abide more than an hour away from his family's cabin."

"If your people already know joy every day…if you have what's purely beautiful, why would you choose to wander and risk—"

"How old are you?" Hugh let himself laugh despite the anxious commotion that their arrival would soon cause.

"Wisdom can come from a child!"

"That's what I'm observing, Miss Troutman!"

The carriage reached a last curve that brought the inn and a handful of other buildings into view. Charles had willingly ridden on back to Macon. Hugh's classmate could be counted on to apprise the Lamars, to assure them that no further danger was unfolding.

Something else was unfolding, and he didn't think he would be able to put it into words for anyone just yet, even this young girl so easy to talk to. He himself didn't know how the near-tragedy would color decisions pressing in at the end of his academy years. He just knew he was changed from the youth who'd fled a ringing school bell that morning.

It was some feeling he had no words for yet, to have wrestled someone from the grip of death, to have pulled someone a distance that couldn't be measured in miles.

"My father will be so happy for you to stay," Joanna said as the rig came to a stop. "You won't believe how many scones Camille can make for breakfast."

He didn't feel like debating with the spirited Troutman girl about the pleasure or wisdom of wandering away from home.

1827 San Antonio, in Mexico's Texas territory

3   Dreams and Headstones

"Alex, darlin', you go on with Delilah. Say, *Buenas noches*, say *Hasta mañana* to the other *niños*," Mrs. Peyton told her son. "The festival is ending. You'll sleep past biscuits in the morning if you don't get on into bed."

Angelina Peyton and her husband Jonathan wanted to stay a while under the stars in the dusty plaza of San Antonio. They had candles. But there were also *luminarias* lining the square and many side streets. The 16th of September, the day for celebrating Mexican independence from Spain, was an occasion lasting well into dark. All day speeches had been made on the edge of town, out near the Alamo mission, which was the sturdiest building in Bexar, perhaps in all of Texas. After the evening fireworks, townspeople slowly wound their way back to their adobe houses.

"There's more fire in the sky!"

"Show's all over, son. Do like your mother says." The boy frowned, but at Delilah, not Jonathan. The head of the Peyton household owned a particularly short temper.

Angelina Peyton knew her husband's disposition well. She was careful about the order in which she brought up topics as the couple lingered in the open before the slow stroll home. At night, Jonathan could have been identified as a man of Mexican descent. He was lean and straight and his hair was dark enough that it appeared black in the shadows. She reached up to smooth her own hair before she spoke.

"Alex will turn five in another few months. He looks like you."

"I didn't mean to sound short with him." They crossed by the *panaderia*, where small round loaves of bread would fill the lane with a sweet aroma before daylight. A family walking more briskly passed them by. Their footsteps and their children's laughter gradually faded ahead of them in the shadows.

"It looks like…" Mrs. Peyton needed to start over. "My best guess is, I'm expecting again." They had gone several of their first years together without children, when Angelina's difficulty in becoming a mother had been just as well. The flight from Tennessee, where there was still a murder warrant, would have been no easier with a baby in tow. But their marriage might not have turned out anything like ordinary, even without the necessity of putting rivers and borders between them and their home state. "My own female calendar is more regular than seasons in Texas, that's certain. I'd speculate May is when there'll be four of us, instead of three."

Her husband didn't say anything. It was not his way to offer words of comfort when they were needed, but he put one arm around his wife's slim waist and patted her wrist with his other hand. Angelina had recently sensed that he was already growing tired of the mission city. After only three months, he had begun pacing again, and letting his temper flair. She'd had little success in helping him adjust to a Spanish-speaking locale. The thin strips of peppered beef and the tortillas, however, had made them converts to Mexican food. Angelina had learned many tricks of the dough pounding process. And the easily repaired stucco exterior of buildings made them shake their heads about the drafty crevices in log homes back East. Nevertheless, Jonathan Peyton was a restless man, and he would likely never change.

"I know it's not forgotten, how we felt when we pulled out of San Felipe," she went on, hoping to get a word in before he announced his plans.

"Tarring and feathering!" He patted her arm again as an apology for raising his voice. "If *you-know-who* had been at home when it all started up, the doctor wouldn't have suffered such vicious action."

"Our Stephen must be the most mild-mannered of all the Austins."

"Righteous in judgment. I could have gone after that entire mob."

"And you'd have been the next tormented citizen riding a pole out to the wide prairie."

"It near soured me on the whole colony." Peyton lowered his voice again. "First, we had to light out from strict American law. Then here in Texas—where we've staked a claim—it's vigilante action that galls me…"

"But San Felipe is like any other Texas colony, Jonathan. Like any place in the world. There'll be puffed-up people you'd like to topple anywhere. Ayish Bayou was no different when we first came across the Sabine."

"Damn Ayish Bayou—I wanted to throw a horseshoe clear through that blacksmith's head!"

"See? Well, I'm surely glad Alex has gone off with Delilah and can't hear us now."

"Around the child, I do hold my tongue," he reminded her. He gave his wife's arm a mild squeeze, and she looked to make sure he was smiling.

"Like I was sayin', Mr. Peyton, we'll have two children under our roof come May. That's the change I have most on my mind." She didn't want to rile him. She had sensed he was ready to move on in their conversation, too.

Still, she wanted to voice a preference for destination before the family loaded up its wagons with provisions and got the slave help overwrought again. Angelina had brought eleven trusted workers back from her visit home to Tennessee the year before. Traveling was easier in their company, but she still feared heading to a place any more remote than this town alongside the Alamo.

"It's good we only rented out our inn back in San Felipe. We surely had an inkling we'd return to our own secured property, and where business already took root."

"Austin's relatives and those other cusses can take a fast horse to hell."

"But, husband," Angelina reminded him, "if we had to choose between a tyrant from Mexico City or any of our neighbors?"

"Not a one gifted in leadership like Stephen."

She couldn't disagree. It was Austin's father, Moses, who visualized colonization in Texas. It was he, the Peytons remembered during their months in San Antonio, who had come on his own all the way out to Bexar, as many knew it. The dreamer had at first been turned away from the governor's foyer—with the Mexican mood about immigrants staunchly negative before 1824. As the story went, it was the well-connected Baron von Bastrop—fluent in Spanish—who had run into the elder Austin in the plaza, and a second interview with the governor's people had allowed the original three hundred American families in Texas.

But Moses had not lived long after, and there was nothing short of reverence for the way his son Stephen had taken up the torch. Yet

Angelina understood how the attitude of some "originals" riled other pioneers.

"There's closeness among Austin's first colonists, I know. It's only a few, though, thinking themselves more rightful to act as judge and jury."

"Hell, we came to Texas before any of the San Felipe originals—even before Moses—Austin himself!" Her husband's outburst only made Angelina sigh.

"I don't want to count the camps we made or rivers we crossed in our first five years here."

"We were here before any of 'em."

"Well, darlin', don't start up that argument with any Mexicans or Comanche chiefs." They were approaching their mud and plaster compound at the edge of town, where the family rooms and servant quarters were clustered tightly together.

The home had been called a *villa* by some. Most townspeople regarded the Peytons as wealthy foreigners, but there was a genuine friendliness from their immediate neighbors. Maybe, because of the new baby on the way, her moods were already changing. Angelina just didn't want to stumble into worse circumstances, Indian hostility maybe. She surely didn't want ever again to endure the horror of fleeing. The Mississippi River would always deliver nightmares, as it had years after their escape, and in the round trip crossings she'd made later to see her family back home. Mrs. Jonathan Peyton didn't want to ease the door open while they still held different views about their next move.

"I don't like the idea of crawling back to San Felipe," he grumbled. "They're likely still swapping tales about how we went off in a huff after the doctor got tortured."

"They acted, knowing he wasn't the one and only doctor in the colony. Goin' back, at least we'd know there's someone to deliver babies."

"I'm thinking we'll pack up and head down to Matamoros before the cold weather sets in. Before travel gets any harder for you."

So, it would be *Matamoros* this next time.

Her husband had answered in a voice to end discussion. Angelina was making a map in her mind about river crossings, even if the family first went down past Goliad, which people here called *La Bahia*. Then, more rivers on the way southeast to the mouth of the Rio Grande. The San Antonio, the Guadalupe, the Colorado, and the Brazos were all unpredictable in any season. She was a tough woman, but sometimes she felt her husband took them both to be indestructible. For longer than the next season, life would become a rough, pathless direction and a string of rocking wagons. She had reasonable worries, but she knew it was no use talking further with her hard-headed husband.

Three months later, Jonathan and Angelina, their son and Delilah, as well as the caravan carrying the Peyton domestics and belongings, had made a half circle in the south and central wilderness regions of Texas territory. Fortunately, the word-of-mouth wisdom about the Comanche had proved true. The fierce warrior tribe had kept their domain somewhat beyond the northern edges of San Antonio. It appeared equally true that the displaced Karankawa were on the wane. From across a mesquite covered plain, a band of Indians, Apache probably, had seemed so unperturbed by the Peyton wagons that Alex was waving before Delilah could put a gentle hand on his arm.

Alongside Jonathan, had ridden Samson, a servant with Angelina's family in Tennessee since childhood. The graying man was superior to her husband, she thought, in judging the banks of the Rio Grande to be solid or shifting, before calling for the wheels to roll. Mr. Peyton, the fretful nomad, and the fifteen people traveling under his protection arrived at last in Matamoros without incident.

The city proved as bustling as New Orleans, its American neighbor up the gulf. Years before, in the weeks the Peytons had spent in Louisiana stocking up for the Texas crossover, they had witnessed cultural divisions and political opinions just as distinct. But French inhabitants of New Orleans had been its first residents. No one could dispute their right to continue their holdings and habits in the city. Yet there, as in San Antonio, a quaint friendliness encouraged the newcomer.

In Matamoros, Jonathan and Angelina judged the atmosphere as chilly as the weather on the day of their arrival. They had to pay an immigrant tax to pass along the main street, and they were escorted by Mexican police to the American section of town—over a third of the city's population—where privilege and pecking order seemed already well established. No discussion ensued without complaints about the treatment of U.S. ex-patriots. Even in the busy mud-baked inn, where the family lodged their first fortnight, the entry of Angelina and Jonathan into the dining hall one evening put no pause in a debate.

"Next they'll be taxing jugs of water."

"General Sesma, if that's the new one in charge, he might be more even-handed."

"I've got half a mind to buy passage on the next ship to New Orleans."

"Better make it *Mobile*," a man in a dingy dress-coat said to the stocky speaker, "unless you forgot the charges up against you from Fort Jessup."

"You got no call to circulate that topic, Ruben." The heavy man struggled up from a delicate chair.

"Don't ruffle so easy. Louisiana officers got no clout here. Down this way, they couldn't order an armadillo out before a firing squad," he laughed. "If you haven't forgotten, that's why you came."

"I've had about enough!"

"I know I have!" It was Angelina speaking. The argument was no particular business of the Peytons, but she recognized the tension in her husband's arm as prelude to a punch. If her tentative Spanish had made her reserved among Mexicans, in American company she spoke her mind.

"We didn't mean to upset your wife, Mr. Peyton."

"There's no one here hasn't seen talk spill into a brawl. I guess you all would have taken pleasure recently in San Felipe." Not a customer dared look up as the woman spoke on. "You like the stink in a street when skin is burnt with tar? Maybe you two would have loved being hauled away next on a cedar pole! All the way out to the wilderness!"

She wore the white tucked blouse and full dark skirt that Matamoros ladies preferred, and with her dark hair and tan complexion, she could have strolled in any marketplace without being pegged as a foreigner. Her fiery speech was her own. A handsome woman by any standards, and as far along as she was in her expectancy, Mrs. Peyton cast a spell on the gathering. She took her husband's hand to calm them both as she went on.

"There's no cause to bring up past threats. Or talk as if our worst menaces are Mexican authorities or law officers back home. The only power keeping any of us from being hauled off or strung up from one moment to the next...is our own decency." Her husband was helping her to a chair. "That being often as thin as a tortilla, we'd best take care to preserve something neighborly!"

The room went silent. No man was willing to dispute her final words. As one and then another tobacco pouch was produced and opened, an appealing aroma overtook the tension and smell of sweat. Two men lit pipes and a third offered chew to his neighbor.

"Well, I'll drink to that," said the fellow who had suggested a trip to Mobile. There was a grumble of assent. When talk resumed, attention turned to the newcomers.

"It's my understanding you took to San Antonio all right. They treated you with reasonable respect? I hear ole Seguin did honor to their governorship."

"Looks like it's his son Juan going in a political direction now," Jonathan said, nodding. "The entire family shows wholehearted support for colonist rights."

"I'd wager on Bexar, maybe the Alamo herself, as harbinger for how the whole of Texas fares." Looks were exchanged among travelers at the table and in the room. They assumed one another to be American sympathizers, but they also knew that Mexico put spies in among their kind as often as possible.

"How long you figure on staying down here in Matamoros?"

"Three or four months, until the weather calms," the traveler answered, without looking over at his wife. "We took the long but safer route here, where we reckoned government patrols would help chase off any Indian attack. A few heathens we saw kept their distance. Turned out it was some of Santa Anna's soldiers that menaced us more, stalking us nearly twenty miles on the banks of the Rio Grande."

"You all looking for passage on to New Orleans?"

"Just goin' north to San Felipe." When she heard her husband's answer, Angelina's head throbbed. The man in a suit coat had risen to give the well-spoken woman his chair. She had made herself sound strong, but suddenly she felt faint.

"We're going back to Stephen Austin's colony," she added. Lightheaded, she smiled at her husband. The unborn baby moved, pushing a heel against her rib cage. She found she could not keep tears from welling, and she was shocked to remind herself that it was the first time she had cried, even quietly, in a long time. After panicked flight from crime in Tennessee, fifteen hundred miles of nomadic moving, childbirth, a bittersweet visit back home, her husband's fits of temper, a disgusting attack on a physician—after all this, she could still not remember crying since the night she had let her guard down in old Natchez, at the home of Mrs. Ann Weeks.

But the thought of returning to San Felipe, to their own tavern and inn, overwhelmed her. The Peytons had built a life there, and she would not let her husband change his mind again until after this new baby was born. Jonathan offered her a handkerchief that was stuffed in his vest pocket, but she just shook her head.

"I don't mind tears when the air is this dry."

After mild months in Matamoros, spring rains fell less heavily than long-time residents of Texas would have predicted. With fortunate weather, the Peyton caravan made it back up north through the territory and along the banks of the Brazos River near San Felipe by the middle of April. In her final weeks of pregnancy, Angelina saw herself as coming full circle back to Mr. Austin's thriving colony. Delilah sometimes sat with her inside the main wagon when Alex took a turn beside his father on the driver ledge. The Peytons' most trusted helper would tell and retell how their exodus from Tennessee had unfolded. She often brought up their brief stop along the Mississippi.

"If I hear an angel sing in heaven, it won't be a voice any prettier than what God gave that little Miss Elizabeth."

"…that same hymn I knew growing up in the Tennessee hills…"

"You and your mama both sang it, though the words changed some, like customs do from one place to the next."

"Delilah, if you ever put into music all the moving that Jonathan Peyton and I have put you through, that one song will fill a hymnal."

"I won't lie and say I'm unhappy about heading back to San Felipe." They were at a bend in the Brazos, where travelers either took a hard turn west to Gonzales or continued their northerly course.

"We'll be back at our own inn, our own familiar home by this time tomorrow," Angelina sighed.

"May the Lord hasten us to a bed that won't rock like a boat, where you can safely bring forth another bold child!" Angelina found the pitching and vibrating of the wagon bearable, as long as home was near.

"Pray this baby comes easier than the first."

"Most men can't lay claim to half your strengths, Miss Angie." The servant laughed at her next thought. "Your baby might come along hat dancing into this dreary world!"

Delilah, Angelina thought, was the strong one when fortitude was most needed—and with a hopeful outlook that could brighten any day.

When the Peyton wagons rolled into Austin's colony the following afternoon, a sudden darkening of the sky seemed to underscore the mood of the hotel's temporary managers, unexpectedly displaced. The pair was obliged to scrounge up scattered belongings and move to the outer rooms of the town's largest inn as if they were mere guests themselves.

But lively talk soon bubbled at the lodgings Jonathan built. The entire population of San Felipe appeared riveted by what could be counted as only rumor so far. Titillating stories about the Tennessee governor Sam Houston overtook any grumblings about Jonathan Peyton's inopportune return. Certainly no one was still calling out judgments against "the nefarious doctor" run off months before.

Current speculation fixed on Houston's bride who had "fled the marriage chamber," as both Angelina and Delilah heard it. The colony's women would wait for privacy to guess what could have transpired between the thirty-five-year-old husband and his nineteen-year-old wife. What the men discussed was Houston's sudden resignation from his state's highest office. And what they all really wanted to know was whether the grandest conjecture could prove true—that Sam Houston intended to leave America altogether and was angling on horseback and downriver in the direction of Texas territory!

News about the squeeze on Texas colonists, it would seem, was making its way well beyond the Sabine River and into the states.

Mexico's Constitution of 1824, the document that had encouraged immigration into Texas, was now disputed. Even though Stephen F. Austin, beholden to his father's dream, had succeeded in bringing three hundred families to Texas, the tide was turning against further immigration from the East.

There was general cursing in the colony about how swiftly rulers in Mexico could shift. A decree was all but signed making slavery in the Spanish-speaking country illegal, and many Anglo colonists from the Southern United States read this as an underhanded move to coerce families back across the border with Louisiana—along with the workers they owned.

But now Sam Houston might be making his way gradually to Texas. Possibly for the express purpose of supporting colonists promised the right to govern themselves as they wished! Changing the major agreements that had worked between Mexico and self-sufficient colonists would be harder than forcing foreigners in Matamoros to pay an extra tax here and there.

Only two weeks after the return of the Peytons to their holdings and home in San Felipe, however, Angelina spent a day with no interest in politics whatsoever. And she was grateful in ways she could never express for Delilah's ability to take her mind off contractions and to make her smile during lapses in labor pain. Neither woman brought up the town's remaining doctor, who was due back from The Place at the Bend, a campground south of San Felipe.

"What is a nineteen-year-old girl going to enjoy from a thirty-five-year-old man?" Delilah asked.

"A fine house."

"Most important room in a mansion—a palace even—is the bedroom, if the wife isn't but nineteen."

"A woman any age…in my condition…might wish she'd never seen a bedroom."

Another pain came and Angelina groaned. Delilah went to the door and opened it enough to ask Jonathan if the doctor had been sighted. He moved his head from side to side. It wouldn't help Mrs. Peyton any to hear what kept the physician away. Whether someone had suffered a crushed leg or partial scalping, it wouldn't matter to the woman about to give birth. Delilah had only been in the background when Alex was born. A proper doctor had been attending, and Stephen Austin himself had been in town then to toast the new parents.

The Peytons' servant had helped bring dark-skinned children into the world, and she knew that the stages were the same for a mother of any color.

"Praise Jesus you weren't with child every time your bed chamber changed location here in Texas, Mrs. Angelina." The expectant woman was panting and trying to smile. "I cannot count how many dwellings you and Mr. Peyton…" Then, there was a change in the expression both women wore. Angelina was struggling to speak.

"…the baby is…"

The delivery of her second child was the merciful kind—far easier than the first, but not with the troubles that often presented themselves during the fifth or the eleventh pregnancy.

Angelina and Jonathan Peyton now had a daughter. *Margaret,* she was soon named. A healthy newborn was reason enough for the Peyton Inn and Tavern to host a celebration.

In the next two years, the child came to be called "Mag." Whatever made conceiving difficult for Angelina Peyton, she was grateful for the space between Alex and the little dark-haired daughter. The tiny girl babbled in partial sentences and gladly held the hand of Delilah or Alex while the mistress oversaw routine and accounts at San Felipe's thriving inn.

Angelina had always shown a good mind for business. In New Orleans, she'd made shrewd purchases as they first prepared to cross the Sabine into Texas territory. After a few anniversaries as immigrants, she had determined to travel back to Tennessee for her family's most loyal and willing workers. She minded her instincts about fair prices and the changing of bed linens in their hotel rooms. If her cooking savvy didn't rival any of the inns where they had stayed in the French Quarter or Matamoros, Angelina had most certainly picked up a number of meal components from the efficient Mexican women she'd observed in the market streets of San Antonio.

Even without official apprenticeship in inn-keeping, she sensed the importance of treating luminaries with special attention. San Felipe would always be considered the most important of the original Texas colonies, and Stephen Austin was often present, ready for consultation. Occasionally, he traveled down south as far as Mexico City to advocate continuance of the self-rule clause established between his father Moses and the Mexican government.

Among the dignitaries who lodged at the Peyton Inn by 1830 was Sam Houston himself. He had crossed the Louisiana border at St. Augustine and then gone the short distance to Nacogdoches, where he seemed at ease with the mix of Mexicans and Americans, and with the mostly friendly Caddo Indians nearby. But later the same year, tension between colonists and Santa Anna's government worsened. The former Tennessee governor traveled to San Felipe to discuss the future of Anglo Texas with Mr. Austin.

Angelina Peyton prepared to greet a tall Tennessee man, and one with the demeanor a new bride might find off-putting. But she was completely surprised by the man's magnetism and friendliness. The sorry shift in his disposition didn't occur until he had poured a fourth or fifth drink. By the end of his short stay in San Felipe, however, she could see that the unwelcome transformation was a daily occurrence.

"Mrs. Peyton, don't let my sitting here at the table cause you to rush," the former governor said amicably one afternoon. "I'll feast on the aromas coming from your kitchen until you say it's serving time."

"We have half our help working on dinner today. Hope you've developed a taste for Mexican cuisine."

"Never been told I wasn't a hearty eater," he said. "I'll just have another glass of whiskey while your people work on the fixings."

While Angelina fussed in the kitchen over the preparation of fajitas and frijoles, she assessed a pile of beets that needed to be cooked or discarded. The combination of bland farm food and ethnic specialties would be odd, but as anyone understood in the wilderness, nourishment of any kind was not to be turned down.

Meanwhile, the atmosphere in the Peyton dining hall grew boisterous. Everyone in San Felipe knew that Houston was visiting, and as many people as possible were squeezing into the inn where the Tennessee legend was staying. Most were not waiting for dinner, but the drinks went round and round, even in the afternoon.

"I'd say it's going to take statehood to get us out of this mess!" There were some cheers, but also grumbles from the crowd.

"Over my dead body!" One man had jerked as if suddenly awake. "How come I crossed the Sabine into foreign territory to begin with? Statehood my hind quarters!"

"I don't think Moses himself would have tolerated much joining talk at this point," Sam Houston added warily.

"Statehood is loose talk. Don't talk foolish. If our speculation wanders that far, we'll surely forfeit the nod of Tejanos like Juan Seguin." The angry man stopped as if checking again for spies. "He's all for independence, though. We're lucky he's on our side."

"By and by—about joining the Union—that's what I meant."

"You've got way too many horses before the first cart!" Another red-faced man suddenly held the floor. "If we don't show enough damn spunk to get treated right by Santy Anna, ain't nobody gonna respect Texians in the future!"

There was a murmur of general accord.

"Mr. Austin's doing what he can at the diplomatic level," Houston went on. "Glad I arrived before he took off again for Mexico City. I don't think the legacy of Moses Austin is threatened enough to warrant statehood talk any time soon."

"It would take a long stretch in a dungeon to put a damp on Stephen's spirit!"

"Even visits from the overbearing Mexican officials don't take the diplomacy out of his dealings—or Seguin's!"

"Here's to our impresario *Esteban!*"

Except for the presence of a leader from Tennessee, the discussion that afternoon was the kind that Angelina and Jonathan had heard often. But when dinner was served, there were mixed reactions to the Mexican dish, and general opposition to its being served up with over-boiled beets. Fiery flavoring did nothing to tenderize the beef strips. Sober men would have known to chew and keep silent, but enough drink had been consumed that several comments, meant to be exchanged under the breath and out of earshot, were overheard by Angelina herself, as well as her irritable husband.

"If this is the best cooking a man in a dungeon can expect, I'd opt for a firing squad," one drunken diner declared. Sam Houston was laughing at that observation while he examined a piece of gristle.

"I wouldn't wager any money right now, which it would be..." He leaned over toward his neighbor at the table, but spirits had made his voice loud. "If I stepped out to where your mount was hitched, would it be a saddle lying on the ground with no horse under it, or your horse standing naked without a saddle on its back? Either way, this tough chunk tells me you were robbed some time before dinner preparations got underway!"

The insult was likely the beginning of Angelina's coolness toward Sam Houston. It was hard to abide newcomers of any stripe—from any American quadrant—who acted as if they comprehended survival better than original colonists did, much less the Peytons. Some loudmouths seemed not to know who first arrived to scratch an existence from Texas soil.

Often enough, the presence of Sam Houston, or talk about the latest magic he had negotiated with the Indians up near Nacogdoches, put the innkeeper and his wife on edge. They fretted over speculation that the former Tennessee governor might defy Mexican military if soldiers continued crisscrossing Texas.

Oddly, young William Barrett Travis had the opposite effect on the couple. His reputation as a hothead made him cautious about where he sought lodging, but visits from the Alabama lawyer lifted the mood at the Peyton Inn. San Felipe colonists, who were the most ardent admirers of Stephen Austin's calm negotiations, widely opposed any stance that Mexican officials could construe as insulting. Still, Jonathan and Angelina found Travis charming. In the next several months, his fondness for little Mag won their special consideration.

"Where'd the little prairie princess go? She was just here? Where is she?" Giggles came from underneath the popular dining table at the inn. The lively lawyer pretended again to lose sight of the three-year-old.

"Find me!"

"I hear that princess voice !" Travis lifted his mug and then the linen napkin that was folded next to his plate. "Could she be under here? Or here?"

The child's laughter brought Delilah, who knelt down to coax the toddler out. A stream of colony residents would be rushing in later to wait for supper, and it was time to hum to the little girl, let her nap during the hot afternoon. Delilah wondered what Mag's expression would have been upon hearing the small brown angel Elizabeth singing away in Natchez. The Peytons' servant claimed no gifted voice herself, but believed it was children who gave the world some soothing grace. As affectionate a cherub as any, the innkeepers' daughter let Delilah lift her from the floor before giving a playful swat at the top of the man's head.

Only Angelina Peyton and Mr. Travis remained in the room. His short temper reminded her of her own husband. But she thought the lawyer was young enough that his irascible ways might eventually change.

He had never spoken of a wife back home, but Angelina knew him to mention a son east of the Sabine. She felt he trusted her, if ever he were inclined to personal talk. Busy as she was, she mostly kept to herself even around other women. Now the lone man in the Peyton dining room studied her cautiously.

"According to letters from home…my boy has a little sister. It appears I have a daughter about the same age as yours," he said, fiddling with the napkin. He didn't elaborate on the older child he'd once alluded to. "My own little girl couldn't be more charming than your *Mag*, Mrs. Peyton, but I like to think she has equal gaiety and cleverness about her."

"If your daughter is mostly cheerful and smart, she'd be taking after her father's best traits." Angelina spoke quietly, trying not to convey shock that Travis had more family back in America than she'd imagined. San Felipe colonists knew the lodger to have registered for a land parcel with Mr. Austin, and he had legally declared himself as "unmarried."

The young man's talk was usually trained on the future—starting up a law practice over in Anahuac, near the Louisiana border, starting up rebellion that could lead to independence. Angelina served him a glass of ale, though she grew wary of a change in his expression.

"I sit here wishing my own daughter might be very much like Mag," he confessed again. "And then I have to ask myself why all wives, in the first place, can't be the strong and trusted kind—like you. I hope that compliment doesn't overstep boundaries." His hand slid near hers where she was removing a platter.

"Well, it counts as flattery but not flirtation. I'll testify you're not the least tempted to court me away from Mr. Peyton." She set the dish at a distance, and they both laughed self-consciously. There was no one to overhear, but Angelina herself would abide nothing more than sibling regard from this rash fellow.

"I suppose it's too early for second drink?"

"Sam Houston wouldn't claim as much!"

"Don't go and malign my hero," he chuckled. "If you do, I'll withhold my toast to your beauty and spitfire personality!"

"All right, Mr. Buck Travis. That's enough fresh bandying for one day." She couldn't deny she was pleased. Handling conversation with men easily, she grew as irritable as Jonathan when she found herself among women recounting their domestic duties. Political discussion held her attention. "So, Austin is going to grant you a land parcel, even though the law just passed last April decrees an end to new American immigration."

"Our commander figures on very little enforcement," Travis conceded. "He's counting on the self-governance clause still holding—a good eight years after being writ."

"Holding somewhat better than the Brazos in an April flood!" Angelina felt the blood rush to her face. "Revolution talk is already over the banks." For the first time, in spite of their earlier banter, William Travis looked over his shoulder to make sure there was no San Felipe visitor of Mexican descent listening from the doorway.

"I count independence as inevitable," Travis said.

Angelina Peyton lifted the napkin from the man's hands and folded it again, the way Mrs. Weeks from Natchez had delicately set hers out.

"You reckon Mexican authorities will cede to us our sovereignty without a fight?" she asked at last.

"Oh…it will take facing off."

She didn't wish to take the topic any further. She had been debating nothing else with her husband for weeks, trying to calm him. It wouldn't soothe Jonathan any for her to get equally wrought up about strict Mexican law enforcement. And if the conflict turned violent, few in San Felipe believed Stephen F. Austin possessed adequate military knowhow. But neither Peyton could feel easy with a leader like Sam Houston, should colonists and Mexicans ever square off. How could a man with his weaknesses organize and lead a movement sufficient to deter government aggression?

The innkeepers had heard vehement colonist views over threatened property rights—plenty of anger and almost no agreement. If slavery could be abolished with the stroke of a pen, did that mean that the land several hundred families had toiled over could be relinquished to a swaggering general sent north from Mexico City?

No immigrant from the United States could dismiss as unrelated the hard choices of American colonists in 1776 or the more recent war with Britain in 1812. Every night Jonathan came to bed with heated opinions about who had said what at his supper table that evening, especially once whiskey and ale began to flow. Not every visitor had the discretion to look over a shoulder before conversing, the way the Alabama lawyer was apt to do. Even an English-speaking dinner guest, in the swirling atmosphere, could turn out to be a spy for General Cos. All Mexican officials were on alert for treasonous discussion. Staunch supporters like the Seguins of San Antonio hardly added up to protection against centralist threats. Hotels and whole cities could be burned to the ground. If there were enemies to central control, such danger could be eradicated.

"Give me liberty, by God! Or else death!" Angelina's husband had come to bed that night, hissing through his teeth. "Your Spanish is getting darn good, missus. Never mind that a Mexican general doesn't know Patrick Henry from Napoleon." He sat up and punched at their quilt. "You could shape the sense of it into Spanish words that these strutting officers can understand!"

"Hush, darlin'. You need some good sleep."

She had tried to calm Jonathan. Not often, but on some nights, Angelina settled into bed grimly assessing the challenges of a marriage contract. Since childhood, she'd loved her husband with an affection not unusual for cousins. Their bond was indisputable, but occasionally she let herself admit that matrimony was a long stretch of difficult concessions. Occasionally, she imagined a second life, her own life, at the end of long appeasement.

She went to bed worried that her husband would still be grumbling in the morning. Never forgotten was a sunrise back in Tennessee, not long into their venture as a married couple, when Jonathan had awakened angry. He had allowed a grudge to build up as the day wore on. By nightfall, there was a body, a knife wound brought by Jonathan's hand. The couple had gone running for the Ohio River.

Angelina often dreamt that they were again rushing down the wide Mississippi. This night she suffered another dark illusion that an angry man had burst into the Peytons' hotel and was pressing a knife against her husband's chest. She awoke wondering if half the men in Texas hadn't been jolted away from their home states by a failed marriage or a blade thrust in a fit of temper. Tales about William Travis suggested that he had fled both in Alabama. And wasn't Jim Bowie now drifting from town to town in Texas with much the same rumors trailing behind in Louisiana and as far north as Natchez? The innkeeper's wife lay in bed shaking her head.

Heaven help the peace-loving families that came to Texas on the grandiose whim of Moses Austin…if the likes of Sam Houston, Travis and Bowie come to be our protectors!

Her husband was breathing noisily, on the brink of snoring it appeared. At least he wasn't coughing. A flare of temper only provoked his coughing fits.

When she dreamt next that her husband and William Travis were menacing a Mexican militia with nothing but hunting knives drawn, Angelina Peyton opened her eyes and was relieved that it was daylight, that her husband lay undisturbed in the bed beside her. His fine black hair had fallen over his eyes. His pale skin made him look more peaceful in sleep than he ever appeared awake and brooding.

She could hear Mag's cheerful morning chatter in the next room, and Delilah talking to the child in a near whisper. Angelina gave herself a few calm minutes before easing herself out from the covers. She knew that Alex would knock before coming in to hug her and ask his father about the stars or the vegetable crops, but she wanted to recover from the series of nightmares that had kept her tossing and turning. One minute of perfect morning calm might help her sustain self-possession during the course of the day.

Suddenly, Mrs. Peyton sat up and threw her legs over the edge of the bed. She sprang to a standstill for a moment, shuddering, with her back to the covers. She balanced stiffly, as if a cruel danger had crept into the room and still lurked in a corner behind her. Then, she walked across to the door latch. She had to swallow before she could call out softly.

"Delilah, you'll keep Alex with you all for a while, won't you?"

"Yes'm. Of course. Mag and I will go on into his room."

"I'll be dressed in just a few minutes. I'll be out shortly."

When she turned to look at the bed where Mr. Peyton lay, she could see from a distance what had not been clear while lying by his side in the gray morning light. He was resting so peacefully. His expression was without agitation and his chest stayed calm. Her Jonathan, always struggling so for ease of mind, had mercifully slipped into the arms of angels—that is what she prayed for. This was how she reassured herself.

She went back to her side of the bed and sat next to him. His hand was already cold, and she cried just a little before reminding herself how much she had already endured in this sputtering, startling territory. She made promises to heaven about what she would be strong enough to manage, for the sake of Alex and Mag and Delilah.

In the next two days, many of the same San Felipe townspeople who had stormed against a foolishly outspoken doctor a few seasons ago stepped in to help. Angelina's neighbors brought chopped wood and hot dishes and hymnals to the inn. Stephen Austin had been preparing to travel to Mexico City, but he delayed starting out to attend the funeral of Jonathan Peyton.

The tall cedars at the edge of the cemetery in San Felipe stood guard, or so it seemed to the lone woman. She drew some comfort that the trees had grown far taller than the average specimen. Her husband had been one-of-a-kind, and memories of their unpredictable life together would prevail. And there were solitary red oaks, so stately that, in their years together at San Felipe, she had often walked to the graveyard from the couple's tavern. It had already proven itself a place of some serenity in the middle of a chaotic day. She had a powerful feeling that the setting would abide unchanged.

Six headstones in the cemetery had names and dates engraved, but only rustic wooden crosses identified other mounds. On one grave an unfinished stone had rested askew for two years. Someday there would be a marker for Jonathan, but such arrangements required time.

It was property and debts that would now demand an accounting. Papers had to be signed and hotel responsibilities officially verified. Members of the other Texas colonies were aiming to pass through San Felipe in the following week. The status of the entire Texas territory urgently needed discussion. Delegates, eventually on their way up the river to Washington-on-the-Brazos would look for overnight lodging at least.

Pausing in the cemetery shadows, Angelina was already trying to remember whether there were two or three hogs in the pen that could be slaughtered and dressed for the extra cooking that Peyton Inn would face.

In Texas, one could afford no languishing during seasons of grief. Life was a current rushing downstream—on and on as unstoppable as the Mississippi. You had to let duties take life in its destined direction. You couldn't allow the dark eddies, even disasters, to drag you and your children on down to the bottom.

1835 Natchez, Mississippi

4   Gone, the Old Moorings

"Wait! Can you see the notch? Is it lined up?"

"Don't lift. Just push. One very easy push." Apokta was helping Shelby Whitmire assemble a canister cabinet. Mr. Todd, down at the river had ordered another. The hotel was expanding its lodging services, and there were several good women from under-the-hill, some from the Indian's extended family, who prepared grains for hot porridge.

Other orders for Shelby's carpentry came in steadily—tables, chairs, bed frames, trunks, washstands, and rocking cradles. It had started with the timber left from flatboats coming to the end of their journey at Natchez. Houses were built from the lumber of lapped and tied flatboats, but there were always boards left over that Shelby couldn't let rot slowly alongside the driftwood. Besides, sawed planks would never wear down beautifully like a curving limb. Mr. Todd had passed along a pile of tools abandoned on his porch. It was Apokta, though, who first mastered the woodworking instruments.

When Shelby's father and stepmother were among the first to succumb to the yellow fever of 1831, the rough cabin not far from the Creeks' edge of town had become all Shelby's. His sisters soon relocated into the Mississippi interior. In the dignified level of town, they would always have been regarded as from "under." He couldn't blame them for finding husbands whose first goal was to move on. The woodshop and small adjacent room, constructed on sturdy pilings of the same style that crowded the Natchez shore, provided him home enough.

"Sizemore!" In the carpenter's doorway stood Apokta's older son, already tall like his father. These days, he was also the industrious youth who'd become driver of Mrs. Weeks' cart. He had rushed up the steep stairway and into the open cabin, but he knew to wait until his father finished easing the cabinet notches into grooves.

"May you one day have a son like Tail Feather," the Creek man said to Shelby. "Such a son will lose all words when he sees wood worked into beauty." The grown boy at the door smiled, but he was eager to deliver a message.

"Your wife wants to speak with you."

"My wife is your mother," the older man said patiently. Shelby thought the two could be brothers. They looked so much alike, even in dress. They both wore striped woven shirts that came to their thighs, and buckskin leggings tucked into high tasseled boots. Whitmire thought his friend's son needed some lessons about tying the sash at his waist. Apokta had removed his waistband before handling saws and chisels. Absent the contrast, Tail Feather's shiny cloth belt folded over smartly enough.

"She said you will come without delay, if I call you by your married name." The father noticed his friend's puzzled expression.

"She is *Sizemore* in the Alabama country. Our custom is wise compared to whites," he went on. "We men take our name from the wife's family."

"Mr. Whitmire probably knows."

"I'd forgotten. I've called you…just *Apokta* for so many years."

"Only to my wife, I am *Sizemore*" He turned from Shelby to his son. "Tell your mother I long to hear her words."

Tail Feather nodded at them, and the three seemed to understand that the boy would deliver precisely that message. But the older man's movements were unhurried. His wife would wait a few minutes. When his son left, Apokta set down the two notched pieces that he had been holding steady. He reached for his sash.

"Remember, civilized neighbor…" Shelby had heard his friend's mildly mocking tone before. "When you marry, take the name of your wife." He was tying the satin material at his waist in a meticulous fashion. "Less war in the wigwam."

"You do keep peace in a big family—with two sons, and I remember how many daughters you have—two, besides Fleur, but their names…"

"More Sizemores."

There was no worry about Shelby ever forgetting Fleur. Almost the entire Creek family had gone east along the great trail for a month some years earlier, to see a great-grandfather living his last weeks on the edge of Alabama. Fleur, expecting her first child, declined the trip and stayed to mourn her own husband, drowned only weeks before. By all calculations, nothing else was to happen in the month the family was away. When her early labor pains began, she had pounded on Shelby's cabin door. The baby boy that Shelby helped her deliver was named *Thank Ye the Lord*, but they all called the child *Thanks*.

"By first names or last…your family has been a better part of Natchez as far as I can remember."

"For under-the-hill, 'better' sparkles like gold on donkey hide."

As a youngster, Shelby had not understood how often his neighbor's words, much less his silences, indicated irreverence. Now they were both thinking the married man had better hurry to his wife. Any discussion alluding to Natchez proper drove Shelby's thoughts to the Weeks household.

"If it weren't for Tail Feather, you and I couldn't keep at all apprised of life in town, up on that hill." He shook his head. For almost a decade, fair work arrangements with Mrs. Ann had benefitted the industrious Creek family as well as the lone Whitmire, but he winced about the topic he'd broached.

"I have many worries for you, Shelby," Apokta spoke up kindly. "Man worries." He paused before pressing the theme. "You are no wagon boy, like my son. A grown man must give his heart a voice." This habitual conversation opener usually went no farther.

"Go talk to Mrs. Sizemore," Shelby said, shrugging and waving him away.

The older man went out to the open doorway, but he turned suddenly before going down the steps.

"I cannot believe you forget the names of my other daughters. Besides Fleur, I have Lily and Dawn Rose."

The grooved joints, to be brushed with glue later, could not be well placed by just one carpenter, so Shelby picked up a plane and began to smooth the edges of a china shelf he had taken on. He had tried to convince the Monroe sisters—the women who eventually bought old Mrs. Greenfield's house—that his craftsmanship was not the quality they imagined, but the new ladies told him they were in no hurry. They liked the shoe shelf he had fashioned for Mrs. Ann next door, and they had confidence in what he could design.

He ran the plane in a steady, even stroke. Pine peelings fell to the floor. He never minded sweeping up after a day's work. Occasionally, he still longed for the company of his father. But he'd come close to rejoicing at the death of his stepmother. He did celebrate the cabin's transformative calm. With Apokta and the good man's relatives in their secure huts and cabins nearby, no dangers common on the Natchez shore encroached.

As Shelby moved the plane rhythmically along the edging strips, his thoughts shifted from Mrs. Ann's neighbor, who had freed her slaves, to the singing girl who had gone with her abolitionist mistress to Philadelphia. He was smiling about his Creek neighbors, the extended Sizemore family, and then about the shoe shelf Ann Weeks had praised when he realized that her son, his long-time friend Thomas, was now standing in the threshold. The carpenter briefly paused with the tool in his hands but he didn't speak right away.

On some days, he encountered Thomas three times, and the younger man would do all the talking. But then Shelby wouldn't see him for weeks, and Ann's son would show up at last moody and silent. Thomas had shown himself disposed to an erratic demeanor since childhood, though before the era of slate tablets and classrooms he had been allowed to chatter and to let his whims play out. Discipline requirements of primary school and eventually the academy had set the youth on edge.

What was worse now for twenty-six-year-old Shelby was that the widow often requested him to counsel her son. The former hired boy was the best friend of Thomas and his happiest influence, she would declare. At times when she confided her worries, Shelby hoped the premature gray in his sideburns made him look older. Yet it was impossible to declare a different and abiding kind of affinity for the mother—just *Ann,* Shelby wanted to call her… *dearest,* someday, *beloved.*

That was the step that Apokta had been suggesting since Shelby himself had turned twenty, about the same age Ann's son was now. On this morning, Thomas had placed something on the landing before moving to the cabin's open doorway. He wasn't smiling, so Shelby waited for his friend to speak. The morning light was only halfway to its noon peak, and Thomas appeared to have the glow of expectation behind whatever he was about to say.

"Did you see the *Natchez* pull in yesterday, just downstream of Todd's?"

"I surely did. There's one steamship you wouldn't need a lookout piece to spy. I'm almost accustomed to its Vicksburg turn-around these days."

"I'm glad it was named when it went no farther north of us," Thomas said. Shelby smiled and ran his fingers over the surface of the pine edging.

"Put together in New York. It's made to last. If Louisville shipbuilders get to copying its side-wheel, so many steamers will stop at our docks we'll need thirty hotels on the strand."

"The *Natchez* won't be unraveling. Remember when we used to see them come apart? It's modern times now and most are seaworthy." Shelby nodded, still wondering at the reason for his friend's morning visit.

"Makes it from here to New Orleans in two or three sunsets, I suppose." Marveling, he shook his head.

"Shelby, you seen a paper from New Orleans, lately—*The True American?*"

"You're the one with the school diploma and the habit of reading. And the leisure time."

"Only a primary certificate. I'll be damned if I can finish academy!" This was the kind of language that Shelby would scowl about in the presence of Mrs. Ann, but he let himself chuckle.

"The best I can figure is…most of us come into this world with either mismatched families…peculiar gifts…fortune or happiness just beyond reach."

"It was you always displayed the temperament for schooling," Thomas agreed. He appeared in a state of nervous energy, and Shelby wasn't yet sure whether his mood bent to cheerful or morose. His young friend stood bracing his hands against the door frame.

"Anyway," the carpenter went on without complaint. "I didn't get offered academy tuition. And I might have fainted if I had been. With time, it's all worked out. Fate has proven me not half bad with a saw and a hammer."

"You could have been an architect—like my father."

"What I recall about your papa…I remember him paying you affectionate attention." Shelby was always cautious when Thomas brought up his other parent. "All I meant about mismatches was…it seems most people have one serious thing or another to rise to…" Lately, Shelby Whitmire was also wary of conversations that might touch on how he felt, and for how long, about Thomas' mother. Something made his younger friend nod in agreement.

"Coming of age, a man might need to battle some doldrums before striking out on his own."

"Then…have you decided on a trade? Is it an apprenticeship that you're—"

"I've got my bags, right here, and packed for New Orleans," Thomas announced. He leaned toward the outer landing and dragged in two long travel satchels.

Shelby set the plane on his workbench and clapped the woody residue from his hands. It now seemed that Tail Feather's mother had no urgent message to give Apokta. The youths in both families had apparently entered into mild conspiracy. This private conversation now at the Whitmire cabin was all their arranging.

"You're leaving Natchez?"

"Already bought my ticket. I've been helping with the lift wagon for more than a fortnight. I saved from tending Mr. Doyle's counter at the grocery, too, if you want to know. And some nights I come down to guard the porch at Mr. Todd's, even though I know you wouldn't advise the risk."

"What do you aim to hire yourself out as in New Orleans?" Shelby was trying to keep his voice even. He wanted to ask right away if his friend's mother knew he had plans to travel downstream.

"Here's what the newspaper said three weeks ago, and the next two issues have the same ads, Shelby." He was again the nonstop talker he had been as a child. "Dozens and dozens of dock workers have joined up in one militia or another. There's near a whole battalion—the Greys are already off to Texas. It says so on the front page."

"You're not volunteering for— "

"No, but they need dock workers now, all over New Orleans! So many are joining the militias—gone to raise arms against all Mexico, if it comes to that. So, now they're in bad need of loaders at the wharf. At least in the American district. I've been working around docks and landings and ship ropes all my life!"

"All nineteen years."

"I'm near twenty," Thomas said, primed for debate. Shelby's heart was racing, too. He didn't want to cast the discussion in a negative light.

"Our town, ancient and thriving as she is, and on the edge of Mississippi territory, that's one thing—but New Orleans?"

"There's no school that teaches imagination. No diploma hands that out. I can picture a big city…"

Thomas strode farther into the workroom, sat on a stool, and folded his arms across his chest. In the back of Shelby's mind was a warning not to say how some young men found trouble in places like New Orleans, or places like New York, in the case of his friend's father.

Just a trip down the river and back would not be such an outlandish adventure for a twenty-year-old, he thought, taking up the plane aimlessly. Young men in Natchez considered the trip a rite of passage, those whose lives unfolded under-the-hill as well as the ones with academy diplomas. Why Shelby himself had an aversion to floating away toward the ocean, he couldn't say. Possibly too much of his life had already rushed away on a current.

"You'll need money for the return trip. Something must be put aside, so that you never lack that fare. That's a wise measure to take, no matter who the man is or where he's headed—to never depart without a way to get back home. Once back, you may hold a different view of your first prospects."

"You sound like a father," Thomas said, smiling. This was a compliment and complaint the younger fellow had been voicing since he was four.

"Since you mention a parent's concern…"

"Yes," he sighed. "I've already talked to Mother. She knows I'm going."

"She does?"

"She's not happy, but you could have guessed that. Anyway, she's got Sara and Levi yet, and one sister still unmarried." Thomas seemed to have more to say. But his expression changed again. "She made me promise to see you before I drag these bags to the dock."

"Otherwise you'd have gone downriver without a word?"

"Here…" He reached down into one satchel and pulled out a shallow box with a lid of ivory inlay. It was nothing Shelby recognized. "Keep this for me. She says it's papers and letters my father left me. I know what she hopes, that I'll read what he wished for me and won't have the heart to set out on a different course." He put the box in his friend's hands.

"You didn't read any?"

"It's something to have in safekeeping, as a grown man."

"Listen, Thomas, whatever your own father…"

"It's you that's been my father, Shelby Whitmire. Mismatched—you put it to words—but it was still always you." He was busy retying the straps on the bag, yet he brushed his sleeve across his face. "The box will have something…I know… something giving me an even more tender view of Mother…" His voice had trailed off. "As if either one of us could take a more tender view…"

"All right then, *son*—little brother, anyway. Let me give you fare for getting home. I'll keep the box for you, but I don't usually store valuables on the premises. Apokta says that's why I never get robbed."

"I made the firm decision yesterday," Thomas went on pleading, with himself really. "Nothing will make me change my mind. I'm turning twenty. So I might as well start doing…acting on my own true knowledge."

Too much was happening too fast. Shelby doubted that he could ever have been the architect of an entire building, much less his own destiny. He couldn't, for the life of him, think of any argument or action to dissuade the adventure Thomas Weeks had in mind.

"Well, take this cash, at least. And shake my hand like family would."

"You'd better go talk to Mother yourself in the next day or two," Thomas suddenly admonished him. "I don't know which one of us is more due…some action, at last."

He was out the door and down the double landing steps to the shore level before Shelby had time to admit that he wouldn't make progress today on anyone's cabinet. He put away his tools and struggled against the impulse to follow Thomas to the shore. He could confirm the worthiness of the well-known steamboat. But he had admired the vessel the previous afternoon, and he had already deemed the boat quite fit.

In a whirl of competing conclusions, he closed up the log building, climbed down the weathered steps, and walked briskly in the direction of Mr. Todd's inn. He slipped past the taverns, and then past the cabin where immodestly dressed women leaned over the railing and dried their hair. They recognized Shelby Whitmire, not just as the sturdy, appealing workman who wouldn't have needed to pay for female company. He was the one who ran a shop with the Indian. A woman too sad to have such pretty blond curls had given up trying to entice him a second time. She rarely turned to the street, unless it was him…the boy who had grown up with an endearing loyalty to some lady up in the proper part of town. As he passed by, he made a nod to them and to a man staggering alongside the pilings. Nobody above or below called out.

It was one of Mr. Todd's sons now often shifting trunks and parcels on the hotel porch, but the commotion of the wharf area never changed. Scurrying and scolding interspersed with threats or peals of laughter. Shelby had no interest in late debate with Thomas Weeks. He felt compelled, though, to watch the steamboat eventually stoke its fires and pull away from shore.

In the crowd, he stood inconspicuously. At last, he spotted his friend. The nineteen-year-old had taken his hat off and was leaning at the rails closest to the bow of the ship. Two other fellows were talking with him and gesturing in the direction the current took. Shelby couldn't let himself believe that the trip was cause for great concern. Unlike the architect father from New York and unlike the Peyton couple running off to Texas years ago, this young man was freely choosing adventure. It was a reasonable step for a young man turning twenty.

When the *Natchez* left its docking spot and began to steam on down the Mississippi, Shelby wondered at his own resistance to travel. He told himself that the season for taking fanciful risks in life had passed him by. His own youth had been mismatched with hardships and longings of the kind mostly worn out by adulthood.

"But now you must go talk to Mrs. Ann," was what Apokta advised him at the shop later that afternoon.

"Thomas told me that she already knows."

"No. You must now tell her, what else we both know. Let Tail Feather show you how he handles the cart these days. Tell Mrs. Ann you rode the cart up the hill, for the sake of old times. This will start the beginning."

Shelby's last stop at the Weeks house was when the Monroes, next door, sent word about wanting a china shelf. That was only a month ago, but when he knocked at the shiny door—set and first varnished long ago by Thomas' father—he felt it had been years since he'd worked up the courage to wait for Ann's turning of the latch.

"I thought you would come on up," she greeted him. She held a dripping hand mop. She was wearing a full apron and her red hair was wrapped up in a muslin dishtowel. One section of the floor was wet, and she dragged a bucket nearer the stove before sitting down. Shelby didn't think she looked thirty-five, but he didn't think she needed to be scrubbing wooden planks at her age either.

"Sara and Levi could be doing that if there's no one to hire for the chore," he suggested, pulling out a chair for himself. "School won't keep them occupied for another month."

"God bless Mrs. Greenfield," she said, catching her breath. "I guess I'd have servants like everyone else in Natchez, if she hadn't been so vocal against slavery."

"Did you get a new letter? Is it settled she's a Quaker?"

"It's official she's joined a Friends Society. Official, up there anyway, that Miss Elizabeth has her freedom, too." She smiled, but Shelby thought she had probably done some crying earlier in the morning. "There's just no taking hold of this world, is there…to make it sit still," she wondered, shaking her head.

"That's the kind of thing I was telling Thomas a few hours ago."

"I don't know why I feel so torn about his going. Every male in Natchez his age runs off to see New Orleans."

"That's the other thought I had. Every man, except me, maybe," Shelby laughed. "He was already with some other Mississippi boys when the ship started out."

"You saw him leave? Had he shown you the newspaper clippings?"

"About the need for dock help in New Orleans?"

"Clippings his father passed on to him. Well, I suppose he will keep them pretty much private."

"Some things feel so private…they're hard for a man to bring up, even to someone close."

"He had a box of papers. In one paragraph, it was his own father's hand that put a little line under the mention of *drink*. I have to hope Thomas won't be taken in by any taverns rougher than what we have right here under-the-hill." Ann stopped herself, and tossed the hand mop into the bucket. She grabbed at the knot that held up her hair and shook her head. "I scoured every inch of this floor not three days ago. I believe I'm just throwing myself into toil to prevent a fit of idle worry."

"Ann, you should have peace of mind about your oldest child not taking to alcohol." Dropping the formal address after all these years was instinctive in the circumstances. Sara and Levi, nearly grown up, were not in the house. And the way their mother's hair fell about her shoulders would have made any admirer risk familiarity. "Thomas heard enough about drink being the ruin of my own papa—heard me complain about it every day when we were little."

"Only one person, Shelby, could treasure your friendship as much as my darling boy does, and that's me!" She stood up and came over to put an arm around his shoulder. "I'd have felt sick to think he left without taking in some of your counsel." She kissed him on the cheek.

Standing up, too, he took one of Ann's hands in his. She smiled at him and reached up to pat a place in his hair just over his ear. She was shaking her head, but she kept smiling.

"At first, I thought he came to the decision over New Orleans, because of my news…about Mr. Harris."

"Ezekial?" He was an older gentleman, in business on the eastern edge of Natchez.

"I stayed a widow so long after losing my first husband. I think it fairly shocked all the children that I would ever agree to remarry." She walked over to one of the front windows, and Shelby began to feel as if she had traveled past a mythical barrier into an unreachable realm. "But, what Thomas said was that he was happy for me. Then he just hugged me, and went on to tell me he had been planning on New Orleans for months and months." She turned around, and there were fresh tears in her eyes. "Tell me the truth, Shelby. You don't think he ran off because he can't tolerate the thought of my marrying Mr. Harris, do you?"

"Your son…has more care for his mother than that."

"I'll put my mind at ease about it then," she said, coming across the room to hug Shelby once more.

"Thomas loves you, and we all do. You deserve to be happy, Mrs. Ann."

"Look at me—near thirty-five and feeling like a school girl again."

There had always been plenty of world for Shelby to navigate between the Weeks house and labyrinth of pilings found under-the-hill. From up in the Whitmire cabin, he often filled idle time by just observing the incline to the bluff. Like Thomas, he was not without imagination about the past and purpose of people traveling the steep path connecting the two parts of town. If he needed company, he knew he was welcome at the enclave of Creeks. And on the other end of the shore, if he ever needed to tamp down his own restlessness, he could walk by the drab windowless shacks where slaves being shipped were kept overnight.

As Shelby had come of age, he preferred to answer any messages or orders sent from upper town through Tail Feather. Apokta's son could get word to Mrs. Ann if a need arose to relay information farther into the proper streets. Shelby Whitmire had maintained the Weeks place or its neighboring house as the limit point in his ranging, just as he had enjoyed watching for ships, only to suppress any urge to sail beyond home.

But something in his way of looking at life had just broken loose.

When he reached the end of the path where there was a short stretch to the familiar edge of the bluff, he turned instead up a residential street toward the business avenues of upper Natchez. He walked at a fast pace, as if he had a mission on the far end of town. He had kept his plain wool hat in his hand the entire time he'd been in the Weeks house. Now, he wore it mashed onto his head, and when the window display in a ladies shop made him blush, he tipped the brim at the next woman hastening by.

Shelby felt sure that he understood nothing at all about females, either what they wore in layers to keep their skirts flowing or what they kept in their heads to keep their dreams alive. And he knew it was absurd to fantasize about running into Mrs. Ann's prospective husband on these confusing brick and dirt roads. He had only once observed the fellow Ezekial Harris from across a crowded porch. He had heard that name only in the context of calm approval among innkeepers and tavern owners on the shore.

Still, the ridiculous thought that he might encounter the man kept Shelby walking—past Des Rosiers Grocers, past a leather shop and a crockery storefront, past a half dozen mercantile windows, an apothecary, and a dentist. If he recognized Mr. Harris strolling in his direction, he would stand in his way and beg to know if the gentleman were ready to lose life itself should the sacrifice rescue a beauty named Ann.

If Harris took affront, they could face off in a duel, Shelby imagined. James Bowie had squared off against an archrival near Natchez! In this very town, Aaron Burr had steeled himself against charges of treason! If this Mr. Harris proved too cowardly to even meet on the infamous sand bar a quarter mile past Todd's inn, well, who would call him worthy?

Shelby Whitmire knew such thoughts were absurd.

He would always belong with the cast-offs and orphans, the other boys from under-the-hill who'd had no chance of schooling beyond primer and no business mixing in with the gentry of Natchez proper. His future would reach no farther than the first street on top of the hill, where early dwellers like Ann's father and then her husband from New York lived. Eccentrics lived at such extremities, like the stubborn abolitionist Mrs. Greenfield and her odd replacements, who looked down the bluff instead of on into town for a shelf that might adequately display china.

Shelby didn't know what he was doing, but his legs kept taking him farther and farther into the only town he could call his home, a place he hardly knew. He passed what he thought was a palace, and might well have housed royalty during Spanish rule. A stucco chapel on the grounds could have been where President Jackson and his wife—too in love to wait—had exchanged vows.

The cast-iron gate continued the length of the street where across the way a dressmaker, a candle shop, and a millinery boutique streamed by. A store offering liquor displayed its wares in glass windows and tables under awnings. A sixteen-year-old would not have been able to contain his excitement, but Shelby felt revulsion at how his own destiny had narrowed. Only a fool would have dreamed so long of an impossibility coming to fruition.

Self-absorbed, he had walked nearly two miles, and he gradually realized he was passing the outskirts of town. A great trail going northeast would soon start up. This much geography anyone born and raised in Natchez knew. There would next be a smaller village—Washington, Mississippi—where Ann's father had gone to live with a second wife and stepchildren.

It would be dangerous folly to wander on to another town and yet another unfamiliar village along the Natchez Trace. Shelby wanted only to find a different path that curved back in the direction of the Mississippi. He couldn't bear the thought of reversing his steps through town, stupidly tipping his hat again in front of the ladies dress and foundation shop. Then he realized he was coming to a fork in the road and to a collection of buildings that was not the work of any architect like Levi Weeks or any Spanish builder known for decorative grillwork.

A hodgepodge of pens and roughly built huts stretched far along the path ahead, and besides white men on horses and some speaking from sturdy platforms, there were only dark-skinned people bottled up, multitudes—women together in some corrals and men huddled in other pens. A dozen carriages and wagons were stationed on the opposite side of the path, and plantation owners and managers moved with purpose from the edge of one confinement area to another. Occasionally a speaker on the platform called out an age and a price.

"Next—one prime field worker, a mechanic, and a housekeeper—all young, docile, and in good health!"

Two wagons, one for males and one for females, were being loaded on the edge of the enterprise, near where Shelby stood. The hands of men and women alike were tied behind their backs, and the youthful males wore shackles at the ankle as well. They were being guided to their respective wagons, but Shelby noticed one woman step over to the men's line and stretch her arms so that her fingers could intertwine with those of one dejected captive. His head rose at her touch, and he appeared unable to stop tears from streaking down his check. The exchange was brief, since the women were urged forward by those loading the transports.

The chained man watched her being led off, and in despair he looked up and away to where the carpenter stood, transfixed. Shelby recognized, in the captive's expression, his own mental state. If he had honesty and courage, he admitted, he too would stand upright like the slave before him and let the whole world see tears flow unabated. The men's eyes met for a few moments, long enough for compassion and shame to stab at the individual with the freedom to walk away.

Shelby made his feet move, but his thoughts were fixed and leaden.

On his way back through town to the bluff, Shelby tried to console himself by imagining what changes Mrs. Greenfield was championing in Philadelphia. A recent letter to Mrs. Weeks had said the girl was singing before white audiences, as well as in freed-slave congregations. He drew the energy to walk on by imagining the effect that child's song might have had on the cruel scene he had just witnessed.

But by the time he reached the top of the incline, where the Weeks house was just down the path, his own sorrows again flooded in.

Choosing to go back down the hill on foot, he knew he wouldn't shake the image of Ann Weeks—*feeling like a schoolgirl*—for long. From the beach landing, Tail Feather looked up in concern. He wanted to know why the carpenter was walking on the rough edge of the incline, when all he had needed to do was whistle to the cart-boy below, wait for the Weeks rig to be brought up, and take the safer way downhill.

"The bluff edges are too soft for walking! You will fall on your head and kill yourself!"

"That would be too easy…"

"What?"

"Look, Tail Feather," Shelby said, once safely down, "if your father asks, don't tell him I came down looking—ready to string myself up at Mr. Todd's pier."

"Mrs. Ann told you about marrying Mr. Harris?"

"How did you know?"

"Thomas told me this morning," the youth said. "Why do you think he caught the steamer to New Orleans?" Shelby felt himself drained of all energy, or he might have stalked back up to the top of the incline to stumble over loose rocks on the way down this time…to see if he might manage to break his neck on the next trip down.

"Mrs. Ann looks happy," he admitted instead.

"That's what Thomas said."

The Creek boy, almost grown, was so much like his father. He was honest to a fault. He had sympathy, but he also had a sense of humor. It was one thing to lose a chance at love. It would be another thing to throw away a friendship that was real and at hand, and apparently true enough to endure into the next generation.

He shook from his mind the image of shackles. He tried to nurture gratitude for choices that he himself still had.

"Don't say anything to your father, to get him worried on my behalf." Tail Feather could see that Shelby was not headed to the friendly edge of under-the-hill, toward the huts and cabins of Apokta's extended family and the Whitmire shop.

Feeling childish and ridiculously old at the same time, Shelby gravitated toward the Mississippi River. Once, there had been a crowd near the shore when a passerby who had lost a fortune at cards let himself drift out across much of the wide water, to a still spot. The gambler had taken a dark bottle with him and a knife. Then the depressed man had cut the lashings on his log raft one by one. He had slipped into the deep water and held on only briefly, before letting go, before disappearing.

"Where are you going?" Tail Feather wanted to know.

"To one of the taverns."

"That is not your usual way, Mr. Whitmire."

"I'm going first to take a good look at the foreign news. I plan to memorize any jobs for hire," Shelby said as cheerfully as he could. "I'm still considering whether to start up drinking."

1835 Knoxville, Georgia

5   So Many Hearts to Win

The weather in early November provided the Troutman Inn several days that were perfect for airing quilts and bedding from the upstairs guest rooms. The ebb and flow of overnight guests was largely unpredictable. But because of candlelight speeches scheduled for November 10 in nearby Macon, any travelers who made it to the smaller town recently, waited for a late coach in Knoxville or hired a horse to ride on to the courthouse town. Several village residents lent out their own trustworthy wagons and paid drivers to take people on to the location setting up for fiery oratory. No one wanted to miss the dramatic event.

Those few keeping each other company at the Troutman Inn talked of nothing but Texas independence and the recruitment of volunteers. Colonel Troutman usually divided his day between the family plantation closer to the Flint River and his inn at the center of town. He was proud to have earned his rank while deterring British aggression in 1812, and now he had a keen ear for developments in Texas. Since July, when newspapers printed an account of the skirmish between an American lawyer named Travis and Mexican officials, it was only the news from Texas that piqued his interest. Shots had been fired in Anahuac, just across the Sabine River from Louisiana. More and more often, he rode in early to take breakfast at the inn.

Newspapers in New Orleans were also releasing articles about a Georgia man. James Fannin, from neighboring Columbus, was distinguishing himself in Texas standoffs. In only a half hour, he and none other than Jim Bowie sent ill-prepared Mexican officials running at Concepcion, a place much deeper into Texas territory than previous skirmishes. That tale generated exuberant talk at the Troutman dining table during the cool week before Macon's speeches.

One afternoon, the kitchen help stepped closer to the doorway to better hear parlor discussion. The colonel's oldest child Joanna put down her embroidery to absorb details when Hugh McLeod spoke to her father of late developments.

"I have to say, sir, that West Point debate about Texas is heated. No one sides with the Mexican dictator, of course, but most are wary of interfering." Joanna's father was shaking his head. "But my mother and I have heard the Lamars boldly stating the cause."

"John and his brother have a cousin in Columbus, do they not? He's written some quotable articles."

"Mirabeau Lamar, yes. He's been the editor there for some time. He and Fannin have been friends a while, I think. Mr. Lamar even went out to Texas on his invitation—to see the trouble bubbling up firsthand. When the fight is personal, the case to stand back and watch doesn't hold up."

"I hear Fannin has moved his wife and daughters down the Texas coast already." Hugh appeared vexed as he smoothed his mustache, but he nodded to the colonel.

"Please don't misconstrue what I'm about to say—I won't make light of a man who has proven his valor against Mexico's military." He glanced in Joanna's direction. "It's just…I might count James Fannin as the only leader on Texas soil who gained less honor while at West Point than I did!"

"No need for humble talk, son, you've graduated…with a commission."

"Much to my mother's relief, sir, I can promise you that."

"Well, none here would disparage Fannin either."

"No, Colonel, and I only meant to convey some humility about wearing this officer uniform." His blue lieutenant's jacket was newly tailored, and he was still not sure where to tuck the required white gloves.

"You met standards in the classroom," the innkeeper said. "I've no doubt you'll prove yourself worthy on the battlefield."

"It's true there was conflict between our instructors and Jackson… friction that put my success in the academy at some disadvantage."

"The President has his hands full with politics—"

"It's action that interests me."

"See there! No blame on you for losing patience with books." Hiram Troutman spoke warmly, "We're of the same mind about that!"

Talk among a few women moved out to the comfortable chairs that stretched across the porch. Seven pillars rose from the entry-level flooring to the upper hotel rooms, making the Troutman Inn an impressive sight from any direction. Some suggested that the Knoxville building was stately enough for grand speeches, that American flags could have been draped from the upper railings as easily as colorful guest quilts.

In the deepening afternoon, Hugh politely announced his intention to start back on the road to Macon. Joanna followed him out to where he had hitched his horse.

"Inside a while ago, I was just shy of telling your father and everyone working downstairs the whole sorry truth about my West Point record."

"I recall your shock at being admitted at all," she teased.

"How shocked are you that I graduated…last place?" She had to smile at him. He possessed the same piercing eyes he'd owned as a boy, the same earnest brow and unruly dark hair. Something about his demeanor made his words impossible to resist.

"In an elite institution, just as in the lowliest school house, someone holds the final rank," she reminded him. "I stand with my father. Any day I can call a personal friend a West Point graduate, I am proud."

He swept away all impulse to apologize. As they tarried by his horse, they talked instead of the speeches coming up and other efforts being made to raise volunteers for Texas. From Milledgeville, the capital east of Macon, cannons were being inventoried so that some artillery might be discreetly sent with Captain William Ward, leader of the Texas movement. Behind the scenes, Ward's own family pressed wealthy friends to contribute financially. After a march to Montgomery, and voyage down the Alabama River to Mobile and then New Orleans, ships would be needed to transport a volunteer battalion down the coast of Mexico to a point safe for an American landing. Velasco, where James Fannin already had control of a fort, was the likely point of entry.

More than anything else, Texas needed recruits. Everyone in the United States understood that shifting political tides in Mexico increased oppression against immigrants. In the Southern states, Georgia in particular, and in the western territories like Tennessee and Kentucky, rugged men had always kept their eyes on the expanding horizon. Now, they thrust open newspapers and scoured columns for every word under "Texas and Liberty." A successful revolt, one that would put control into the hands of American colonists, would take a wave of volunteers signing on for the trek to Mexico's coast.

"If ever we are to upend tyranny in Texas," Hugh said to Joanna, "we must answer these cruel threats. We don't need dozens to defend their freedom. We need throngs! If a ruthless central power threatens independence in the Texas colonies, surely we must fly to their aid. We must proceed as if our own dear liberty were at stake. If not we Americans, who else will help?" He was in the saddle and, with his hands free, had gestured to emphasize his conviction in the matter.

"I do hope you are among the speakers on Tuesday next, Hugh McLeod!" He was surprised at how grand her suggestion made him feel, and his face grew warm as he turned aside, smiling.

"Captain Ward will speak, and Eckley, either before or after."

"Your West Point exams might have left you in last rank, but I can't think of another man whose oratory is more likely to pluck young men looking idly on."

"You think I should ask to speak?"

"Let the more experienced officers know that you've already worked out a speech!" Her enthusiasm brimmed, as Hugh's had moments ago. "Tell them you feel called by heaven to address that crowd!"

"I've seen the handbills going up already," Hugh said. He wanted to jump down and waltz her along the street, but he swung his attention back to logistics of the Macon speeches. "People stop to look them over, those who have already been reading about the Texans' plight. But other strong fellows—the very ones we need—have probably been too busy plowing to keep abreast of foreign affairs."

"What will you answer…when they want to know where your own course of action leads?" Joanna asked, her eyes suddenly growing wide and solemn. Hugh was already considering this obvious question. He had just received his commission, along with orders to report to Fort Jessup in Louisiana—not far from the Sabine River border with Texas. An American officer was sworn to follow protocol.

"First, I'll take command of my company. Then I'm going to request relief from my commission. Once I'm free of my U.S. post, I can join the volunteers bound for battle in Texas."

The colonel's daughter looked at him with equal parts admiration and wistfulness. She then glanced skyward for a moment to gather her thoughts, and Hugh knew whatever words she spoke would prove she was no longer anyone's little girl.

"Women are forever denied such action," she said. She reached up to pet the horse's neck, though her hand came close to where Hugh held the reins. "But as dearly as I treasure the home hearth, I doubt I would be the kind of female to step forward even if we were allowed."

"Ladies in Macon are helping," he said. "If you bring it up, your father might make a donation to the cause." Her smile made the thought of dancing flicker again. "I don't know how he could resist. The Wards and several other plantation owners between here and Milledgeville are contributing already."

"You should have asked him yourself, Hugh. He couldn't have wished for a son of any better caliber—"

"It's you he dotes on."

"I do adore riding in with him to the inn. I love to be there when fresh news arrives from Montgomery or Mobile…or Savannah…"

"I forgot!" Hugh turned his attention to his saddlebag. He had been struck by the wild notion to lift her up behind him and gallop off in the direction of the Flint, to see if the cypress trunk still lay in the creek. A woman had come from the hotel kitchen out to the porch to shell peas, and if the two young people stayed out in the dirt street engaged in conversation any longer, more adults might come outside as chaperones. "I put one of those handbills in my saddle pack," he said fumbling. "Here, let your father peruse the copy. Then, you can post it in view of any travelers coming through before next Tuesday."

"Colonel Hiram Troutman will offer a handsome sum—that I know." To make sure his response was not overheard, Hugh leaned over in his saddle, as he had years ago when Joanna offered him a bundle of scones.

"If his donation is as handsome as his eldest child is pretty, the volunteers will have enough funds to sail a dozen ships from here to the equator!"

Hugh's heart pounded as he raced away from the Troutman Inn. He was so eager to get on the path back to Macon that he had to make himself slow his mount to a trot at intervals and then a walk. He repeated the speech lines he had tried on Joanna, and then he thought further about how to phrase the qualities that make a man.

More fine words came to him about graves freshly dug for heroes of the American Revolution. He and every young man of recruitment age would have indelible memories of a Fourth of July just one decade past. Thomas Jefferson and John Adams had expired within hours of each other. Lieutenant Hugh McLeod was forming a question he might pose to a rapt crowd, about whether elegant words spoken in tribute to past heroes were indeed just fine prose for mourners' ears. "Or," he practiced aloud, "are the beloved revolutionaries just recently interred still listening from the grave? Are our heroes still watching from a higher place, to see what course their descendants will take?"

He was thinking about men like Colonel Troutman. Those who had joined the effort to stand against England's second challenge in 1812 deserved applause and admiration as well. "Do not the hardy souls in Texas," he went on speaking to his startled horse, "those hardy souls in Texas who were promised self-governance, do they not deserve to retain their land and their independent way of life?" The logic and wording came powerfully to him. *Had these American brothers and sisters not toiled over and tamed the raw land of Mexico's northern wilderness?*

In three hours, he was approaching the outskirts of Macon, and he had a full speech he wanted to practice before someone. He thought he might ask in town, at the newspaper office or at one of the dining halls, whether his academy classmate Charles still worked at his family's small farm or if he'd taken on a position in the business streets of Macon. The two had become friends since their jaunt to Knoxville years before. But Hugh McLeod was the kind of young man who won friends wherever he went. He had been rehearsing an address that would win new allies against Mexican dictatorship. The new officer sensed he was rehearsing language that could spark momentous change.

During the second week of November in Macon, Georgia, the townspeople witnessed an astounding surge of visitors. A comparable gathering could not be recalled since ten years earlier when the Marquis Lafayette stopped at Mulberry Street to enjoy a luncheon before traveling on to Knoxville's inn. Governor Thorpe, the last surviving general of the Revolutionary War, had accompanied Lafayette on his tribute tour of Georgia.

November 10, 1835, in the open space by Macon's simple brick courthouse, was not to be forgotten either. The sequence of events went by in a blur for Hugh McLeod, as he waited for his speaking turn. In candlelight, he was introduced by Captain William Ward to a wildly applauding audience. Every Macon resident appeared to be present—men, women, and children—as well as soldiers from Milledgeville, leaders from Columbus that included Mirabeau Lamar, and families from as far away as Darien.

Hugh nodded to one of Knoxville's inhabitants in the crowd, the Spillers man who had worried so about his wife during rescue at the creek. He was among those who'd offered to drive an extra carriage from the Troutmans' livery to Macon. Such was the demand of travelers nearby to get to the larger town by any means and hear speeches about the Texas cause.

McLeod's winning line may have been his fervent pledge to resign his United States officer commission as soon as he made it to Fort Jessup. He did not search the crowd to see where his mother stood, possibly shaking her head, but there were other ladies in the gathering, whose teary-eyed admiration added to his conviction that he was doing the right thing. The wild jubilation of the throng, when he finished, and the moving spectacle when man after man stepped forward to sign up for service in Texas, would have stood out in anyone's mind as a pivotal moment in life.

There was no lapse in Hugh McLeod's euphoria for the next two days. People still gathered on Mulberry where the speeches had been given, and the walkways were far more crowded than usual with people recalling who had spoken, what had been said, whose delivery was most rousing, and which young men had stepped forward to volunteer. Everyone anticipated Thursday's issue of the *Macon Georgia Telegraph*. A red-blooded American who had somehow missed the event firsthand would want to read carefully its column on the liberty speeches. Those who had been there were eager to possess a memento.

Captain William Ward's speech was mentioned, as well as the small fortune that his family was contributing to the cause. Though it was not reported, McLeod learned from Ward that the same Knoxville man, John T. Spillers, was the courier entrusted to carry a worthy donation from Colonel Troutman. As the article stated, more than three thousand dollars had been collected for the Texas bound volunteers by Tuesday evening!

Concluding the report was a list of the Macon men who'd approached the podium to volunteer for service. They would not be sworn in until they reached the fort in Velasco, Texas, since respectful distance was the only official position the United States could take in Mexico's affairs. Those pledging to stand with their "brothers and sisters in peril of losing liberty" would be risking their own legal reputations, but for what a cause! And, as Hugh McLeod's own speech went: "Was that not precisely the position, the same honorable risk that revolutionaries had taken against England in 1776?"

"Look at this, Mother," Hugh said, as he found the page where the candlelight meeting had been recounted. "Listen to the names on the volunteer list…"

"I did stay for much of the signing, though the roar of the crowd was beginning to deafen me."

"Both Bullochs, Uriah—also a captain—and his nephew Monroe. And you know Mr. Hunt, from cotton dealings? One of his sons signed up—F.M. is the second brother. Francis, I think, and Sam Hardaway…"

"Sam? That child's not but fifteen! His mother needs to know where he put his name, so it can be expunged!"

"We have to be proud that two Lamar names are printed from the list."

"Indeed, I am as proud of Basil as you are, and he has some military training. But I intend to talk to John about his own haste in signing. He has some responsibility already spoken for in looking after our family, Hugh, as well as his own. And John's sister, Rebecca, can't afford to be without a brother on hand, not with their father already lost, as your own was."

"I don't think it will do our Mr. Lamar any dishonor to offer a monetary sum, instead of his physical presence," Hugh agreed. He had been tempted to toss his own officer epaulettes into the crowd and declare himself an independent fighter for Texas, but his mother was right. Protocol and pledged responsibilities of any kind had to be taken into account. "His family duties were carved into stone first."

"And I rather thought…" Mrs. McLeod hesitated before bringing up a subject that her son might have been wavering about. "I've always thought that Rebecca Lamar might one day become…*your* responsibility, Hugh."

"I don't know if she'll ever develop an interest in a younger man," Hugh said evasively. It was true that he'd been smitten by her in his earlier school days, but like other older girls, she had paid him little attention.

"She's not your senior by any more than four years, and grown men and women don't suffer a trifling handful of birthdays to foil a good match." The next thing Hugh's mother said made him think she was able to read his mind. "I would be cautious, dear, in any farewell embrace you might bestow on Colonel Troutman's sweet, young daughter. Her parents think she's the one who painted stars in the sky, and I wouldn't approve your tempting her attentions away from home."

"I'm just out of West Point!" Hugh protested. "And as we both know—but barely so!" A future with either Rebecca Lamar or Joanna Troutman was the farthest thing from his mind. "I need to write a request for immediate leave from Fort Jessup, if I can make myself sit down long enough. I've no time for females of any age right now," he went on. "I wonder how long it will take President Jackson to sign off on my permanent resignation?"

He withdrew to another room in search of good parchment and a fine pen. His mother looked at her hands in her lap and decided she might need some new embroidery to diffuse her deepening worry.

"Let all us surviving McLeods pray to God," she said to herself, "that no official signing off comes until Texas is won—and all this uproar over." She reached instead for the newspaper to take one last look at the article about Tuesday's speeches when she noticed another headline on the same page: *$50,000 reward for the capture of abolitionist from New York!* She read on about the dangerous, impromptu proclamations the northerner was making. "It looks as if there will be plenty of battles yet to wage on this side of our border with Mexico."

With distractions bubbling at home, there was no time for Hugh to lose before riding ahead to Columbus, where he could help with the same recruitment effort. He would then hasten on to Montgomery and, finally, he would cross over into Louisiana to report at Fort Jessup. An officer could not request permission to resign a commission, until he had shown up for that post in the first place.

McLeod had spoken regularly with William Ward, and the two settled on an arrangement to continue together as far as Columbus. Captain Ward would take official command of the Georgia volunteers once they arrived there, where they would again make speeches, inspiring additional recruits. Knowing his mother didn't hold up well to long goodbyes, Hugh avoided her for a few days. Their opposing hopes for the resignation request were best left without further discussion.

There was no other lady to bid farewell in Macon, since Miss Rebecca Lamar now resided mostly in Savannah where his own sister lived. Only one person worked back into the new lieutenant's mind as he packed satchels for departure ahead of the volunteers.

Hugh McLeod felt he must speak one more time with Joanna Troutman. He had an extra copy of the Macon newspaper, and more urgently than if he'd had a love letter to deliver to her, he yearned to see her expression as she read about his oratory. His words, among others, had been noted in the *Macon Georgia Telegraph* as having elicited an astonishing response.

At midday one week after Macon's speeches, Hugh McLeod found himself at the Troutman Inn. The aroma of pork roast came from the hotel kitchen, and he knew that Camille, the colonel's main cook, liked to serve the innkeeper's favorite sweet potatoes alongside. This might be a last chance to enjoy muscadine jelly. There would be fresh mint with tea. Hugh was laughing to himself about his mother's warning regarding romance. He thought a fine meal would likely tempt him away from honorable duty on the battlefield, sooner than an attractive lady of any age. Still, he wished to see Joanna sitting with her embroidery hoop in a chair by the dining room.

The desk clerk told him, however, that the colonel was in the plantation fields that day, and that Mrs. Troutman was down with an inflammation. Miss Joanna was out at the family's private home, making sure the younger children were looked after. Their father was a tender husband, so there must have been something in the fields that required his presence.

Hugh had only ridden in the direction of the plantation once, a few years before his West Point appointment. The main house was a fine structure, with columns and porches along three sides. He preferred talking with Joanna at the Troutman's inn, where both their roles were more relaxed than in a domestic setting, especially with a mother as watchful as his own nearby.

But there was no question in his mind about taking time to speak with Joanna Troutman before following the long trail toward Louisiana. There was a particular question he needed to ask the colonel's daughter. The door to the entry hallway was open, and when Joanna walked out from one of the side rooms to greet him, Hugh almost forgot what had made him brazen enough to ride out to her home.

Joanna Troutman was seventeen. Her forehead was pale but her cheeks flushed as if she too had just risen from bed. He had seen her only two weeks earlier, at the chair reserved for her when she worked embroidery, but she had never looked as lovely as she did standing before him. Her hair was loosely tied back with a ribbon. All he could think to do was hand her the Thursday paper and tell her that the news was on page three. He said that he didn't trust the hotel staff to keep the issue for her father. The colonel, he thought, would want to read it over in his leisure.

"I hope you'll tell him that John Spillers made it safely to Macon with the Troutman contribution. We didn't want to name separate benefactors making up the three thousand collected, but surely part of Texas liberty will be won through your father's generous donation."

Joanna studied the article while Hugh nervously chatted on.

"And look what it says about you!" she interrupted. She came farther out on the porch where they could both sit down. "Your name is right here in one of the first paragraphs. I wish I could have been there in the crowd, but I've heard you out in the streets of Knoxville before. I could tell you'd found words with the power to move mountains."

"Everyone was clapping and cheering," he laughed. "It's a far cry from the response my name brought in West Point's main hall when the ranking of cadets was called out."

"Then listen to me, Hugh McLeod—no more of that. You're an orator and a born leader, and don't you ever forget what gifts God put into your hands!"

Hugh was elated to hear that view voiced by a good friend. Maybe Joanna had idolized him since they were children, but he couldn't have felt grander if President Jackson or an archangel had applauded his calling. He jumped up with such enthusiasm that Joanna clasped her hands to her mouth.

"I've no right to ask you for anything, Miss Joanna, but…"

"We're talking loud enough to wake my mother," she said, putting a finger to her lips. She stood to entwine her arm with Hugh's, and she led him down the wide porch. She had probably washed her hair that morning, the officer was thinking, because he caught the scent of lavender.

"Suddenly I feel as if I'm…fighting a river current," he stammered. "I can't help thinking of that summer day when we both waded in." Pulled underwater, the cousin had opened his eyes to terror, and now some emotion akin to fear made Joanna's eyes widen as Hugh spoke on. "What I can say so easily to a crowd of strangers, and what's been welling up… things I've been wanting to say…" His inability to finish the sentence left him dazed. He couldn't feel his feet. He was surprised, when he looked at her hand in his, to see how small her palm was, how delicate her fingers, still like a little girl's. His own eyes were growing wide, and a sensation too much like drowning made consciousness flicker.

"And I was longing to tell you," she broke in, "something extraordinary happened last night—a singular star—I hoped you were watching."

"I noticed before I spoke to the Macon crowd." He had to catch his breath. "That blaze in the sky made me think I might rouse Columbus men, too. It's the main reason I rode out here…" When his hands slipped briefly into his pockets, he was relieved to find the officer gloves still there. "The night sky was like a great flag! Hundreds were cheering, and at times no one could hear. Candles were quivering everywhere." Then he took both Joanna's hands in his, "…do you think you—with other Knoxville ladies—could you make the Georgia volunteers a banner?"

"Of, course."

"Who knows how many more might sign on in Montgomery and on down in Mobile? Once they reach New Orleans, William Ward can use a flag to champion our battalion. And there's James Fannin waiting on recruits at Velasco, off the Texas coast. Do you think—"

"Will you wait for it in Knoxville? I'll need a few days, Hugh."

"No," he said putting his hat back on. He was still adjusting to the weight and heat of the West Point uniform, and he stepped back formally. He felt the sharp tug of his assignment in Fort Jessup, but another purpose nudged him away from her as well. "I've got to keep my horse headed in the direction the Macon boys will go. I'm riding back through town and on to Columbus if I can make it there tonight."

"Then I'll…"

"If you sew a banner for the volunteers, Captain Ward can accept it while he and the men march through. Your father's inn will be the first stop."

"I have some inspiration for the design!"

He rushed back onto the veranda to embrace her, and he couldn't keep from giving her a quick kiss. He thought he heard again the roar of the approving Macon throng. In a flash of prescience, though, he envisioned a clump of toddlers reaching for his coat lapels or letting their kisses linger on their mother's pale cheek. His thoughts racing, he turned to hoist himself into the saddle. The horse pranced in place for a few moments, and then responded to his flick of the reins.

Lieutenant Hugh McLeod wouldn't have pictured his childhood friend's action in the next minutes. Joanna returned immediately to a sitting room near where her mother lay ill. She lifted up her layered beige skirt to feel the silky material of her top petticoat. It had been sent recently from Charleston, where she expected to attend a young ladies' academy in the coming year. With all central Georgia in turmoil about Texas, she had found no time to discuss her own finishing school plans with the lieutenant.

Joanna wasn't thinking of Charleston now. She was pulling at the waistband of her petticoat and examining the side seam where she could cut threads in order to lay the cloth out flat. There was a section large enough for a banner and its hem. There would be a single star…a blue one if she remembered where a scarf remnant was folded—one star against the white silk.

"Joanna? Did I hear a visitor?" her mother called weakly.

"It was a message from an officer." She touched an edge of the petticoat lightly to her eyes. "Just a moment…I'll be right there."

"Was that Lieutenant McLeod? You're too young to marry, Joanna. I hope you didn't promise him anything." The daughter was looking at her hands and trying to steady herself for a calm voice.

"He came about the boys going to Texas, Mama. It's a battalion flag he needs."

And the words were coming to her, because she wanted it to be something that Hugh would appreciate. A man with such a gift for words should have a worthy banner. Something along the lines of the American Revolution's battle cry, she decided. Yes, *Liberty or Death*. But she also wanted to express the sense of freedom's pull on an individual.

She had never seen a person as inspired as Hugh McLeod of Macon, Georgia, and she couldn't contemplate his departure toward the battlefield without sending along words of comfort: *Where freedom abides, there is my home.* She would work on the Latin, before she asked friends to help her sew the letters.

Soon, there would be soldiers marching through Knoxville, on their way out past the borders of Georgia—soldiers determined to trudge and sail on until they entered the turmoil in Texas.

November 1835, Knoxville, Georgia

6 Embrace and Farewell

John Spillers sat in near dark on the cabin stoop where he could rest his feet on the lowest step. A thick candle made the tin lantern glow. Touching the place where one toe pressed against worn leather, he was doubtful about his shoes holding up on the long march to Columbus.

Some people in Knoxville were saying that the path then from Georgia's border to Montgomery, Alabama, was at least one hundred miles. He couldn't judge whether that was just a story. The entire volunteer enterprise, though he had heard the Macon speeches himself, somehow still seemed like a tale spun by a traveler at the Troutman Inn.

In the crisp air just before first light spilled through the trees, Spillers found it hard to believe that civilian enlistees were already gathering in the town a few miles east. They would pass through Knoxville by midday, but their purpose would eventually take them all the way to Mexico. He wondered if any Texas colonists desperate for help had awakened with a vision of the rescue army on its way.

The father of three, Widower Spillers now, was trying to imagine what his wife Matilda would have said about his joining up with Captain Ward. Instead, his thoughts drifted to their past conversations, small talk taken for granted just one November ago:

"The beans are good yet for picking, John. Another two weeks anyway. The children will help Martha and me."

"Both boys—even little Will—should be fillin' buckets for their mama. I don't want you down on your knees."

"Baby's not due until after Christmas."

"Youngsters learn easy. About feeling proud to help at home."

"Ours do. They're like their papa." She had patted his arm. *"They're sweet children."*

"If all folks were as kind as you, not one cross word would be invented."

They sat out on the stoop, waiting for the sun. When she hugged his arm again, he'd reached up to tuck a strand of fine auburn hair behind her ear.

A year later, beans as well as squash yielded well until the heavy rains in late October. The baby daughter that Matilda had so wanted was flourishing. Eliza was a pretty little thing. "Like her mother," John Spillers said quietly to himself. But he was not easily reconciled to the hard fact—his wife was gone. It was difficult to concede that the fiery glow in the east still managed to emerge and make its way slowly up, dissolving every day in the blue Georgia sky. Matilda was no longer in this world.

On this late November day in 1835, Spillers was in a state of disbelief about his own destiny. When recruits from Macon stopped near Colonel Troutman's inn for a noon meal, John was planning to slip into the ranks. He would be marching with them to Columbus and beyond. Like any patriot, he believed in the cause. Convincing, too, were handbills about payment in land scrip. The sum was promised to those who survived the military effort in Texas, but also to dependents of those that heaven took along the way. Most volunteers would be barely past boyhood, and John didn't think too many of them considered death a likely outcome. A year ago, he too might have shrugged off the odds of early demise.

But no sweet wife now clung to his arm. John Spillers was shaken. He judged no loss to be harder on children, except being orphaned with no inheritance whatsoever. Johnny and Will and Eliza would not suffer that hardship. He reminded himself to sign clearly on any volunteer roll set out in town. The official muster would wait until their arrival in Texas.

A door squeaked from down the path where the other Spillers cabin stood. The children's Aunt Martha would be coming with little Eliza, still too young to sleep beyond the reach of maternal care. The baby was cheerful by nature, unlikely to sense impending drama. Matilda's sister had told John T. that she would come just before sunrise to sit and be there when the boys awoke.

John's satchel and musket lay on the narrow cabin porch beside him. He hoped his sons would dream peacefully until he was already at the inn. He wished he could stop worrying about his shoes, so worn down at the heels. At first, his eyes fell on the dear child still asleep and leaning her head against the aunt's shoulder. The blanket drawn up around Eliza was one the two sisters had kept from their own mother's hopechest.

What dangled from Martha's other hand caught Spillers' attention next. The woman shifted the baby's weight in order to balance her dual loads. She held tightly onto the tops of her late father's shiny boots, sturdy footwear that had sat for two years atop the mantle in John T.'s cabin. When Matilda died, he had passed them on to the surviving sister. His felt guilty that officer boots from the Revolution gave him a jolt of hope. But his sister-in-law held them out and took a seat next to him.

"It came to me as clear as an angel's instruction." She could see he was shaking his head.

"These should stay here and polished, the way you and Matilda kept them."

"Well, see if they fit at least. I suppose these were made even before 1776. Could be you can't walk but two steps in them."

When John leaned down to unlace his shoes and wiggle them off his feet, the baby lifted her head and reached down toward his sleeve. Martha pulled a pair of thick socks from her apron pocket. The volunteer soldier was too embarrassed to ask if they had just been lifted from a keepsake box or if her own husband was going to ask later what had happened to his good pair. At the homestead where two sisters were married to two brothers, sharing was as natural as seasons. For some time, though, John had been wearing socks in need of darning and had struggled with a needle himself. If the boots fit as easily as the socks went on, he would indeed be fortunate.

"I may never ask a horse to carry my weight again."

"Don't you speak on what you'll never do again, John T." Her lip was pursed with worry. "Such predictions are best kept silent. If you mean your feet sit right well in the boots, that's a blessing." The baby began to babble, and both adults were glad for the distraction as John moved onto soft ground to try walking.

"They do feel ready for my feet, not stiff like a new pair would be."

"It's a good sign. It means you'll make the full circle and come on back to this family." She paused for a moment. "Your brother's awake, but I don't reckon he'll come on up the path."

"Not much for men to say to each other." He worked to regain an even voice. "But I can't thank you—"

"This would make my sister happy." Dabbing at her eyes, the woman rose and gave the baby's father a quick hug. One thump from inside the cabin was followed by another.

"Can you get them back under the covers?" He paused to swallow. "Sister, would you…"

"You go on. You need to set off without excessive goodbyes." She was at the top step before calling softly, "It's just Aunt Martha, boys. I'm comin' on in with our favorite baby girl!" She made a shooing motion to her brother-in-law before speaking again, "Now, hop back under the blanket. I'm just here to rock Eliza a while."

John Spillers quickly gathered up his weapon and his knapsack. Since it was such an early hour, he had stepped only twenty feet away from the stoop before darkness enveloped him. Turning his back on the cabin he and Matilda had built, he fought the urge to steal one more look at home. He would lose the battle to stay quiet, though, if he saw either John or Will come to the doorway and lift the lantern. The night before, he and his sons had played hide-the-thimble after supper. It was best they memorize that tender evening.

Spillers stayed on the move. He found the edge of the trail and ducked into the tree-lined path at a pace his officer boots handled well. The sky was lightening to deep gray, and the red dirt of the main road began to reveal its color. At the pace he was taking, the outline of the Troutman Inn would show itself in half an hour.

Not long after he made out the Knoxville landmark, where windows were already fully lit, a field torch danced a ways off in the opposite direction. From along the other trail cutting in from Macon, there appeared to be two travelers, one on horseback and another on foot, carrying the flame. He was hesitant to move a step farther until the two individuals traveling the eastern road drew close enough to identify. The family man chided himself for his plan to enlist as a soldier. He was hardly trained for throwing himself on the ground to await combat. He had no instinct for ambush—of that he was certain. Maybe these two were bringing news that the expedition had fallen apart.

The travelers were talking as they made their way closer to Knoxville's road, and when they laughed, they sounded out of breath. They were young men, though, maybe just boys who were coming in from a nearby farm to watch developments at the inn.

"Hello!" The man called out in the gray light. He didn't want to be mistaken for a threat. "John T. Spillers here. You expected at Troutman's?"

"Mr. Spillers?" Even when the pair ambled into view, the father could not say how one spoke to him with familiarity. "Charles Wentworth— Remember me? I was with Hugh McLeod down by the river when you rode out to help. It was five years ago—you probably don't—"

"We dragged that tree trunk off the colonel's nephew."

"You two are acquainted?" The lad on foot held the torch higher.

"He has a hero's reputation already," Charles explained. "Without him, there would have been a drowning that day." The older man shook his head.

"Fast work on McLeod's part and yours." After hearing the young lieutenant's speech in Macon a week earlier, Spillers had replayed the creek rescue in his mind. "Is it just five years?"

"The way from Macon to Knoxville seemed as long."

"…by torchlight and taking turns in the saddle."

"You two come to watch the battalion move through?"

"Me, yes," Charles admitted, "but Sam here has already signed on."

"No official muster until Texas," Spillers said. "But I'm joining up, too." He didn't want to doubt the age of the younger fellow, though he felt relieved to have spoken his own intention. He had begun to worry that he might just wish them well and retrace his steps homeward.

"Sam Hardaway," the youth on foot reached out to shake the Knoxville man's hand. "My father is all for my going, since I'm too young for any serious help at his cotton enterprise. This will land me some respect when I return." Then his expression changed. "My mother's another matter. It's been cat and mouse ever since the speeches last week. I've managed to evade her, thanks to Charles. He's come to catch a word with Hugh before the parade starts down to Columbus." The talk about parental permission left John Spillers feeling sheepish.

"What my people might conclude…is that I'm too old for all this."

"I'm months shy of sixteen yet, so it was my father's assurances kept my name on the roster."

The fellow on horseback dismounted and took the reins to walk the distance to the inn. Mr. Spillers couldn't really say that he recognized him from the creek emergency. His hair was now dark. His voice seemed to have darkened some in just the last few minutes.

"It's hard to say what my own mother and sisters think of me," Charles confessed. "They wouldn't let me put down my signature." He kicked at a pecan shell. "Probably won't look me in the eye as they used to back in Macon. I might be the only male still in town of a soldier's age."

"I've been telling him that's not the way to look at it."

"I rode in to tell Hugh, if he hasn't gone on yet to Columbus…to tell him…" He looked away out at the gray field again. "After his speech, it must have been hundreds crowding in to congratulate him and the other officers."

"It sounds as if your family is in your care," Spillers broke in. "A man has to mind the needs of his own people, too."

"That's what I've been telling him." The boy gave his friend a pat on the shoulder. "His horse and torch helped me get this far. I might have been scalped or drown in a creek myself otherwise."

The three reached hitching posts alongside Troutman Inn, and the noise of unusual activity inside brought an end to their conversation. Several voices came at once from the kitchen, more than the usual flurry of breakfast preparation for guests. From individual rooms up at the balcony level, people who might have ordinarily slept late walked briskly out to the railing beyond their chambers. With no spectacle yet below, they then retreated to their privacy. From the parlor downstairs the colonel's voice occasionally rose above other speakers, and John Spillers thought it was Mrs. Troutman asking about progress in the kitchen. Camille and other family cooks were orchestrating a special dinner for the officers expected to march through.

A murmur and clatter grew steadily as the sun rose. Charles was barely able to edge into the parlor and discover from the innkeeper's daughter Joanna that Lieutenant Hugh McLeod had already ridden out from Knoxville three days earlier. The girl, grown woman now, was working feverishly with a half dozen females her age. They had a white silk banner still shy of its final hemming.

"She said McLeod has posted a request for leave from Fort Jessup. He needs President Jackson's permission to join the Texas fight." Subdued by the news, the three men sat on the smooth planks at the edge the inn's porch. In the morning sun, they unbuttoned their coats, losing the inclination to chat as young men and onlookers streamed into town. They shared biscuits that were for the taking in the hotel dining room, where batch after batch was laid out. Charles suddenly rose to dust crumbs from his vest. "I should start back to Macon. If I let the horse amble, I'll most likely meet the battalion half way." Mr. Spillers and the youth stood, too, separation suddenly proving awkward.

"You should stay and see us off from here," Sam suggested. "I smell pork roast, and in the kitchen, dough was being set into pie tins."

"Maybe if the colonel's daughter were to ask me…"

"The banner's a beauty, but she's the fairest thing I saw."

"No wonder Hugh has an eye for her," Charles agreed. He went to his horse to secure the extinguished torch in a saddle loop. "But I can't say she made half an impression that first time."

"Five years can reshape the whole world, let alone one girl," Sam laughed. "That long ago, a general's order couldn't have made me sit next to any female."

"I'd best escape before Hugh rides back to duel other suitors." Carts and wagons were beginning to come down the Knoxville road from both directions. "Good to see you, Mr. Spillers. Sam, I'll keep all your Macon sweethearts safe!"

"Four months, or five! See you then!" In the rising street commotion, his horse's hooves appeared to make no additional noise.

In the next few hours, John T. Spillers and the Hardaway boy walked the length of the village and back a dozen times. They stepped into the blacksmith's to ask if there had been any special wheel repairs, and to see if his estimation of the cavalry numbers met with what they'd heard. On one return trip to the inn, they had seen Miss Joanna rush out to the veranda with her friends in order to test the unfurling of their single star flag. By noon, tables had been set out on the porch as signing desks for new enlistees, and a young officer told the Knoxville father they should wait for Captain Ward's arrival with the troops. Soon, new volunteers would amass there from every direction.

Mr. Spillers and Sam peeked in once more at the dining hall, now set for dignitaries. Then they moved to the end of the thoroughfare where the Macon formation would march in. The father of three was lost in his own thoughts, though the youth keeping his company chatted enough for the two of them.

"The colonel's wife looked at me sideways when I went in for one more cold biscuit. And Miss Joanna appeared ready to challenge me about my age, so I told them I was going along under the protection of my uncle."

"Your *uncle?*"

"Well, what I came up with was that you and my mother are really only second cousins, and that we're just getting to know one another, but I've always heard you referred to you as my *uncle*…that this adventure seemed like a good opportunity for better acquaintance…"

"…I am your uncle?"

"If you don't put it like a question, it sounds more like truth."

Mr. Spillers could only shake his head. His own children would be this youth's age in another ten years. He was wondering if little Will would end up being more talkative then than he was now at age three. The older boy, John, had taken to speaking up in the last year. There had been so much time to fritter away waiting for the parade to arrive that the widower was berating himself for not lingering in his own cabin. He could easily have joined in on familiar chores and still had time for the walk into Knoxville.

But the bustling street suddenly fell silent, as someone on the long inn porch had hushed the crowd. Stirring drumbeats grew louder from the east, and bystanders gathered near the Macon road stepped back to make room for approaching soldiers. John recognized Captain William Ward riding in the front, and Captain Eckley had come along as an escort. More mounted gentlemen seemed no older than Hugh McLeod—including one of the Lamar nephews.

Behind the recruits on foot rolled wagons with cannons, the likes of which only a man such as Colonel Troutman would have seen before on the battlefield. John's grip stiffened on his firearm as ammunition carts creaked along. Official state weaponry and rows of young men stirred the Knoxville audience. A great cheer went up for volunteers marching eight abreast. They looked worn from the half-day out, but they had twitched to alertness for their first appearance beyond home.

Mr. Spillers felt his heart race. His face flushed as he imagined himself part of this battalion. He hoped he could look as proud and bold as the men before him. Despite the tumult, Sam Hardaway was pointing and saying something to him, but John couldn't help looking behind the outer fringe of bystanders to the road leading home.

Then, he doubted his eyesight. He wondered if angels had brought him another fine image—since the rows of soldiers seemed appointed by a supernatural source. He looked again down the path he'd taken at first light. This time he was sure he saw a boy walking briskly in their direction. After the father took a few steps, he started to run toward the child, but now the boy stood still holding out a bundle.

"Johnny-boy!" When the man reached him, he could see that his son's face was streaked from tears. "Does your Aunt Martha know you've come to town?"

"She has Will searching for any good squash that's left. She knows right well where I went to."

"Your little brother wouldn't understand where I'm going."

"Me neither. Aunt Martha made me come." Suddenly the child broke into sobs and he threw his arms tight around his father's waist. John Spillers had seen the youngster wrap himself around his Aunt Martha, but men and their sons rarely made such a display of affection. He touched the boy's light brown hair. "You didn't tell us goodbye. You didn't say you would be coming back." The child stepped away and turned to put his sleeve to his cheek. Before him now, a crowd gathered around the cannon wagon to see the metal stocks up close.

"No duty with the cannons will be mine, no danger of that sort," the father said. "Only officers worry with working those." He was relieved that the awkward hug had passed, and he was desperate to reassure the stricken boy. "Likely there won't be any shooting at all, but it might be better not to tell your aunt you saw weapons."

"She has Will looking for squash, because she keeps her handkerchief up at her face."

"Well," he said to little John, "let's save our own hankies for sneezing." His son suddenly remembered to hand him a piece of cornbread with a dollop of blackberry jam. It was flattened inside a pouch of butcher paper he'd held inside his coat.

"I only came…to give you this…" Then, the child began to inch backwards down the red dirt path. "If you promise you're coming back…"

"Well then." Mr. Spillers was battling the impulse to dash down the path with his son. "I'm going to save this for the next stop. Take care of your brother, then, Johnny—and your baby sister." Someone had come up behind the pair.

"Is this your son? Young Johnny, is it?" Spillers was proud the child knew to come forward and shake a hand when Sam Hardaway extended his. "I'm a lucky fellow that your father is coming along. He's promised to look out for me since I'm the youngest volunteer so far."

"My aim is better than fair, but I'm not as good as Papa."

"I'm letting on that your Mr. Spillers is my uncle, that he's watching out for me. It's brought my confidence up where I need it." He shook the boy's hand again.

"I have confidence. I can shoot, too, can't I Papa? Let me come with you."

"You take care of Will and Eliza." The father laid his hand gently on the child's shoulder to turn him again in the direction of the Spillers homestead. The boy whirled around suddenly.

"Anyone can see he's not your nephew. And he's not but a foot taller than me. Let me come along with you, Papa. I bet this boy couldn't shoot a rooster off a molasses barrel."

"Go on home, son." John Spillers felt his chest tightening, and he wondered if he had time to walk the boy back to their cabin, to hug them all goodbye in the privacy of the woods. The child had turned as instructed and was walking down the path away from the crowd.

"Your father and I will watch out for each other!" Sam called, but the boy looked determined not to turn around again.

There was no way to tell if the child's eyes were filling again with tears. John T. Spillers kept watching his son. He watched until the boy's hair blended in with the color of branches. He could see his son reaching the last curve in the path, where he turned but wouldn't let himself raise either hand in a final wave. The father could only determine that his first child stood stubbornly facing town. The man glanced down, fighting the impulse to run in his son's direction, but a moment later the boy had moved on out of view.

Whatever sorrow might next befall the Knoxville father, he believed he could feel no more lonely than when he looked up to find the red dirt road deserted, when the rush and pull of tides only drew him to the company of strangers on their way to foreign territory.

During the noon meal and handover of the banner, Sam Hardaway held up both ends of conversation. He reported to John hearsay as well as what was right before their eyes. A wagon traveling along with the battalion as far as New Orleans carried a family of women, the Harpers—a girl of school age, it appeared, as well as her servant and her aunt. That news traveled quickly to those joining up in Knoxville, but only the most youthful volunteers conveyed interest openly.

"They say it's twelve days from here to New Orleans," Sam observed to his adopted uncle, "but it'll be at least another two years before a young man could tell whether that Macon girl makes a contest with Miss Troutman. Did you see how the girl took to a stroll on the arm of the older woman, though, before Captain Ward's speech?"

John Spillers was on the verge of asking the young man if he believed they were signing up to attend a cotillion at the capitol in Milledgeville, but he decided it wasn't right to dispel anyone's high spirits. He could admire such confidence. The youth had a naturally hopeful perspective that the despondent father thought he might very well come to lean on.

At Columbus, Lieutenant McLeod's speech inspired more volunteers, but a wave of regret soon swept over the battalion. He'd also announced the necessity of his parting from them for a while. He bid adieu to the swelling ranks and retired to his tent for the evening. At daylight, he rose and spurred his horse on toward Montgomery, where he intended to cross the Alabama River and travel with his orderly through the northern part of Louisiana to Fort Jessup.

"I was loitering near the officers' tent last night," Sam admitted to Spillers. It was McLeod himself spotted me and called me in, just as if we were on the docks at Macon. He was writing a letter to Miss Joanna, to thank her for the fine banner. Don't I wish I knew whether she'd be putting her lips to that signature."

As the plainclothes soldiers made their way past the Georgia line into Alabama and across in the direction of that state capital, the shortfall between shoe quality and what was required for a hundred mile march grew apparent.

"The Harper ladies are practiced with the needle, Mr. Spillers—I mean, Uncle—and the girl is ingenious. I've put my name on the list for getting a patch or two. They'll sew the buffer layer into a man's socks or shoe leather, whichever works best." He was rubbing his instep. "Those boots of yours, though…you could likely trudge to Persia and back."

Montgomery was so different a community from Milledgeville, much less Macon or Columbus, that most in the Georgia ranks just kept quiet and took in the scene.

"You'd think this was the crossing station for the whole country. It's not that I haven't seen slave traders before and their transports, but I never counted so many Indian savages cuffed into submission." The youth suppressed a cough. He and the Knoxville man solemnly witnessed a group of Chickasaw males being led single-file to the boarding pier. "I had forgot we're on the route to Oklahoma territory, as well as the commercial districts of Vicksburg." Both onlookers were more than ready to board the *Benjamin Franklin*, a sturdy steamboat, and get on down the Alabama River away from the dreary docks, even if water travel made them queasy.

Chugging down the river gave the original Georgia men time to recuperate from the march, a sobering first leg of their trek. New recruits picked up in Montgomery were eager to chat about the Texas adventure, but watching several Macon volunteers gingerly remove shoes and socks curbed their enthusiasm. From their groans as they lifted or set down rifles and packs, sore shoulders could be surmised, but bleeding blisters on feet offered grim evidence of worse hardship. Reserved by nature, John T. nevertheless spread the news about the patches that some enlistees had.

"Sam Hardaway—my nephew—he's floating along behind us on the sick barge. The doctor says it's just a cold and a precaution. But in a few days, he'll point you to a Macon girl onboard, Miss Adeline. She's figured a way to stitch patches opposite any blister. When we reach the coast, we might stay long enough to take up formation practice. You'll know soon enough whether you need the Harper women to see what can be done with needle and thread."

In Mobile, there was indeed time for marching after the city's elaborate banquet. The surf had turned too rough for ships meant to hug the shoreline toward New Orleans. In addition to the family of women, there were other clumps of relatives in the growing volunteer army. Two shared the last name Bulloch, including an experienced officer who would surely be in contention for a commission once in Texas. Sam Hardaway also recognized the second son of John Hunt, another Macon cotton dealer. That youthful recruit and a Stovall the same age were first cousins. Adeline Harper pointed out to Sam the presence of three other cousins among the men. They were former neighbors of hers, where their tobacco field had abutted her little homestead. During the banquets at Columbus and Mobile, the battalion had seemed like a traveling family reunion.

Captain Ward was proving himself to be Hugh McLeod's rival in oratory, and the battalion was nearly two hundred strong before ocean steamers readied to carry the volunteers down the gulf to the last American port.

"I hope we don't get separated again, dear uncle, though it was a heavenly thing to hear soldiers and females converse. Adeline Harper's aunt peppered the captain with questions the rest of us were too shy to ask. Uriah Bulloch was down with bronchitis, according to the doctor, but I've no doubt he'll be voted a captain when we get the chance to elect our own officers."

The Georgia men had been impressed by Montgomery's busy docks and moved by the gracious welcome in Mobile, but New Orleans left them speechless. Everywhere were cobbled and gas-lit streets, ornate building facades, extraordinary clothing, and a flurry of accents. The Southern soldiers mostly stared, their lips parted in astonishment. Stationed in a multistory building off Lafayette Square, the volunteers tried to steer their attention to maneuvers. Even the reserved Knoxville father took another turn starting conversation.

"They say the Mobile Greys formed up here and already made their way to the Texas border."

"But they didn't journey down the coast as we'll do in two weeks." It was a Lamar nephew speaking up. "They went up from here as far as Natchez, and then they marched west toward the Mexican line near Fort Jessup."

"You suppose McLeod met up with them?"

"No, they left well before Macon speeches were even made," the serious youth said. "But they would never have checked in at Jessup, if they were wise."

"Trouble there?"

"No more than we'll face if we were to encounter American military. President Jackson doesn't see how we can flout our treaty with Mexico over its Texas territory."

"We'll stay in our own coats and breeches, I suppose," Sam added, "until we meet Fannin in Velasco. Our uniforms are probably stored out of view."

"I can't say I approve of such secret maneuvers." Spillers said quietly. They were watching the Sunday marching practice of smaller Louisiana companies whose uniforms were far from inconspicuous. Military ranks in cardinal red marched one direction, while others in cornflower blue strutted off at a different angle.

"Don't anyone ask the older Spillers boy," Sam said, "if his daddy left home in secret to join this army!" When John winced, the Macon youth regretted making the jest. "My cousin, young Johnny…he came to see us off, though. He felt more of a man for having walked to town on that mission."

In the next few days, whenever Sam motioned to John Spillers from across the brick paving stones of Lafayette Square, the Knoxville man could imagine his older son in another six or seven years looking almost a man, like Hardaway—yet still full of energetic leaps and gestures and the enthusiasm of a child. Those three cousins from Macon helped anchor his thoughts, now that he found himself in a swarming city population whose individuals could not be identified. Occasionally he caught sight of John Hunt's son, not so much older than Sam, but with a solemn and intense demeanor that Mr. Spillers recognized as how his own disposition struck others.

When they'd watched the Harper women ride off in their carriage to the French part of the city, the girl's dark braids reminded Spillers of his sister-in-law who had worn her hair down until married. The Macon women's servant had spoken French to their driver, and Spillers recalled how the Troutman's cook Camille sometimes spoke in a musical dialect to the other help. As he tossed on his cot one night, Spillers dreamt that all the Knoxville women were walking toward him on the red path, calling out to him in French or in some other tongue. His sweet wife Matilda was in the forefront, but as she broke into a run, her words were nothing he could decipher.

On another night, a dream made him toss and sweat. In fitful sleep, he saw himself and the Macon men in deep consultation about supplies for the mission in Texas. Miss Harper's neighbor Francis Gideon, who was known for his accounting ability, and others were trying to predict what emergencies might threaten their survival.

If food is scarce, we'll be glad for a long knife to dig for grubs or skin a snake.

Should water prove hard to reach, that same knife could split a gourd into a scoop.

As heavy as oil cloth is for carrying, you'd be lucky to have one layer come between you and a freeze.

Or something to smother a fire…started by a floating ember.

I can almost smell the stench of fire…

"'Tis smoke I smell!"

"We're on fire!"

"Fire!"

John T. Spillers was shouting in his sleep. But none of the soldiers stretched out near him had been soundly at rest. The barracks was packed with uneasy men, and more than one was dreaming of fire.

"Mr. Spillers! Uncle!"

"A terrible dream…a barn engulfed!" Now others were rushing to the window to look in the direction of the square. Footsteps thundered from the stairwell where some had gone down and then back up to report a blaze not far off. A bitter smell wafted into the barracks.

"It's not us. It's not a building." One battalion man knew more details. "There's a boat gone up in flames at the main port."

"Not the *Pennsylvania?*"

"No schooner—a steamer, at the dock where they come down the Mississippi." There was a wave of relief that it wasn't a ship readying for Texas. Still, if an engulfed deck was close enough to smell, embers could float beyond the wharf to buildings. "A southerly breeze brought the stench in this far. But cooler air from the north seems to be taking charge again."

"T'was the *Natchez,* they said, a steamer that's been a regular here for years. She's charred down almost to the hull."

"Better get back to sleep, boys, if there's no threat to land sites."

"We'll go have a look in the morning," Sam said quietly to John. "After maneuvers, we'll see what's left of her." Then he pulled a blanket back up around his shoulders, but he turned once more to the older man's cot. "Whatever you were dreaming…it took real fire to pull you out of it."

Late the next morning, knots of men from the Georgia Battalion headed down to the old docks. Some thought they might learn whether anything lost in the fire had been provisions intended for loading onto the *Pennsylvania.* They wanted no delays for their trip down the gulf. It didn't matter which way the wind was blowing once they reached two streets from the wharf. The acrid stink of charred woodwork and upholstery permeated the port area. Ash drifted thickly in the air.

They found the steamship still smoldering, its top level having crashed in ghoulish tatters to the deck below. Unlike scenes where flames still angrily devour their surroundings, the ship workers moved in slow motion. They were gingerly pointing out any pieces of timber or hardware that could be put to use again. Several Georgia soldiers wondered whether the remaining blackened floorboards might be in danger of caving in, too. No doubt many of the laborers had invested their best energies during the night in a futile attempt to halt the fire or unload cargo and furnishings. When some battalion men offered to help with the salvage, maybe come back the next morning after the wreck had cooled, they were politely refused. Cleaning up would take at least a fortnight, and that effort would still be paid work. Besides, someone recognized the onlookers as being among the Texas volunteers. They were advised to conserve energy for their own toil and danger.

"Now there's someone sorrowful enough, if not old enough, to be the ruined owner of the *Natchez*." Sam Hardaway gestured toward a young man sitting on a jettisoned cushion. If he had shed tears earlier, he now appeared too numb. There was no doubt about his dejection as he propped up his head with both hands.

"Were you working this boat?" Spillers asked. The dark-haired youth had piercing eyes. He let his hands fall to his lap.

"Any ship that needed unpacking or loading. I've been working them all for over two months."

"Those doing salvage appear protective of their wages."

"It's not that," the stricken fellow said. "The boys know me. They'd let me pitch in for a meal and more."

"At it two months? Your home's not New Orleans?"

"No, and that's the shock. I came down on the *Natchez*—on this very ship—from the Mississippi town by the same name. But I'd had enough of…seeking my fortune." He coughed and then forced an odd laugh. He turned away and passed a hand across his cheek. "This steamboat was my transport upriver. I was going to tote luggage for the passengers in exchange for the return fare."

"Surely another steamboat goes that far," Sam suggested.

"Did you put any away from your wages?"

"You sound like my friend back home." The young man stood up. He smiled somewhat as he stuffed his hands into his pockets. "Can you believe I have a friend so true he gave me cash for returning—in case of any such catastrophe?"

"Then…"

"You can spend that amount for only three days room and board in this city, if you let the sumptuous edibles entice you." His grimaced again. "Or if you let the roulette wheel catch your eye."

The two lingering by the docks to talk with the youth exchanged worried glances. Neither Macon nor Knoxville hosted any gambling enterprises. Captain Ward had been wise enough to station the Georgia volunteers close to the square but in the direction of Esplanade, a thoroughfare on the side of the city opposite where high stakes gambling was established.

"Why don't you come along with us, then? To Lafayette Square, if not to Texas. More and more are joining us."

"Stay for the day at least. We're mostly from small towns. Come along. It'll lift your spirits," Mr. Spillers suggested.

"Name's Thomas Weeks." He straightened up and began shaking hands.

"We have a Weeks gentleman in Macon. Maybe you'll find some kin among us."

"I only know about my mother's side." The young man's expression had been brightening, but now his dark eyes grew somber again.

"Well, Master Weeks," Sam broke in, "when was the last time you ate?"

"Yesterday morning…before the fire."

"There's a bakery only one street off the square. My uncle and I will treat you, let a little Georgia hospitality brighten your day."

They paused for a last look at the smoldering hull of the *Natchez*. The Mississippi youth seemed to be deciding against any need to tell the salvage crew where he was headed. He could write a letter home if he threw in with those bound for Texas. The removal of blackened timbers unsettled the battalion men. If rebellion ignited full war in north Mexico, there was no telling what might fall to ruins. But they turned aside without speculation, making their way from the dock toward the brick avenues near Lafayette Square.

Thomas Weeks looked a bit faint as they came up the side street to La Marguerite Bakery. A line of customers was almost out the door, and Sam guided their new acquaintance to a corner of the boardwalk where they could sit and wait for Mr. Spillers to bring out some beignets. The Knoxville man took his waiting place in the doorway.

"It's one of your Texas soldiers stalling purchases," the lady ahead informed him.

"Quite a big order," another woman said. "But he's counting out the payment, so we'll be moving along soon."

"You're a brave bunch, all that are going—"

"Patriots!" The two ladies nodded to each other and smiled at Spillers. "I'll be glad when you can take off to Texas and put an end the whole sorry trouble."

"And leave us to our short bakery lines!"

Soon a Macon man exited the shop, tipping his hat to the ladies and apologizing for extending the wait. His curly hair was distinctive, and Spillers recognized him as one in their company who was often at the center of some lively exchange. But when the older private came out twenty minutes later with two beignets apiece, he was surprised to see the Macon volunteer still there, standing alongside Hardaway and their new friend.

"He's a *Weeks!*"

"We told him all you from Macon would be trying to make a connection."

"Well, we can't let him languish here in New Orleans among strangers. Come along with us."

"I'll need to write my mother," Thomas said. He pushed his dark hair from his eyes. "Last she heard from me, I was making wages on the wharf, but likely to get back home by spring."

"We'll all be home by spring, lad." Malacai Mulholland was the volunteer's name. He had spent early years in his native Ireland, and still had an accent.

"Uncle," Sam said brightly, "he's just ordered up a mountain of beignets for our departure day!"

"Compliments of William Ward—captain right now, but I'll vote for him to be general of all Texas if we get the chance."

"Tell about the ships!" The Hardaway youth had risen to his feet.

"The *Pennsylvania*—and the other three—they're going to be ready for loading within the week."

"Maybe day after tomorrow!" Their enthusiasm made the young man from Mississippi stand, as well. Malacai gave the newcomer's shoulder a friendly pat.

"And beignets all the way around the morning we sail out."

"For all two hundred? Or is it three hundred now?"

"Well, Ward is kindly taking care of Macon and Milledgeville men. No doubt the other officers have some confection in store for the men aboard their ships."

"No such pastries in Texas, I suppose."

"Maybe no bakeries! They say you can't find but one in the whole wilderness where we're headed," Malacai declared. "Anyway, it's likely to take a week at sea before we reach Velasco. We may have no appetite at all until we reach dry land."

The Southerners didn't know which fact was hardest to believe. The hungrier men worked to swallow. When they had dusted sugar from their trousers and vests, they headed for battalion quarters. They did not speak of the ghostly *Natchez* remains. In the narrow streets before the great opening into Lafayette Square, locals were buzzing about the departure of the Georgia Battalion. One local couple showed disdain for American citizens venturing into foreign territory, but their objections were shouted down. Applause broke out for patriots willing to aid colonists across the border.

"I can't forget to send a letter home," Thomas repeated. He was still walking the emotional plank between grief and exhilaration and the others wondered if he might not be better off finding his way home.

"Maybe your mother needs to see you in person." Spillers couldn't help worrying. "One of the other barge captains in town would surely let you earn your way."

"Or if you sign on with us, you'll have a small fortune in land scrip to show your mum when we return." The fellow with the Irish accent spoke with infectious optimism. "The whole lot of us will be writing until we board ship. Don't worry about getting an envelope to the post. They say thousands in sympathy will see us off at the docks. Anyone will be glad to get your message on its way."

The father from Knoxville considered what he might say in a letter to his children. No, a letter to his sister-in-law, he decided, a letter that she would read to his sons and baby daughter. The words *liberty* and *forefathers* came to mind, because the speeches had inspired every volunteer. But his thoughts had swirled in the last six weeks. He did not understand how some men sat down and composed page after page, how anyone could record enough words to convey all the hope and danger this course of action posed. John T. Spillers thought that if he found the time, and if someone from his hometown or from Macon had just a single page and one envelope he could purchase, he might write out a very short message—that he loved his family dearly and would think of nothing else while he was away, that he would see them all in the spring—after the cause of freedom was won—and that their sweet mother's soul would forever be their comfort.

1836 the Louisiana-Texas border

7   The Sabine at a Splash

In the chill of late February, pine trees along the river separating Louisiana from Texas exuded a potent scent. The winter had been unusually bitter and wet on both sides of the border. Smoke from a spitting campfire drifted slowly toward the riverbank, the same direction that Lieutenant Hugh McLeod wished he could be charging on horseback. Just waiting for the sun's first glint was hard enough.

"It's good to see that you quit pacing." The officer speaking was in charge of the bivouac near the banks of the Sabine and had just come out of his tent. McLeod liked Lieutenant Bonnell. He wasn't so sure he would get along as well with General Gaines, due to return next month to Fort Jessup proper from clashes with the Seminoles in Florida.

"Coffee should be ready in a few minutes."

"Sit down, Hugh. I'm just hoping you didn't sleep on that stool."

"It's more comfortable than the cot. Only two months at Jessup, and I'm starting to get a paunch."

"There's nothing much to do back at the stockade, except eat," the senior officer agreed. "Not much action out here by the river either, not since last fall with the Caddo treaties signed."

The new officer responded in respectful silence. What Lieutenant Bonnell had managed to accomplish was impressive. Staying within the limitations of American involvement in Mexico, he had secured peaceful dealings with the Indian group just across the border around Nacogdoches. But Sam Houston, now the Texas Army's general, had appreciated the American's negotiation style enough that he'd called Joseph Bonnell his aide-de-camp.

Hugh McLeod wondered how he, too, could participate in the unfolding revolution across the river, while still adhering to United States protocol. Several times during a mostly sleepless night, he imagined himself slipping noiselessly up on his horse, ambling in the direction of the ferry crossing, then picking up speed on the opposite shore.

"You don't think Jesse Burditt will go on to the fort without stopping here, if there's any news?"

"No reason to," Bonnell said. "We can't expect Gaines for another three weeks at the soonest. I told Jess last time we'd be out here in the tents through February. He'll come straight up to our campfire if there's anything urgent."

"Well, my men and I won't head back to the fort until afternoon, if you don't mind."

"Might as well stay to see if there's a post. If he's bringing reports from Nacogdoches, he usually gets as far as San Augustine where he sleeps over. The ferry isn't but an hour or so from there. If there's any further word about San Antonio, we'll likely hear by noon."

McLeod was trying to picture whether the post rider, Mr. Burditt, had been galloping or taking a stroll last fall in delivering his report of one New Orleans battalion. Avoiding U.S. military, half the Greys had already filed across the trail between the fort and the bivouac, and crossed the Sabine considerably north of the Gaines Ferry. Once in Texas, they cut down toward Nacogdoches without entering the city and then moved on west along the Old San Antonio Road. Other companies from Louisiana, McLeod knew, had been waiting for fresh recruits at Velasco.

Now, volunteers from Macon and other Georgia towns were there under Colonel Fannin's command. William Ward managed to get a letter posted and through to Fort Jessup confirming their arrival during Christmas. From Velasco, the battalion expected to move inland to Refugio. But a rumored plan for Texas soldiers to invade Matamoros was currently considered folly. Streams of messages from General Houston's force in Nacogdoches had to be believed—at least two Mexican generals already quelled rebellion as far along the gulf as Matamoros. The question now was whether Santa Anna, Mexico's military leader for the last year, was brash enough to move an army inland in the direction of the Alamo.

McLeod was on his feet again and refilling Bonnell's coffee cup. The Macon man hadn't really slept at all, but a level of energy was building anyway. He'd felt a similar surge of intent the night before the candlelight speeches.

"Word came last week about Crockett making it to San Antonio. You figure he's been there more than a month?" The slow pace of Texas' postal delivery shocked Americans.

"About a month, I'd guess." Then the officer in charge shook his head. "When I heard we had lost Ben Milam—right before our boys forced Cos to surrender the Alamo—I was worried about William Travis holding San Antonio on his own. But I'd forgotten about Jim Bowie's involvement, forgotten about Seguin and the other men raised right there and being with us all along. And now Crockett and some other Tennessee men have come across in answer to Houston's plea." The senior officer went quiet.

A corporal walked over from a group of guards and stooped to stir the fire. The metal coffee pot was moved to a cast-iron trivet, and then the soldier leaned a fire poker against a rock before going to check where fresh horses were secured.

"All this talk is unofficial," Bonnell went on in a low voice, "and I do have to remind myself not to get quoted as sounding like General Houston's aide-de-camp."

"Even though you are?"

"Well, curb what you say around your men, Lieutenant McLeod." His manner was entirely affable. "If we were just now to see a company of American volunteers, carrying a Texas independence flag and marching toward the ferry over that rise, we'd be obliged to order a halt and to relieve them of their firearms."

"Not having seen battle yet, that might be the hardest duty I'd face so far."

"Lieutenant Bonnell!"

The corporal who was seeing to feed bags heard shouts from the ferry landing across the river. From the Louisiana side, a soldier's horse galloped toward the campfire in the half-light. Both Bonnell and McLeod approached the rider as he made it to the clearing.

"It's Burditt, sir! He's coming on across, but you can hear him yelling from the other bank!"

"He must have slept in the woods to be so close to our camp by dawn."

"Says Nacogdoches was going crazy the day before yesterday!"

Lieutenant Joseph Bonnell was strapping on his sword. His orderly stood by with the officer's rifle.

"It's not the Indians, sir," the rider said. "Ole Burditt is yellin' that Santa Anna has his army all up around San Antonio. He says General

Houston got word from riders that looked half dead from the race to tell him!"

"Houston's headed out? How far did he figure to go?"

"He and his company rode out fast toward Washington-on-the-Brazos and San Felipe! They're taking as many as will join them on down to Gonzales, sir." The rider slid off his horse, and stood shaking his head in disbelief. Bonnell assumed an authoritative demeanor that he had not conveyed a few minutes ago.

"Lieutenant," he said to McLeod, "If you'll keep my company in order here, I'll go speak with Mr. Burditt about the how the Caddo are handling the disruption. Our job is to make sure there's no turmoil on the American border. Understand?"

"Yes, sir."

There was a crowd around the campfire by the time the messenger and officer in charge walked their horses back up to the bivouac area. Hugh McLeod had requested them to form up in rows to await any announcements. He was barely used to ordering his own company back at the fort, and he wasn't sure if he would ever adjust to commanding strangers. His own words spoken to Georgia boys, with hope of inspiring them, had not yet helped him adjust.

"Men, " Bonnell already had their attention, "the news is that Sam Houston left a reasonable patrol in the city, and there are plenty of other citizens able with their firearms. There's no trouble with the Caddo so far, but we're going to keep our posts near the ferry to offer security if any Indian threat spills over."

His message was impossible to misinterpret. There would be no reactionary dash across the border to assist revolutionaries.

"How far is San Antonio from Nacogdoches, sir?" The corporal asked what many in the ranks were wondering.

"Could be four or five days normal riding when the roads are good, but you'd have to take the mud and some swollen rivers into account." The lieutenant appeared to consider the next question likely. Sympathy for Texan colonists could not be dampened. "So, we won't have any word about how Travis and Houston fare for at least a week, I'd say, probably longer." Mr. Burditt had caught his breath and his attitude contrasted with the officer's calm.

"I was right next to the general when news came in about Santa Anna. He stood up straight like he was near seven foot just to hear the Mexican despot dared ride into the heart of Texas."

"Let my orderly get you a biscuit and some coffee, Jesse. You've had one helluva ride. We appreciate your getting word to us fast." Bonnell walked across the front row of soldiers while he continued speaking. "Lieutenant McLeod is going to take his patrol back into the fort and pass this latest news to Company B," he said. "Meanwhile, we'll step up our daily maneuvers here and be on alert for any problems unfolding along the river." He gave the Georgia officer a nod, and the two saluted each other.

A half hour went by before Hugh McLeod and the three privates who had accompanied him to the Sabine Camp altered their single file formation. The man in front of the lieutenant slowed down to let the officer's horse come alongside. Two other soldiers followed, out of earshot.

"Permission to speak, sir?"

"Speak, Dilworth."

"If you was to get official word, allowing you to resign your commission," he started out, "not that I overheard any higher-ups discussing it..."

"I don't know what you're talking about."

"Right. Yessir." He thought for a while as they rode. "But if you *ever was to get permission* to show Santa Anna...how any tyrant threatening Americans gets dead right quick..." He looked at McLeod to read his expression. "You wouldn't go racing across the Sabine without taking some of us with you, would you, sir?" Lieutenant McLeod couldn't help smiling. "Lots of us in Company B hope you wouldn't."

At Fort Jessup, a compound of cabins surrounded by a barrier and lookout stockade, word traveled quickly about General Santa Anna's moves. From a window in the officer's cabin, Hugh could see the men undertaking ordinary routine—raising buckets from the well to take to the laundry stand, men along the upper stockade ledges switching positions at timed intervals, small units of men practicing their marching or rifle positions. But he could also see two or three men at a time, when they were at ease, talking in an animated fashion. He knew they weren't conversing about whether or not the cook might have a wild turkey to pluck for stew. They hungered for action in Texas.

By the fifth day back at Fort Jessup, inactivity had worn on the lieutenant from Georgia. He could make only so many trips from his desk in the officer cabin to the cold pane of glass looking out on muddy parade grounds. Slumped in his chair, he jotted down a list of dinner dishes that might be ready to taste over in the kitchen. Then he recognized some commotion among the gate guards and warned himself against expecting a bulletin from Texas or sealed documents from Washington D. C.

He cleared a circle in the fogged window to observe three privates on the lookout ledge. They were running back and forth and, on the ground, men rushed to pull back the log securing the fort's eastern gate. McLeod was already reaching for his jacket when a riderless horse, with a pack mule tethered, sauntered past guards and into the enclosure.

"I'll see to it, sir." A corporal rose from a small table nearby where he had been studying supply ledgers for the first quarter.

"No, I need to get out. Too much sitting as it is, except for round trips to the dining hall."

"Is it finally ole Matthias with the Mississippi mail?"

"It's not anybody, so far." Judging the scene outside, McLeod grabbed his gloves and his neck scarf. "Just a mount and a mule. Don't know how to interpret the horse's gear, fringe tied in tassels." He set his hat firmly on his head. "It's been a while since I've ridden the trail east. I may take a couple men with me. Two who didn't go along to the Sabine a few days ago." As he buttoned his jacket, he looked once more out the window at the loose mounts. "Could be someone on foot—or dead—between here and the Donnelly's stand."

At intervals all along the trail to the Mississippi, crudely built rest stands offered travelers a source of water, food necessities, and news. A double shack run by the Donnelly family had been established on the trail since a year after the fort itself was completed.

More rough structures popped up along the Trace between Natchez and Tennessee, but even on the Louisiana side of the big river, enterprising individuals or families staked out spots where they could set up to offer passersby some respite. Such stands would have let an aimless wanderer know of the fort's proximity. And anyone bringing news up from New Orleans, from Natchez, or as far away as Vicksburg would have known Fort Jessup to be near.

"There's no sign of military mail!" called the soldier checking saddlebags. "Just a keepsake box with letters, it looks like. And a spyglass of good quality." McLeod nodded and chose men for a small patrol.

"It could be somebody smart enough to have documents tucked down inside his jacket," he said. "Just not too wise about tying up his horse."

The lieutenant braced himself for signs of foul play along the way. It was only Texas action he wanted to see, and he sincerely hoped they might make it all the way to Donnelly's before evidence of the rider. The horse may have strayed while the traveler was resting.

Not four miles out, McLeod and his patrol met a family and their wagon headed to the fort. The wife, clearly pregnant, held the reins and the husband cradled his arm in a sling. There were at least three children peering from underneath a canvas cover.

"We're on the lookout for a man who might have been taking mail to Jessup from the Mississippi border. You carrying anyone with you who might have lost his horse?"

"We seen a horse and mule running along together."

"They showed up at the fort."

"My boy tried to latch onto one, but the mule had a fit and both animals just kept a'runnin'."

"Didn't spot the rider, then?"

"No sir. When the two critters passed us up, there was no one in sight." McLeod thought the children looked too cold to smile.

"You all plan to stay overnight at the fort?"

"Hopin' to rest up closer to the Sabine, maybe wait for this last chilly spell to break…if my wife can manage the wagon that far. My arm only suffered a bad sprain—I let a molasses barrel slip away from me a couple days back." He tugged at the sling. "Should be good before we get to the Texas border, though. We're counting on making it to St. Augustine… before the misses has her…confinement."

"Don't count on making it across the Sabine just yet. Jessup's waiting to see how Texans over near the Alamo hold off Santa Anna. Could be our army won't allow settlers to cross until the border calms down." At that news, the woman took one hand off the reins and rested her fingers over her mouth. "The Mexicans have been sent running before, so I don't doubt the outcome. But the San Antonio Road is a straight shot to Nacogdoches and they might wave swords at us up this far."

"They'll get word at the fort?" her husband asked.

"With these children in the weather, I'd set up there until the next report on General Houston." The parents were nodding and looking back into the wagon flap. Even the horses wanted to move on in the cold, and they strained in the harness.

"Hope you find the rider before the sun sets. Saw ice in patches two days ago. Guess that's what made me lose my grip on the dang barrel."

"Oh," McLeod said, reaching into his back satchel, "you recognize this type tassel?"

"That horse goin' along on his own, they was all over his saddle."

"I know," the lieutenant said. "I mean, do these tassels look like any you've seen before?" The woman, reserved until now, shook her head about the leather decoration.

"I grew up in Alabama, where the Creek Indians mostly live. I can't say as I've seen any tied to a saddle before, but I seen plenty like that up around the tops of their moccasin boots."

"Creek Indians?"

"That's where I've witnessed the like," she said again.

The family's wagon moved along on the trail in the direction of Fort Jessup, and Mcleod's men checked the angle of the sun to gauge the remaining time they had to look for the missing rider. The trail was no wider than the wagon wheels had been, and the soldiers took formation one behind the other. But the private behind McLeod edged up alongside.

"You don't think that leather work could be some kind of Indian ploy, do you?" His commanding officer didn't answer, and the enlisted man waited so that he could read the look in his lieutenant's eyes.

"Maybe you ought to ask *them*," McLeod said at last. But his expression meant hush and don't react in a startled way. So the party of three continued without changing their pace. One by one they took furtive glances up a woodsy north slope where the movements of scout horses could be detected.

Ambush by white men most often came without warning. A thick bush by the side of the trail might transform into two armed thieves firing off shots before any introduction whatsoever.

But an attack by Indians could sometimes start off calmly enough, and look at first as if a scouting party had drifted accidentally in the direction of travelers and would soon ease back the other way. Anyone on this extension of the Natchez Trace could just as easily bet one way as the other about the outcome of such a sighting.

McLeod and his men did not look steadily at the half dozen Choctaw scouts, or Chickasaw in these parts. But all three Jessup soldiers leaned so that their jacket flaps rose up to expose their rifle butts. They were ready for an engagement, but didn't want to invite conflict—not with numbers stacked against them. The fort's military patrol waited tensely for any sign that the ridge riders intended to fight.

"Hey there!"

One private dug his heels into the sides of his horse in surprise, and the animal reared up. The soldier had some trouble regaining his balance in the saddle.

"Are you who we're looking for?" McLeod asked a man who had been sitting on a tree stump. The stranger rose to his feet and rubbed his hands together. With no other horse in sight, there was general relief—mixed with tension about the onlookers—that they had found the rider of the stray mount. The man bent over to pick up an easily recognizable United States mail satchel. McLeod felt a surge of anticipation that he knew he'd have to master until returning to the fort.

"I lost my horse and pack mule a ways back," the stranded man said. "I'm the temporary carrier from back at Natchez. Did you get word that Matthias Jones took a leave of absence from postal delivery? He had to see about some losses in New Orleans."

"Yeah?" one private responded. "I figured Jonesy would head down that way for good one day. But he loved the trail."

"Anyway, name's Shelby Whitmire." He was dusting off his breeches or just slapping at his legs to keep warm.

"Your horse seems to know the way to Fort Jessup as well as the regular mount that Matthias rode."

"Just trail instincts. It's *me* the horse isn't too sure about."

Hugh McLeod had been studying the man. The fellow seemed not too embarrassed about being on foot in the middle of nowhere, though he had an appealing humility about him. His hair had a touch of gray at the temples, but his face was young. He looked strong, but not overbearing about how he might put his muscles to use. The Indians, McLeod noticed as well, had come to a halt above.

"We've got some company up on the ridge just now," he reminded the whole group calmly. "Pretty soon, we ought to look as if we know each other and are headed back together in the same direction."

"I think they'll be plenty relieved to hand me over to you," Whitmire said.

"How long ago you spot them?"

"I thought I heard them laughing about ten miles back, when I stepped into the brush to relieve myself—the damn horse took off and I heard laughing. They found my predicament funnier than I did."

McLeod and the other soldiers were looking warily from the mail carrier to the incline where the watchful scouts stayed in a cluster. The lieutenant himself couldn't help smiling as he assessed the weight of Shelby Whitmire, and decided the man should take a position behind one of the more slender privates.

"You'd be better off pissing down your leg than to let your mount horse run off out here."

"I did have to pass water all the sudden," Shelby admitted. "If I'd known the horse had an evil sense of humor, I'd have tethered him."

McLeod had gestured to one soldier who was hoisting Whitmire up behind him on the saddle blanket. It wouldn't be too comfortable, but it would be preferable to walking.

"How long you been carrying mail? How long you been riding trail?" the man with the reins asked.

They were heading back in the direction of Fort Jessup and all four men had hope that the next time they glanced up the slope they wouldn't see any threatening observers.

"Never been on a horse until two months ago."

"What do you mean, *never?*" McLeod had let up on the pace of his horse so that he could hear this Shelby Whitmire's answer.

"I've lived on the Natchez shore all my life. Not much use for a horse there, and not much means to buy one." The three soldiers took a minute to mull this information.

"When I came over this way from Montgomery, I went through Natchez myself," Mcleod said. "Most horses are too smart to keep company with men that wild—at least down along the shore." He wondered where Whitmire fit into that scene. "So that's not your saddle, with all the tassels?"

"Pack mule, horse, and all the tassels are most surely mine now. A neighbor, a good friend from down along the shore, gave them to me. Named the horse Sawdust."

McLeod liked this man, and the disappearance of the Indians on the ridgeline made him cheerful, too. He didn't much want to catch the Natchez fellow in a lie, but an officer's job was to size up a situation, to assess any changes in circumstances and company. He had to put one more question to the affable stranger.

"All gifts, you say. Mind if I ask your generous friend's name?"

"Apokta. Apokta Sizemore."

Over the next few days, Second Lieutenant Hugh McLeod had a hard time consoling himself that the Natchez mail had included no reply to his resignation request. If military approval were on its way from President Jackson to the Mississippi, with Shelby Whitmire stuck at Fort Jessup until the weather cleared, there would probably be no official word for many weeks. A stretch of freezing temperatures and sleet locked down any movement from the fort, except to get word that Bonnell's men were managing at the river.

Challenges to maintaining posts in the hostile weather meant the Sabine Camp men were likely too busy to fret over Texas. Lieutenant Bonnell oversaw morale in a way McLeod admired. At the fort, he too tried to carry on like a West Point graduate. He put sergeants and corporals in charge of exercise and maintenance details, but the new officer could not deny the restlessness growing within Company B. Arguments about who would dispatch General Santa Anna fastest, given the opportunity, kept the men agitated long after lamps were extinguished at night. Some had relatives living in the Texas colonies. One man knew his cousin to be among the men Colonel William Travis depended on. No one at Fort Jessup expressed disinterest in the outcome at San Antonio.

Appearing in Hugh McLeod's mind were the faces of Macon men who had stepped forward after his speech. When he couldn't stand the idle wait, he would go to the stable and talk to his horse, check the animal's ankles and shoes, make sure that his saddle and blankets were stored and kept dry. He couldn't allow himself to speak to the enlisted men about Texas. Except for the stranded family and the agreeable mail carrier, little distracted him.

The Natchez man was good company, though. McLeod had heard him talking about New Orleans with the private who knew Matthias. Whitmire also had one friend in the big city, though late word was the Mississippi boy had volunteered with the Georgia Battalion as it headed for Texas.

One morning, out in the stables along the southern stockade walls, McLeod found the rescued man repacking a saddlebag. He couldn't get a bulge with sharp corners to rest where he wanted it.

"Whatever that is, you'd be better off shedding the container."

"It's a box, with letters I'm responsible for. Not regular mail," Whitmire added, "just personal writing—keepsakes."

"Nothing more valuable than that?"

"I promised to hold onto them. Could be none of it matters much to anyone. It's my word I hate to give up, I suppose."

"You lost your horse and nearly your life," the officer reminded him. "I'd have let a pile of letters see hell first." The man he spoke to laughed while reaching inside the large leather pouch to pull out a wooden box. He turned it over in his hands.

"I couldn't leave it back in Natchez."

"All I'm saying is," Hugh went on, "those corners poking up are no good. You'll call attention. Someone aiming to ambush would otherwise let you pass."

"Oh."

"Besides, you might need to get off your horse in a hurry, bed down without moving at nightfall. A box won't make a decent pillow, but a satchel of letters could."

"I did. Took the box out along the way and…"

"Being at your leisure is *a mercy*—as my mother says—but it sounds as if you haven't had to throw down in a hurry yet."

"It was a peaceful stretch," Shelby conceded. "Monotonous. My horse probably ran off to find entertainment."

"Any horse is keen to shed extra weight. That's my only counsel," the trained officer said, leaving the civilian to make his own decision about the box with the inlay top.

Later that afternoon, Hugh McLeod noticed the Mississippi man out where the stranded family had secured their wagon in the last two sunny days. The man had his hat in one hand and was handing the pretty box to the woman, who sat near a rear wheel on a leather trunk. Her middle was distended with the child expected soon. She smiled when she took the gift, and the officer was startled to see how different the shift in expression made her look. Left alone with the empty box, she soon called over her children. Enjoying a warmer spell, they had been tossing marbles in the dirt, and when they wanted to see how the shiny globes looked inside the box, the expectant mother made them wipe the marbles clean before setting them down.

McLeod had worried at first about a man who could claim close friendship with a Creek Indian, but he trusted the mail carrier's demeanor. After keeping his company for just a few days, the officer sized the man up as no one with a secret side contradicting outward appearance.

"You ever think about signing on with the military?" the lieutenant asked Shelby Whitmire one evening. The civilian had happily accepted a bunk spot on the floor of the officers' cabin, where there was only a cramped space to stretch out blankets. Most men would have grumbled, but the good-natured fellow didn't seem to need special treatment. Before pursuing the topic, McLeod offered him a glass of port, but he had waved it away. "Never tempted by a muster roll, I take it."

"I guess I've been following my own marching orders too long."

"You don't get riled up? With all this talk about soldiers from Mexico City threatening Americans who don't obey?"

"Didn't say that, though I guess I don't rile as easily as some." The Whitmire man was sitting on the floor. McLeod would finish his own drink in another few sips. Nearby, a corporal and sergeant were collecting paperwork so they could check off watch duties.

"With you having no experience on horseback, it must have been some kind of fever making you ride out this far from your hometown." The lieutenant and the other men chuckled again about finding the Mississippi man sitting on a tree stump. McLeod kept wondering how the newcomer could befriend an Indian, yet know nothing of wilderness travel. "I can't think of one reason why a peaceful man like you would strike out from home," he joked. "Though I've made speech powerful enough to fire the appetite for adventure!"

"Didn't say I was immune to inspiring words."

"And I can't picture you nursing an insult." The officer studied him while he finished with his glass. "If I learned you'd taken revenge or fled a crime, I'd fall out of my saddle. Mind you, a good many American men cross into Mexico for just those reasons."

"You're right that I've no interest in returning to Natchez for the next satchel of mail," Shelby Whitmire admitted. McLeod was preparing to turn in. He was almost ready to face another sleepless night, wondering if tomorrow would be a day with news, when his sergeant spoke up.

"On my count, it is my lawful wife making me glad for far-off duty." He winked before going on, "and a far sweeter female giving me dreams of home." Mcleod shook his head, but suddenly wondered whether the smiling young mother with the inlay box had reminded him more of Joanna or Rebecca.

"You have yourself a lady in Natchez, Whitmire?" he asked. "One who misses your sense of humor?" The lieutenant didn't hear an answer, and he was about to tell the pleasant civilian to take another blanket from the shelf if he needed it.

"My Natchez lady was waiting for someone," the Jessup guest finally said, stretching out on the floor, "just not *me*." He shook out the blanket. "Can't say I gave her a smile more than twice, but at least I never made her cry."

McLeod tossed in his cot before drifting off. Both ladies who had been important in his youth—Joanna and Rebecca—remained estranged from his priorities. Only the name *Texas*, finally, absorbed his attention. The lieutenant slept fitfully but dozed past sunup. He had heard children's voices. They were playing out near the laundry shed where the family wagon had been draped with hides against the cold. Light was beginning to seep in, and the officer's head throbbed only a little when an urgent pounding brought him to full consciousness.

It was an older boy at the cabin door and, from his expression, McLeod thought an arrow might be protruding from the child's back.

"Where's your doctor at?" He slapped his own sides to underscore the question. "My daddy's having a fit of worry. It's Mama needs help bad… where's your doctor? The baby's comin', but Mama needs help!"

"Doc's out by the river camp," McLeod said. "We can send a rider out—"

"Ain't no time for that. The last one—my baby brother—needed turning—this one's likely stuck, too. Ain't you got no one else…no woman who knows?"

"Tell your pa that I'm on my way." Hugh McLeod looked at the mail carrier as if he hadn't heard right.

"You can't stay on a horse…but you…?"

"Get someone in the washhouse to bring me some clean towels." Shelby Whitmire took time to put his hat firmly on his head. No more words came to McLeod, and he felt his jaw slacken.

Outside in the parade grounds, several soldiers with sheepish expressions had gathered around the distraught father. The low moans and then the sustained howl came from inside the covered wagon.

"Even bear skins wouldn't warm it enough for tonight, not for a week or two likely. The wind's kicking up. After the next pain, help me carry her into the officer barracks." The men looked at one another. McLeod could only gesture to his corporal to do as Whitmire asked. "My blankets are rolled by the shelf. Fold another one into a pillow." After a brief respite, the woman had started to moan again and Whitmire entered the wagon. "Never mind," he called out in a moment. "We'll carry mother and child in shortly."

An hour later, a stunned group pressing against the walls of McLeod's office included the relieved father, the other children, and the lieutenant's mute staff. They all kept their distance from a makeshift partition shielding the pallet with mother and infant daughter. They kept their distance from the implausible scene: the mail carrier kneeling beside her, the only one who had known how to turn the baby's head and guide its shoulders. The Natchez man was telling her that the baby was as fine as any he'd seen, that they both needed to stay in the warm cabin. When he assured the woman that all would be well, the older children began to hug their father, and the displaced soldiers began adjusting their buttons and pockets.

The ranking officer suddenly felt no older than the boy who had come knocking in the emergency. He had perceived the age difference between himself and the civilian, but this morning he believed he would never catch up in experience with the older man wise enough to guide fresh life into this world. If any new warning sound had begun out in the courtyard, nothing registered inside Fort Jessup headquarters. From the infant came a clucking noise that made each soldier ponder the range of courage. Then insistent pounding on the cabin door caused everyone to flinch.

"A letter!" the breathless messenger shouted. "I've brought a fair copy! Is Lieutenant McLeod up and about?"

"Never slept, but the morning woke us full steam." The private was one of Lieutenant Bonnell's men, and he stepped in to salute McLeod. The unlikely nativity scene held his attention only briefly, and he repeated the statement he had been ordered to make.

"It's fair copy of a letter Bonnell gave me to deliver." Shelby Whitmire pulled a blanket edge up closer around the resting mother and stood up. "Back in Nacogdoches, when they got this letter, they could tell it was already a duplicate made in a rush." The messenger stopped to inhale fully. "We took time to write out the gist, though some lines are quoted—they're hard to forget." He had been fishing in a leather pouch, and the document he handed to Hugh McLeod was curled at the edges. The officer moved to the windowpane for enough light to read.

"This is from the 24th of February."

"Yessir—ten days ago. It's the second letter from Travis that's made it as far as Nacogdoches."

"We already knew that Santa Anna was closing in on San Antonio—" His voice trailed off. Then he read aloud.

Fellow citizens and compatriots:

> *I am besieged with a thousand or more Mexicans under Santa Anna.*

"Travis says a surrender was demanded," McLeod told the others grimly.

> *I have answered the demand with a cannon shot, and our flag still waves proudly from the wall.*

When the lieutenant finished reading to himself, he handed the letter to his sergeant and sat down to pull on his better boots. The next Company B man to look at the parchment paper read some to himself and then quoted, *"If this call is neglected, I am determined to sustain myself as long as possible and die like a soldier who never forgets what is due his honor and that of his country."*

McLeod knew what the last three words were. *"Victory or Death,"* he recited. When the Georgia officer was on his feet again, others in the room appeared to hold their breath. "My orderly has the best handwriting in camp." He reached for his heavy coat. "Fetch him, will you, Sergeant? I need to leave General Gaines a letter before I go." He faced everyone assembled. "I'll be taking a leave of absence. I know you men will carry on. Tell Lieutenant Bonnell," he said to the messenger, "that I may or may not be coming through Camp Sabine. If I don't see him today, let him know…that I won't do anything to discredit the U.S. military."

Three hours later, Hugh McLeod and thirty enthusiasts from Company B urged their horses on through the thicket at the river's edge. They had skirted Bonnell's camp and the ferry named after General Gaines. Upstream another hour was a narrow point in the Sabine, shallow enough for cavalry to get across. An unlikely break in the bitter cold boded well, and the soldiers nudged their mounts toward the water. McLeod intended to get close to Nacogdoches by nightfall. If General Santa Anna had taken revenge successfully on the Alamo, he might well march his thousand men up the old road toward the northeastern border city. There was no telling what protection citizens there now had against punitive Mexican troops.

McLeod couldn't help wondering whether the Georgia volunteers under William Ward had been able to come to the aid of Travis. He only knew he had to head in their direction. He only knew that heart-wrenching words had to be followed by action.

At the edge of the Sabine River, his horse hesitated, stamping its hooves on the cushion of smaller pebbles. Then McLeod's horse was in at a splash, and thirty Fort Jessup men followed. Watching to see how high the water rose on the legs of his mount, the lieutenant shook off the ghastly image of a submerged face from the past, the trapped cousin of Miss Joanna from years and years ago. He flicked the reins and concentrated only on the rescue now in motion.

Coming along as well was the pleasant man from under-the-hill at Natchez. Shelby Whitmire brought up the rear, hanging on to the saddle horn and turning to check for the bulge of letters inside his saddlebag. He was just as likely to cross paths with Thomas in some stretch of Texas, than to ever see his friend again at the threshold of the old carpenter shop. Then another departure came back to him, and a scene from childhood days washed over him. He was oddly cheered to think what he might say to the Peyton woman who had stolen down the Mississippi with her husband. She had been fiercely secretive about their Texas destination. Shelby Whitmire urged his horse on with one hand and led his tethered mule with the other.

It was the 6th of March, and the American men angled their horses to cooperate with the current. Cold water splashed against their boots and leggings. In minutes, they had crossed more than half of the watery border and were about to meet Mexico firsthand.

Witness the Maelstrom

Map of Texas, 1836

Map of Texas, much as it appeared during its years as a republic. Artist Karen Boudreaux.

~ John T. Spillers

far from the sandy path ~

March 1836, the embattled territory of Texas

8 Hell from Any Angle

Once the rifle assault let up, soldiers from inside the church could call to the company pinned down at the perimeter wall and ask how powder was holding. But the Mexican attack was steady from the town's main street, where General José Urrea's next line maneuvered. Out in the wide path before Refugio's church and open courtyard, the general's reinforcements kept coming in waves, crouching behind the bodies of those who'd attacked initially. They took special aim at the low rock barrier extending beyond the chapel door.

Urrea's losses were crushing, and now his troops retaliated with vengeance. Surely they were keeping in mind the outcome at the Alamo, a mere ten days earlier. Battalions under Santa Anna had suffered unspeakable carnage there, too. But the final obliteration of Texians on March 6 was news that riveted revolutionaries and Mexicans alike. The volunteers under William Ward fired into the street at each assault, but Urrea's trained replacements appeared endless. Then, inexplicably, the barrage from Refugio's main road let up. There was no telling how long the Mexican onslaught would pause.

The next American to take a turn, to press his elbows onto the cold dirt and belly crawl toward the church doors was Private John T. Spillers. He had to find out how many boxes of rifle and musket balls could be dragged out to the perimeter wall before the siege continued. And ammunition needed dry powder.

Some Georgia men were now expert with the new percussion firearms borrowed from state artillery reserves. Joseph Tidwell, one of three Macon cousins, took down so many of Urrea's infantry that one body pile in his sight grew and twitched regularly. Another cousin was among the company sergeants now leading in the churchyard. Their lieutenants were absent, having taken an urgent message to General Houston—that the endangered men at Goliad were never able to reach the Alamo defenders. They would retreat to Victoria, as ordered.

At Goliad, though, Fannin's men were delaying their retreat until one development, the return of Ward's battalion from its emergency mission at the village twenty miles west. That task should have taken under forty-eight hours. But the rescue of desperate Irish families at Refugio was not unfolding well.

"Spillers?" The voice of Lieutenant Colonel Ward was enough to hearten any Georgia man. "Is that you, John T.?"

"Yes, sir. It's Spillers. Ready to drag the next boxes out to the boys? How many of us do you need?" Just inside the massive door, the battalion leader lowered himself onto the sanctuary floor to communicate at a hoarse whisper.

"Just the two of us."

"I can get more, sir. It's a lull. Hardaway's been out here for a spell, and the Weeks boy." He had not needed to add that the youths were less lethal at their firing posts.

"No, Spillers. Let them rest while they can." The prone men, each at one side of the door opening, took a moment to breathe. "We're down to a partial box. And just enough powder to make use of it," Ward went on, his voice altered by worry. The Knoxville man was at a loss at first.

"The lull may last overnight. Could be the next wave won't be until morning."

"You and I can drag the box out."

In the next few minutes, the two wriggled toward the low rock wall somewhat enclosing the sanctuary grounds. Dragging the box and resting, they drew close enough that they and the company with aimed rifles could communicate in hushed tones.

"It's gone quiet." It was Sergeant Hunt who spoke, one of the Second Company men in charge during the absence of commissioned officers. "It might stay calm until daybreak…"

"Not this pack. They're too angry, they'll come at us again," another man said before recognizing Ward, who looked at the bedraggled defenders around him.

"We'll be making our own move before then." His weary men did not respond. The eighteen left appeared not to hear the statement at all.

Surely, he did not mean that the half-starved volunteer battalion was to charge into village streets and assault Urrea's infantry head on!

"Two of our boys—that's our own losses, sir."

"I've been working it out since the last full box was brought out," Ward replied to the First Sergeant. He also looked where the Tidwell man silently kept post. The soldier with the mustache was the company's best shot. He'd had his turn crawling to the mission door just an hour ago, and apparently was also good at holding the news of dwindling ammunition. "Losing two of you—two of my little brothers—that's too many. Your rider Trezevant scouted out behind the church for us. He says the riverbanks in that direction are unguarded. " The battalion leader cleared his throat. "With the odds as they are now…we'll retreat… tonight…after their last rush."

The Second Company soldiers could raise no rational objection, though the two fallen soldiers in the courtyard made leaving and staying equally painful to consider.

Ward wriggled back to the stone building where one massive door was being held ajar. Still at the wall, Bulloch's company could not find words for a while. They needed some discussion about remaining together in the creek-beds behind the church. They wanted time to say something about looking out for one another. They had come a thousand miles to winter on the Texas savannah, someone needed to remind them. Exhausted as they were, they had been helped through the last day by pride and controlled panic. Fewer than two dozen men—and their officers absent—had kept General Urrea from overrunning this open courtyard!

Inside the church, Ward's other companies had done their best to retaliate after each barrage, choked each time by plaster dust. Fannin's men waiting for the battalion back at Goliad would surely cheer them for protecting Refugio's threatened Irish settlers. But all knew the final furious assault was coming soon.

Private John T. Spillers looked at the shadowy forms crouched down along the low perimeter wall. The man with the long mustache still concentrated on the street, and appeared lifeless himself. Next to him, the First Sergeant, who had watched over his two cousins, now held senior rank in the company. The young fellow started out as an orderly, but when Captain Bulloch fell ill on the coast, and when the two lieutenants left to apprise Sam Houston, the whole unit came under his command.

Spillers thought it a dreadful fate—to be a Macon civilian barely past youth, now facing such responsibility. Yet the calm man had taken on the burden and was holding up, directing the others. The Knoxville father felt such weight of care for only two of the youngest. He was heartened to see how Sam Hardaway and the Mississippi lad Thomas Weeks had struck up their own friendship over these months. The Macon boy, assigned duties inside the church, was presently pressing himself against the low wall alongside the others. As the soldiers awaited further direction or the next assault, the older volunteer let his thoughts flit to New Orleans, to cheerful exchanges outside the beignet shop. It was then that he looked to the position at the rock enclosure where the man with the Irish accent had posted himself. The curly-haired cousin had lifted the unit's spirits during the last forty hours. No other man in the company could have eased the dark lulls.

But even Malacai remained unusually quiet at his post. Whether his voice would have seemed devoid of its usual optimism, no one knew. Spillers was reassured to see that the two under his own wing were quietly helping each other, preparing for the necessary move soon back across the mission courtyard. They readied as best they could for an evacuation and escape into the bitter night.

Thomas assisted Sam with his jacket buttons, so that pockets would sit straight and not let anything precious drop in the dark. His fingers, stiff from trigger use and the cold, worked clumsily. The Macon boy then turned to help Thomas pull his coat together in the front. His finger touched a middle button, Spillers saw, when a scuffling sound out in the street was followed by several cracks from Mexican muskets. From within the besieged barrier, return fire was immediate. In the seconds before he could reach for his weapon, Thomas flinched and an odd look came over his face. Spillers saw the youth's eyes hold their flash, but they stayed open in a peculiar way. He had seen the boy's coat button jerk from Sam's fingers at the moment every able man gave full attention to the onslaught from the streets.

After an hour of blurred chaos, the mission village fell silent again, and none of the men in Ward's Second Company were surprised when the hoarse order came for them to remove themselves from the cordoned off yard. They were to retreat at once to the sanctuary. Any attempt to fall back to Goliad would be suicide. At some point later, in the still of night, they would trickle out into the rocky plains and riverbanks in the direction of the coast.

Better able volunteers from inside the church scurried out toward the surrounding wall to help men from the perimeter take cover inside. They also dragged into the sanctuary two bodies, the first battle casualties suffered by the entire Georgia Battalion. No one knew the accurate count of men who had perished along the one thousand mile trek from Macon to Goliad. Men had been buried or had wandered off—rib bones protruding from hunger. Others, gone looking for water, had disappeared into the repetitive landscape.

At first, Spillers thought Thomas and Sam were lingering at their posts to give other retreating soldiers in the courtyard some protection. But he could see both their faces now and their expressions of shock.

"My leg…it won't work," Weeks said, his voice rising as if he'd posed a question. On his jacket, a patch of blood was spreading. "They hit me in the back somehow, but it's only my one leg not working at all." Sam Hardaway was turning his friend away from the rock barrier, so that his head was closer to the church door where they would have to crawl. When Spillers took a look at the place where the pellet had entered, under the shoulder blade, he put a hand gently on Sam's arm.

"No, turn him the other direction, so we can pull from his ankles." Another young company private, the one returned from risky scouting on horseback, crawled up to help with the effort.

"He only lost a button, Trezevant." Hardaway's voice was pinched with anxiety. "He'll be all right."

"Just…get me…inside."

In the sanctuary, families pressed together to make space on the benches or on the floor wherever soldiers were not already clumped together. The dead were drawn aside in the cramped foyer. An Irish youngster, among the Refugio colonists that Ward's battalion had come to rescue, had also been killed. His family, the Finnissees, were in shock and Father Orlando consoled them in a side room. While Sam Hardaway and John T. Spillers propped the Natchez youth against a blanket roll, they saw two of the Macon men bending down over their cousin. There was far more red on Malacai's jacket than on the coat Thomas wore. For a while no one spoke about the sad fortune of the curly-haired fellow.

"Only one of you should stay behind a while with the wounded," William Ward said kindly, but in haste. He was making rounds, and he nodded to Spillers. "We'll leave from the rear of the church within an hour." Sam Hardaway opened his mouth to plead. "We're proud you joined us, Thomas Weeks," Ward rushed to add. He bent down by the boy. "We'll all join up with Fannin's men soon enough." When a woman from a nearby bench approached, the lieutenant-colonel went off to another cluster of volunteers waiting for next commands. She knelt beside the wounded soldier.

"From his hard breathing, it looks to be a lung lost its air. I've seen such mend before, in time. His backbone was nicked, maybe, with the feeling gone from his leg." She put her palm on Thomas' forehead and brushed his hair back. "He looks very like my own boy—Lord knows how he's faring," she said, pulling back a bonnet to reveal her dark hair. "I'm Mrs. Molloy, Fiona. After the Mexicans break in—" She stopped, because she could see their horror. "If they do manage to get inside, I'll say the lad's my son, that he's one of us Irish—but you mustn't speak, young man, or…"

"When Ward starts us out the back," Spillers said to Sam, "I'll see that Thomas is all covered and…"

"I'm staying with him!" the Macon youth insisted. He brought the sleeve of his jacket up to his face, and the three men could not keep tears from sliding down their cheeks. They dabbed at their eyes and fixed their attention on the woman while she brought a thick quilt from the family's belongings.

"Now, when you two come back in a few days…," she started. Her husband sat with several younger children on the dirt floor near the last sanctuary bench. He had a surprised look and seemed not to comprehend his wife's actions. "Just a few days. Don't you be fretting about your friend here," she said. "We'll keep a bandage over his wound and he'll get his breathing back within the week. Like as not he'll be doing a jig by the time all this… sweeps away in another direction."

"I'm staying here, too."

"Oh, no you're not—young master Sam, is it?" She finished securing an embroidered towel inside Thomas' jacket, and when she stood up, she took hold of his friend's shoulders. "My husband is already gone from his proper mind, over shame at not being able to help the Finnissee boy. Nobody could have stepped in fast enough, and 'twas the boy's own gun that went off is my guess. But…" She tugged at her apron tie and collected herself. "It was when one of the Urrea's guards laughed about it—one cruelty too much—my poor husband wasn't the same afterwards."

"I could stay and say I'm your son as well—"

"No, you and—your uncle, here—help me move your friend into our family's spot. You'd give us away with that dreary face of yours," she said to them. They gently shifted Thomas G. Weeks to a bare section of dirt near her family's household boxes. "Look—some already heading back to the altar." Sam's shoulders were shaking again, and when he looked down at Thomas, he broke into quiet sobs. "None of that, now."

"I'll stay here until the last, until all from Georgia are out the back," John Spillers said. "See there? Even Tidwell has gone for the door. Ward is motioning to us all." Only one cousin now leaned over the curly-haired man, while Father Orlando held a crucifix and recited last prayers. "The ones with poor feet or no shoes must head out," the Knoxville man went on. "Mrs. Molloy is right. It wouldn't do to have a clump of soldiers still here. If we had wagons and oxen…Ward knows how our best chances sit." Sam was accepting a handkerchief from the Irish woman. "And we'd better not forget what cause brought us to Texas," Spillers said finally to the Macon boy. "Once we meet up at Victoria, some of Fannin's men can bring carts and horses back here for any in Refugio needing transport."

He nodded to the Irish mother and to Thomas, and motioned for Sam to go on ahead of him. Men from the Second Company were moving silently toward the benches by the altar, and Sam was swept along with the others in exodus.

The young sergeant stood not far from the Molloys. His feet were planted next to his lifeless cousin, Malacai. John T. Spillers thought the Macon man might be able to stay in the sanctuary, after all, and be mistaken for a religious statue. But the First Sergeant moved suddenly and was now nodding to them both, making it clear that these two were to be the last of Ward's men to exit the church.

"Bless you, Thomas. Mind Mrs. Molloy. You'll need to stay quiet."

"Shelby always said…I could talk the ears off a mule." The woman had turned aside to get the better of her emotions.

"Don't speak any more, son."

"When you take off for home—I know you'll get there—you're sure to cross the Mississippi." A final burst of energy was making him chatter. "Remember the name Shelby—he might as well have been my father. I looked up to him—if you come across a man named Shelby Whitmire, it'll be a blessing."

"All that know you…are proud."

"Tell Shelby—it was for the Weeks name—for him, too. He'll pass word on to Mother."

"Don't talk any more, Thomas Weeks."

"Tell Sam…"

"Mrs. Molloy and the good Lord are right here."

The dark-haired mother was patting the soldier's forehead and he had closed his eyes. John T. Spillers was exhausted. He wanted to kneel down again by Thomas and stay, but execution would be certain for any Americans that Urrea's troops might find inside the sanctuary. His presence would only worsen the boy's chances of going unnoticed among the stranded Irish colonists. Spillers needed to follow the young sergeant. He needed to overcome his dire fatigue and fall in with the retreat. Other men panting and struggling in the dark ravines were in worse shape, had fled without shoes of any kind and would need his steady shoulder or words of encouragement. Sam Hardaway, if he caught up with him, would need consoling about Thomas Weeks.

Somewhere, five hundred miles to the east, Spillers told himself, the Mississippi River would mark being halfway home. He couldn't let his thoughts dwell on the dead men strewn along Refugio's streets or American bodies littering the hostile stretches of Texas territory. He wanted to think of his own three children. He hoped they'd not forgotten their own father. Spillers had to keep going in the night toward Victoria, no matter how confusing the frigid creeks and patches of stunted oaks. He had to scrub from his imagination any images of pursuit by Mexican guards. He ordered himself to hold another thought—that his own son had come back to the end of a red dirt road somewhere, a thousand miles to the east, that he had lifted his hand to wave.

1836 Texas spring on the battle plains

9   Between Flight and Labor

Men in the scattered Georgia Battalion rested in creek beds by day and staggered toward the coast during night cover. One week out from Refugio, a handful listened to the movements of a single individual thrashing toward them along the muddy banks of the Guadalupe River. Most likely a messenger had information from the advanced position. They knew Victoria was near. After days of wandering without food or fair water, they were in need of every necessity. Ward's men were so exhausted that just stopping to listen in the dark brought relief. A sergeant from First Company called out upon approach, but men waiting in the swamp were mostly Bulloch's, and they didn't recognize ranking soldiers from other companies. The shadowy figure leaned on a tree before sliding down the dark embankment to the mud.

"You men, pass the message, scouts have moved in toward the city."

"We need to get outa this bleedin' muck—tell Ward."

"It won't be long, boys," the sergeant said. "We'll soon get word."

"I could drink the whole Guadalupe."

"It's stagnant here, so don't let yourself…"

"We'll freeze in this wet sooner than die from any bad water."

"In no time, you'll drink from Victoria wells. You'll have fires—food." The sergeant bringing word stayed a moment to catch his breath. He wanted to be sure desperate men didn't cup their hands at the swamp. "See those lights a ways up the shore?" He was moving toward the next clump of spent volunteers, but he turned suddenly. "Say, anyone know a man name of Spillers?"

"Over there." One private pointed in the moonlight to a mammoth cypress tree. "He's with us. He only looks dead. Asleep, I reckon."

"Don't disturb him." There had been little sleep on the frantic escape from Refugio's church. "When we move on, just let him know his nephew has been asking around. Sam Hardaway is up front near First Company with Ward. Will you tell him?"

There was a murmur from the listless soldiers.

"Hardaway was overwrought," the sergeant went on, "about a boy left at the church. He wants to make sure at least his uncle made it out in one piece."

They were in no hurry to wake John T. Spillers. The men within earshot knew it would take Ward's officer an hour to get word to the string of spent men straggling behind. They needed to stay put until commanded toward city boundaries. Leaders of the starving volunteers were close enough to make out Victoria campfires, and no one at the front thought they'd wait long for a city escort. After the nightmare crossing of the savannah, they smiled about their proximity to the Texan-held city.

Most of the battalion had missed their first cutoff out from Refugio to the drier plains. Their direct route to the coastal town lost, they had wandered two extra days across desolation before reaching the Guadalupe swamps. The retreat left them mostly ruined, and they had not yet tallied those lost forever. Hope surged at the prospect of joining Fannin in Victoria.

But there was no gentle waking for John T. Spillers an hour later. A jolt of panic shot through the entire line of stragglers. Victoria was securely under military control, but not by the Texas battalion. It was controlled by General Urrea's forces! His cavalry and marchers had hastened from Goliad to Victoria. When Ward's men heard the boom of artillery two days earlier, they had hoped that Fannin's army was defeating any Mexicans in pursuit. But now it was clear the Texians had been overtaken. Those captured were likely marched back to Goliad.

Expectation of safety and recuperation within the city walls of Victoria evaporated. A groan rose up from the men following Ward. Hunkered down in the Guadalupe riverbed, they despaired. No direction offered another exodus.

"Spillers?" There had been the appointed man coming first with a hopeful report. Then an hour later a wretched corporal brought the news of the worst reversal. Now someone was sloshing through the swamp and calling out a man's name. "Is John T. Spillers among you?"

"Sam! It's me! Over here!" The young man lifted his knees and sloshed briskly to the cyprus tree where the Knoxville man sat.

"Uncle John!" The two men embraced and clapped each other on the back. "Out of Refugio, I had to walk fast…to keep from thinking about who was still there…"

"Mrs. Molloy was looking after Thomas Weeks."

"He looked like her kin."

"They likely took him for her son."

"But you…you look half dead."

"I'll grow into this trunk if I sit any longer."

"Ward says…" The Hardaway youth stopped himself. Those stunned men nearby were listening. The cruel truth about Mexicans controlling Victoria had sunk in. Dread paralyzed them. "The officers are deciding. It may be…we're on our own." He looked at Spillers and then turned to the others slumped nearby. "Whether we can make a stand…or if it's best to light out on our own. That's what they're deciding." He looked at Spillers again. "It might do to take the Guadalupe back inland ten or fifteen miles, and if any men could then cut east, they might skirt Victoria patrols…and any from Goliad."

Mention of Goliad wrung only silence from the watery resting spot. The stranded volunteers appeared to have ceased breathing.

"They figure Fannin's men were taken back there. The artillery we heard but a few days ago…must have been closer to Goliad than here." Suddenly, he looked down and put his hand on Spillers' boot, where the man had begun to tug at a lacing eyelet near the top. "What are you doing, Uncle?"

"Loosening the tops…to see if they'll pull off. My feet might be too swollen."

"What are you doing, then?"

"If it's every man for himself, you should be in better shoes."

"Don't you dare…" He stopped the motion that John's fingers were making and put his other hand on the older man's shoulder. "The twine wrapped around my own shoes is in knots. They won't come off." He patted Spillers on the shoulder again and leaned in to whisper. "Don't you dare. Johnny is waiting for you in Knoxville, and two more." The older man's hands drifted from his boots to his eyes.

"I see their faces sometimes. I wish my boy hadn't been crying that morning."

"If we cross a desert escaping Urrea, could be we need your boots to carry drinking water."

In other circumstances, the image of men drinking water from a boot might have generated a chuckle, but Sam Hardaway and John T. Spillers only let the image halt discussion. They waited, without speaking, for the next instruction coming down the line.

A sergeant who'd gone forward to hear Ward's order firsthand soon came struggling back through. What shape the men's powder was in and how their rifles were holding up hardly figured into the decision. When the command came back for every man to manage his own survival as best he could, it took a few minutes for the exhausted soldiers to respond. Sam Hardaway was first to stand up. He repeated to the others what he had told Spillers.

"The Guadalupe angles over, as she goes inland. If we give the river a dozen miles, no more than a day's progress, we should then cut due east. We should miss the inland edge of Victoria and any western patrols from Goliad."

"We need water."

"The flow is drinkable a short distance inland. Where sea water and fresh meet here, it's rank enough to tear your innards."

"Damn if I can stand, much less march for miles." Several heard the frank admission, but no one answered.

"Every man…as best he can." Sam reached for the hand of John Spillers and helped him to his feet. "Let's not lose each other again, Uncle. Let's move and rest…and think about Georgia."

No significant distance would be made that night, but those able took the Guadalupe immediately, knowing the farther they got from Victoria, the less likely they'd be found by patrols in the morning. Only three miles from where they had started, several fell in a knot to breathe and test the water.

"We're too close together." One man spoke in a flat tone. The band had kept a somewhat steady pace as they sloshed along the muddy bank. "One guard alone could round us all up. We need to separate. The first to reach our cutoff north can wait some."

"He's right. If we stretch out, a patrol won't guess how many we make."

"How the hell many are we?"

Had they not been so worn down, they would have smiled at the question. There were five from Bulloch's company, they thought; the unit still went by their absent captain's name. No one had seen the sergeants, Gideon and Hunt, or their cousins. Not far behind, though, the private who'd ridden barefoot to scout back in Refugio had finally found the company remnants.

"Trezevant is back there. He only got hold of one boot and one shoe, but he's moving better than those men from Columbus."

"Seven all together, maybe. Who knows how many more? If it comes to getting questioned, say you got separated from any others, that you're lost by yourself."

"Move on ahead." John Spillers was addressing Sam. "You've got some energy still. When you count fifteen miles—tomorrow—hide in the river brush and call out to us."

"I won't survive fretting again over whether you made it."

"We'll find you, and we'll all wait a spell… to see who's coming along behind."

The man wearing boots couldn't gaze long in the direction of Hardaway's departure, and he was filled with regret over not swapping footwear. He didn't see how the rounds of twine could hold the boy's shoes together. In the darkness, he couldn't tell whether Hardaway had himself turned to detect any men behind him. When Spillers could no longer hear sloshing sounds from the boy marching on ahead, he rose and followed in the dark as he had promised.

It was some hours before first light. They would all need to hide once the sun rose.

Only a mile later, the Knoxville man sank down on a flat rock and heard periodic sloshing sounds or dreamt he had. He knew he must have dozed off, because when he opened his eyes again, darkness had shifted to a gray wash. Gradually, he became aware of hoarse voices, not farther up the Guadalupe toward a northern cutoff, but from the direction of the swampy coast where some of the others still followed. The battalion had been instructed to flee, but a new alarm was sounding.

"Spillers!" Muted groans and splashing came next. "Hardaway!" The man at rest could tell there was fast progress to where he sat. "Hardaway! Spillers!"

"Over here."

A ragged private sank down to the flat stone where Spillers sat. The man catching his breath was from Milledgeville, one of the first to step forward at Macon's candlelight speeches.

"Colonel Ward—he thinks we can make a stand…after all."

"Make a stand—here?"

"He's called back as many as can be reached. We're to assemble near a landing, where Urrea's watch isn't thick."

"It's likely not everyone took the same fork back there. Some are already out of earshot."

"He knows. His order is—however many hear the call—to come back. We'll see how our ammunition counts up. There may be a better chance," the man said catching air again, "if we give them some pain before we show a white flag."

John Turner Spillers experienced an equal mix of sorrow and relief. He felt sure that he would never see young Hardaway again. Certainly the Macon lad had progressed beyond where any summons could be heard. A pang of grief got hold of the Knoxville man, until he pictured Sam's better prospects of survival. He wished he'd given him some messages for anyone gathering back home to meet Texas survivors. If he had only swapped footwear, he thought. Martha Spillers could take some comfort in having the family keepsake returned by as fine a youth as Samuel G. Hardaway.

But Private Spillers did not have long to embellish such longings. He and the Milledgeville man went back down the Guadalupe in the growing light. They came across more stragglers in the band that had started upriver together. It took the entire day to edge up on the diminished battalion, where they had initially gathered to assess their chances. Whatever wisdom William Ward first figured in a coastal approach to Victoria, the advantage of staying undetected suddenly evaporated. The lieutenant colonel and his men were spotted. Mexican patrols pinned them down by nightfall, just a mile from the city proper. At least eighty American volunteers found themselves in an untenable position, knee-deep in the coastal swamp.

Whereas fighting outside Refugio's church only days earlier had been governed by tactical shrewdness, the new fight in the saltwater swamp was disorganized and futile from the start. By the next afternoon, a Mexican official with a flag rode out to meet with Ward. The word "surrender" filtered back. Though the lieutenant colonel had wished a do-or-die skirmish, his exhausted officers believed deportment from Texas to be the army's better prospect.

Most of the Georgia Battalion could not imagine beyond a drink of fresh water and a piece of bread or dried beef. If they were rounded up now, after all they had survived, if they were to surrender to General Urrea at this point, no honor would be lost. Every American volunteer had weathered battle and harsh travel. No honor would be lost in sharing these grim tales.

Even if the Americans had been issued fresh uniforms upon their arrival in Texas, the procession of captives into the docks and streets of Victoria would have been a sorry sight. But the farmers and cotton accountants had served in their homespun clothing, which now hung in nondescript rags. What clung to their bodies was more river mud than cloth of any kind.

Spillers, shuffling behind a Columbus man, had barely noticed two half built ship hulls near the boardwalk, when a portion of the surrendered battalion was halted. A Mexican officer ordered them to stand straight, an easier position to maintain since they'd been relieved of their weapons. But the minutes it took the guards to select a dozen prisoners seemed an eternity. It appeared they needed more men.

"You!" The guards knew this English word and used it with gestures to be understood. John Spillers saw they meant for him to move forward.

When he stepped off to the side, one guard looked down at the Knoxville man's boots. He tugged at the tops fitting snuggly around the man's calves. Maybe they preferred to take his boots and return him barefoot to the ranks, but they shrugged and motioned him to join the sturdier young men already called apart. After seventeen had been culled from Ward's survivors, the bulk of prisoners trudged to a cluster of low buildings on the city's edge.

Spillers and the other sixteen were led back where ship hulls had been erected. Nearby was a log shack. The men were led inside at gunpoint, though there would have been no resistance if one of Urrea's guards merely pointed. A half hour later, Spillers and the others had drifted into a repose that shelter from the elements allowed. They were shocked when freshly cooked rice with slivers of pepper and beef were brought in.

But it was water they were most grateful for. A clean bucketful sat in a corner. Ward's men drank long, at first in fast gulps and then slowly once they realized there was no limit on their intake. After drinking, they could easily have slept twenty-four hours without eating. But fearing the withdrawal of food, they ate without questions. The battalion had surrendered on assurances of deportation to the United States. Whatever they were to endure in the meantime they thought bearable. Each understood his job now was to somehow survive until reaching the United States border.

By the next day, the detainees understood they were to help with shipbuilding. A wooden trough with hand tools was brought in after the feeding, and each prisoner was required to prove he could move a saw across wood and hammer a nail. Without water and a meal, several might have been unable to lift an arm high enough. They sensed their treatment depended on their usefulness.

With better protected feet, Spillers had been chosen for the most punishing tasks since their original trek inland to Refugio and on to Goliad. During Fannin's fortification of La Bahia, he'd steadied heavier beams while those with damaged feet made trips with plaster or rocks. It took the Knoxville father two swings to drive in a nail, but Mexican officers were satisfied with his fitness.

When the evening guard brought food again, a slender boy, most surely his son, accompanied him. The small child, no older than five or six, held the ladle for a thick porridge carried in a kettle. His forearm looked to be scarred from a burn. He had apparently been instructed not to look any foreigners in the eye, as he ducked while offering the father of three a portion. Though Spillers never claimed a gift for languages, he'd heard common words.

"*Gracias,*" he said. The boy stole a glance at the prisoner, whose voice seemed to surprise the child and Spillers himself.

"*De nada.*"

"Eduardo—no!" The guard chastised his son firmly but not harshly. He hesitated to let the little boy within reach of the desperate men again.

None of the crew selected for carpentry were cruel enough to endanger a child for bargaining, but the Mexican soldiers could not know. And Spillers did not blame the man for calling the boy to his side. The prisoners passed the ladle and kettle to each other. Still, the child stole glances at the man from Knoxville. In a few minutes, the remaining porridge and bucket of water were removed, and the cabin locked under guard for the night. The dirt floor of the cabin was dry and the log walls protected Ward's men from the wind gusts tearing through the prairie and creek beds nearby. The captives fell into a deep sleep. If they had any worry about the battalion, it was that those pulled aside for shipbuilding might miss the general evacuation to a ship bound for New Orleans.

On the first morning of ship carpentry, those chosen for Victoria's docks moved slowly. Their muscles stiff, and with little feeling yet in their fingers, the men awkwardly handled planes for smoothing the ship planks. But there had been bread and a half-cup of thick coffee in the morning. To their surprise, a real meal was offered again at midday—more rice and two kinds of peppers that were sweet and mild. The Americans spoke quietly to each other while they ate. Where, they wondered, had the rest of the battalion been sheltered?

Spillers made an oath to remain silent about Sam Hardaway. Let those still with Ward suppose the youth had come back to join the shipbuilding ranks. Let those in present company assume the boy had not been called out with his "uncle." He would never divulge that the Macon youth had gone on ahead before the desperate change in orders trickled through.

"I don't know why they've put me to labor," one man said. "Have you seen my feet and legs?"

"Whoever stood straight…that's what called attention."

"A corporal next to me slumped down. I was afraid they'd shoot any not standing."

"Now I wish I'd fallen on my face," the first man went on. "I've been thinking about the rest of the boys all day. Probably still sleeping—I'd give the next plate of rice for some straw to lie down on. There might be blankets where the others…"

"Don't be so sure who you envy."

"Just so we know when our deportment ship comes in—"

"That's my meaning. It was English one guard spoke. The other soldier had some different accent…German, I think."

"Shh." Talk ceased immediately, as the watch approached. They went back to spooning rice with their fingers, until the sentry moved off.

"What one of them said—about the others—that they would be marched back to Goliad."

"There's no place in Victoria to corral us all—Fannin's men, too, after they gave up out by Coleto." Imagining that battle left the prisoners quiet. Their colonel surely anticipated nothing more glorious now than the expulsion of every American from Texas.

"Not too many were lost there. Every man who surrendered was sent back to La Bahia." The man shook his head. "I'll bet not one Goliad man gets enough water to quench his thirst."

"Whatever keeps us breathing until transport to New Orleans gets set up…whatever it is will do." The man spat on a rough plank.

"It's the *whatever* that stops me envying those boys. Staggering back to the fort only to cover the same ground soon to get back here—"

"I'm not complaining." A Mexican private was gesturing for them to get up and move again toward the pile of raw lumber. "Still—"

"Shhh."

"If this is the only guard assigned to us," one whispered, "we could run down to the swamp most any time, then find our own way along the beach to New Orleans." Silence after that jest added seriousness to the possibility.

"If they make us miss our ship, I'll damn well give it a try."

Within a few days, the group of men ordered to shipbuilding fell into a routine. After sleep, protected from the elements, a bit of nourishment for the first half of the work day, and a hot meal early in the afternoon, they labored again until dusk when another modest meal was allowed. Among these Americans, most had hailed from regimens no more luxurious. As diminished as their health and appearance in Texas now was, their hope recovered enough that they could imagine heading home—being home.

Eduardo continued to accompany his father at mealtime, and the guard appeared less worried that the prisoners posed any danger. John Spillers couldn't help wondering if a mother waited nearby. He couldn't help noticing that burn scars went far up the boy's narrow arm. There was a mark on the child's forehead, too, somewhat hidden by his thick, dark hair. The little fellow knew now to refrain from speaking to the "pirate" captives, but he let his eyes dart to any man who nodded in thanks. Spillers smiled, realizing the impulse was no different from the greeting he would have given any curious youngster walking along Knoxville's dirt road.

On the sixth workday, during the morning stretch, Eduardo came along with his father to watch the final lathing of one ship mast. Sitting on a crate, he was rapt while the careful shaping took place. In another two weeks, ropes and pulleys would be arranged to set this new pole and deck at right angles. But now, bark chunks and peelings created a tempting pile underneath where the long trunk was being whittled. Scraps peeled off like snakes gliding down from low hanging branches.

Then, the boy's father was called beyond the starboard to confer with a foreman. Men working lathes and the prisoners' guard followed. In a moment they had all stepped out of sight. Knowing the ground to be muddy, the boy kicked off his sandals and left them by the crate. He dashed underneath the half-shaped mast to forage for a curling wood prize.

The mute American workers had been stealing glances at Eduardo. As soon as the boy slipped off his shoes, Spillers felt a stab of worry and he stood to watch directly when the child rooted around in the wood shavings. But the child suddenly grimaced in pain, hopped on one foot, and tried to inspect the other while still standing. If he sat, his soiled trousers would tell his father he had disobeyed. Spillers rushed over to him and at first simply let the stranded boy hold onto his arm for steadiness, to get a better look at the injury. There were certainly water moccasins and cottonmouths where the Guadalupe met the ocean, but this was a coarse splinter that had driven in a half inch under the skin of one heel.

It was not punctures indicating a snakebite, and the two looked at each other with relief. Spillers gestured toward the overturned crate where the boy had been stationed. "Eduardo," he said, pointing to himself and then to the spot.

The child did not respond, except to regard him with the same cautious acceptance he'd given his father during the prisoners' mealtime. The man bent down and picked up the boy. Mud slowed the private's movement, as did his weakened condition, but the child seemed only mildly alarmed by the adult's decisive action. When Eduardo first resisted the idea of letting him try to remove the splinter, the Knoxville father instead helped the boy put his other sandal back on. He could tell that the youngster was torn between calling out to his father, perhaps receiving a scolding, or letting this prisoner handle the delicate emergency procedure.

With one shoe on, the boy relinquished control to Spillers. The sliver was wide, making it painful, but its size also made it easier to grab and tug out cleanly. Not much blood appeared, and no fragments seemed imbedded. The man then went to the bucket and ladled clean water over the boy's foot.

During the episode, the other battalion men nearby worked their tools in slow motion. The crisis had taken only fifteen minutes, and when Eduardo's father came at last around the tip of the ship hull, the child sat calmly where his father had left him. The lead guard looked nervously where the captives shuffled to ready more boards for shaping. He seemed gratified that all remained at their stations. No man in either army dared being found derelict in his duty, but nothing looked amiss after the sudden conference.

The rest of the day unfolded as the others had, but in the evening those forced into labor found an opportunity for secretive discussion.

"I heard a different company talking—the ones doing the heaviest work on the ship—they were taken under guard even before Ward and the rest of us showed up. Just in from a New Orleans ship and they were taken as surrendered. They'd no time to unload their rifles. So, once docked, they were identified as unarmed hostiles."

"The last of the Mobile Greys?

"Maybe, but they were talking about us—any with Fannin's army, they said."

"God knows when we'll see him again."

"These new men thought it would be soon…but that's not the—"

"Blast it! What is it?"

"Ward and his companies were sent to Goliad just this morning. While we worked at the docks." The news was unsettling, but they tried to piece together the logic.

"Where they can keep watch on so many until a ship comes in."

"No…" The fellow stopped himself. He looked afraid to speak the rest of the sentence. "So they can corral us…until time to follow Santa Anna's execution order."

No man spoke for a long spell. Spillers could not believe that they had been treated decently, fed, and given reasonable shelter, only to be amassed and shot.

"If we're the only ones left here? What in God's name…do they mean to do?"

"Keep us useful with the ships, maybe, but there's no guarantee."

"I can't believe they heard right. Urrea doesn't act a butcher. He doesn't seem such a bad sort, but even if he doesn't want to preside over—"

"If any chance comes up, we need to get away…make our way out of here one by one…take advantage of the guards relaxing or getting distracted—by anything else that happens near the bay."

No one spoke of what opportunity might have been missed that very morning in the minutes a playing child had held their attention.

"A smaller mast is to be set tomorrow. The new boys from New Orleans, they're in better shape than we are. All eyes will be fixed on deck when the post goes up."

"Find your way up the coastline. There are scrub trees and rocks. It's no good now to head back up the river. On the banks of the Guadalupe, more patrols go that-away than before."

"We'll stagger our cutting inland, for fresh water. It's no use staying in a clump."

"*Silencio!*" A rifle butt had been jammed against the door of their sleeping quarters before the soldier shouted. Ward's men ceased their conversation and took turns sipping from the water bucket. They shared what rations and defense tools could be hidden inside clothing or in blankets. Large clamshells, halved, could be used as knives or as scoops.

The next day began as any other had. After coffee and a piece of bread, seventeen men from the Georgia Battalion were led to planks being stacked. Most carpenters and stronger workers were already on the ship's deck awaiting placement of the salvaged mast. Other parts of the captured New Orleans schooner were to be tried in the new ship, as well. Since a main contingent of guards had left the day before to transport prisoners back to Goliad—even Urrea—there was far less military supervision in Victoria than usual.

One by one, Ward's men slipped away up the beach. Two had at first made visible tracks from their quarters to the banks of the Guadalupe. Then, they circled back to the pebbly strand north of town. By midafternoon, they were all on their own. John Spillers was the fourth man to take off from the prisoner crew. His boots soon put him at the front of the escapees, where he stole farther along the rocky coastal edge. No man was in sight of any other in the group. It made the retreat lonely, but allowed hope that all made fair progress away from Victoria. Spillers reached into his trousers pocket to touch the leaves folded around a fistful of rice. He commanded himself not to eat until he reached a cove where it might be safe to turn again inland.

As distance from Victoria increased, commotion from the town grew faint, and Spillers stopped to eat. Beyond exhausted, he fell asleep, dreaming of Knoxville and Sam Hardaway. When he awoke, he hoped he was still dreaming, because a familiar Mexican soldier on horseback sat erect and looked down at him. It was Eduardo's father, wearing an expression of frustration or anger. For a few seconds Spillers thought he was going to be shot, but the man abruptly reached down to help him up on the horse, behind. A mile or two inland, a rough cart was waiting with three more American prisoners, only one of whom had been among the shipbuilders. The Georgia man slumped down in the wagon, feeling nothing but relief at not having to trudge along on foot.

The back of the little boy's head bobbed next to the driver, Spillers noticed. He believed himself headed either back to Victoria or across the plains to Goliad where he could wait with Fannin's army. This guard, the boy's father, had probably been swept along by crisis and diminished choice, too. The prisoner could not let himself believe any fate lay ahead other than the deportation Ward had agreed to in their surrender.

Despite the lurching of the cart, Spillers and the others slept during the heat of the day. Late in the afternoon, they reached a grassy field called Coleto where it was obvious a battle had raged. They were ordered to join a wide search across the prairie area to check for any additional American survivors. The carcasses of oxen and horses bloated in the sun and stank, as did several corpses. Spillers thought he recognized one body—but no, he was grateful to acknowledge. Ward's battalion had already been engaged in Refugio before this struggle was lost.

Just two poor fellows were found still breathing, and one could only be given the water he pleaded for. He was left moaning in the grass. Even the solemn captives knew his wounds were too grievous for surviving the ride to Goliad. He would have died en route to the fortress La Bahia, they told themselves. They had let him sip water, and Eduardo's father looked sympathetic about the man's shivering. He had let them pull a bloodied coat up around the injured man's shoulders

Every now and then, the guard's son Eduardo would change from the wagon seat to a place behind his father in the saddle. Spillers wondered again whether this child, too, had lost his mother—whether the father was his only family.

When they reached Goliad they next day, Spillers swooned at the sight: over three hundred wretched men clustered in filth. He wanted to feel heartened that so many of Fannin's army still lived. They had numbered more than five hundred while the fortress was being fortified. But their condition was pitiable. Gaunt and half naked, they leaned to keep each other upright. No bonny white flag waved from the presidio's front lookout. All things American were now gray tatters.

Spillers helped carry the wounded man into the tiny sanctuary where some care could be given. But cramped conditions inside were even more horrifying, and they were ordered to simply deposit him against a wall and return to the open grounds. As they edged out of the foyer, one captive whispered that Fannin was kept in a side room with better ventilation. Word was that the colonel would recover eventually from his wound. Just arrived from Victoria, William Ward was also in the room separate from growing pestilence in the little chapel.

A handful managing to walk, including Spillers, were suddenly given buckets, and a guard led them down to a creek on the northwest side of the fortress. The prisoners called aside to fetch water did their work without speaking. Only three weeks earlier—it was impossible to believe— Fannin's army had made a valiant effort to move with artillery up the same Goliad banks in the direction of the Alamo. So much disaster was impossible to believe. When the water crew returned to the main grounds, they circulated among the thirsty prisoners. Many took the fresh drink listlessly.

Well water from inside the garrison was reserved for Mexican soldiers. Even though Fannin's men had endured a February there in harsh conditions, they now judged their own colonel's strict edicts with nostalgia. The task of fortifying La Bahia had been brutal work, but they'd had plenty to drink, and their cooks worked over hot kettles. They'd taken turns emptying slop buckets at a reasonable distance, and they'd all enjoyed fresh air by day and a solid roof at night. Here they were exposed to the elements at every hour. There was no escaping the squalor.

But later that night, hope made three hundred twitch to alertness. News circulated that tomorrow they would all head out for the port of departure—Would it be Velasco again, or Copano? Spillers felt some relief, at last. He rejoiced about the fifteen Victoria captives who appeared successful in their escape, or who had maybe been escorted back to the shipyard. But he thought himself fortunate to be with this largest contingent. The American prisoners began singing "Home Sweet Home." Those who could not sing moved their lips. Some could only breathe somewhat more deeply and weep.

In the morning, John Spillers was ordered to the quarters for wounded Mexicans. He was carrying a pail of water while Eduardo handed the ladle to each resting soldier. The Knoxville man was nervous because it looked as if all the captives were being roused and told to stand. They were all being grouped and lined up for a march out of the Goliad fortress. He didn't want to get stranded from his battalion, and he even hoped to find Bulloch's company and rejoin them on their march to the sendoff port. He had nodded to the Macon man with the long mustache and several others who had fought in Refugio's churchyard.

But as they came out of the Mexican barracks for another trip to the well, Eduardo motioned instead to a root cellar. Baffled, Spillers went down three steps with his empty bucket and could not fathom the door closing behind him, the sound of a lock clicking. He protested by putting his fist against the wooden door, but it was the boy's father who answered, "*Silencio!*" Spillers had earlier noticed the bayonet newly fixed in the guard's rifle. "*Por favor,*" the man beyond the door hissed, "or you die!" Spillers could only slump down in the dark, making the overturned bucket a stool.

There he sat, waiting for a prayer to come to mind. He heard the shuffling steps of three hundred, and he understood the Texan Army of regulars and volunteers to be marching away from Goliad. He fought the urge to pound again on the cellar walls. His own Texas experience had been threat of demise followed by reprieve, and Private Spillers made himself concentrate on breathing in the dark. *Why pound if a bayonet were the next certainty?* He waited, feeling a nightmare close in on him.

The first shots and the first wrenching screams were distinct and clear. He had heard these sounds before from both sides of battle—rifle fire from inside and outside the wall at Refugio, agony out in the street and inside the sanctuary. Now he heard a volley distinctly from Mexican guards. The shrieks that followed were so many as to be unintelligible. In the next half hour, John T. Spillers wanted to disbelieve the roar, horrifying enough to immobilize an observer on either side of the presidio walls. Fannin's army was being methodically shot down. A slaughter was underway of men who had been paraded out beyond the fortress hill. The volleys went on and on.

In despair, Spillers slid to the dirt floor and put his hands over his ears. He was still in shock two hours later, when a new commotion rose from within the chapel courtyard, just a few feet away. On the other side of a wall separating the root cellar from the officer barracks, wounded men from inside the little church were now being dragged out and shot. When pieces of English came through, he realized that William Ward and Colonel Fannin, as well, were outside the chapel doors. More shots rang out. There were shrieks, and then silence, except for the curt orders of Mexican officers.

By later in the afternoon, a sharp smell of smoke and of burning flesh permeated the fort. Spillers wondered how long his thirst and hunger and his need to relieve himself would allow him to stay confined in the root cellar. He tried to convince himself that the discipline to keep from crying out meant his mental faculties were intact. If he could know he'd be shot, he might let himself pound on the door. But he wondered whether any Mexican officers were murderous enough to order him thrown onto a fire to be burnt alive.

He was numb late in the afternoon when he realized that the door was creaking open. It was Eduardo's father. He did not have his rifle at all, and it looked to Spillers, as his vision adjusted to light, as if the guard's eyes were red and swollen. The boy behind him, letting the water ladle dangle in his grasp, had surely been crying. His other hand clutched his father's jacket, and the child let out a sob when Spillers emerged. The guard motioned him forward. He gave the captive a rough gray shirt, loose but clean, to pull over his ragged coat. There was no one that day to speak to except God, so Spillers just followed where father and son led. Off the barracks entrance was a cart hitched to a stout horse.

The Knoxville man could not gaze upon the woods and fields outside the walls of La Bahia. He did not want to look where the piles were growing near the banks of the creek running off the San Antonio River. Already, he was not sure he wanted to go on living. If he asked to be shot and then thrown atop the pile of burning bodies, he wondered whether anyone would decipher his English. Beyond the Goliad perimeter and well past the riverbank, the cart Eduardo's father drove came to a stop. Down a short ravine and close to the water, soldiers were attending to grim salvage work. Urrea's men dutifully washed blood from coats and ragged breeches.

Eduardo's father gestured for Spillers to get out of the cart. The two men went down to the river some distance from the others, and the guard pulled out a bloodied overcoat before dipping it back into the icy water. The prisoner thought he'd made the boy stay in the wagon, that he'd not wanted his child to see a man shot. But after wringing water from the salvaged coat, the father next took a bundle from inside his own jacket.

He was pointing up the hill where a ridge of small oaks rose. The other Mexican guards seemed consumed by their duty. Stunned soldiers moved in short steps and did not lift their eyes. Eduardo's father pointed again up the riverbank and handed the American a gourd of fresh water, the wet coat, and three tortillas wrapped in brown paper. Spillers understood it was only a small chance. He took the package and uttered the word *"gracias."* He simply walked, as running would flag attention. He still wore the billowy cotton shirt he was given outside the root cellar. He kept saying "gracias" to himself, "gracias" to any sympathetic angel. He was thinking of Eduardo's shy curiosity, his dark hair, his unexplained scar, his playful eyes.

An image rushed before John Spillers that almost brought him to a halt, the sympathetic eyes of Matilda the first time he met her. He had scraped his arm when a hoe fell from an armload of tools. He had held the cuff of one shirtsleeve down to stop the bleeding and when he looked up she was there in a sunlit doorway. In her eyes was tender worry, but also happiness, as if that were the expression human beings deserved.

1836 in the spring of the Texas Revolution

10   The Cruelty of Circles

Private Spillers was leaning against a rock that protruded from one bank of the creek, and he dozed off again. When his teeth began to click, his eyes opened. It was early daylight. He tightened his fingers around the hackberry stick he carried. During the long night, he cradled it the way he had his rifle before a Mexican guard tore it from him near Victoria.

Unlike the man lying nearby, he had not really slept. He only drifted off, even though shots could be heard from three directions. A stick was no defense against any soldiers from Matamoros, the ones searching for escapees and now shooting everything that moved. But a sturdy branch might be swung to ward off a wolf or a wildcat. If he could keep his arms from quivering, if he could get feeling back into his fingers and know for sure that his grip on the hackberry limb was steady, he might survive an animal attack. There was no telling whether it was his fear or the cold making his teeth chatter.

He didn't know if he could be of any help to the other man, whose bare feet were brown from dried blood. The rest of his companion was still hidden from view under a mat of decaying leaves made heavier from dew. His eyes oozing, Spillers blinked to verify that it was only blood staining the two exposed feet and to assure himself that the other soldier's skin had not turned blue, then black overnight.

The Knoxville man did not believe death visited on the grim stretches of Texas the way it had back home in Georgia. As cruel as the end had been for his wife, Matilda, she had at least been surrounded by family. Or when the plague of fevers came to a town, or even the vilest Indian depredations, friends or family were usually with one another as earthly lights went out. Even if the end brought a fruitless struggle, companionship was a lit candle. Back in Georgia, the land itself could figure as a friend.

Here, death was different, the older man felt, ought to be called something different. He was sorry he hadn't asked his companion's full name. If the man suffering under those leaves had expired during the night as they hid in the creek bed, Spillers knew he would be unable to properly record the poor fellow's passing. Another man named "John," was all he knew. He rejoiced that it was not the young man from Macon. Sam Hardaway, who had managed to stay close until the battalion's retreat from Refugio, still lived as far as he knew. Their separation during the first retreat—and suddenly the absence near Victoria of the Georgia youth who called him "Uncle"—was no easy loss to bear.

Spillers did not want to look at this other man's feet until a noise came from the leaf pile. He didn't want to give death the satisfaction of seeing him gaze hopefully upon a corpse. Instead, he studied his own boots, the clothing article that had survived the hostile winter in Texas. He could not feel either foot, but he supposed they were intact, inside the footwear his sister-in-law insisted he take. He considered what direction was best for two Goliad survivors. He tamped down surging images of the massacre. Would it be safe, he wrenched his mind to consider now, to head where shots were fired the night before? Surely Mexican patrols had then gone searching elsewhere.

The alert survivor did not want to stumble upon a scene they'd encountered the day before—two wolves tearing at a mass of bones and rags. What made a scene of horror so compelling, he wondered. What made a man unable to turn aside? He looked again now at the bare feet in view. The blood looked dried. Spillers hoped no animals would sniff them out. He thought the other escapee might wake later in the morning and give a full name. He let himself drift again into half-sleep, but he hoped he wouldn't dream. A short dream of beignets at New Orleans was followed some nights by a nightmare about desperation at the church in Refugio, then a dream with all sights murky but with clear thrashing sounds growing louder. The fate of the Georgia Battalion just two days earlier at Goliad he knew was no dream. He prayed that calamity would not replay while he rested.

In the afternoon, the barefoot man awakened and John T. Spillers tried to keep him quiet. A Mexican search party had filed along the ridge of the creek an hour earlier when only one of the escaped prisoners lay awake. Later, the less able man had mumbled a few words. His name was John Holliday. He had come to Texas as a volunteer with the Kentucky unit under Captain Duval. Before the looks of his feet began to distress him, the northerner was gasping for water. A creek current, however enticing, could prove lethal, the older man knew. When he had first splashed the cold water on his own face and neck, there had been a faint stench, distinctly different from the odor of composting river ferns. A decaying body could contaminate a stream for a half mile. A spring would be safer, but worse danger lay in any daylight search.

By the third evening that they were together, there was fair moonlight. The pair made slow progress toward a stand of small oaks not far from where the creek curved. The weaker man braced himself against the other. It was not easy in the evening to determine direction, but if they made it to the spindly trunks, there was a rise just beyond. They could shelter there and get their bearings at first light.

Even though the sturdy boots held up past all expectation, Spillers struggled on the rocky turf. Holliday said it had been weeks since his own feet had feeling. Frostbite could have ruined his toes during the bitter month at Goliad, when fortifications were made for a siege. Then, five hundred men, hungry and half-dressed, had leaned into Fannin's orders to rebuild the perimeter walls, restructure the parapets and garrison doors.

"My shoes held together then," the Kentucky man said, "by lengths of twine. So many had naked feet."

When they reached the straight oaks, it was the older man who seemed more out of breath, collapsing onto the brushy ground. Widening at the base, the tree trunks would make it hard for a search party to spot them, even when the sun rose. But Spillers assessed the stand as too spindly to support an animal looking for prey. The Kentucky man was already drifting off with his mouth open, and the rasping noise gave the older man a sense of urgency. He inched to the top of the short rise and was cheered to see a cluster of larger trees an equal distance away. It was barely April, too early for such oak trees to be thickly leafed out, but the canopies appeared full in the moonlight. If that were the case, the trees might well be fed by an underground water source, he reasoned, nothing reeking of contamination. He figured a peculiar rumbling hum to be the labored breathing of John Holliday. Orders barked by Mexican officers, had there been any search parties nearby, would have eclipsed night sounds. With no noises, other than the odd hum, both exhausted men fell into deep sleep.

At first light, the Georgia man was surprised again by the looks of the treetops. Live oaks would be shedding last year's leaves in the spring, and solid blotches upon branches at the next rise struck him as eerie. He thought his own vision might be affected by lack of food and water, because the dark clots then appeared to expand and retract. Spillers realized, too, that the strange rumbling noise was growing louder. Suddenly, as if an invisible whip had been cracked, a hundred buzzards lifted off from the clump of trees and began to flap and ascend in a spiral just beyond the ledge where he'd thought a spring or a rivulet bubbled. As the ghastly birds rose, branches were left in their true state—nearly bare, skeletal.

"What's…happening?" Holliday asked.

"Buzzards."

"They seen us?"

"No, they're circling. Must be water on the other side."

"I need…water."

"Stay here." He still had the spilt gourd Eduardo's father had given him. The next source might be drinkable, no matter what carrion the birds spotted. A spring was not easily ruined. But he had to move quickly or risk being sighted by an early scouting patrol. "I'll drink while I'm there and get back to you with the gourd."

"If you see…Duval. Tell him I made it."

The father from Knoxville was sure he was not about to meet up with Captain Duval from Kentucky. What he doubted was that either this John Holliday or he would make it to anywhere safe.

Somehow his legs minded his own command to move fast. He had run more in the last ten days than in his first ten years of life as a farm boy. The boots were salvation. If ever he did make it out of Texas, if ever he saw his Georgia family again, he would polish the boots before every Sunday. He would say a prayer often at the mantle in Martha's cabin.

When he reached the hilltop and looked down the ravine, he clutched at the concept of gratitude. The grim birds circled, their flapping wings and bickering now making a racket. What came into focus, atop the next dominant rise, just beyond the squabbling birds, almost brought John T. Spillers' heart to a stop. Dark rock walls loomed. There was the same high gloomy arch that lately haunted his dreams. A crucifix atop the taller interior structure accentuated his despair. He and the soldier from Kentucky had hobbled and inched their way across the cold and hostile plain, but they had moved, it was clear, in a punishing circle from the cruel scene they had fled four days earlier. La Bahia, the presidio at Goliad, stood on the hill less than a mile away!

A wave of nausea gripped Spillers. He thought the fortress might be a grotesque vision, chastisement from God for the folly of leaving home. But thirst, he reminded himself, had to be dealt with in this world. If he could suppress the news, he would not inform his weak companion of their bearings. The Kentucky man might go mad, run out onto the prairie, or charge down into the smoldering scene below.

There, the buzzards descended lazily, where one company had been marched out from the fortress walls. Nothing about the mound reminded Spillers of the men hoping for liberation early on Palm Sunday morning. Carrion birds and wolves had not needed to tear through much clothing to get to flesh. A shift in the breeze made him think Holliday would soon guess how close they were to these pyres. But the rivulet branching off from the San Antonio River might not be spoiled. Spillers slid down the ravine to take a long drink and to fill the gourd. Then he pulled himself back up the slope and scurried back to his companion.

"I heard…commotion," the Kentucky man said between gulps. "I thought that a patrol…"

"More birds."

"Don't say…turkeys…I could eat—"

"No," Spillers said. "But a ways back, I may have seen—smoke—in the direction of the sun," he said. "We'll rest a spell, and follow along where it could be a cabin with a chimney, maybe a tilled field. I had a dream about collards and turnip greens."

"I could eat a turkey leg."

"It wasn't a swarm of birds to tangle with."

Spillers wanted to get up and start walking in the direction away from La Bahia, but the two needed rest. He shook from his consciousness a new fear that Sam Hardaway might have been recaptured between Victoria and Goliad.

He fought against wondering whose limbs and torsos lay clumped a quarter mile from the hilltop presidio. As he drifted away from consciousness, he concentrated on the afternoon he had been on the run alone, on the hopeful moment he had first spied another survivor of the massacre.

Following a creek bed after the executions, Spillers had noticed a floating log, stalled by its branches. While crossing, he studied the bobbing trunk before discerning the arm of a man. He was no longer alone in the wild struggle to avoid recapture and a bloody finish. The two had barely acknowledged each other when a patrol began to descend the ravine. Just as suddenly, the Mexicans had moved on. The soldiers must have judged the sodden embankment too risky for their ponies. They were gone.

In the next days, Spillers and the Kentucky man supposed that some others escaped the initial slaughter. A few might have gone enough distance to hide well in brush or clumps of trees. They, too, could be making some progress. One unfortunate fellow, however, had already met his end. When they came across his remains, his trouser leg was pulled up to his knee. A pair of needle-like punctures was still visible on the swollen ankle.

At present, Spillers and Holliday knew of only themselves. At least two had survived Palm Sunday. The pair of escapees now lay off a shallow embankment, near where they had spied a cabin and garden. Bed linens and a blanket flapped in the wind on a cedar corral fence. The older man couldn't shake the image of the red and green flag he'd just seen atop La Bahia.

"That pretty white flag we had. I don't know what made me think of it," he said. "Made by a Georgia girl, from my hometown."

"It kept us going those weeks we were getting the Goliad walls strong."

"You think the colonel took it along? That morning you broke out toward Coleto?" Spillers pictured the Troutman girl handing Ward the banner when Macon volunteers marched through. Holliday coughed before answering.

"It was nothing but fog everywhere at sunup. And the wind had mostly tore it to pieces by the time it was lowered. Not much but the blue star left."

"Such a pretty banner," Spillers said, shaking his head. "The girl who made it, too."

"When you get home…I wouldn't tell her."

"No." He looked away, back to the fence and flapping blanket. "There's enough sad stories…"

"I ain't considered home yet. Don't know if I'd still be…me."

"Not a one of us could have foretold…"

"They'll want to know what Texas was like," Holliday went on. "They'll never quit asking about all the others."

Spillers imagined Martha would be the one to gently bring up the subject of what he had been through. He would say the ordeal was beyond words, and she would let the others know—his own children—never to ask, never to start up talk on what had happened in Mexico territory. Then his expression changed. Chances were he would soon starve to death anyway. Chances were he would be captured again, only to be thrown at last on the growing piles outside the gray rock walls.

The Kentucky man, John Holliday, promised to stay in the brush while Spillers crept close to the isolated homestead. When two women came out of the cabin and began to scrub a woven rug, Spillers lay flat alongside their cultivated patch and braced for hours of waiting. The rows were mostly corn in early stages, but he pulled a fistful of lower leaves from a prickly lettuce and shoved them into his pocket. He had eased three green onions from the dirt when the women's voices went louder and made him freeze. They were speaking Spanish, but he knew that language did not necessarily define what side they took in the conflict. Females were often more sympathetic than the men, but he had seen one officer's wife spit at a Señora Alavez for giving soup and tortillas to the starving Goliad prisoners.

And how could he explain Eduardo's father? Maybe the child had confessed about collecting wood shavings after being told to sit on the overturned crate. His father likely knew about the prisoner who'd extracted a sliver from the boy's foot. If not for that exchange, Spillers wondered, would he be lost somewhere in the mound of bodies? As he waited for the women to go back inside, his thoughts returned to other battalion men who might have staggered to safety. Bitterly, he admonished himself to make certain he and Holliday now headed east. Help from a Mexican guard had been rare fortune. Death was sure to greet them if he became confused in the undulating prairie and circled back again.

At last, the women finished their work on the rug and went back through the cabin door, calling in four children who'd scampered out to the stoop. Though menfolk could be riding in from any direction, Spillers made a dash back to the cover of the woods. When he reached the first line of trees, he thought he must have angled back differently because he could not find John Holliday. He spent most of the afternoon edging north and then south along the shallow ravine, looking for his traveling companion of the last three days. In one spot he thought the loosened rocks and pebbles indicated departure by a man on foot, but by then he could not be sure of the signs. Was it only where he himself had stood and turned looking for the other wanderer?

Captain Duval's man must have panicked when he heard exchanges in Spanish. He must have hobbled away. But how far could he have gone? In what direction? Spillers kept stealing along the creek bed, but his thoughts spun from his wounded companion, to the face of Sam Hardaway, to the poor Weeks lad, to his own son watching and then turning to go. He thought he might be going mad. In the late afternoon shadows, he climbed out of the creek and followed a faint, easterly path.

Just before dusk, he detected horses coming along behind, from around a bend at the edge of the mesquite line. Spillers stood still. He could only envision what a short ride it would seem back to Goliad. They approached from the direction he had left, and he thought the women might have spied him in their garden, after all. They had probably sent a patrol after him. He would be too exhausted to resist being apprehended. He would try to keep the images of friends and home until he sighted the mounds at La Bahia.

Two soldiers on horseback and one driving an unloaded artillery cart wore Mexican jackets. Their gray riding pants were mud-spattered, and the chinstraps of their caps were tight to protect them from the wind. They rode like any other unit of guards lately crisscrossing the savannah. The three calmly approached the man wearing a common peasant shirt. Spillers thought he would shake his head, no matter what they asked. Perhaps if they thought he'd gone insane, they would ride on. But his shirt appeared not to fool them, and they came to a halt where he stood.

"You are Americano?" He could only nod and brace for immediate execution. "We passed near Goliad this morning. It is God's mercy you were not there."

"I…was there," he found himself admitting. One guard tugged at his chinstrap. The others looked away and then at their hands.

"I am sorry, *amigo*," the lead man said. "The Alamo. And now La Bahia." He dug the heels of his boots into the stirrups and shifted himself in the saddle. He was of slight build, though Spillers guessed he was muscular, and his tightened expression made the escapee again predict a rifle blast. But the officer swore instead. "No one can count the men of Texas who wish Santa Anna dead. If the honor comes to me, I will dispatch him to hell."

The man speaking was Juan Seguin, Spillers learned, a Tejano clearly siding with the Americans. On the orders of Colonel Travis, his unit had left the Alamo just before the siege to find Sam Houston and testify to their desperation. Now, they formed a spy group sent from the Texas general to find out what had become of Fannin. What was left of Houston's army was already heading farther east, expecting to be pursued by Santa Anna or one of the other Mexican generals. Surely a decisive battle would erupt somewhere between the Colorado and the Sabine, where settlers now fled and the wounded were being transported.

"Houston's going to the coast?" Spillers asked. An odd pulse pounded in his ears.

"Perhaps. He is not so distant yet, coming from north on the Colorado," the wagon driver answered. Seguin nodded and looked into the bed of the transport, where it became clear someone else lay.

"We hope to intercept him at San Felipe, or across the Brazos if he removes the army farther." When he said something in Spanish, the man with the reins climbed into the open wagon and made rearrangements. "Your boots, Mr. Spillers, are they what holds you together? Do you have family in the territory?" The man addressed just shook his head before thinking of his frantic search for Holliday.

"But there was someone else running with me…" The Knoxville father felt his panic subsiding and exhaustion taking over.

"It is only you and this poor man we have seen all day." He pointed down in the wagon. "He could be one of Ward's or Fannin's. He was under a mass of branches, wolves gnashing at his sleeves. We bandaged his head and face, but he is in God's hands." Spillers couldn't say he recognized the man. "Jorge will travel on to Galveston with him. Let us help you up, too. If you keep talking to him on the way, he might make it."

"Is Galveston…a ways yet from all this?"

"If the men under Houston's orders meet defeat, any left this side of the Sabine will try to find the island. Ships in favor of Texas drop their anchors there. Survivors might well sail up the coast to New Orleans." The new passenger looked at the pitifully bandaged man prone in the wagon bed.

"You figure Santa Anna will catch up with Houston's army?"

"We shall hope it falls the other way. But we must hasten now. The general needs to know Fannin and all his boys are lost."

"Sir, you didn't hear of a young volunteer," Spillers had to ask, "by name of Sam Hardaway?"

"No time for roll call. By tomorrow, I might forget my own name, as well as yours," Captain Seguin said in a sympathetic way. He spoke to the driver and the other soldier on horseback. "San Felipe in two days. Perhaps." The three Tejanos tipped their hats to one another and saluted the officer, before he and the other mounted soldier rode off into deepening shadows.

The next morning, John T. Spillers rearranged two sacks of dried beans in the wagon, then leaned against them to ease the bounce of wheels over prairie terrain. He wedged another sack and an oilcloth tarp under the head of the injured man, who remained mute. He only moaned as his eyes flickered, but when the private named Jorge brought the wagon into a place called San Bernardo, he managed to get the weakened soldier to chew some bitter lettuce. He could not learn the man's name or determine features under the bandages, other than guessing the matted hair was light when washed.

"Maybe you joined up in New Orleans or in Mobile," Spillers said to keep the fellow listening. "I was familiar with faces until we got to Montgomery." The man's haunted eyes told that where he had originally come from was not as significant as what he had seen. Spillers predicted that a long series of nightmares awaited the few managing to clamber away from the slaughter. "If you're from Georgia, I apologize for forgetting." He was encouraged by the injured man's attention, so he talked on. "Maybe it was Columbus when you put your name down. There was so much commotion over Hugh McLeod going off to Louisiana. We lost track of others joining up."

The wounded man fixed his attention despite the bandages. When his lips trembled, it was clear he was trying to speak.

"You going…home?" he asked.

"I've been thinking about the route," the Knoxville man began. "Up the Alabama River, that won't be easy." The weakened soldier took some water.

"They'll ask…about the rest of 'em…"

"Another man and I spoke on that just yesterday," he said. "It's my own boys on my mind…the older one might still be sore I went at all. Might be he's waiting right in the road …standing there, stubborn…"

"You have children?"

"This other man, Holliday, was from Kentucky…Captain Duval's company…He said doctors were protected from the massacre. One named Shackleford had his own son in the company…lost with all the others likely. That would take some prayin'…to go home after a thing like that." Spillers refolded the oilcloth, and the makeshift pillow made it easier for the weaker man to speak.

"…all shot dead…"

"When you get home," Spillers said, "you can tell folks it was Seguin who…"

"I was thinking…"

"My fault you've been talking too much. You need to rest." The eyes of the wounded man brightened, but Spillers fought off rising dread. He had heard Thomas Weeks ramble, on the brink of death.

"Any like us in Galveston, more dead than alive," his spurt of lucidity went on. "If Mexican scouts don't find us before then, I expect we'll get doctored there." He closed his eyes again. "Will you do something for me?"

"…anything I can."

"When you get to Georgia," his eyes stayed closed, and it looked for a moment as if he had fainted or expired. "Mail me a letter next year, if you recollect to," he said at last. "The island gets its post regular. How your Knoxville fares…"

"Son, I don't even know your name."

"Write to…*F.D. Bahia*…If I'm still breathing, I'll collect it."

"Goliad also went by the name *Bahia*. But if someone asks about the *F.D.?*"

"*Fort Defiance.*" He inhaled deeply, about to lose consciousness. "What Fannin called the fort after we had her fixed up…when we thought cold and starved…was the worst we'd get."

In the next bumpy miles, Spillers wondered if the wagon had already crossed the River Styx. He was alarmed that he could not visualize the face of Sam Hardaway when he concentrated on the name. The bandaged man made him brood again over John Holliday, equally transformed by bloody struggle and hardship. He judged the last several weeks to be punishment enough for anyone deserving hell—to wander endlessly, alone or crossing paths with other wasted souls too broken to believe in home. Home, he kept telling himself, was a father sitting on porch steps not far from where his children slept.

Knoxville's red dirt pathway came to him. He erased the cheering crowd from his imagination, the rows of proud and eager volunteers as well. He blanked out the moment Sam began calling him "Uncle" only hours after their first handshake. John T. Spillers spent the next half day, as the wagon lumbered over the prairie, trying to picture his children's faces.

But when he struggled to envision a hand waving at the end of the sandy road, it was burnt arms and legs interfering with his chosen memory—somewhere beyond all that tangle was Johnny's tear-streaked face. All the father could imagine when he closed his eyes was his son's voice, "You didn't tell us goodbye. You didn't tell us you would be coming back."

~ Angelina

on her own ~

April 1836, on the banks of the Brazos

11   Flames of Remembrance

When Angelina sat up suddenly and threw her legs over the edge of the bed, she was breathing heavily. She couldn't remember if the scream she had heard was real—maybe her own—or if the terrible cry had only been in her dream. She was wearing her burgundy wool skirt and fitted bodice, both damp. If she loosened the ties, she thought she might lie back down and rest a little longer. Delilah had warned her that the bodice was too snug to wear to bed. But since the funeral two years earlier, Jonathan Peyton's widow had been slipping into bed each night fully clothed.

There was no telling when the sole innkeeper might have to greet a late traveler. Recently, there was no telling what clamor would arise in the middle of the night. No husband now saw to such alarms. Mr. Peyton would certainly have chided her for leaving on her stockings and laced boots, no matter her state of exhaustion. But what action the next scream might call on her to make, she refused to speculate.

An unearthly wail had drawn her from bed little more than a fortnight ago, when scouts from Sam Houston's army rode into town on a moonlit evening. They brought word of the Alamo calamity. That night in San Felipe a collective moan cut through the thickest dreams. Since then it seemed nothing could wring further grief from Stephen F. Austin's original colonists, yet there had come just yesterday at daybreak news of Fannin's need to abandon Goliad and retreat to Victoria near the coast.

Angelina and other town leaders worked to rally spirits during the long day, but some of Captain Moseley Baker's men came through next with additional warnings. There weren't nearly enough men crossing the Brazos and heading northwest to join General Houston. If the Colorado barrier had to be abandoned, how would the Texan Army keep Mexican soldiers from pursuing in the direction of San Felipe itself? Already, a few citizens had packed their belongings and taken the ferry across the

Brazos up near Groce's plantation. Now some were stacking chairs and trunks into wagons and heading down the riverbanks on the town side.

"Miss Angelina?"

"I'm all right."

"The moon's still up. If you start walkin' this room now, you won't have energy to last through breakfast."

"I'm all right."

"Was it a noise made you sit up?"

"Only in a dream."

"Even Alex and Mag fret through the night."

Angelina couldn't imagine any San Felipe citizen sleeping soundly since that second week of March. Like her, neighbors closed their eyes in dread of continuing calamity. The next screams might be orders in Spanish to take aim. Jonathan Peyton's widow didn't feel honest promising the children that everything would be all right.

"I've been trying to think of what else we can melt down or pound into rifle shot."

"That pewter tea set has traveled too far to end up fired from a musket…all the way from Tennessee…and to think…" The servant's eyes went to a hutch that stored silverware, and she kept herself from trying to read Angelina's thoughts.

"Oh…the clock weights will melt, too."

"I'll bury that clock first…"

"Let's not fuss at each other this morning, Delilah." The Widow Peyton was out of patience for conversation if it veered toward sleeping in a tight jacket. She stood to take a deep breath as she secured the ties and fasteners. "Have you already been to Celia's? I wonder if Dolly Ann is still rolling out hard bread for Captain Baker's order? You'd think our army was readying to cross an ocean."

"I was on my way for any yeast loaves or corn bread, when you called out."

"I'll see about it, before it's all taken." Braiding her hair would have to wait. "With so many families on the move, it could be today we're left to see what our own oven can produce."

"When you get back," Delilah said, "I'll find out if Mr. Tindle has any pork to roast. I hate to take down another hog so soon."

"Going without meat is likely to be our least worry. Celia will know what other supplies are hard sought."

The Allen Bread ovens were just down the street and around the first corner of the town square from Peyton Inn. Angelina went past the door that had been William B. Travis' law office. A mountain laurel wreath hung from a nail. At Bake and Borden's printing shop where she rushed by next, she had been one of the first individuals to look over the Declaration of Independence headed up to Washington-on-the-Brazos for signing. What a stunning rush of events life had become in only three weeks. What a terrifying flood of death at the Alamo!

Angelina still couldn't let herself imagine the despair of Colonel Fannin's men at abandoning Goliad. Sam Houston was not the only one expressing tactless doubts over the colonel's leadership, but she was fed up with the feuding between the two leaders. Who could sort out the rivalry between their factions? The Council, Governor Smith's supporters, Houston, Fannin—they all seemed ready to tear the fledging republic in opposite directions.

Unity would be their only salvation. She chided herself about holding a grudge against the general. But what business owner here was not galled by his shifting the independence convention to Washington, a town north along the banks of the Brazos? Hadn't all the documents and discussion up to that point taken place in the hometown of Stephen F. Austin? Why San Felipe wasn't chosen as the place where the declaration would be made official, Angelina could not fathom. She felt the illogical change was due to Houston's stubbornness and his vain wish to have his orders contrast with Austin's. The original impresario, now the republic's secretary of state, had already gone to the United States capital to ask for help.

Well, where the independence document was signed affected present concerns very little. San Felipe residents prayed Houston could hold off Santa Anna's men at the Colorado. Since events turned as they had for men like Jim Bowie and Travis, no one could expect mercy from the Mexican dictator. She had seen the last Alamo plea for reinforcements, script in the hand of William B. Travis—the same neat letters he had drawn many times on his lodging receipt. Angelina could hardly let herself recall the banter she'd exchanged with the fiery lawyer.

The last time Travis stopped at her inn, he and Houston had been much in agreement about what could not be tolerated from Mexico's army. Bowie was then monitoring the Bexar settlement after his early win over Santa Anna's brother-in-law. Houston had sent the young Alabama attorney only to take stock firsthand of San Antonio. Surely her charming hotel guest never suspected he was riding west toward annihilation.

In spite of tragedy at the Alamo, she couldn't let herself doubt the hopeful view now that forces under the Mexican general could be whipped once they came face to face with Houston's army. They would make any of Santa Anna's generals regret moving east as far as the Colorado River.

As she came up on the town's bread ovens, she wondered how Miss Celia was taking all the dreadful news. William Travis had been the only lawyer willing to file *manumission* papers on behalf of the dark-skinned woman. Her owner, Captain John C. Allen, had arranged to free her. The freckled daughter, also working the ovens this morning, looked a lot like Celia—and, Angelina often thought, as much like the captain now off with Houston's men.

"Morning, Miss Dolly. You and your mama been out here by the fires all night?"

"Not much time to sleep, ma'am." The girl was almost as tall as her mother. Her arms were slender and strong, brown and graceful like Celia's.

"I shouldn't even ask about yeast loaves."

"Right busy with the squares of hard bread, yes'm. Not too many know the recipe, but Mama learned as a child, near the coast. Captain Mosely says they'll need it whether the army stays over near the Colorado… where they'll try to hold or…"

"These days, Mosely Baker himself chokes on words."

"Or if our men have to go back across the Brazos…"

The pang Angelina felt was mixed with relief. Her son was not yet this girl's age. Alex was still too young to fully grasp their peril or to join the fight.

"Whatever you can spare, we'll purchase. Delilah plans to get a stew started, even with the rationing …we thought we might as well cook up what pork is already cut. But any bread would be good."

"Is that…?" Dolly Ann was pointing and her expression made Angelina take in air through her mouth. Other early risers near the end of the main path gravitated toward an officer on horseback.

"Looks like just Captain Baker…saying we can breathe easy, I hope."

"That's Mr. Mosely, for sure," Celia's daughter said. "But I don't recall him ever waving his hat down that-away. It looks to be other soldiers riding up behind him."

Angelina had tried, ever since her husband's passing, to keep a calm demeanor for the children's sake. But if she had not had two young ones to look after, she would have thrown herself into keeping up the inn to maintain her own sanity. She certainly had no patience for men who seemed unable to master their emotions in the midst of emergency. After settling the bread order, Angelina Peyton strode out into the muddy path that was San Felipe's main street. Early risers now spilled into the center of town, and the narrow boardwalks could not long accommodate the crowd. Mr. Shannon, the livery owner, was on the edge of the throng.

"News about Houston's movements?" she said to him.

"His army ain't but fifteen miles from here, according to those scouts."

"They've held off the Mexicans from crossing the Colorado?"

"Not hardly."

"It can't be anything worse than…" Angelina rarely searched for words, but she could not bring herself to utter the syllables…*Alamo*.

"It's about Fannin's men, too," the liveryman went on. The woman's eyes flashed without blinking, and anyone speaking to her would have flinched.

"Are they fortifying Victoria?"

"Never made it that far," the man said.

"Never…"

"There was a shootout halfway there." Mr. Shannon wished he were working on a harness and could say he was too busy to talk. "Urrea won the day…Last word we have is the volunteer army was marched back to Goliad. They say Fannin himself took a bullet near a Coleto Creek. He was carried from the battlefield."

"So, there's no help?"

"No one left of any use but Houston's own companies—it appears they're retreating in our direction. Once he heard the colonel's army had been captured…" The man took off his hat, ran his fingers down his scalp, and glanced in the direction of his livery stable. He seemed ready to take the fastest horse in any direction. "Some declare Houston is on the run, but others swear by him and claim it's best to bide time for any encounter with Santa Anna. It's Filisola or some other general that's run Texas boys off our way."

"Maybe the Mexicans are aiming for Washington rather than here." Angelina felt guilty now for her grudge against the town a bit north. Yes, once Washington-on-the-Brazos had been designated as the republic's meeting spot, her business had fallen off sharply. But who could envy a location targeted for attack. Still, she couldn't shake her growing contempt for General Houston's decisions.

"Mrs. Peyton…if enemy soldiers do come directly for San Felipe…"

"Delilah and Alex can pour shot. We'll be ready for—"

"No, what they did to Gonzales right after the Alamo went down. Rather than let supplies fall into Santa Anna's hands."

"We won't…" Angelina Peyton's wide eyes grew fierce. She opened her mouth and tried to form words. "You're not saying Houston would…"

"Could be he orders everything burned down, anything that might speed the enemy."

"Burned down?"

"Some fear the whole of San Felipe." Another resident was elbowing his way toward the liveryman.

"You still have that spare wheel, Shannon? The one you were repairing?"

"Got it hanging."

"Well I'll take it, before someone else asks." He wheezed and put a rag to his mouth. "Elsa and I are fixin' to follow the river south before the crowds thicken up."

"Why don't you try in Groce's direction first? They figure the Yellowstone, or another steamer, will ferry the army and any of us over to the safer side."

"Could be that's where Santa Anna forces a fight. He's not crazy enough to try the muddy banks downriver."

"No tellin'."

"No telling what will be torched and left to cinders."

Angelina Peyton had already turned to make her way around panicked townspeople and back to the inn. Alex's face and Delilah's were pressed up against a windowpane. She was trying to decide if she would tell them to spend another morning pouring shot or whether she would order them—calmly—to abandon that task and set their energy to packing the dearest and most useful belongings. She glanced in the direction of the cemetery a block off the main street, where Jonathan's headstone was only recently set. But she could not allow herself to picture the grove and markers surrounded by smoldering cabin timbers.

Texans would certainly make a stand and beat back any attackers. There had been barely two hundred men defending the Alamo. There were at least four times that many soldiers rallying under Sam Houston's command.

By midmorning, the first waves of Texas Regular Army were moving into San Felipe. While most sodden men from the Colorado headed immediately to Groce's, many were too weary to pass up a respite in town. The manufacture of munitions came to a halt at the Peyton Inn to accommodate a packed dining hall. Samson hauled in a side of hog from Tindle's, while Alex helped Delilah cart bread loaves from the Allens' ovens. Angelina opened a crate of Madeira that she and her late husband had dragged into the cellar upon their return from Matamoros. She didn't think any future occasion would make her wish she hadn't opened such special wine. Who knew when these liberty fighters would see their next hearty meal?

An hour after tin plates were cleared, Sam Houston himself—a head taller than any other man—was spotted in San Felipe's main street. Angelina felt he must have eaten for midday at a less prominent inn, perhaps sensing her coolness to his company. Reacting to news of his presence, colonists went back to readying their wagons. The steamer *Yellowstone* had navigated the turbulent water halfway up to the common ferry and positioned itself to transport soldiers across to the eastern shore. Exodus toward the swollen river was underway. Suddenly, Houston's voice boomed out on the streets.

"Men armed for Texas! Move out to the *Yellowstone*! She's just north of town! Hoist your gear and march upriver!"

"Near town, the current's like flood rapids, General! The plantation ferry might be a better bet!"

"If time goes to waste, we'll have to dog paddle—drag the men out or threaten to shoot 'em. Get them north on the riverbank, whatever it takes!"

"Once we reach the other side, do you aim for us to retreat some more?" The man spat emphatically from a tooth gap. He was not the only one peeved about bolting from the Colorado.

"Who says we're in retreat?" one of Houston's lieutenants blurted. "The general can judge the best time to wup 'em!"

"Evacuate San Felipe!" Houston roared again, before turning to the man in doubt. "If Santa Anna's cutthroats make it here, every hog and musket will be put to use against our boys!"

"General..." It was Miss Celia speaking up. She had just filled several cloth bags with squares of bread and was setting those down inside oilcloth pouches. "It's best to let them cool completely. But I don't expect you all have time." Dolly Ann filled the next enlisted man's order as her mother again addressed the imposing man in the saddle. "Will we end up like Gonzales, Mr. Houston?"

"We won't put a torch to a thing if we don't sight any of Santa Anna's men. But their scouts can track a lone coyote in a blizzard." The general leaned and nudged the horse's flank with the heel of one moccasin. Draped in a tangle of fur, he moved his horse toward the nearest path from town. Soldiers near the bread ovens seemed as stunned by Celia's temerity as by the crisis itself.

"They could miss us by one mile as easily as a hundred..." she observed, "unless they're coming right behind."

"We're ahead by hours at least."

"Gather up whatever you can into a wagon!" an officer was shouting. He was as likely a corporal as a colonel right under Houston in rank. It was impossible to tell since the Texan army had never been issued uniforms. A civilian might as well have been told to look for the tallest white man wearing moccasins, if he had sought General Sam Houston himself.

This evacuation unfolded like nothing Angelina Peyton had ever witnessed, though the horror of flight was not new to her. The Peytons' desperate escape down the Ohio and Mississippi Rivers flashed in her memory, but the fears she and Jonathan shared were secret. Calm surroundings had helped shore up their own fortitude. On this day, extreme agitation gripped every San Felipe inhabitant. *Keep your wits. Keep your wits,* Angelina told herself, as she instructed the children to help pack up blankets, dried beans, the lightest pots, tools—a sharpened shovel.

Delilah and Samsom directed the other family servants, all doing their best to secure the innkeeper's survival goods. She glared at one couple chaining their slaves at the ankle. Surely a responsible master could engender allegiance. She felt it shameful that any owners resorted to irons, but she knew the case of Miss Celia had worried many San Felipe colonists. Even Captain Allen's work partner had split from the business alliance over the issue of granting her freedom.

Delilah scanned the street periodically in the direction of the ovens.

"I suppose Miss Celia will be taking all her bread tins," Angelina said, shaking her head about a heavy, blackened roaster.

"She's not packing a thing, Miss Angelina."

"Not shutting down the ovens? Is she waiting on the captain's return?"

"Not likely to wait on anything." She couldn't help smiling as she fixed her gaze. "Or pay attention to any lights but her own." They both took a long look. The two dark-skinned women bent and straightened and placed baked items into outstretched satchels. Mother and daughter appeared disinclined to budge from their property.

On this March 29th, the clamor of early afternoon never subsided. Usually, dining was offered for several hours, but midday menus shut down early. Too many dishes and cooking utensils needed packing. Angelina and Delilah busied themselves figuring what could be served from the back of one sturdy wagon, wherever it might be headed. In front of the inn, they set Mrs. Peyton's footboard on a barrel as a serving table where pintos were spooned for customers too late for any pork stew. Others had to be turned away, and Angelina worried that the Ingram family next door had not taken time to eat while any meal was offered in town.

Celia Allen, they said, was now rationing out baked goods only to the military stragglers. Then Captain Mosely Baker made a last round to ask how many hogs were in the Peytons' pens. What she could let go to the army amassing at the eastern edge of town would be paid for later, he assured her. Angelina said to take them all, wherever Houston aimed to lead them.

"Not too many using the word *lead*, ma'am."

"If it's Santa Anna or another general coming at your heels from the Colorado…"

Maybe Miss Celia could stay calmly defiant about orders to leave. Maybe the woman's new freedom gave her the nerve to stand alongside her daughter Dolly Ann and coolly stare down the devil himself. Angelina felt any Mexican general would see the hostility and danger firing in her own eyes.

Each half hour rushed by. The innkeeper, her children, and seven Peyton servants had loaded two wagons with the one feather mattress, her tin bathtub, two changes of clothing for everyone, and more pots than plates—cups that would do for soup or coffee. Chairs were left behind, since she reasoned that she could sit on any dry ground. People she might feed would squat or stand to take a meal, but at the end of a day she was going to get a few hours rest on familiar bedding. That and a weekly bath would make waiting for the outcome tolerable.

She hoped that the Texas Army, after vanquishing each soldier sworn to Santa Anna's orders, could send San Felipe people home. As Texans owning their own country and constitution, they would honor this day. There would be recollections and lively talk at the inn's long table, like the debates she'd witnessed many a time among Travis, Jim Bowie, and the general.

Word came back in the dying afternoon that the Houston's men had been successfully transported across the Brazos. The river raged, but the *Yellowstone* had managed eight crossings to get the army of Texas to the safer bank. The steamship had already made two more round trips with folks from Washington and San Felipe. Even some from as far as Nacogdoches had come seeking greater protection near the general. Others were now directed toward the ferry at Groce's, as the steamer had left on its risky return downstream.

Poised in front of their hotel, the Peyton family believed themselves on the verge of departure, but one additional item after another kept them from pulling away—a set of wooden horses Alex loved, Mag's baby clothes. It was dusk before Samson took the reins of one wagon and Angelina directed the other horses away from the log structure. She consoled herself that the two wagons would best fit on that ferry anyway, and then heavier rain began to fall.

The innkeeper's people were squeezing onto the floating platform, when a cry went up from the center of town that Mexican scouts had been spied at the northwest edge of town. Mosely Baker and another captain had stayed behind to protect the last of the townspeople. Forces traveling with Sam Houston and nearly all San Felipe now stretched beyond the eastern shore of the Brazos.

There was just enough light for Mrs. Peyton's servants to see where the edge of the raft touched ground again. On horseback, one soldier and Mr. Shannon urged clumps of evacuees to move on and make room for the late crossing. Others held torches to see where the wagon wheels were about to roll. Once the Peytons reached a firm, grassy level, there was nothing to do but collapse and turn in the direction of the abandoned colony. With nightfall encompassing the landscape, onlookers could only speculate where the first flames took hold—or guess which men set torches to which homes.

Angelina Peyton and her family held one another, taking in a scene that was as strangely beautiful as it was horrifying. They guessed it was the two smaller inns at the northwest end of town bursting into orange first, then the printing establishment, the livery, and maybe Mr. Travis' law office. A loud blast came from windowpanes shattering in the heat. Thick bitter smoke stung their eyes. But Celia and Dolly Ann weren't shouting for help from the opposite riverbank, so they assumed the two refusing evacuation now stood defiant against any threat to their bakery. In a few minutes, the entire town was an inferno visible from miles away. If the whole Mexican army were still toiling to locate only Austin's colony, they would easily find their target on this dark night. Holding Mag, Delilah sat next to Angelina. The two women linked arms. One dismal fact was slowly becoming clear. San Felipe buildings were being torched by their own friends and Houston's men.

Makeshift protection from the elements made the long night uncomfortable, but it was dull outrage truly thwarting sleep. At dawn, nearly a thousand Texans opened their eyes and surveyed sparse woodlands just east, where they would likely head next. Exhausted from the previous day's struggle, soldiers and families stirred, dazed. Light rain had fallen throughout the night, and many were grumbling that the job of torching the town—unless done expertly—would have failed. Across the Brazos, the charred gash that had been San Felipe was the result of torches placed strategically inside the worthiest buildings.

By full daylight it was clear that Santa Anna's soldiers were just then arriving. If it was as true as it appeared, that the first alarm had been woefully premature—that there had been no urgent reason to torch so many structures—the flames had surely served as a guidepost to San Felipe. Two local volunteers, acting as rear guards, lay on a small rise. From that vantage point on the eastern shore, they observed through a spyglass the happenings in the burnt town. Not far from the last ferry to unload, Angelina moved close enough to hear them.

"That could be Santa Anna himself," one said, "judging from the fancy uniform—gold epaulettes and all—though I suppose it's another general."

"Celia Allen is still there by her ovens. It looks like she was right about their not wanting to interfere with a Negro who can provide bread."

"If they're taking time for edibles, dammit, we should too." The men commiserated about missing dinner during the evacuation. Angelina had knelt down, well hidden from sight of anyone in the streets across the river.

"There's a neighbor and her in-laws in the wagon ahead of us. I don't think they ate a bite yesterday. It's Mr. Ingram's mama and daddy. They've been at San Felipe no more than a year—so much harder for older folks—and now this." She talked to steady her own nerves. One watchman turned toward her.

"You all get that hog out of the mud?"

"Mr. Tindle's favorite palomino went downriver, too," she said, shaking her head, "water up past its belly. Samson says a quarter mile down shore from here, three cows followed each other into wet clay. Not enough spring grass yet to make the footing steady. One will pull a hoof out and the other legs get stuck." The man with the spyglass kept his observation steady.

"Those son-bitches aren't goin' anywhere with the rain at it again."

"Lucky we had use of the *Yellowstone* part of yesterday. She'll have to make it down past Brazoria to the coast and wait all this out."

"There won't be any settlers making use of a steamer for some time."

"No ferries neither, not until down by Fort Bend."

"Could be Urrea tries that crossing, too, once he knows which side General Houston took to.

"We're sure to stick east of the river. Santy Anny is likely to slice through any settlers on down the trail like he—"

"Well…" Angelina broke in. Alex had followed her. She didn't know how to dispel his anxiety. "That hog you were talking about. We should put him from his misery and get something on the fire for later. It appears the Mexican army is going to rest up in what's left of San Felipe for the afternoon."

"I wouldn't be so sure," the soldier with the lookout piece said.

"What is it?"

"I've been watching six fellas steer a cannon barrel over to Celia's bakery. You know that bee hive oven she only uses for drying hardtack?"

"She made all she aimed to for a while. Unless they're forcing her do another batch special for them."

"They've had her at the regular ovens, making brown loaves…and cornbread."

"Where's the cannon now?"

"They're settin' it up top of…," he sucked in air, "…they've got their own spyglasses. Looks to me like the barrel is—facing right at us!"

"Move on out! Pass the word along!" A moan spread out slowly, east toward the woodlands and down through the ranks of the Texas Army. But the first space available and out of cannon range was south along the riverbank from where they had stopped. Angelina and Delilah got the children into one wagon while Samson and the other Peyton servants readied themselves by the hefty cart. The men each shoved at wheel rims as the two women flicked reins and shouted. Before the family had moved the width of a building from their resting spot, one thundering blast came from Celia's.

A heavy weight splintered the railing on the boarding dock a short distance away. Once on the move with the other fleeing Texans, the Peytons risked no time looking back. The Ingrams' wagon had moved off at an angle with them, and the three covered transports stayed together. Cholera had almost taken Vera Ingram's husband two years earlier and now she refused to lose track of the army he'd joined. It wasn't difficult to follow Houston's direction on the muddy prairie, but the young wife struggled to keep pace. Inside their lurching wagon, her in-laws clung to the side panels. The two neighboring families felt some consolation in keeping known company.

Mrs. Peyton suddenly stopped her wagon, though. There was no time for proper dressing of a hog, but she had forgotten entirely about the stranded animal. One soldier bringing up the rear warned her that retreat was imperative, but she brushed him off as she unharnessed a single horse from the lighter wagon.

"I am not obliged to follow the general's orders." Samson let Mrs. Peyton step into his locked hands to mount. He clearly intended to walk along with her. "If I left a poor beast in the mud with no sense left but fear of wild cats, I could never close my eyes again, much less sleep."

"Ma'am, we'll have to keep these last wagons moving on."

"Go on and catch up with Mr. Houston—if he's not already sunning himself in the Floridas."

By the time Angelina and Samson made it back with two buckets of pork flank, heavy rain had shifted all worry to how many settlers were getting stuck. No wagons or horses made measurable progress. But from word passed through the ranks by scouts, it grew clear that the menacing army had no interest in slogging past masses of townspeople to confront Houston's men. River crossing up this high on the Brazos was suicide for anyone. Maybe Santa Anna's general had spied the palomino being knocked from its feet by floating debris and swept downriver. Spanish ponies were shorter than most Texas mounts.

Mexican forces had backed away from the riverbank altogether, to head south as quickly as possible, probably aiming as far as the coast. The shale surface in those parts was preferable to muddy banks inland. It was rebel fighters they meant to slaughter, surely not hysterical colonists in retreat. No one was ready to wager on Sam Houston's intent—whether he was heading southeast determined to stand against the Mexican Army, or making the speediest retreat possible across the Sabine to Louisiana.

Regardless of Texian destiny, Angelina and other refugees with any strength did their best to take charge of the fleeing settlers, a few clumps at a time. After a meal, old Mr. Ingram showed more fortitude than his wife or daughter-in-law, but Angelina asked Samson to take their reins while the family found some rest inside the rocking wagon. Alex helped Delilah manage one of their own. At the other front seat, Mag whimpered at Angelina's side. The next day and the next, the wheels took them through a shocking blur—pleas for food or water and sobs of despair. People resorting to escape on foot, trudged alongside the Peyton wagons. Angelina sometimes stopped altogether to let a family shelter briefly under their awnings. She did not know whether her own determination would sustain them as far as the Sabine.

One dusk during the first week out, the mass exodus halted to make an encampment before the next river crossing. Not far ahead of the Peyton-Ingram pairing, some commotion was starting up. A young soldier had been given permission to ride several hours back along the retreat lines, as long as he promised to return to Houston's command the next afternoon. It was Zachariah, the printer's nephew. He and an older daughter in the Niederwald family had planned to marry in early April, but alarms and packing postponed all such festivities. The soldier couldn't abide not knowing how his betrothed fared, though, and the Texas general granted him a two-day furlough.

To see firsthand, Angelina strode up the haphazard line of wagons, many of which had been abandoned for more predictable progress on foot. She wound her way past trunks and furniture discarded to help wheels inch forward. On one scuttled piece of luggage, a man with a gray beard sat cradling a fiddle. She wondered if he had refused exhortations to toss it too into the mud-caked debris. When Angelina saw the young Niederwald woman sobbing on her sweetheart's shoulder, the need to do something on their behalf washed over her with urgency.

"You sir, with the fiddle—play us something merry, won't you? And you," she said to the would-be groom, "ride back on the line, if you're in love—see if there's someone who can preside over a legal wedding—if not a preacher, a lawyer or a barber who quotes scripture." The two sweethearts had begun to smile. "Lord knows we're toting Bibles a-plenty in this scramble!"

Before sundown, the private returned with a wiry, silver-haired gentleman sitting behind him on his horse. One of his coat sleeves was streaked with mud, but his stiff white collar still gleamed in contrast. In the meantime, Angelina and Mag had gone up and down the string of wagons asking if anyone had a lace shawl or veil, as the trunk with an heirloom wedding gown had been left behind—likely now in cinders. At last light, two sisters gathered a bouquet of Indian paintbrush and Queen Anne's lace. Some early tickseed mixed in the yellow, which went well with the bride's red hair.

A fiery sunset charged the scene, and unexpected joy rippled out from the knot of people close enough to hear vows. Hunger and blighted dreams were temporarily soothed. The sudden merriment was tinged with desperation, and as many old men as women let their tears flow. Celebration continued well after the couple retired to a wagon for privacy. Long into the night those with instruments took turns strumming. After guitars were put away, a lone voice would lift in song out of nowhere, making the fitful dreamers smile. Until a person no longer drew breath, Angelina consoled herself, such camaraderie could rekindle hope. Such fellowship, she knew, had stitched together the early colonists of Texas in the first place.

During the third week of exodus, the townspeople of San Felipe and parts more northerly on the Brazos had lost all trace of General Houston's army. Angelina was consumed with worry for the Ingram family. One day it would be the wife Vera moaning that all was in futility. The next day, she was the one trying to convince her in-laws that their only son had not been lost in battle. Settlers knew nothing except that Texian forces had made it to the banks of the San Jacinto River still upwards of the coast. Many feared that Santa Anna would swing southeast on their heels. They would not openly review the worst fate known to befall those fighting for a republic. Most were too ashamed to keep talking about Houston's apparent unwillingness to make a stand. Some remnant of fierce pride among the runaway settlers kept them making progress toward the final eastern river of the territory.

A private had left Alex with a spyglass that wouldn't fold up properly. The boy wouldn't have tucked it away even if it had been in working order. He kept lookout in every direction as if he were following an assignment. Angelina couldn't help recalling her stop in Natchez, Mississippi, years earlier and the twelve-year-old equally pleased with the lookout piece Mrs. Weeks gave him. She smiled to recall how she almost jumped from the river barge to shake the boy Shelby and make him promise never to talk of their Texas destination. Surely the Natchez youngster used the birthday gift to monitor the riverboat's departure down the Mississippi. At that time, Angelina had believed the couple's escape to be the most stressful and unpredictable turn life could ever take.

Suddenly, Alex called that riders were coming. Angelina and the other able-bodied adults stood up, steeling themselves for the worst possible news—that Santa Anna had defeated all but those two soldiers riding post. Perhaps there was no time for any action except a nonstop dash for survival toward Louisiana. She was looking to make sure that Delilah had Mag by the hand, that Samson was ready to unhitch the horses and leave every possession behind, when the shouts of the riders began to be made out.

"We licked 'em!"

"Houston and the boys won the republic!"

Angelina wriggled her way in among the other astonished settlers, who had to hear it from the men again once they had dismounted and recovered enough wind to recount the events.

"Only lost a handful on our side, and there was a mess of Santa Anna's men begging for mercy. We were fresh out of feelings."

"*Remember the Alamo! Remember Goliad!* That's all that was a-ringing in our ears!"

"So Fannin and his men joined you?" Angelina asked. Many had hoped cautiously over the last weeks. "Did the battalions break out of Goliad and join with Houston?"

One man looked for a place to sit and the other took off his hat and looked down at the ground.

"Goliad was inspiration, ma'am, like the Alamo and what all was lost there."

"The colonel's men were captured, we heard that," Angelina said. "If they couldn't break out, we'll need some party of men to head down southwest…if they've been holed up for more than a month."

"It's certain we're a free republic now," one rider rushed on. "Ole Santa Anna was caught the day after we trounced them. Put him in irons as he was tryin' to get back across the Rio Grande, dressed out like a lowly private but when other prisoners went to saluting him, well…" The seated man let the sentence go and forced a chuckle. But the man still on his feet avoided Angelina's eyes.

"What about the Goliad volunteers? Most were from Georgia…they came over a thousand miles, some of them and—"

"They got killed, ma'am."

"Santa Anna had 'em all walked out and shot to pieces."

Joy over defeating Santa Anna at San Jacinto was immediately diluted in the pooling grief. Over the next few weeks, news of what had happened to the men at Goliad only magnified the myriad woes of settlers slowly returning to the colony sites. Angelina, Delilah, and Alex did their best to console their neighbors when word came slowly up through the mass of families that the younger Mr. Ingram was one of the few Texans lost in the San Jacinto triumph. Whatever might have been burnt in a hometown, there could be no news as devastating as an only son slain in battle. Alex took to sitting alongside Samson on the driver's seat of the Ingrams' wagon. Angelina and Delilah offered the family of three some bean soup that they managed to cook on the journey back toward the Brazos, but the widow and stricken parents could do no more than allow a spoon to be held to their lips.

Whenever Angelina Peyton felt that the return to San Felipe took longer than she could bear, she made herself think of the three hundred unarmed volunteers marched out and executed at La Bahia. Families of those slaughtered might not have heard yet of the frightful outcome.

Their lives might unfold hopefully for another week or two. The sorrow that her closest neighbors were experiencing, the grief that families in Georgia would soon meet, had life of its own and would hound the survivors beyond borders and time. Exhaustion, Angelina reminded herself, could be forgotten after rest.

After their wagons rolled at last back onto the charred remains of San Felipe, Angelina hid from view to sob quietly over the blackened rubble. Before letting anger consume her, she again contemplated the desolate feelings her own neighbors struggled to rise above. The ghastly scene Stephen F. Austin's first colony had become was nothing as cruel as the final seconds of so many lost.

Houston's ultimate win for the republic left few willing to denounce whoever had given the order to torch San Felipe, whether setting the flames had been premature or necessary. But victory for all those returning was tinged with bitterness. Angelina had seen some familiar faces while crossing back over the Brazos—the Whiteside brothers, one of the Kuykendalls, and the older of the two Millican men. Reaching what had been the main path of a bustling and proud town, most hung their heads. Each San Felipe inhabitant seemed to be drawn to his or her own former dwelling as one visits a cemetery.

Dozens more returned to the charred landscape during Angelina's brief stay. She kept to herself, along with Alex and Mag, Delilah, Samson, and the other Peyton workers. Except to console Vera Ingram, who shook off enough numbness to decide that she and her in-laws would follow a string of families on up to Nacogdoches, Mrs. Peyton threw herself into small salvaging tasks. At least there was no more reason to flee. She and Delilah decided against prying black tiles from the wide kitchen hearth that had been a source of pride in town. The Peytons' place had been the first structure in town erected expressly as an inn and tavern.

"Those oven bricks," Angelina mused, "blackened but set even as the day Jonathan and the masons laid them out. We could put up a sign that we're ready for the next slow bake of a pork side or tray of yams."

"If it hadn't been for the ease of trading with Miss Celia, we could have taken on a helper and made yeast raised for the whole town. Your Mr. Peyton set these bricks to last." Angelina knew she would soon leave behind all nostalgia over her first love. She needed another day or two to say farewell to it all.

"I can smell fresh bread right now."

"She's down there, ma'am. Samson just walked in Miss Celia's direction to tip his hat." Delilah knew she could safely speak on. "Shake hands too. Her freedom declaration hasn't made her too proud for the rest of us."

"She's a good woman, Delilah." Celia Allen had done what she needed to for her own survival and Dolly Ann's. Angelina would stand up for her on that.

"Santa Anna's general told her to bake for his troops if she wanted herself and her daughter to see another sunrise. That's what our Sam heard tell."

"None of our men were near town by then. I don't know what woman left alone wouldn't grant an enemy the wherewithal to move on."

"She and Dolly ask forgiveness about the cannon going off. They had a terror of any on our side being struck." It was a full minute before Angelina responded. The innkeeper had turned away again to take in the sweeping view of blackened timbers, to glance in the direction of the lot with headstones. She felt certain she would not stay to nudge the town's revival forward. The aroma of baked bread wafted their way.

"If we can't forgive friends for a rare ill-advised step, our hatred of enemies will eat us alive."

Delilah pulled a heavy kettle from the ash and decided not to speak any more just then of Celia. Angelina didn't wax philosophical very often. What she liked about her mistress was that she kept her statements short about right and wrong. As a habit, she would look at the truth that was in front of her and tamp down broad sweeping statements. Speechmakers were bound to get caught up in a pile of half-truths and hypocrisies over time. Of course, Delilah had turned over the question of slave ownership in a country where the practice had been abolished by Santa Anna himself. And now Texas was its own country. No doubt slavery would be declared legal again, with such contradictions as *manumit* perhaps thought of as treason. She could see Angelina's admiration for Celia's fortitude and maternal care—that was something. Delilah reckoned it good fortune to work for a mistress with character and one who was tough enough to live a long, long time. The chances of her or Samson ever standing on an auction block were remote.

"When I heard that little slave girl sing years ago on our first trip down the Mississippi…" Angelina was remembering while she worked with a damp rag to get soot off the kettle. "The girl must have practiced the evening before Mrs. Weeks held a birthday celebration for her hired boy. You must have heard her practice."

"The first and only night I ever did spend in a white person's house," Delilah said. "Not without you were in a guestroom. I won't be forgetting that night, no ma'am. How I felt after hearing that child sing—my faith before that would tally up as wishy-washy." Angelina was surprised to see Delilah's eyes glisten now, after all they had been through, and the widow was embarrassed that she had not spoken more often about the remarkable song. Now, she needed to shift her attention away from the ruined hearth.

"Sometimes those words come back to me as clear as the day that child sang. I wish I could put voice to melody...but I do recall the lines—"

All good gifts around us

Are sent from heaven above,

Then thank the Lord, O thank the Lord,

For all his love.

"When that little girl sang, I felt shot through the heart. We were running because Jonathan had killed a man, and I felt shot through myself. Her voice made it seem that every angel in heaven must have skin as dark as hers—and yours and Celia's." When it looked as if the kettle might fall from Angelina's grasp, Delilah reached for it and their fingers touched.

"I don't doubt the Lord loves a child of any color."

"My own world was upside down then. But the girl's singing could have melted every chain in Mississippi and Tennessee." She looked for another piece of cookware to scrub. "Well, go on down yourself and tell Celia and Dolly...Tell them I said, 'Be well.' Go on and say we love them." Angelina turned away and put her palm to her forehead. "With everything San Felipe folks lost, we'd better love each other. Tell them both goodbye. If I go, I might burst into weeping."

"Goodbye? What do we...Where we gonna head to?"

"Down the banks of the Brazos a ways. There's Columbia, before the trail reaches Brazoria."

"And what's there for us?"

"A room or a roof, people of a mind to build a new cabin, likely—but on fresh, pretty land. No scars from fire. Nothing but life at full pitch, like it was here for so long. Law offices where I can get papers ready after a time, if anyone wants to buy the Peyton lots here. A few will start the rebuilding. Someone will stand in this spot before long and have the heart to wash soot from every hearth tile." They'd restored only one colorful tile brought back from Matamoros before restricting their toil to more practical salvage.

"But what will we do in Columbia to get by, to make our way?"

"I heard talk about its being named capital. It's one of the few places with meetinghouses erected. If we've got a new country and a new government on our hands, it won't be long before the men need a place to gather and argue again." Delilah hadn't pictured their leaving San Felipe.

"No, it doesn't look like such doings will go on here any time soon." She turned again in the direction of the street, but she had one more thought. "I do praise God that Mr. Austin isn't astride out there right now, taking in all this ruin." Angelina hugged her, just for a moment. Delilah seemed to take her word that leaving was a firm decision. The Widow Peyton didn't want to give away how close she was to despair, how tenuous her hope was that another town could revive her. She chased the image of a heartbroken Stephen F. Austin's by speaking aloud to herself.

"Stephen is a man with enough optimism to lift the weary. If he were to walk up right now, he'd say 'There's that beautiful wide hearth your Jonathan and the neighbors built. Don't you doubt that another family will come through here in time and put such a masterpiece to lively use.' "

But, no, Angelina went on thinking as she watched Delilah move down toward Celia's ovens, Mr. Austin would not be cheered by the vibrant green and yellow painting on a single Spanish tile. A year in the Mexico City prison had robbed even that great man of his hopeful air. There was a limit, she told herself, to what the boldest individual could bear before having to admit that a fond dream had fallen to ash and cinders.

~ Shelby

adrift ~

Summer 1836, Nacogdoches

12   Losses Less Glorious

The two men sitting outside a printer's shop in Nacogdoches had become acquainted in the last week. With families beginning to move back into town, and General Houston returned to finish recovering after San Jacinto, any bystanders could enjoy the steady stream of activity in the street. But Shelby Whitmire had begun posting himself there in the mornings to be available for carpentry inquiries. The young soldier keeping him company was courier for Houston. Messages from a cabin in town where the general recuperated were sometimes formalized by the printer before being taken to McLeod's bivouac a few miles north.

The Mississippi man appreciated the private's ability to share a bench mostly in silence. He was curious, though, about the document the soldier was waiting to have legally copied. It was something meant to calm hostilities between disgruntled Cherokee, Caddo maybe, and the new republic. Townspeople were speculating about how a talk might go between Chief Bowles and the new Adjutant General of Texas, Hugh McLeod. Whitmire thought the document might be something for the two to sign, but he knew not to question a soldier about orders.

Across the way, a pregnant woman ambled from a mercantile out onto the muddied walkway, and Shelby was suddenly keen to avoid comments about his unique medical skill. With a short green stick, he had been scraping horse dung from one shoe onto last week's newspaper, and he made a thwacking sound that caught the private's attention.

"How long had you lived in Brazoria when things went haywire?" he asked.

"A year and a half almost." As the soldier turned to the window to see whether the printer was still hunched over a table, Whitmire glimpsed his sketchy whiskers. He didn't think the private could be more than sixteen. "We drifted over from Arkansas, so this ain't my first stay in

Nacogdoches. My folks tried Columbia for a few months, and before that we camped out at a little place just down from San Felipe."

"You must have had your fill of moving," Shelby said. "It was the opposite for me, born and raised in the same spot."

"New Orleans was grand." The ordinarily solemn youth was smiling. "I wouldn't say I was glad General Houston got his foot shot at San Jacinto, but me and the other men who went with him to the Louisiana port got an eyeful we won't forget."

There was something now about the private's distracted look that reminded Shelby of his friend Thomas Weeks. Probably it was a look that any young man took on when conversation turned to New Orleans. On the opposite side of the street, two little children and a husband were now walking alongside the pregnant woman. They stopped in front of a millinery shop, but the courier seemed not to notice.

"McLeod told the general about you," the younger man said. "When you didn't take one of the new shirts delivered for us, Houston wanted to know who the hell you are. McLeod told him…how a friend of yours… was lost along with William Ward." Shelby Whitmire nodded and the soldier watched him take the sturdy stick to his other shoe. "How did you come to know a fellow from Georgia?"

"Thomas Weeks and I both grew up in Natchez. But he went down the Mississippi."

"Joined up with the battalion in New Orleans?"

Like everyone else in Texas, the private talking to Shelby understood that a conversation about men under Ward and Fannin could only grow increasingly somber. Talk often slid away quickly before the word *Goliad* could be spoken. No one in the new republic had much stomach for delving into what had happened to the volunteer battalion. The dead at the Alamo and the victors at San Jacinto were hailed. It was best to let mention of Goliad, the La Bahia slaughter, lapse into silence or chatter.

"Glad you weren't hurt in the last battle, Zeke," Shelby finally said. "We didn't lose too many that day."

"Did I show you the scar where a wild hog scraped my ankle?" The Brazoria youth was rolling up a pants cuff and sliding down a sock. "Had it by the ears but it whipped around and gave me the mean part of one tusk."

"Looks like it took some doctoring."

"That's my only scratch." From inside the printing office, a customer was talking to the typesetter. While Shelby scraped, the courier watched and went on. "A pretty teacher in Brazoria broke my heart a little once, but nothing hurt me at San Jacinto to brag on." He stood up, sensing that he would be on his way soon. "What are you going to do after you finish with your shoe?"

"Dab more glue onto this front bench leg, I think. It has a wobble that won't help my reputation any." The boy's question was a friendly inquiry about the day, but Whitmire had been mulling bigger decisions. His skills with woodworking tools were only mediocre, and he surely wanted to be done with delivering babies. He felt an urge to move on from Nacogdoches, but he couldn't decide whether to take the trail back east to Natchez or follow where the republic's army would trickle next. The printer came to the shop doorway to hand the soldier a compact leather folder. "Come to think of it, Private Moreland, I'll ride out with you, if you don't mind. I haven't seen McLeod for a week or more."

The soldier opened the folder and took a look at the document, as if he'd been directed to see that it was clear and legible, but the fellow's lips were moving as his eyes stayed fixed in the same spot. When he looked up, he appeared relieved it was Shelby and not another soldier watching him refold the paper into its holder.

"That Brazoria teacher never got around to showing me cursive." He and Shelby rode up the main street toward the northern outskirts of town. The horses soon relaxed into their own pace, and the military messenger seemed content to have company.

"They say your McLeod has less use for town now that Houston is back. Never seen two men send out more fighting signals without really coming to an argument."

"After learning how enemies cut each other down, I can't understand fight among friends."

"Some of McLeod's boys stopped me the other day," Zeke declared, "They declared their 'Hero of Nacogdoches' was ten times the fighter Sam Houston would ever be."

"We did do some hard riding out here in early spring to protect the perimeter," Shelby said, surprising himself by his defensive tone. "Don't think we weren't worried that Filisola was on his way up the Camino Real—even I carried powder and shot on my saddle horn."

"I didn't mean to get you riled." The young man ahead of Shelby rode silently for a few minutes, and it was clear neither wanted to join the local debate—whether Houston or McLeod was the more courageous defender of Nacogdoches. That the town had been Sam Houston's home for some years, no one could dispute.

"We'd all better show Mr. Houston some respect," Shelby said at last. "He's likely to be the country's first president, though I suppose it's Austin's job if he wants it." The younger man groaned and shook his head.

"I'd rather get shot in both feet than slung into a Mexican prison the way Austin was. Just hearing about a dank cell makes me want to curl up like a dead leaf." After his release, and only weeks before the revolution's decisive battles, Stephen F. Austin had gone to Washington D.C. to seek American aid. The last holdout for peace between Mexico and its colonists, he had been changed by eighteen months in a Mexico City dungeon. "My mother and father have a picture of Austin by the fireplace. People love him, that's sure, but the president will have to be a man physically fit to charge."

Conversation stopped as the two approached a shallow thicket of pines bordering an open stretch. Knowing that attacks from disgruntled Indians could erupt at any direction or distance from town, they scanned the far trees for flickering movement. They directed their horses at an angle toward where the trail picked up again at the forest's edge.

"I've heard the name Mirabeau Lamar mentioned as well," Shelby went on.

"Don't say that name around the general! He might practice his charge and aim right at your head." Shelby couldn't put his heart into politics, but he had learned Texans wanted to talk of nothing else. Even this youth, ordinarily calm, grew animated. "Sure, Lamar did himself proud in the last battle. He was a picture on his horse and waving his sword. But he'd be lying if he said he'd been in Texas for a full season, much less a year. Could have been the day before San Jacinto that he rode over to this side of the Sabine."

"That's about how long I've been here."

"But you ain't tossing your hat into the ring for president!" Not much about the light-haired boy reminded Shelby now of his childhood friend, except his confidentiality. "If there was no one else up against Lamar, I'd run for office," the soldier laughed. "I'd surely put my name in as representative of Brazoria…if that teacher hadn't left town before she got me past primer."

"No." Shelby's short response and tone of voice made his companion sit up in the saddle and slip his rifle from its leather sleeve. Riders were arriving at the treeline across the way. They paused at the turn in the faint path McLeod's company had gradually worn. The mottled color of the ponies, the buckskin leggings on the brown-skinned men identified this group as Caddo or Cherokee—none of the Texas enlisted men, that was certain.

As the two approaching riders kept their direction and pace, Shelby's attention was fixed on the figure in front, a tall sturdy man wearing a beaded vest plate, as well as a dramatic black hat set sideways, Napoleon style. His braided hair, not quite black, caught the light and glistened. The regal individual had stopped with both hands on his pony's neck, though the other half dozen with him let their mounts stamp nervously. Shelby reined his horse in a direction that would give berth without the need to talk, but he also extended his arm slowly to point where he and Zeke Moreland wanted to pass.

Shelby could not take his eyes from the individual he thought surely must be Chief Bowles. Later, he chastised himself for not looking sooner in Private Moreland's direction, to tell the boy not to raise his rifle as far as shoulder level. Shelby could have shouted to the young soldier to keep his weapon low. He could have held up his own empty hands at the group of Indians to assure them no hostility was intended.

The single arrow that pierced the courier's new shirt seemed only to stun the boy into lowering his rifle. When Shelby spun to face continued attack, he saw instead two Indians dismount, on the chief's orders. They rushed their comrade who had used his bow and dragged him by the foot off his horse. They were kicking him fiercely when one raised a knife and looked to the man with the beaded vest. But Shelby had also rushed down from his horse by then and could only pay attention to the soldier beginning to slump from the saddle.

He let the Brazoria youth slip down without putting pressure on the arrow, but Shelby could see his injury left no dilemma, as flesh wounds often did—whether to pull the arrow out or push it through. It had gone as aimed into the chest, and all Shelby could do was turn the boy's head so that he could better breathe, before racing to get his medic bag where he carried a bottle of laudanum and bandages for survivable wounds. Then he sat so that he could pull the youth's upper body up against his own knee and hold the soldier's mouth open to give him a drop of the numbing liquid.

One of the men in Chief Bowles' escort had directed his horse to the disaster scene. He slid down and squatted next to Shelby a minute before producing a knife in a way that conveyed no threat. Something in his solemn eyes and nod convinced Shelby that he had no intention of trying to dig out the embedded arrow. Gently, the Indian placed his thumb on top of the shaft about two inches from where it had gone in. He pressed and turned the slender wood so that the feathered extension came off neatly, even though blood now oozed from his own thumb. There was no saving Private Moreland, but some horror from his last minutes was removed.

"Is the medicine helping?" Shelby asked the boy, who blinked back. "All right. It can do wonders." The young man's breathing was labored but steady. "I'll talk while it's working some good. I don't want you to try…"

"Brazoria…"

"I'll let your people know…you've been hurt," Shelby said. "I don't know how that young teacher could have left you behind," he rushed on. "You were surely her favorite." The wounded man had his face turned toward Shelby but his eyes were going blank. From the boy's throat came an odd sound that the Mississippi man had heard a few times since riding across the Sabine with Lieutenant McLeod. After the threat from Mexicans vanished, the skirmishes with disgruntled Indians had started up. Young men falling, fatal wounds on either side left Whitmire in equal distress. He wanted to head in any direction that led to fewer such scenes as this.

Chief Bowles and every man in his escort now stood next to their horses, not far from where Zeke Moreland's final minutes played out. Only the Indian who had let an arrow fly sat on the ground, staring at his feet. Shelby Whitmire surmised that it might be up to him to decide the killer's fate, though it was the boy from Brazoria who had first set the tragedy in motion. And if Shelby had only warned him about lifting his rifle; if the two had not been talking politics when the Indians first came into view; if he had not started up distracting conversation in an effort to steer talk away from the delivery of babies—the man displaced from Natchez knew he would blame himself plenty in the days ahead, so he didn't mind letting the chief's hothead dread punishment a while.

When three of Bowles' men helped to wrap the boy's body in one of their own blankets, Shelby noticed two others in the escort examining his saddle tassels. They were slow-moving, and the gravity of the scene kept them silent. As the pitiful bundle was being draped over the horse and secured, the chief approached Shelby, who had readied himself to communicate about the man sitting on the ground.

"I speak your language," Bowles said. His eyes searched Shelby's to confirm he had made himself understood.

"The boy…the soldier raised his rifle. Your man," he said pointing, "was only protecting you."

"You will say this to Houston? To McLeod?" Bowles looked again at the wrapped body. Shelby nodded.

"I distracted him with my talk. It was my fault."

"We can give you this man." The shamed assailant sat motionless. "We can give you his death now, if…"

"No." The others flinched at his interruption of their leader. "No. I will explain to McLeod. He will believe me, but…" A leaden weight was settling into Shelby's frame, but he thought suddenly of the youth's saddlebag and the document. He had heard the revolution's death counts—one hundred times the number of men now on their feet in this clearing. "Let me take a look at what this soldier was carrying," he said. "It was something General Houston wanted you and McLeod to sign."

"More papers," Bowles said, and his tone made Shelby doubt that any good could come now from a treaty. When Whitmire looked over the scripted paragraph set on official stationery from the printer's, he shook off the image of the youth mouthing out words earlier in the day.

"It's about our ceremony soon, when Texas leaders are going to see the new president, the chief of Texas and the other leaders sworn in."

"Papers and leaders my warriors do not follow." But then the chief said, "My men will not fight when you have your ceremony."

"That's all Houston says here, that when the new leaders gather… our generals…"

"McLeod…"

"They won't start any fight either, and…if your men agree not to attack—"

"I cannot speak for Caddo or Tonkawa. No one will speak for Comanche. I am the voice for Cherokee where the forest and river meet the buffalo. We were pushed to this place."

"If you sign this, then," Shelby said. "McLeod will sign, because General Houston wants him to." He looked at the make-shift shroud and the motionless form laid over the saddle. "I will explain what happened here." He heard his own words as if from a distance. The dull weight in his head and throat made it hard to speak further. "It may be that Houston will be the highest leader of the Texans."

"He knows about Cherokee," Bowles said, "but he is one general. I am one chief. Many ride with me. I cannot hold the arm of every man."

There was nothing else to say, Shelby thought, nothing else to get settled after the chief put his mark on the document. Anger would flare up when he rode into the army's bivouac soon, but not as much as if the body were paraded back through town. He hoped that soldiers under McLeod would trust friendly testimony and that their impulse for retribution would be mollified by the signed paper. The Indians, with the culprit riding in shame behind the others, stayed to make sure Shelby knew the way toward the encampment. Bowles let his horse go a few steps further in the direction Shelby led Zeke's horse.

"I can find it from here." Shelby thought he might be only two more miles from the soldier camp. He wondered what a practiced diplomat might say after a tragedy. "I go in sorrow…but in peace."

"My father, too, was from the place called Scotland," the Cherokee leader said before turning back to his escort. "That is the only sorrow McLeod and I share."

When Shelby rode into the Texas encampment a half hour later, it took all of McLeod's speaking fire to dissuade his men from taking immediate revenge. Several of the irate soldiers were likely the same ones, Shelby thought bitterly, who had recently accosted Zeke about the contest between their man from Jessup and Sam Houston.

"That half-breed chief needs scalping!"

"Stake him and his damn killers to the ground. Flatten that hat of his and then the whole lot of 'em!" Hugh McLeod fired a single shot near enough one man to make him put a hand up to his ear.

"If you boys don't stand down, you'll face worse from me than from the Fort Jessup court just now taking up your desertion charges." There was grumbling, but the threat of vengeance cooled quickly. "Get to digging out by the other memorials. I'll come say some words when the grave's ready." Shelby, signed pact in hand, followed McLeod into the officer's tent.

"More papers," the officer said, looking at the document.

"That's exactly what the chief said." Shelby had never before seen the look that McLeod gave him.

"You think it's all even? Maybe you should slide your collar around, Shelby, and take up turn-the-cheek preaching full time! Maybe you'd like to say bygones to relatives of the Parkers…bygones about one whole branch of their family hacked to pieces or kidnapped—to forget about ever finding their girl Cynthia Ann."

"It's the Comanche that took her off somewhere, not the Cherokee."

"You think these savages will have a church pageant to sort out those niceties, take a civilized vote at an afternoon tea with linen napkins?"

"And there's nothing uncivilized about the rancor between you and Houston—"

"Neither one of us would rape old women or slice off private parts! You think those tassels on your saddle wouldn't be used by a Comanche or Karankawa to hang your eyeballs from a hackberry branch?" Hugh McLeod was known for maintaining good humor, even before battle, but his face had gone florid and his hand squeezed into a fist, deforming the latest peace document. The last time Shelby Whitmire had been in a small room where fists flew, it was moments before his stepmother took a cast-iron pot to his father's shoulder.

"I can't begin to understand the difficulties of your position," he said calmly, waiting before going on. "I should be safe enough riding back to town by myself." McLeod was turning away to a shelf where he put the signed paper. "If you don't mind," Shelby said while the officer collected himself, "I'll go with you and your men when you take the trail to Columbia."

"It'll be another week or two, maybe a month," Hugh McLeod managed to say.

"If it's as close to Brazoria as they say, where Zeke was from, it may be some of his people still live there."

By September, there was a growing stream of travelers on the trail to Columbia for swearing in of the first Texas government. Not far north of Brazoria, the town had been spared in the widespread burnings, and its buildings included several big enough to seat officials. The first adjutant general Hugh McLeod and Sam Houston, the newly elected President, both set out, but they journeyed in separate contingents. During the last weeks of summer, their rivalry had only sharpened. The general's foot was all but healed, though his drinking habits picked up and his temper worsened. McLeod had become disenchanted with the Nacogdoches townspeople, who'd voted heavily in Houston's favor and against the Georgia publisher, Mirabeau Lamar.

The adjutant general looked forward to candid talk in Columbia with Vice President Lamar, who saw westward expansion in the future of Texas. They could keep one another abreast of any news from parts around Macon, but Hugh McLeod wanted to hear from Lamar's own lips his vision of final borders. Having been released officially from his American commission, the former Jessup lieutenant relished the idea of an expanding republic.

But Lamar, he reminded himself, was also an uncle to the woman most family members pictured as his future wife. Hugh vowed to discuss matters of the heart with no one. As he rode alongside his company and then closer to a pocket of men belonging to Sam Houston's contingent, he only nodded to the mail rider—or carpenter or physician—who had come west from Mississippi. The two had been awkward in one another's company since the unfortunate death of Houston's young courier. Suddenly, McLeod was glad he had not spoken at length—that night when too much port had been poured and officer chat had steered toward women. He was glad he had not gushed uncharacteristically about Joanna Troutman's large eyes, her pale skin, and her childlike hands.

Still in sight of his own officers, he rode just close enough to hear the kind of conversation that probably had Columbia's political fires plenty stoked, too.

"I don't like rumors I've heard," one Houston supporter said, "that Lamar sees Texas sweeping all the way to the Pacific one day."

"Four months after the Mexicans damn near have all our hides, they still don't concede us the land we're sitting on, and now we're aimin' to stake out the entire west?"

"The United States can scoop up all the northern holdings, for all I care."

"Well, if Sam Houston has his way, Texas will be just another state before long."

"President Jackson is friendly to that notion."

"Then don't talk about taking a swath of the continent west of us," one man warned breathlessly. "We're all likely to get hauled before a court like Aaron Burr was—maybe strung up."

"His problem was not looking far enough in our direction. Anything east of the Mississippi is dang sure holding under one flag."

"You men talking about increase in this-here territory are plain fools!" The man getting riled was wobbling in his saddle. "You think two thirds of the men who crossed the Sabine to come aid Texas would have lent a hand if they thought they weren't helping the United States?"

"Americans are already at each other's throats as it is over where slavery can and can't be legal."

"Now that's another issue entirely."

"Mirabeau Lamar visited across the Sabine well before the revolution. He had Fannin show him around, talk about the plantation prospects, as well as the importing of slaves."

"Slander! But talk of Aaron Burr reminds me he knew how to come out of a duel on the winning side."

"Cool down, boys! What I know is we've got to start thinking like an independent republic. Our decisions don't necessarily follow America. We need a president who puts our independent country first."

"Well, I say that's General Sam Houston!" As McLeod's ranks rode up closer to Houston's stragglers, the adjutant general himself fell back in line to the lead of his men.

"Mirabeau Lamar!" one of his corporals shouted. The riders just ahead, including the civilian Shelby Whitmire, kept their gate without turning around. The government of Texas was settled for the next three years with President Sam Houston, and with Lamar to serve as vice-president. Few doubted that the friction between these two would quit giving out sparks before the next election. They were still a good hour from crossing the Brazos and then finding their way to Columbia, but the countryside didn't give them much to take their mind off political controversy.

Whitmire had listened to the debate among Houston's last riders without feeling tempted to enter the argument. It shocked him to hear public talk about expanding Texas all the way to the Pacific, but he had grown up dismissing the boasts of drunkards on the Natchez shore. So much Texas talk seemed made of similar bluster. He had kept an eye on Hugh McLeod and figured him to be listening as well. But why wouldn't he be? As the top army officer, he would need to keep informed of political tides that touched on military schemes. Shelby, however, was not the least drawn into their speculation. The only lingering reflection the Natchez man carried deeper into Texas was his own slow response to Private Zeke Moreland's raised rifle. He couldn't take his mind off the shock of that deadly arrow.

In the three-day ride from Nacogdoches, a much less consequential shock settled in. Just a few miles west of town, pine trees had come to a sudden halt. Instead, solitary live oaks dotted swells of grassy plains. September was no cooler than most summer days had been, but a pelting rain helped settle the dust one afternoon. As the Nacogdoches companies drew up along the Brazos River, there were more and more wagons going in the same direction. The blackened remains of buildings where Washington and then San Felipe had been were stark reminders that bluster could lead to lethal reckoning.

Shelby watched both military lines follow the riverbank for a crossing somewhat south of what had been Stephen Austin's colony. A short distance north, however, he joined a smaller band of soldiers where they crossed the river at a ferry they said was vital during the revolution. Though San Felipe had been gutted, there were numerous wagons and makeshift domiciles, and word was true about ovens in the main street where round loaves were put out night and day. If the crowds were anything like predicted at the swearing in, a man would feel a fool for not having stopped to buy bread where it was available.

Later that afternoon on Columbia's perimeter, Shelby Whitmire let his horse come to a stop near three wagons securely arranged. Visitors pulling all the way into town were already circling back out to the edge of activity. There was adequate shelter in Columbia where the inaugurations and legislative gatherings could be held. The well-constructed collection house had served even during Mexican rule, and there were two well-established inns. But those spaces were not nearly enough housing for all the officials and representatives, much less family members and onlookers who wanted to say they had witnessed the new country's first assembled government.

Shelby had four loaves bundled in a blanket behind his saddle, but he thought it might take as many men to coax him toward the ground and teach him again how to stand. Only once before had he been in the saddle so many days straight. He let his feet dangle from the stirrups. As he stretched his legs and back, he looked more closely at the travelers already settled in.

Gradually, the Natchez man grew spellbound by the wagon arrangement before him. He observed every movement of a tall woman and the servants surrounding her, especially an agile black woman who was taking special care of a little girl. An older boy had to be the girl's brother. The tall woman, the apparent owner of the wagons and crew, steadily ladled beans and thin beef strips into flatbread. A line inched toward the serving spot, and Shelby dismounted gingerly, giving a fellow two coins to tether and water his horse.

"Sir!" The woman in charge gestured to the customer now ahead of him. "If you elbow anyone else, this ladle will flatten your ear. My son had better manners when he was two!" Only once before had Shelby seen the lady with dark hair and olive skin, so he doubted himself. Then he realized that her helper—Delilah?—was squinting in his direction.

"You can come back and get a piece of cornbread, too, for a penny, but why don't you wait and see how you fill up?" The woman was talking to a stout man. "I'll take off a quarter from the price for any two who are sharing in the first place! Let's see how far we can stretch this." Her expression softened as a family moved up to the kettle of beans. "And where are you all from originally?"

"You mean Kentucky? Or you mean once we got here to Texas? We'd been pretty much set up in Harrisburg, but they turned it to cinders just before San Jacinto." The mother spoke. Her hands went to her apron.

"Don't I know about charred remains! I think about my oven hearth every time I try to find room for more than two pots of anything over open coals."

"Where'd you live?"

"San Felipe wasn't fit for a single bed after. Our bakery women stayed, though, and I wouldn't doubt a handful of good folks like you are bringing it back to some life."

After the man who'd taken a scolding, Shelby Whitmire moved up and stood before the woman with the ladle. He wondered if Mrs. Angelina Peyton's eyes would signal some recognition.

"That'll be fifty cents," the dark haired woman said. "Or a quarter, if that's all you can find. If you don't have it, I'll take barter." She had turned to straighten a ribbon on her daughter's bonnet. When she looked up, she appeared startled but puzzled, and not by the two loaves of bread Shelby had placed on the table.

"I was a bit younger than your son there, the last time you saw me, ma'am. I wouldn't recall that I was twelve, except you were there at my birthday celebration." The woman shook her head slowly. "I never told a soul you all were headed to Texas," Shelby said, smiling, "but it looks like I caught up with you."

"I don't…" The crease in Angelina Peyton's brow relaxed, and then a broad smile spread across her face. "My Lord." She was coming around the table to give him a closer look. A passerby and the boy who looked like her were beginning to attend to the conversation, and Shelby grew worried that her husband's secret was still a topic safer not discussed.

"I never told anyone that you and your husband were headed here," he repeated.

"Four years ago Mr. Peyton was laid to rest in San Felipe. I've been on my own with my son and daughter, and my good help from Tennessee." Shelby had assumed she was not the kind of woman to throw her arms around a virtual stranger or break into sobs. But he found himself grateful that she asked her son Alex to help Delilah finish ladling. She wanted him to sit with her on stools where the Peyton wagons touched, making a windbreak. While he got situated with a plate of beans in hand, he didn't mind her silent study of him.

"It was hard losing Jonathan. But I can't say my burned out home didn't take as big a bite from my heart," she admitted. "And to tell the truth, it may be I'm best off not having the cemetery a short walk from my front porch." She turned quiet again, as there was too much to put into easy words.

It's best to get on with life, Shelby thought, but it didn't seem a platitude worth speaking. He looked over at his tethered horse and thought about the bulge in his saddlebag. He would find out what he could about the fate of Thomas Weeks, he suddenly felt sure. Somehow he would find peace about the private letters that had been entrusted to him. He would mourn the loss of his earliest friend, and then, *Get on with life*. Hearing Angelina Peyton talk of her husband's place in a cemetery, he dismissed with more certainty the notion of seeing Mrs. Ann once more, to place the family articles back in her hands. In the conversation he had overheard as a boy, Ann Weeks had said herself that it was better to let some stories drift out to sea. If more could be uncovered about the final days of Thomas Weeks in Texas, Shelby thought, it would be for his own sake, for some clarity about letting life move along.

"Men with McLeod! We're set to bivouac south of town!" An officer coming from Columbia's main street called out. Alongside him was the adjutant general himself, Hugh McLeod, who directed his horse toward the Peytons' dinner wagon.

"Mrs. Peyton? Ma'am," he said tipping his hat to Angelina. He glanced in Shelby's direction, and the civilian suddenly began looking for a place to put his empty plate. "Captain Eberly is setting out soon to make a quick ride down to Brazoria—for any post from Velasco, any supplies we need." Mrs. Peyton was nodding, so Shelby wondered with some relief whether the officer would address him at all. The two men had not conversed since the day Private Moreland was felled with a single arrow.

"Did the captain ask you to pass that message on to me?"

"This is Hugh McLeod," Shelby spoke up. "The general here wouldn't be running messages for anyone. It would be the other way."

"Eberly will be over here, ma'am, as soon as he rounds up any stragglers. Sorry I didn't introduce myself," he said amiably. "The captain said I should look for a handsome woman and a line at the feed table." He still found it difficult to look directly at Shelby. "I mostly came by to make sure Mr. Whitmire knows about the speedy mission to Brazoria… if he still has a wish to go that way before festivities in a couple days."

A strange feeling came over Shelby Whitmire, that he had stepped back only minutes before from a strong current but was now being invited to walk back in, to see where a rushing stream would take him next.

"I think I'll wait until after the inauguration," he found himself answering. "I just promised Mrs. Peyton…that I'd scrounge any scrap wood and fashion another couple stools for her."

"We've been catching up some from earlier days," she said. She smiled at the man who had changed much since his twelfth birthday. "Mr. Whitmire hasn't yet accepted my offer of work at the inn I aim to open here, but…" The other officer had crossed the congested path.

"Good afternoon, Mrs. Peyton."

"Captain Jacob Eberly," Angelina said, and then she turned to the man in plain clothes. "This is our good friend from Natchez, Mississippi, Shelby Whitmire. If he stays here in Columbia, he may hire on at the inn, keep a watch on us when the military thins out."

"Mr. Whitmire." The captain had nodded to the newcomer, but he seemed more interested in reading the woman's expression. "I've come out regularly to check on the lady and her people this last week," he said to the men, "but I'm gone to other parts often enough. You can never have too many gentlemen looking out for…the families on their own."

"This is your friend…from Natchez?" McLeod couldn't keep from asking. He looked as if he suddenly perceived how volatile the interaction could become, if this was the unrequited love that had spurred Whitmire westward.

"We enjoyed the company of our mutual friend, Mrs. Ann Weeks," Angelina said wryly. "Now, there was a lovely woman. Any man looking to protect her needed to stand behind angels in a line longer than this."

"Well, Whitmire" McLeod said. "I may have missed my chance to enlist your services." His tone was oddly formal and tinged with uncharacteristic regret. "Lamar just let me know there are more cannons up near Cincinnati promised to the republic. I thought you might go along. I thought you might not mind passing by Natchez." Shelby felt he had been nudged closer to a rushing river. "Mr. Shelby Whitmire is my Indian expert," Mcleod explained to the others.

"Apokta." The name had come back to Angelina. Hearing it spoken, Shelby felt steadied enough to tell the soldiers that he appreciated being apprised of the jaunt to Brazoria and the upcoming mission to Ohio, but that he was inclined to stay in Columbia. He felt very much inclined to stay in the company of the Peyton family.

Both soldiers tipped their hats and got back to the errand of directing ranks to the southern extremity of town. Shelby hadn't felt so much like laughing for a long time. Somehow, an image came to him of the blur Angelina Peyton would have made. Had she acted on her first impulse long ago, back on the docks at Natchez, and leapt to squeeze her hands around young Shelby's throat, she would have made a dazzling blur in those suspenseful seconds. He had changed almost beyond recognition over fifteen years. Mrs. Peyton was the same woman, except that lifted secrecy had changed her expression.

"It won't hurt any for Captain Eberly to weigh you as a competitor for a while," she said.

"I like his manner. He didn't seem to itch for a duel."

"Like Burr and Hamilton," she nodded. So much of that night in Mrs. Weeks' house was coming back to both of them. "The captain has taken to riding out once a day to check on us. I like his manner, too. I've aged enough to appreciate a man with no hothead reactions."

"Your suitor might be right to consider me a challenge," Shelby said, making the lady smile. Gradually his grownup features were making sense to her. She had reconciled herself to his darkened hair and gray-flecked whiskers, and the slower, more deliberate movements of an adult.

"I'm trying to think if I heard more than twenty words from you when you were turning twelve. I do remember what a help you were to the Weeks family. That was an honest offer I just declared, by the way. We'll pay for your help and handy work."

"Thomas did most of the talking when it was the two of us out together."

"Inside their home, I recall you as mostly tongue-tied." Shelby had felt stricken when McLeod mentioned his "Natchez friend." It seemed only Captain Eberly let the reference pass unnoticed.

"Apokta used to tell me to speak up more. We ran a carpenter shop together, until last year." Angelina didn't take her eyes from the Mississippi man, and she wouldn't let go completely the topic they were both avoiding.

"You don't have to explain early love to me. Jonathan Peyton and I were sweethearts from the first times we played together as children. A whole piece of me was buried with him," she sighed. "But it was also the end of a burden I'd be best not explaining. Something weighing on my spirit for a long, long while." The little girl Mag came up to hug her mother's waist and then went off in Delilah's direction again. "It was clear you were in love with Mrs. Ann."

"She's Mrs. Harris now," Shelby managed to say. "And Thomas ended up with the Georgia Battalion—with those lost at Goliad most likely." Even Apokta had not made so clear a statement. *You were in love with Mrs. Ann.* "How did you know?" he asked Angelina.

"You weren't the only one with sharp ears and sharp eyes," she said. "How you felt about her was as easy to read as print in daylight." And then she added, "I can read your misgivings, too, about following soldiers where they're off to next. I know what it's like to be swept from one dilemma to the next. My marriage was like that." She looked in the direction that Jacob Eberly had ridden. "If I pledge matrimony ever again, it'll be for the serenity of a placid pond, not the thrill of a waterfall."

Suddenly, Shelby could picture the Columbia road in a few weeks, after the government trickled away to see about their far-flung electorate. There would be time next month for a ride down to Brazoria to see if any of Private Zeke Moreland's family still resided there.

He thought his carpentry skills would prove useful in the town where the friendly widow intended to settle and that his mere presence at a Peyton inn would deter any casual male nuisance. He had heard no mention of medical expertise in town, but he had grown secure about methods of preventing minor scrapes from becoming lethal infection. He could set a broken bone reasonably well, and he had already picked up some herbal remedies for light fevers from Apokta's family and from the Caddo in northeast Texas.

Having observed the captian's expression upon greeting Angelina, Shelby Whitmire was glad he still knew almost none of the answers to questions a female might ask a real doctor—what precautions an older bride might take to avoid pregnancy. He felt sure he would not advertise his experience with guiding babies from the womb into the chaotic world.

Never a Still Shore

Fall 1839, Austin, Texas

13   How the Heart Flickers

Busy as any Sunday was in the republic's new capital, it offered some rest. The Methodist Reverend Haynie and the Presbyterian "Sunday School Man" James Burke did not need to advise Austin against conspicuous drinking or public arguments. Even the regular loiterers who sat on a log in the open area outside Bullock's hotel on Congress Avenue needed no reminder to hold off from loud swearing.

But Shelby Whitmire had come to count on the following day as his respite from work. On any day other than Monday, Angelina—Mrs. Jacob Eberly now—needed his help at their inn just around the corner and down Pecan from Bullock's sprawling hotel. Only three years ago in Columbia, the captain and the new Mrs. Eberly had needed Delilah and Sam, as well as Shelby, to corral the brood of children from combined families. Mag stayed somewhat shy around her stepfather, who was often away on military assignments. She and the captain's daughter Julia grew partial to Shelby, as did Angelina's son Alex. So much concentration was required to keep up with all five children and to maintain their inn at Columbia that the family and Mr. Whitmire could hardly stay abreast of politics in the first years after revolution.

It was clear that President Sam Houston and Vice-President Mirabeau Lamar were never likely to sit down at the same cozy dinner table together. Shelby detected nothing conciliatory in how one faction discussed the other. Houston was characterized as "an Indian loving heathen hell-bent on turning the republic over to the U.S. government." Those siding with the first president thought Lamar was "a weakling poet who fantasized about sending muscular men all the way to the Pacific with the Texas flag." Nothing had changed since his days in Nacogdoches, as far as Shelby Whitmire could assess.

There was a peaceful stretch in Columbia after President Houston moved the capital to Galveston and then to the new town named after him, not far inland from where Santa Anna had turned Harrisburg to cinders. The Eberly household calmed enough that the newly married couple had time to consider their own investments and future. The captain had seen some beautiful land along the banks of the Colorado farther north. Though not as enthusiastic about those real estate plans as the captain, Angelina was appreciative that her new husband thought consulting with his wife to be a requirement. Though she stayed candid about matters of the heart affecting others, she seemed never to articulate her own deepest feelings. What Shelby quietly observed was an Angelina mostly free from worry. She enjoyed life as the wife of Jacob Eberly in a way she never had as the bride of Jonathan Peyton.

Even the new elections and the family's relocation from Columbia to Austin could not alter the convivial atmosphere at the Eberlys'. With Texas disallowing consecutive presidential terms, the second election went as predicted. Mirabeau Lamar achieved top office, and Houston won representative from the Nacogdoches area. The ensuing struggle about where next to locate the capital mostly had amused the captain and Angelina. They only shook their heads about Lamar's preference for an encampment off the northern Colorado called Waterloo, until the rumors proved fact. In a blur of transactions, Captain Eberly sold his own Colorado investment land and sank all their savings into lots where the renamed capital, Austin, was being planned by the visionary architect Edwin Waller.

Captain and Mrs. Eberly often patted one another's hands and marveled at their changes. One factor easing the family's move to Austin was that the children had matured. The captain's eldest daughter was already married and settled not far from Columbia, and the other girls were fond of Mag who enjoyed minding them. The Eberly boy was a good friend to Alex, now as tall as his mother. The youth looked like Angelina and appeared to have her verve for taking charge, too. Shelby Whitmire felt he belonged with this family. He, too, enjoyed more peace than he had known since a child helping out at the Weeks place.

Mondays allowed him time to follow his equal inclination for solitude, and he often let his horse meander west of Austin's main street. A wide embankment gradually cut way down to a picturesque stream flowing eventually into the Colorado. The stretch of land was punctuated by great twisting trunks of live oaks, and Shelby wondered whether this was where buffalo sometimes ambled in to drink, perhaps the great animal that the new President Lamar had spotted on his first hunting party here. The setting would have inspired a sermon from either of Austin's preachers about Eden and God's gift of natural beauty. After a group of peaceful Tonkawa and some Apache settled into an encampment closer to the Colorado, fears about Comanche raids as far in as town dwindled. Late one morning after a solitary ride, Shelby came back up into the far end of West Pecan where his friends' buildings were clustered. A man on the other side of the dirt road was shuffling after two squealing piglets and an angry sow.

"Where you been, Whitmire?"

"Along the creek."

"You take down any Comanche warriors?" Captain John Holliday, a regular at Bullock's, had asked him this question before, so the Natchez man just shook his head. His horse plodded to a stop near the smaller inn. A rare survivor from Fannin's doomed ranks, Holliday appeared to be driving the hotel owner's pigs back toward their pen across the way. "Come over here and threaten to take a tomahawk to these swine."

"What are they destroying today?" Shelby slid from his saddle and walked his horse in the direction of the hog pens.

"A box of books Mr. Burke had ready to move into his reading room, for one thing."

"They ate books?"

"Just some papers they were wrapped in," Holliday said. "Mrs. Bullock shooed all the drunks off the sitting log earlier—including me. Otherwise, I wouldn't have been easily engaged to stop these bastard pigs from—Git on in there!" Three more piglets were finally going in the direction of another sow finding the feed bin full.

"What did she bribe you with to take up this task?"

"Any half bottle I choose, but these animals are under my watch until after Burke's grand opening this afternoon. I'd better find McLeod and sign the next muster if I don't want *p-i-g* carved into my epitaph." Holliday could drink plenty without losing his mild disposition, and Shelby liked the man who was usually staggering. He felt a bit sorry for him now, because the whole town had been in agreement lately about the destructive powers of Bullock's pigs and their infernal ability to escape a pen. Frequent ransacking by the ungovernable creatures had become the greatest frustration for most Austin inhabitants.

Everyone in town still knew, though, what measures to take if the cannon were ever fired to signal a Comanche raid—they knew how fast they could move women and children to the government buildings surrounded by a ditch and spiked pickets. But consensus held that the warring Indians had been frightened off to some distance west of the new Texas capital. The day that oxen pulled fifty carts from Houston loaded with the republic's archives proved a thunderous din that could be heard for miles in any direction. Anyone marauding in Austin while the Texas government was congregated would face deafening and deadly repercussions. Treaties and posted bulletins paled against such a firsthand warning. The written word, Shelby thought, promised no more security in Texas than it had on the rough banks of the Mississippi. Still, he had wondered in the last weeks whether a copy of the *Natchez Gazette* might turn up at Austin's new reading room.

"Burke opened yet?"

"There was already a line at the front and along the windows," Holliday said. "He has some mercantile goods out for shoppers, too. But ole Sunday School Man says the doors can't open until straight up noon."

"Who's in line? Mostly your log sitters?"

"You don't see any other regulars sent to discipline pigs, do you?" The soldier laughed. "My drinking brethren probably just want to see what all that window glass looks like from the inside."

"I didn't help with the frames, but I had time to build half the benches in there." Shelby declined to say how much sturdier they were than his first efforts back in Nacogdoches. "Burke was smart to set so many panes—catch the daylight along Pecan and get the western sun in some. Hospitable reading light nearly all day."

"I might be the only sitter who can read more than my own name on a muster roll." John Holliday rarely made reference to anything military unless he had a bottle. There was never a reasonable time for Shelby to ask him if he'd met a private named Thomas Weeks while Fannin's army was at Goliad. "There were four ladies waiting, too. Started out five, but Doc Robertson came out of his office and called that assistant of his."

"She keeps steady at patching men up," Shelby said. With the doctor's dogtrot cabin just cattycorner from Bullock's, medical cases that fell to the physician's female aide made quick news. Shelby had at first paid attention to Adeline Harper with a sense of relief over not being called on himself to assist. But he could not help noticing her expressive movements and alert eyes, her thick hair sometimes still down on her shoulders if a patient called early for the doctor. "Doesn't look like much she can't handle when Robertson gets called away." The Eberlys' handyman was patting the neck of his horse Sawdust, and loosening the saddle, but he sensed that talk had not concluded.

"Whitmire?" Shelby had never heard John Holliday make a crude comment about a pretty girl, even when the man was too drunk to stand upright out by the log. He wanted to keep liking the Goliad survivor, so he wished he had gone on and led his horse to the stable before more conversation struck up. "Listen…I never asked you about something Bullock's cook told me." John Holliday looked as if he needed a drink to even finish asking the question. "Herman told me—is it true you once delivered a baby?" Shelby looked around to see if any of the Eberly brood had wandered out onto the inn porch. "None as ugly as me," Holliday laughed, "or you wouldn't have had the nerve to show it to its mama."

"No time to calculate nerve. Had to be done and I was there," the handyman admitted.

"Damn! You really did that? You really did that once?"

"The task fell to me twice." Shelby couldn't resist correcting the record, but he regretted his frankness right away. "If you speak about it to anyone, you might find yourself asking Miss Harper to set two broken arms."

"I know for a fact you can do a wood splint," Holliday said, "but I won't argue it would be more pleasant to have that Georgia girl leaning over me for an hour." The look that Shelby gave the Goliad soldier conveyed more than a verbal warning. He'd given that glare at least once to a sandy-haired man who sometimes sought company at the log. There seemed to be no topic other than females that the vagrant was interested in. No one liked the turn he was willing to take his musings in public. "All right," Shelby's friend said to him. "I won't broach either topic again."

The man heading now toward the Eberlys' stables just touched his hat brim lightly and went to groom his horse. He knew there would be opening hour crowds at the Sunday School Man's place, with shoppers and readers milling around on into the last hours of daylight. He thought he would edge across the intersection of Congress and Pecan just at dusk to see if Reverend Burke needed any help getting lanterns set. He didn't know what he would hope to read if a copy of his hometown's *Gazette* had made its way so far inland in Texas. He thought he might spot the name *Ezekial Harris*—the husband Ann Weeks had taken—printed in some business report. He couldn't say exactly how he would feel if by chance the Natchez paper might hold the report of a birth from that marriage. Shelby shook his head about the other fantasy that drifted to him—that familiar pages might contain one small announcement about the Texas hero Thomas Weeks, safely back home and in search of his longtime friend Shelby Whitmire.

By sunset, Shelby had spent hours in the hotel livery giving the family's horses special attention and talking to old Samson, whose arms were getting too stiff for the job in the last year. Shelby and Delilah minded the lobby and dining hall after the children begged Angelina to see the reading room. Besides a Bible collection, including one in German and one in Spanish, Mag told Shelby afterwards that she'd counted over a hundred other books.

A clothbound volume of *Oliver Twist* chapters had been donated by the wife of a representative from San Antonio. A set of children's books with pictures on every page stayed up close by Burke's register, and playbills from Louisville as well as New York were displayed nearby. Whispers circulated that Burke had allowed a novel by Balzac on the shelves, but the rumor was not yet proven. Among the newspapers was the *New Orleans Picayune* and one from as far away as Boston, the *Courier*, though the women were somewhat disappointed that it had not been that city's periodical better known for clothing ads and sketches of East Coast fashion. People streaming out of the new reading room were giddy from the announcement that their own first newspaper *The Austin City Gazette* would be kept on the premises, with extra copies given away after a week on display.

By early evening, Shelby Whitmire was ready to have a look for himself.

He could hear the voice of John Holliday over laughter from other men sitting again across the way. Notes from Mary Bullock's piano accompanied the merriment. The windows at Burke's place were showiest in the evening, Shelby thought, with the flicker from several lanterns making the large panes seem to shiver and bend. As he stepped up on the boardwalk, he was struck suddenly by the scent of new construction. He admired James Burke for his judgment about requiring cured pine timbers. The preacher had waited for some hauled in from the Texas eastern pines, rather than opt for the green cuts sent daily from Bastrop. A few experienced carpenters in town refused to discuss what President Mirabeau Lamar's fine house might look like as that raw lumber aged.

But they agreed that Austin's newest establishment would hold its hinges and shape.

Shelby found the Sunday School Man fussing over the cash register, just a few feet from where Doc Robertson's assistant was engrossed in a newspaper, and a family with two small children handled a set of picture books in awe.

"At one time this afternoon, four ladies sat together on that very bench," Reverend Burke said, shaking Shelby's hand. "You did a fine job. If it had been my carpentry, Miss Adeline there would have been too busy removing splinters to relax with her Georgia paper."

"I just thought I'd look around after your opening crowd dwindled."

"There's many won't read except by daylight—gives them vertigo. I judge this will be the usual ebb and flow, with a surge late in the afternoon after work is done."

"Mag and Angelina said you had newspapers from every part of the country."

"Houston and San Antonio, Brazoria and Nacogdoches—even half a paper from San Felipe— if you mean Texas," Burke said. "Lots of American papers, too, but I can't claim one from Mississippi." He knew what Mr. Whitmire would be looking for. "We might get an issue from Vicksburg before a Natchez paper makes its way here."

"I'm just now finished with this page in the *Macon Telegraph*," Adeline Harper said, gazing his way. Her expression was always cheerful, Shelby had observed before, but not given to silliness as young girls could sometimes be. "I'm going to savor no more than one page at a sitting." The physician's assistant began to neatly fold her paper up.

"Then I might ask Shelby to tend shop while I walk you home," the shop owner said. "I can't testify to the safety of these streets after the sun goes down." The young woman stood up and waved away the offer. On her feet, she looked no more than fifteen, even though she wore her hair up and carried herself seriously enough for her profession. She put her hands at her slim waist and gave the preacher a look that shortened both men's breath.

"If I can't cross the street and walk two cabins away after dark, I might as well be living in New York City and reading about the untamed capital of Texas."

"Don't ever try to argue with this precocious lady, sir." The preacher was putting on his blue velveteen jacket. "She'll be winning the debate before I get her over to the doc's office." Adeline shook her head, but her eyes sparkled. The family was also beginning to stand and notice the dark windows with surprise.

"I'll guard your readables," Shelby found himself addressing them all. His offer made Burke smile.

"I've asked Pastor Haynie to look for a Natchez journal next time his circuit takes him to the coast. We could get a paper in from your hometown before Christmas."

"The Ocmulgee isn't quite the Mississippi," Adeline observed to Shelby, "but Macon's shipping news and social postings might quench your nostalgia some." Angelina Eberly's handyman was suddenly struck with a lapse of easy words, when a raucous round of laughter came from those sitting across Congress in Bullock's side yard.

"I'm going to see you home and wait until I hear your door latch click," Burke said. "I'll bet your Aunt Maggie is worrying away, and Yarico, too."

"My aunt isn't herself if she's not cultivating a worry." She nodded to both men and slipped her arm through the preacher's as they turned to the door.

"I can vouch for the harmlessness of most that loiter at Bullock's, but a bottle and the dark is a dangerous mix." Shelby couldn't believe he'd made the comment or deny his pleasure when the Harper girl paused to face him again.

"Yarico will walk a mile off her path to stay clear of where spirits are being uncorked."

"Let Mr. Whitmire tell you sometime what he grew up with on the lower banks of Natchez." Adeline Harper glanced back into Burke's reading room once more as he led her out onto the wooden walkway. The family had buttoned their wraps and headed for the doorway, too. The November evenings cooled quickly.

For the next several minutes, Shelby enjoyed the peace and pine smell in the grand room, and he found the front section of the *Macon Telegraph* as soothing a read as Doc Robertson's assistant suggested it might be. The ads for steamboat travel and delivery of goods did remind him of his hometown. New shops were opening "only blocks from the courthouse on Mulberry." And among the more personal announcements was an article about a choir director, who had "just moved with his family from Natchez, Mississippi, to our Georgia town." The man was expected to lead the singing at a new Methodist sanctuary on the main street.

Shelby Whitmire could only wonder at the whims and callings that shifted the human population across borders so. He marveled at how he and Thomas had ended up in Texas; how the first Mr. Weeks had worked first in New York and then built homes in Natchez; how Hugh McLeod's father had chosen to move from Scotland to America. He wondered how in the world three women from a town in Georgia could now be living in the remote capital of a new republic—where a village only a year before been little more than a cluster of primitive cabins. He sensed that the reading room would nurture the Eberly children's interest in geography, much like the Mississippi back in his hometown fed his boyhood curiosity about travelers who might next be floating around the bend from upstream.

"What was it like in Mississippi?" Mag asked Shelby two days after Burke's opening.

"The sky was blue. The trees were green. But Natchez by the river was different from anywhere else I guess."

"I found a paragraph saying two murders happened in New Orleans on the same night."

"That's in Louisiana, but bad news can happen anywhere. Were you reading that by yourself?"

"Alex showed me. Anyway, I can sound out words on my own."

"Your brother should have found a lady's page for you."

"I made out the word "fire" easy enough…and "funeral.""

"Maybe you should read with Julia next time."

"She and Mama were looking for fashion pages. Oh, and there were three pages from a San Felipe paper with an announcement about this baker woman they call Free Ann, who used to be a slave. She went and married a Mr. Lopez, just like any lady might. She already might have a daughter—I remember Dolly, but—"

"Hush, Mag…what's that shouting?" The bell in Bullock's sitting yard was being flailed, too, but, there was no cannon going off. It didn't sound as if an attack was underway. Then Mr. Whitmire caught the sharp smell of pine smoke, and Mag put her arms around his waist. There was very little other than the smell of burning buildings that could make the innkeeper's daughter react in terror. By the time Shelby and Angelina's family ran to the corner, people were racing from every direction with basins and buckets. Reverend Burke was out in front of his new store, wringing his hands and pointing at the smoke spewing out from the roof.

"Help! Help me get my books away from the fire!"

"Someone take the water wagon down to the river!" Captain Holliday was shouting. "Wet down anything nearby! The whole street could go up!"

In the next hour there was a massive effort to retrieve stocked items from Burke's main floor, where he had stored dry wares for fully expanding as a mercantile. Bolts of chambray and calico were carried across the way and set on Mrs. Bullock's piano. The lower shelf of her china cabinet was crammed with parcels of sugar and coffee. The closest building with shelves for the preacher's books and newspapers was Dr. Robertson's office. Outside the front door, the doctor himself participated in the chain passing reading material away from the quickly engulfed building. Inside the medical office, the Harper women were scurrying to find places for whatever could be saved. When Shelby Whitmire came in with an armful of newspapers too fragile to be passed off, he stepped onto the porch of the dogtrot to find Adeline Harper taking charge of emergency arrangements.

"Any books bound in leather should go up off the floor. A western storm can send water under the door—"

"How about newspapers?"

"Better put them up on the apothecary ledge for now," she said pointing. "I don't think they'll be too heavy. But if they go on the floor, people are likely to forget what's being set on top of them."

"I think the last of the books got out." He set the newsprint on a shelf, and worked his empty hands into his pockets.

"Thank the Lord!" The girl's Aunt Maggie had been pacing in the walkway between the treatment room and the women's quarters. "Adeline would have gone into pure mourning if any more books were fed to flames." For a moment it looked as if something was too painful for the Harper girl to speak of.

"I had to leave my mother's volumes in a makeshift town near the Brazos," she told Shelby. They were all out of breath. "When the scrape came...and there was nothing to do but run east and save lives, nobody had a right to try to take books. When we finally came back through—"

"We could hardly tell where our half cabin had been," the aunt said, squeezing a handkerchief. "Who could tell if a charred pile had once been *Robinson Crusoe*."

They could hear shouting in the street for everyone to stand back. As night closed in the air remained still, and there was surging relief that the fire would be easily contained to one building.

"Miss Angelina came back to cinders in San Felipe," Shelby said, sympathetically. "The ruined linens were what pained her most—the blackened hearth. I don't think she had many books."

"Or time to read them if she had been in possession of a library." Maggie pulled her shawl tight around her shoulders. Her last name was Linder but she was more readily identified as one of the Harper women. "I've never seen a woman throw herself into work any harder than Mrs. Eberly does. If I didn't go over for a coffee at Bullock's near the same time Angelina does every day, I couldn't testify that lady ever sits for a minute."

"Looks like they've cleared the place out!" The doctor came in to announce the end of the retrieval effort. "Nothing left to do now except watch the place burn to the ground." He was distressed, but also cheered that there had been no injuries. Formerly Waterloo, the entire capital might have been consumed, had the wind been gusting as usual.

"Come sit on the porch and rest some, Mr. Whitmire," Adeline said an hour later. "My own head feels light, and you've hauled several loads at a run." She took one end of a bench Shelby thought might have come all the way from Macon. "I often stay put here. Since the doctor is off representing the Bastrop district so often, I try to stay where his patients can find me." They were both looking in the direction of the burning shop, and Shelby had a sudden dread of turning his head too soon and having to look directly into her hazel eyes. "I've seen enough of blackened buildings," she said quietly. "I suppose we'll all be witness to the charred remains being cleared and hauled away. Poor Mr. Burke."

Miss Harper was the first person, Shelby realized, to directly state concern for James Burke. Of course, everyone had joined the effort to recover what was salvageable and make sure the fire didn't spread. Without warning, the wind could kick up in the middle of Texas. Water had been drawn from the river several blocks to the south. Rushed in wagons up Congress, any left would be used to douse embers. The whole town would sleep better knowing that nothing else was catching fire.

"I'll be fixing some wash basins, Miss Adeline." It was Yarico who had stepped onto the porch. Shelby had noticed that the family's helper was always with the other two, much like Delilah was never far from Angelina. "There will be enough perspiration and soot that you and your aunt might want a basin before bedtime." She herself often sat out alongside Maggie and Adeline in the evenings, but only if the doctor was conspicuously present next door.

"Thank you," Adeline said to the woman. Then she turned to Shelby, and he felt his chest pinch as if he had inhaled smoke. "Mr. Burke keeps his horse at Angelina's stable, doesn't he?" He nodded and brushed a streak of soot from his pant leg.

"I didn't understand that about men, how important a horse was, until we started our journey from Macon. Then in wide open country…" She didn't seem to be in a rush to finish her thought, and Shelby realized he would be willing to look off toward the ruins of the reading room and wait a long time for her to speak. "When everyone was crowded at the Brazos and the ferries were threatened, we couldn't have crossed without our own horses, worn out as they were." Her voice didn't waver the way her aunt's had earlier, but she glanced away toward the river end of Congress before saying any more. "Did you grow up riding, Mr. Whitmire?"

"Never sat on one until I headed in the direction of Texas." There was a popping sound and hissing as water found a hot spot in Burke's charred store.

"Our poor Sunday School Man," Adeline said again. "He's talking like he'll rebuild. I suppose he will."

"Cabins on the shore at Natchez sometimes went up. Even right on the water, there's not much you can do most times."

"That town was mentioned in Macon's paper."

"Due east from here, I figure. Right in the middle of the state's river border."

"It's old, like Savannah and New Orleans, isn't it? Lots of French and Spanish buildings. My aunt and I, and Yarico, we couldn't believe what fine structures New Orleans had. So many people speaking French. Made it seem like another world—we might have been happy to stay there."

"I didn't know where you ladies came from originally. Mrs. Eberly said Bastrop."

"It was Macon for most of my childhood. That was all I knew as home, off the edge of town in crop land mostly, then in town for just a few weeks, really—I believe close to half of Fannin's army came from that part of Georgia…some from Alabama."

"John Holliday—the captain partial to Bullock's sitting log—he came from Kentucky with Duval's company. The only Fannin man I knew from way back…was a friend from my Natchez home." He didn't bring up Thomas very often and he felt a shield slipping away from his emotions.

"How did that come to be?" She had asked Shelby in a way that surprised him. She was asking more than the route he had taken, more than geography.

"He was just a boy, at loose ends…after a change in his family." Suddenly, Shelby felt a wave of reasons not to tell Adeline Harper about the woman who was Thomas Weeks' mother. "Lots of young men raised on the Mississippi… just out on their own…would take a riverboat down to New Orleans—take on one odd job or another, enjoy the city, and come on home with some tales to tell."

"Like so many Macon boys getting the urge for adventure after William Ward's speech in November, '35. By the time every glory speaker said his piece, I was near ready to sign up for Texas myself."

"My friend's family got one last letter from him." Shelby turned to see she had looked up at the star-filled sky. "My friend Thomas said he'd met up with some Georgia volunteers—that his steamboat home had burned at the New Orleans dock and there was no way home any time soon anyhow."

"We all thought our boys would be home by spring."

The young woman stopped talking then, and they could hear Aunt Maggie softly snoring where she had settled in a rocker. Workmen who had built Burke's store gathered not far away with other townspeople to discuss rebuilding after a burn. Most spoke as if they had experience. Over at Bullock's, a charred piece of counter was placed in the outdoor fire pit, and jars of ale were served as consolation to Burke and comfort to those who had fought the blaze. There was plenty for Shelby and the young Harper woman to watch silently.

Shelby's face grew warm in spite of the evening chill. Somehow he didn't want Miss Angelina, kind as she was, and as good a friend, to happen upon the scene on the doctor's porch—an aunt sleeping while a man and a young woman kept company easily without words.

"Well, thank you for letting me sit a spell, Miss Harper."

"Wait—what you just told me, it means we each had a friend at Goliad that terrible day."

"Miss Adeline?"

"If they weren't together on that Palm Sunday, they were surely with Ward in New Orleans and went to Texas together as far as Refugio and Goliad—"

"Thomas Weeks was as much a brother as…"

"Weeks! We had a Mr. Weeks in Macon. Your friend likely had kin in our town. My neighbors would have thought so…Francis Gideon, Joseph Tidwell, Malacai Mulholland—tell me again what your friend looked like. We might have spotted him with our Macon men there in New Orleans."

"I hadn't figured you to know the Georgia men that Thomas signed on with. You're saying you came all that way at the same time?"

"We were fortunate to ride by wagon. My aunt and Yarico and I had been stitching blister patches ever since our men marched across the Alabama line. While the schooners were being stocked for going on to Velasco, more shoes were sent to where we lodged across town, maybe even your friend's shoes."

"Adeline? Are you telling about our lost boys? Are you telling Mr. Whitmire about my nephew Matthew Linder?"

"I'm sorry, Aunt Maggie." She turned to Shelby quickly and shook her head. "The fire got me to thinking…how loss of belongings is a much lesser sorrow…."

"Mrs. Linder, Miss Harper, I appreciate your letting me rest."

"You come back some time soon," Aunt Maggie said, getting up weakly. "Next time, I'll tell you about the brave boys in Gonzales."

"I've heard some," Shelby said. "They rode on in to the Alamo to help."

"But we think my nephew went south to help on the mustang ranges, or…"

"Nice to talk a bit, Mr. Whitmire." Adeline had stood and was smoothing her skirt. "Dr. Robertson gives your medical experience good credence."

"Friends of friends…" The older woman started to say. "Oh, that's Yarico tapping on the window. She's drawn a washbasin for us, Addy. Goodnight, Mr. Whitmire."

During the next few days, the entire population of Austin appeared to be on edge. The odd euphoria over having banded together during the crisis and of having escaped widespread conflagration subsided into shortness of temper and malaise. Few in the newly built capital moved near the acrid ruins without recalling a smoldering wreck in their own history. An Austin resident could appear to be going about daily routines and then suddenly explode in a fit of worry or disgust. Angelina Eberly thought her handyman Shelby Whitmire had taken a morose turn. She didn't like to see him brooding so, and it was well worth having Alex and her stepson care for the stabled horses, if an extra day off would soothe the nerves of the Natchez man.

"Why don't you ride on down to your spot at the creek?" she said to Shelby. "It'll be another week before all hands are needed to haul off the blackened beams over at Burke's. There's nothing going on here, except readying a room for the Refugio widow."

"I think I will."

Angelina was surprised at how quickly her industrious helper took her up on the suggestion. She knew the man had known hard times as a boy, and there was no telling what might trigger a dark sense of loss. The day was beautiful, and she was glad to see him harness Sawdust and ride off.

After letting his horse amble for a half hour, Whitmire came up on the ridge where he could look down to the familiar creek bed. The commotion of Austin subsided to nothing, and he found the scene below unusually quiet. On Mondays, Tonkawa children sometimes played upstream from where the women washed clothes. The sounds of their activity would echo through the ravine, but this was Saturday. Shelby always welcomed the solitude, and he didn't mind the extra quiet today. He wished, though, that his own thoughts would take on more calm. He had been chastising himself since the day of the fire for feelings he thought he had abandoned at the Mississippi.

It was one thing for a boy to develop romantic longings for an older woman. Shelby didn't know how he would forgive himself if he allowed his admiration for the doctor's assistant to flourish. If he wasn't too old for Adeline Harper outright, he was too worn down by a bad start and heavy torch to appeal to her. He chastised himself again for the conflicting thoughts that had swept over him on the Harpers' porch. When Dr. Robertson's young assistant spoke the name of Thomas Weeks, he'd felt an oven's heat on his face.

Today, he wanted to discard such vulnerability to emotion. Alongside a creek, an impressive row of mature live oaks rose just far enough apart to let their wide limbs angle off curving trunks and reach out toward each other.

"You almighty fool," Shelby muttered out loud. "Is a curve of any kind going to make you think of girls barely past childhood from now on?"

He wanted to ride down into nature at its loveliest today, and to be able to laugh at himself when he came back up the embankment. Later, he would give little Mag a pat on the head and do an unexpected favor for Angelina Eberly. She would accuse him of trying to win her away from the captain, and he would count himself lucky to enjoy such platonic affection.

Angling farther down the embankment, Shelby Whitmire found the rustling leaves of giant oaks uplifting, and gradually the ripple of the fine wet creek struck him as melodic. The last time he'd so readily welcomed nature's solitude, was along the Trace west of the Mississippi when he was delivering mail to Fort Jessup. In these last three years of bustling activity, there had been little chance for reflection. But he felt himself moving toward peace.

He let his horse move at its own pace and they made easy progress along the edge of the winding brook. The animal, too, seemed energized by the scene. The crowns of the live oaks were broad enough that the green canopy allowed only scant underbrush, and the creek banks appeared lovingly tended. The man from Natchez gazed upon this landscape as if it were startlingly new, yet he sensed that the trees and rippling current looked much as they had in early autumn for the last two centuries. It was a pleasant contrast to the mile-off town recently just a clump of crude structures. None of the six hundred witnesses to Mirabeau Lamar's inauguration would bet on Austin's standing as long as fifty years.

The handyman and his horse Sawdust ambled down onto softer ground that would surely be covered with water whenever the heavy rains fell. Shelby dismounted and picked up two pebbles not far from where the brook gurgled. He didn't doubt that they had been warn smooth, maybe washed downstream to this point, by some deluge in any season but summer.

Shelby's untethered horse followed along behind him. The pebbles made clicks against its hooves, so that the man did not hear any separate sound at first. A soft thudding came from another horse finding its way down off the ridge on the opposite side of the creek. In fact, Shelby had kneeled down to look at a particularly interesting rock, one Mag might like—it was pink with tiny clear sparkles, and it seemed to weigh more than a sandy piece. The handyman did not even look up after a faint whinny came from the opposite shore. He thought it was his own horse that had wandered off to nibble a tuft of green. When he looked up to find the lone, mounted Indian with a taut bow, Shelby only had a moment to stand and raise a hand as if the motion would halt action long enough for him to rethink defenses. His rifle was still slung alongside the saddle, out of reach. Sawdust was equally slow to turn and notice they were not the only creatures in the creek bed!

The arrow struck Shelby's right kneecap, but it was unlikely that the Comanche missed his mark. He had plenty of time to finish the white man off however he pleased, and he let his mount plod across the creek where Sawdust watched warily, his leather straps hanging loose along his mane and neck. Even when Shelby made an agonizing effort to stand, even when he managed to aright himself on his good leg, the Indian did not appear threatened or worried. He only edged up within a rifle length of the free horse and leaned over to reach out for its reins.

"No," Shelby said. If the aggressor did not understand that word, it was clear that Sawdust did. "He's mine. Don't take my horse."

The Indian looked briefly and with only casual interest at the wounded man, probably understanding the one word very well. But he seemed curious, perhaps somewhat jarred, about the absence of malice in the horse owner's voice. When the lone Comanche leaned far over to secure the harness strands, Sawdust stamped and backed up suddenly. Two hands taller than the pony, the white man's horse made it awkward for the stranger to gather the leather strands. The menacing hooves then came off the ground and caught the Indian off guard. For a moment, the thief looked shocked that the man with an arrow in his knee spoke to soothe the animal, but it was too late. One hoof struck the mounted man in the forehead before his spotted pony could back away from engagement. Now both men were on the ground, but only Shelby stood, wobbling, as the other man appeared to have taken a blow that knocked him from his mount and consciousness as well.

Shelby hopped and hobbled, the arrow still protruding from the fleshy part of his knee. He had never known such pain, and a dull admission came to him that his stepmother's whippings had caused mostly humiliation. He wanted to cry out, but what he had seen women endure in childbirth and men suffer on the battlefield made him growl instead like a groggy bear. He staggered to his rifle before the Indian came to. In his acute sense of urgency, he had no confidence that he would be able to fire off a lethal shot before his assailant could send a second arrow flying. Maybe this Comanche had heard about the giant buffalo Mirabeau Lamar felled a year ago on what was now Congress Avenue. Maybe he had been warned about the terrible harm most white men could do with rifle shot. When Shelby got to his horse, he pulled hard on the saddle horn so that his weight was only momentarily on his right leg and knee where the arrow still protruded. With his left foot in the stirrup, he was able to pull himself astride.

When his dazed adversary came to with a groan, Shelby was mounted and the rifle barrel was aimed down at him. He regarded his attacker carefully before sliding the weapon back along his saddle. With Hugh McLeod's men, Shelby Whitmire had met groups of Caddo in their huts, and Cherokee to the north of Nacogdoches were often watching from their horses. He had spoken with Chief Bowles of the Texas tribe and watched as that leader's mounted men sat ready to strike. Why Shelby should have felt surprised to see a human face so unlike his friend Apokta's he didn't know. His friend's smooth features and quizzical brow suggested a capacity for humor. His hair sometimes went out of place as he worked with hand tools. The familiar sash that Apokta set aside before work flashed in Shelby's recollection.

This Comanche wore no shirt at all even in November, and except for a blue paint smudge on his chest and woven leather strings dangling from his earlobes, he wore no decorative dress. He was clothed in leggings and a loincloth. But Shelby examined his face—the pronounced cheekbones and a wide jaw both set low. His eyes conveyed no sign there had ever been mirth, but they prompted a question as Shelby set his rifle aside. The Natchez man held his hand to his own forehead and then gestured at his attacker.

"Are you hurt bad?"

Shelby had Sawdust take a few steps back and he sweet-talked the Indian's pony into moving closer to the fallen man. He was not so foolish or so brave as to get down and help the Comanche back on his mount, but after urging Sawdust quickly up the hill, Shelby turned to see the Indian walk his spotted pony to a low oak limb. He watched the man climb from the thick arm of the tree onto the animal's back, and then sit erect. He couldn't be sure if the Indian spoke to his pony or if he meant the syllables to travel uphill.

"Yoo-ruh," he thought he heard the Comanche say.

The Mississippi man made a sweeping gesture that Apokta had taught him as a peaceful way to signal goodbye. He could not be sure that he was not being followed, and he hoped to remember—to shout a warning to the first person he saw as he came up on West Pecan. Only a minute later, though, the pain in Shelby's knee throbbed to a new level and a powerful nausea overcame him. He began to sweat and an odd taste hung in his throat. If his attacker were racing up the hill to send a second arrow straight into his back, where it would be lethal, Shelby had no strength to take aim.

By the time he reached the first log compound just down from Eberly House, the trees looked like green kites and the dirt traded places with the sky. Just outside Angelina's porch where he tried to dismount, he ended up flat on his back with the pain in his right knee screaming—the arrow jammed farther in. He wondered if his own sustained moan and Mr. Bullock's screeching pigs, as good at sniffing out chaos as creating it, might be the very last sounds he heard in this world.

In the next few days, or it could have been weeks, Shelby distinctly made out Dr. Robertson's voice. He had spent some time in the office of the doctor's dogtrot cabin where books had been rescued from Burke's fire. Then Shelby could hear Angelina's voice and her daughter Mag or the captain's daughter, asking if he was sleepy, if he needed anything. He was then moved to his own room on the west side of the Eberlys' inn, and he sensed there was nothing that could be done about the pain in his knee, so he never tried to work his lips to say anything. On most afternoons, it was Delilah holding a soupspoon to his lips after the captain or Alex came in to sit him up in bed. Even when feverish, he worried that he was taking too much of inkeepers' time. A paying customer would have little patience for skimpy service.

One morning, when his knee throbbed less, he grew aware that conversation out in the hotel dining room centered on "the man with the wounded leg."

"Well, I know Adeline's been peeking in at him since it happened, but Dr. Robertson wanted her to change the dressing this morning." Shelby recognized the quavering voice of the young woman's aunt. "I told the doctor that a lady back in Macon or even in this rough town can't go into a man's bedchamber without a chaperone."

"I've stitched up men before." Miss Adeline's voice conveyed equal amounts of amusement and irritation. "Sometimes there was no one else in earshot, and the man's pants were hanging on a doorknob." The loudest laughter at that observation came from Angelina.

"Addy, one of Mrs. Eberly's guests might hear!"

"Maggie, I'm glad to get to know your niece better in these last two weeks. If I want to keep my reputation for matchmaking," she laughed again, "I'll have to take into account what a rare sense of humor she has. I need to adjust my thoughts about who might meet Miss Adeline's requirements best."

"Uh-oh," Maggie interrupted her. "She has something of a temper, too, if you carry that topic too far." Shelby's knee only bothered him at the moment with a dull pain, but the throb at his temples grew pronounced.

"Never mind, Aunt, just let me step in shortly and see to Mr. Whitmire's bandage, though the doctor says this patient can wrap a wound as well as anyone." But the two older ladies often enjoyed coffee together near Bullock's front window, and the Harper aunt couldn't resist going on with her line of chatter.

"One gallant youth in Brazoria was all but ready to take her as a bride, but she wouldn't even entertain the topic."

"Aunt Maggie, I aim to see to the good man's injury with or without a chaperone standing watch."

"Not that every boy in the schoolhouse wasn't in love with her!" The older woman caught Angelina's look of surprise. "Oh yes, she did school teaching before she jumped up and took tolerable well to all this doctoring."

"Dr. Robertson said after this changing, Mr. Whitmire can probably let the wound finish healing in the open air." The embarrassed niece spoke to Mrs. Eberly, and Shelby heard her step closer to his partly opened door off a short hallway.

"If you find a likely match for her, Angelina, it'll have to be a fellow who pens a more romantic letter than the lovesick Zeke Moreland did back in Brazoria. However, she still keeps that envelope he handed over the day we left."

"No one who can't keep silent is going into the sick-room with me." There was muted laughter after Adeline's stern warning, and Shelby made his eyes close as the door to his room opened slowly. He kept them closed when he heard his name spoken, but he couldn't withhold a soft groan after a chair was pulled up by his bedside and the blanket pulled back from his swollen leg. Other steps settled near the doorway, but Mrs. Linder, must have heeded her niece's warning to stop all chatter.

The doctor's assistant had a natural touch, and she slipped one hand under Shelby's knee while she loosened the layers of gauze with the other. The patient's face flushed with shame over the appearance of his leg and the dank bedclothes. But he didn't resist Adeline Harper's gentle tugging, then sponging and rewrapping.

"Mr. Whitmire?" He looked directly at her, and found her eyes more flecked with green than he had imagined. He knew her hair to be brown, but strands swept up at the side caught light streaming in from his window. When she put her hand on his arm where the sleeve of his nightshirt had been rolled, he nodded to her and thought his fever might have started to tick up. "I hate to see what happened to your knee, sir. But we're all so glad there was no assault on any part more vital. It's healing well, just as the doctor said. I expect you've concluded as much."

He couldn't keep himself from picturing the arrow that had protruded from Zeke Moreland's chest.

"I'll live, it looks like."

"Reverend Burke says his own knees are worn from praying on your behalf." She looked fuzzy when he blinked and looked at her again, because tears had welled. He shut his eyes, hoping she hadn't noticed. Trauma could make any man helpless to conquer feelings. "Well, it's still rest that you're most in need of." Her voice was in the calming tone of a trained medic. "Your leg should get some air this next week. Don't fancy yourself walking without help, though, until the doctor or I come test your steadiness."

He could only nod, and she patted his arm again before pulling the blanket farther up on his chest.

"All right, Aunt Maggie, let's go home and tell Yarico that Mr. Whitmire is truly on the mend. She's usually the tough one." She surprised Shelby with the comment and a sudden turn in his direction from where she stood. "She's done nothing but tie and retie her apron strings since the captain and Mr. Holliday brought you in." When he smiled back at her and quickly shut his eyes, he could not suppress a thin tear from trickling to his pillow.

After the door was closed behind them, Shelby stared at the ceiling he had helped put in. He wondered if Thomas Weeks' father would have admired the carpentry. "Still wondering whether approval is deserved," he chastised himself. He knew emotions ran high in anyone bedridden. Still, he could not bear the way she made him feel. He and the girl had only talked about books that evening on the Harper porch, and about the odd ways people come to travel far from home. "Still wondering if particular eyes are looking at you from kindness only," he said, swallowing.

He stared at the ceiling and wondered if his wounded friend Thomas had lived a while to look up at stars or a friend's face or a fine tree. He berated himself for never having taken on any battle except for the struggle to tamp down his longings.

He could hear the Eberly House door open and close, and his own window jiggled from the November gust that swept through the first floor. "Damn you, Shelby," he said again to himself. "You're already thirty. She likely just turned fifteen, if that." But he couldn't promise himself that he would tell Miss Adeline about Zeke Moreland's death the next time he got the chance to talk with her. He didn't think he would ever work past the pain of climbing onto Sawdust again, not if he first had to let the doctor's assistant cry some on his shoulder in mourning of first love.

1839 Knoxville, Georgia

14   Ritual

"Where you headed, Papa?" Johnny had been watching his father tighten the horse's stirrups. He already knew the answer.

"Just going to ride over to the inn. I won't be long."

"It's because of today, isn't it?"

"What do you mean?"

"The 20th of November."

"How come you recollect so well?" John Spillers went over to the porch steps to sit for a while. He knew his older son had changed in the three years since he had been home from Texas. But he was still trying get over the change he'd seen in Johnny on the day the battalion marched through Knoxville. He waited for the boy to speak.

"I never told you about…the rest of my November 20th."

"There was lots we never told each other about the day I left with Ward's men."

"I took my knife down to the creek."

"After you walked to town with that cornbread?"

"I couldn't go home." The creek was a good three miles from the Spillers cabins. "I went to the creek and sat until afternoon. I carved the date in a cypress tree. Then I sat until it was near dark."

"Your aunt must have been sick with worry."

"She thought I stayed to see you off, maybe to see all the people at the inn."

"Aunt Martha knows you better than that."

"What do you mean?"

"You're like me. You wouldn't have stayed to visit with strangers. You would have come on home."

"She never said anything if I made her fret."

"She's like your mama. They were good sisters."

"I still miss her." The man looked over at his saddled horse, and suddenly he didn't know if he would have the energy to ride into town with his letter. He waited to see if the boy had more to say. "When I walked to the inn that day, I thought you would never come back."

"I feared the same myself."

"But you never talk about it, what it was like."

"It was hard, son." Nothing would ever prove more difficult for John T. Spillers to talk about, not even the death of his wife Matilda. "It was hard to stay alive. It was harder facing up to how many couldn't stay alive." The two sat for a while on the porch step without speaking. Lately, the father had noticed that his son was almost as tall as a man, though his face would still be boyish for a long time. He looked to be turning another question in his mind.

"Did you ever get that Spanish land scrip for your time?"

"I forget it was promised most of the time."

"Mr. Stovall from over in Macon, he's still pestering Texas about paying the volunteers, isn't he?"

"I don't suppose the payment will help him feel much better. He's like a lot of others whose sons are never coming back. It's the honor his boy deserves. That's what he's after. Feels it's his duty as a father, I'm sure."

"Is that why you went?"

Mr. Spillers nodded, but that was a question that had rattled around in his own mind when he was in Texas, and was still unresolved in his thinking. Some of the men who perished had gone for nothing but duty. Some had gone for glory. His son wanted more than a nod.

"I was cross…because I didn't know why you had to go."

"In the worst times over there, I wasn't sure myself," the father admitted, trying to find words that wouldn't keep him awake that night. "That November, we all felt we were going where we were needed. For another thing, I thought the future would be more secure for you and Will and Eliza. We were promised a soldier's compensation." He put his hand to his jaw before going on. "We thought we were headed to a fair fight, that's for certain." Johnny had turned his head away toward the other cabin at the end of the path. The father knew his son was too grown to be calmed with a pat on the back, the way the little ones could be. "Why don't you ride on in to town with me today. Go saddle up Davy. He won't mind a morning walk."

In a few minutes, the two were letting their horses amble away from the cabin and Aunt Martha came to nod at her brother-in-law and wave.

"All I know, is by the time I had sloshed through half the mud on this earth—and done all in battle I ever care to—it was a medic wagon that came along and finally picked me up, took two of us as far as the ferry to Galveston. And then a few days later, a ship was on its way to New Orleans. I guess if it hadn't been carrying Sam Houston, wounded from San Jacinto, they wouldn't have been so friendly about taking along a pile of ragged bones like me."

"Maybe the general himself paid your way."

"Victory made everybody generous. And any coming from…where we'd been…where I'd been…" Spillers' son knew that the word *Goliad* was too painful to speak. The boy was sorry he had made his father think about it all again.

"Are you mailing another letter? You never get an answer back it doesn't look like."

"I can't explain why it makes me feel better to put it in the post." Both horses moved along the path without prompting. "I never do expect one back. But I still feel somewhat better about things."

"How come the other soldier wanted to stay in Texas?"

"*Wanted* might not be the right word. After San Jacinto, more than a few ended up staying. A lot of them boys already had families in Texas. Or it was just too hard to picture being back home where they'd come from." Spillers paused. The father could see that his son was still curious about the letter, and since he never sealed it until it was ready to go directly in the post, he offered the brown envelope to the boy. Johnny read as if he were in the classroom, aloud and slowly so that he could be corrected.

"Dear Mr. F.D. Bahia…Is that his name?"

"Never told me his name. It wasn't very easy for him to talk at all. But he gave me a name no one else would collect letters for."

November 20, 1839

Dear Mr. F.D. Bahia,

Here in Knoxville, there is still some squash coming in. Cotton was a bit poor this fall because of scant rainfall, but it was worse in other parts, so the price is good for those that got their planting in.

The family is doing well again this year. My brother and his wife have four children now. Their baby keeps us all in stitches. My three grow another inch every time I look. John is nearly as tall as I am. He is very good with all the little ones and also with the horses.

I have been talking pretty regular with a real nice woman after church meetings, but I ought not to report any news on weddings except for the one everyone in Knoxville is sure about.

I don't usually make reference to anything about our trials in Texas, so I only ask you to think how fine that banner first looked flying up atop the presidio when we were still together with Fannin. If you picture it, you might remember how some of us from Georgia knew it was a sweet Knoxville girl who took it on herself to sew the white flag with its blue star.

The whole town is happy now that she is set to marry a gentleman from right around here. Colonel Troutman would sorely miss his oldest daughter had she chosen to settle too far from their inn here in the middle of town. I imagine the ladies will do up some memorable decorations. All of Knoxville will be at the occasion.

That same inn is where I go every November to mail your letter.

I keep a hope that you are making your living well in Texas. I stay thankful about how good it was to have some friends along the way when we were all in worst times.

I can't fit but three pages in an envelope, so I will close until next year.

You have a home in my prayers.

Your friend,

John T. Spillers

Johnny had been letting Davy slow to a stop, but the inn was in sight now, and Mr. Spillers waited while he let his own horse nibble at a clump of green. Today, he felt, the boy should speak his own mind first.

"Does Sam Hardaway know about the church lady yet?"

"I didn't even know until I put it that way on paper, son."

"When he comes around this time of year, you and Mr. Hardaway usually ride a ways toward the creek and woods. And when you come back onto the trail, sometimes I see you've been laughing. Usually, it's only the baby can get you to laugh."

"Most times we find something to laugh about, because we just finished shedding a tear." Mr. Spillers took the envelope from his son and creased the flap back down. "Young Sam will keep that spirit of his if he lives to be a hundred, I expect. It's no wonder he's got his father's business going so brisk. Some days in Texas, he kept me alive with his good humor."

"Can I ride out with you this time, when he comes around?"

"I don't think he'll mind. We often don't talk much, but sometimes—"

"I won't talk. I just want to listen."

"Well, I hope you hear what I'm saying now, son. I'm never riding off again where you can't come runnin' with a scoop of cobbler."

Up ahead, the colonel was standing out on the porch of the Troutman Inn. The fellow next to him was likely the gentleman Joanna would soon marry.

"I like her, too, Papa."

"Who's that?"

"Miss Adams. The nice woman after church—I like her, too."

1840 in Austin, Texas

15   When Seeing Is Not Believing

On the day that fifty oxcarts arrived from Houston with the republic's archives, no one living in Austin thought the spectacle could be rivaled. A half year later, though, the approach of a delegation from France brought residents to the boardwalks and dirt spaces along Pecan Street. Alphonse Dubois de Saligny, from the first country to recognize Texas as an independent republic, was due to arrive with his entourage along the Bastrop Trail at the end of winter.

It had been over three months since Shelby Whitmire's injury, and Angelina did not want her handyman and friend to suffer a setback in his recovery. She advised him to avoid the crowd.

"I'll be glad when all this fuss is over," she said to Delilah. Shelby was at her dining table drinking coffee before guests at the inn arose. "Why I ever told Bullock I would help get things ready for French royalty, I can't explain."

"Mr. Whitmire and I can see to company," the family servant said. "Alex and Julia will help, too, though I suppose they'll want to wait in the street with everyone else and say they waved to the king of France."

"He's not the king, but you'd think he was the man in the moon for all the special accommodations being made at the big hotel." She reached for her bonnet and coat. "I thought Mary Bullock had more sense than her husband, but she's had the cups from her china cabinets rinsed and linen table cloths set out. The Harper women have hemmed more napkins than—"

"Miss Angelina, if word got back to France that Texas doesn't know a teacup from a spittoon, next thing they'll believe is we sleep in dirt and give up our beds to the pigs."

"Well, you're not far from the truth there!" The innkeeper was laughing, along with Shelby. "I'll surely die of shame if a band of those creatures run off from their pens just when *monsieur* makes his appearance at the end of Pecan. Though it could be French people won't even know what's attacking them."

"As I recall, the country has a long history with pork, Angelina."

"Well…" The innkeeper squinted at her handyman for his tone. "Since you know all about the French, you won't need to crane your neck to see some firsthand. If I find you abused your leg for a close-up look at royalty, you could maneuver yourself out of a job here." Delilah just shook her head at the outlandish joke. "You might have to hire yourself out as permanent pig tender."

"I've no interest in jostling with the onlookers," Shelby said. "Besides, he'll be in town awhile. We'll all get more than a glimpse of him."

"If his group numbers as high as the Bullocks fear, even their overflow cabin yonder will be past capacity. We can watch French comings and goings while we sip from our own rustic teacups!"

In the next month, Shelby Whitmire was more than relieved he had not put extra strain on his weaker leg in order to see the Frenchman's arrival. There were far more attendants accompanying de Saligny—who preferred to just go by "Count"—than could be housed in Bullock's main building. The hotel man had more cabin lodging in the rear of his two-story structure. From inside the Eberly House, the parade of slender women in lush silk gowns, and occasionally the dignitary himself in a glistening overcoat and elegant hat, could be observed by Angelina's people and guests.

Shelby was half energized, half depressed, by the other activity that transpired often enough within sight of Angelina's front steps. Though de Saligny spoke English easily, most in his company understood only French. A woman in charge of maids and other female attendants could use English, and so could the count's secretary and footman. But there were often exchanges where an interpreter was needed, and all Eberly House had come to understand that the Harper family's Yarico, of all people, was one inhabitant of Austin, Texas, who could speak without halting in both languages.

The women's helper, of course, rarely ventured beyond her own doorstep next to the doctor's unless in the company of Miss Adeline or the aunt. Shelby had seen Delilah's mouth unhinge when talk between Yarico and the count's maids became so animated one afternoon that the Eberly dining guests ceased their own conversation to listen.

"I see it," a woman from Refugio said, "but I don't believe it."

"Most of the count's servants don't understand a word if it isn't French."

"I wouldn't have thought the Harpers' help could speak a syllable in any language until French royalty came to town. Ordinarily, she's as quiet as a fence post."

"She knows she's off the main street," the wife of another guest observed. "I can vouch for her proper demeanor, even if she's laughing too brightly right now. I'll testify she did the best mending you ever saw on my favorite bonnet, one that got torn by wind on our first trip out here."

"But who would have thought her to speak French like that?" Angelina Eberly had noticed Shelby pretending to dust powdered sugar from his sleeve.

"I took a pudding over to the Harpers one day when Miss Maggie was poorly. Inside, Yarico hadn't had time to put her hair up, and it struck me she might be the most comely female that ever was in bondage." Shelby Whitmire had stood suddenly, and then everyone at the guest table could see that Adeline Harper and the companion under discussion were walking with purpose toward Eberly House. There was a soft knock at the door, but the doctor's assistant declined to come in. She just wanted a word with the innkeeper's handyman out on the front porch. It was both knees bothering Shelby equally, and he could feel Angelina's eyes on him, as well as those of the Widow McIntyre from Refugio. The two had been discussing for days what man in Austin might be a good match for the attractive widow, and Shelby thought he would try a long ride on Sawdust once his conversation outside ended.

He nodded to Yarico before he let his gaze meet Adeline's. The servant remained mute as was her custom, and she studied the dirt path in front of the inn.

"I didn't want to put an idea in your head, if your leg is still bothering you for any such travel." The young woman was carrying a book and she put one hand then the other on its cover. "The doctor says there's a group of soldiers going to San Antonio next month." She could see that Shelby was unaware of maneuvers not involving Captain Jacob Eberly. "Something about meeting with Comanche leaders. It could be a treaty that leaves us on more peaceful terms."

"I haven't heard."

"Well, it's not about soldiering that made me want to ask you. It's about doctoring." She went on to tell Shelby that there was a German surgeon in San Antonio who was in possession of a liquid developed from European experimentation. A patient could be made to fall asleep, long enough for a doctor to operate with no conscious trauma to the injured person. "The San Antonio physician is just now trying it for pulling teeth, until he gets confidence about the formula. Can you believe it?"

"I hadn't heard."

"Aunt Maggie was over at Bullock's yesterday, and she heard Mr. Holliday say he was going along with the company that bivouacs northeast of here, up near the Salado stage. Maybe he's already taken a captain's rank again." She stopped as if she suddenly realized how much she had been talking. Shelby Whitmire had been nodding with only half a notion what her purpose was.

"Holliday's going to San Antonio?"

"When I heard that, I thought you might be going, too."

"I didn't know about it."

"Yarico and I are happy to see you on your feet." She turned to the woman behind her and Shelby imagined that when she looked at him again she was blushing. "Any proper doctor would warn you against jostling your knee more than necessary, but you know as much about how folks mend as I do. If you do go," she went on, "here's the name of the San Antonio surgeon." She had written the name *Weideman* on a slip of paper. "If you go and you have time to watch one of his procedures, I'd be attentive hearing how it was done and if the sleeping concoction can be ordered by any means."

Shelby watched the Harper women head down the block toward Austin's main crossroads. He gazed after them just long enough for any observer inside Eberly House to figure he might have been assuring himself of the ladies' safety. But then he decided to move on to the captain's stables and offer his help to Samson. With Angelina and the widow in deep consultation for the last week about how unmarried adults should be matched, he did not want to risk getting interrogated about whether Miss Adeline had lowered her eyes or blinked or smiled at anything Shelby said. He was the one in awe of the young woman's enthusiasm for medicine. If he could have relived the scene, he would have volunteered to look after the fragile aunt and household while Miss Harper traveled to San Antonio to learn firsthand about the latest surgical miracle.

In the third week of March, Shelby took his place comfortably enough on a wagon seat next to one of Hugh McLeod's privates. The adjutant general was in charge of the contingent prepared for two days of travel and a weeklong stay. In Austin, McLeod had only passed word along through a corporal that Mr. Whitmire would be welcome, since a dozen other civilians had reasons to go. When not engaged in medical observations, he was requested to stand by as something of an interpreter while authorities tried talking peace with the Comanche.

In traveling from Austin to San Antonio, Shelby was affected in ways he could not have predicted. The sky itself seemed to open and enlarge, providing a dome wide enough to overhang the earth. It struck Shelby for the first time how different Texas was in the more western parts. Far to the east up in Nacogdoches, one was either in a forest or could see the edge of woods no matter where one's horse was directed. Then, there had been no reason to take the Camino Real, the old road aiming straight at San Antonio. Instead, McLeod's group had angled south that first summer after the revolution, because Columbia was far down the Brazos. Again the undulating land with all its river crossings had required a constant consciousness of changes in terrain. From Austin, though, the route to San Antonio sprawled into monotony. Somehow, once the Colorado had been crossed, uninterrupted stretches allowed a wagon passenger to consider the interior landscape for a change. Shelby found hope welling, despite the nondescript scenery and worrisome conversation.

There were two topics that the wagon driver, a wiry man with nearly white hair, could discuss with no input from Shelby—first, recognition of the republic. The question went beyond whether Mexico would ever concede the independence of Texas. The visit of a dignitary from France spurred musings about how soon the United States would follow suit. Any Texan in his right mind, the soldier contended, would embrace countries willing to promise loans on a grand scale to the new republic.

"Do you have any idea how long it's been since I had hard money in my pocket?"

Shelby shook his head, and tried to remember whether it was as far back as Natchez that he had touched payment coins.

Other talk was about what prompted the excursion to San Antonio— what could be done in the western regions of Texas to squelch hostile Indians. Some recognized no borders whatsoever with settlers, whether they spoke English or Spanish. Most feared were the Comanche, especially after the murder of Cynthia Ann Parker's family. The abducted child had been missing since the year following San Jacinto, and though there were periodic sightings, she'd never been located, much less rescued. Other white captives were known to be held and transported from one region to the other. Since the Comanche ranged freely all along the western plateau, the republic's military felt their primary concern—other than watching out for any new incursions from Mexico—was to reclaim kidnap victims and perhaps convince the nomadic Comanche to leave Texas altogether. McLeod's private said officers couldn't agree about what strategy might work best with these chiefs.

"I reckon your knee being on the mend don't ease your grudge against the savages any." The soldier leaned over to spit, and Shelby weighed his answer.

"My horse evened up the score enough for me. Knocked my attacker unconscious."

"No wonder you're bringing the animal tethered." He looked back where Sawdust trotted behind. The tasseled saddle lay in the wagon.

"The arrow was pulled out from my knee entirely," Shelby went on, "but the flesh that went with it hasn't grown back much. One bone chip was removed before cauterizing."

"Well, the army will likely never take you." He swore and then laughed. "That's curse or blessing depending on how much you like missing meals. Or marching your hindquarters off as murderous heathens wait to ambush."

"I suppose I've been on my own too long for soldiering to appeal."

"Never heard General McLeod say he loves the army, but I'm sure any West Point man would rankle if told he had to quit. Can't see him satisfied selling reams of muslin and sassafras sticks." Up ahead, someone bellowed orders and the man tightened both reins. "The arrow that gone into the general's thigh last year hasn't dampened his career any."

"Into his thigh?"

"Somewhat before you yourself got attacked," the private nodded. "The doc got the shaft clean out but the point is still sitting in his upper leg. Doesn't even feel it most of the time, but he had a bout over the holidays that kept him from taking ladies to the dance floor."

"When did he get in a tangle with…the Indians."

"Half the battalion was called up back toward Nacogdoches—you didn't hear about ole Chief Bowles finally getting his due? All his warriors got killed or run off and the chief, with that big hat of his, just sat down in the middle of a field, just sat down and let the death shot get him, like he deserved." Shelby had heard mention of the chief's death in the previous summer, but the details made him eager to keep his distance from soldier conversation.

That evening, he promised himself he would try riding Sawdust on into San Antonio the next morning. He was relieved that Hugh McLeod had not found time to speak with him or make the awkward compliment about his being "the best help at Indian peace-talks." The Austin handyman studied the German name Adeline Harper had written down. He hoped the surgeon's office would be some distance from the Council House where a dozen Comanche chiefs were to gather for parley about prisoner exchange and lines of separation. To fend off reflections on McLeod's injury and the death of Chief Bowles, Shelby tried imagining a city big enough for a two-story meeting building, a city with avenues and structures almost as old as the Alamo itself.

The one time he walked the length of Natchez-on-the hill, he'd been too distraught to appreciate its Spanish buildings. Three small adobe buildings stood in Nacogdoches outside the perimeter of the original log fort, and Shelby had also seen drawings of Mexico City and the town Santa Fe far up to the northwest, but he had never entered a town made distinct by its mud structures with rounded corners. San Antonio was a shock.

The concentration of adobe and red tile rooftops hushed the forty soldiers that made up General Hugh McLeod's party. Uppermost in their minds, too, was the fourth anniversary of the Alamo's fall. Once the military contingent settled into tents, with most officers finding their lodging in town, several rode to the mission at the southern edge of San Antonio to pay their respects. Though earliest March was celebrated across Texas for the date independence was declared, a palpable gloom descended on the city when losses at the Alamo were recalled. Citizens of Mexican ancestry moved warily, and Shelby was surprised to hear more German spoken in some streets than English or Spanish. The Eberlys' handyman rejoined the soldier steering the military wagon, and an Austin family wanting to view the landmark Alamo rode along in the bed.

"These days, even Juan Seguin can't live hereabouts without hostile encounters. He risked his own neck as much as Crockett or Bowie. Folks just don't know," the soldier under McLeod said. "They say Seguin might be driven all the way to Mexico for his own safety. He was born here in San Antone, you know. It's a shame." Whitmire was thinking it equally shameful how most white settlers could not differentiate between a man as friendly as Apokta and a callous marauder.

Even with his natural gait lost to an arrow wound, Shelby understood each tribe to be distinct, each member no less unique than any individual in an American town. He was remembering Tail Feather and Fleur and the whole Creek family living so close to his Natchez cabin, when he realized that General McLeod was angling his horse toward the wagon paused near the Alamo gates. Shelby touched the brim of his hat before speaking.

"I hope there's some result better than annihilation day after tomorrow."

"That's why I'd be obliged if you stay close to the Council House that morning." They had not really spoken since Columbia, or conversed as friends since the early days in Nacogdoches.

"I'll be watching a German doctor administer a sleeping potion while he operates—a Dr. Weideman."

"If you can just maintain presence in the plaza. With your civilian clothing, you could lend a sense of fairness to the parley."

"I didn't have much success on my first encounter with a Comanche," Shelby admitted. He wondered which thigh it was that McLeod now favored.

"We expect some captives speaking English will be brought along. Sometimes their first look in years at an army uniform strikes as much terror as…"

"I'll come out to the courtyard after Dr. Weideman pulls a tooth. An old chief is expected at an early hour, an elder the doctor treated years ago for a snake bite." Shelby could read the worry in Hugh McLeod's expression, and he was grateful for not having the weight of negotiations resting on his own shoulders. If the two men had been sitting on Bullock's log, Shelby might have sympathized about the general's arrow wound, but the officer headed off to lodgings.

On the morning of the Council House meeting, Shelby went out with Dr. Weideman to the side of the plaza where a cluster of Comanche leaders and some of their family had stationed themselves. A silver-haired man in a European overcoat the same color as his braids came out from under one sun canopy. A boy young enough to be his grandson followed. The Indian dignitary extended his hand to the German doctor and Shelby thought the greeting showed genuine warmth. It was the small child who appeared most nervous about the procedure his grandfather was about to undergo. The doctor, with his bushy beard and oddly shaped eyeglasses, spoke soothingly as he led the way back to his office. His white shirt and red suspenders made him easy to follow in the crowded side streets.

What Shelby observed in the surgeon's treatment room took an impressively short time. Instead of having to subdue a patient writhing in pain, Dr. Weideman used only seconds to lay a clean bandage soaked in the formula over the old man's face. It took little more time for the doctor to secure pliers around the afflicted tooth and pull in one clean stroke. Not until the physician brandished the bloody molar did the boy let his emotions show. He turned to Shelby and let the stranger place a comforting arm on his shoulder. When the grandfather regained consciousness minutes later, a celebration followed as if he had awakened from death.

"Ees goot now, my friend, no?" The patient and doctor shook hands again, and the Comanche elder next gripped Weideman's wrists for emphasis.

In a state of euphoria, Shelby walked the grandfather and the boy back out toward the plaza. As the old man found his way to the shade canopy, the youngster stayed on the edge of the open area to watch three blond boys kick a leather ball back and forth. Meanwhile, the meeting time drew near and tribal leaders more grandly dressed were coming forward on painted mounts.

Riding in first were regal chiefs who wore buffalo headdresses. Their leggings had been painted blue, and one of the men wore a silk shirt with ruffles. The Comanche were reputed to be excellent bargainers, and they appeared proud of the clothing they had acquired in barter. Two younger warriors wore deerskin shirts painted green and yellow. In their braids were woven strips of animal fur, coyote or jackrabbit, Shelby thought. He found himself searching for the one fierce expression that he had seen close up before, but was not surprised that the shapes of their faces and set of their eyes were different from any he had seen before. He could not discern eagerness or apprehension underneath their steely front.

All the warriors were required to place their bows and rifles down outside the courthouse. On a pallet pulled by a palomino was one of the hostages that the Comanche had agreed to bring into town. The captive's head was covered with a shawl, and some of the military men whispered that if she proved to be the only prisoner surrendered by the Comanche, the whole conference could go awry. When the pony was brought to a stop, wives of some of the officers permanently stationed in San Antonio were escorted to the hidden woman. In hushed tones, they spoke to the captive.

Still exhilarated by the tooth extraction he had just witnessed, Shelby was engrossed watching a contest between the local youths and the visiting boy. They aimed to see how far a leather ball could be kicked. Inside the deerskin outer layer, the sphere appeared to be stuffed tight with straw and stitched smooth so that it rolled easily. When the ball went past the Indian youth, Shelby stopped it with his feet and sent it back to the yellow-haired brothers enjoying the competition. All four of them were laughing, as well as some of the citizen spectators gathered by the council building. It was twice the height of other adobe structures on the plaza, though several impressive domes rose up over the earthen buildings surrounding the crowd.

A first sign came that events would spill the wrong way. One of the wives who had gone to talk to the hostage had turned her head and begun to sob. The other woman controlled herself with difficulty, while helping the young lady under the shawl. The hostage's head was kept covered, and she was led to a shop alongside the meeting place where unarmed chiefs had entered and doors were latched.

"Oh dear Lord," one officer's wife spoke to Shelby. He turned to her and her eyes conveyed a wild horror. "...they went and cut her nose clean from her face."

"Who...did ?"

"It's healed. She said they did it more than a year ago." Then the woman broke into tears and took hold of Shelby's arm. "They cut it off her face, poor thing—vile beasts!" The game in the street stopped, and the little Comanche boy, who had been smiling broadly a moment earlier, looked urgently over to where some braves remained on horseback, waiting for their elders. The boy looked next for signals from an older woman who stopped grooming the palomino with the pallet. Every face exuded dread.

Suddenly, a barrage of rifle shots rang out from inside the Council House, and one wooden door was being splintered from the inside. A hatchet blade wedged near the door handle and the entrance fell open. Whatever one chief yelled just before he slumped, his arm wiggling at the handle, his shout made all the Comanche waiting outside yelp and cry out. Propelled by urgency, they made frantic efforts to escape. The woman who had been guardian of the hostage was lifted onto the back of an untethered pony by one brave, and when she motioned to the boy he sprinted toward her. Halfway across the wide courtyard, the little fellow jerked as a bullet ripped into his back. Hearing a man behind him shout, "Finish off the little heathen," Shelby lunged after the child and felt a lead pellet burn into his own shoulder before he fell on top of the small motionless form.

The last Shelby Whitmire heard in the plaza outside the Council House was a shrieking and crying powerful enough to wring the bark from a live oak. Then a dull roar in his ears took over. With his eyesight and consciousness fading, he could only make out futile escape efforts of Indians who had been on horseback waiting for their elders to finish negotiations. In moments of consciousness in the next few hours, he imagined he heard the Mexican soldiers at San Jacinto crying out in despair as they were backed up against Buffalo Bayou. He imagined the nightmare screams of Fannin's volunteers scrambling a step or two toward Goliad's river before being cut down.

He did not know whether it was hours or days later when he began to make out distinct voices, but once again he was disoriented. He could not understand the words of a bearded man standing over him.

"Ya…ees goot." Then Shelby was aware of the speaker lifting a bandage from his shoulder and speaking directly to him. He felt a wide hand move gently where the gauze had been. "It swells, Mr. Whitmire, but not too much. You will sip some broth today. Tomorrow or the next day, maybe sit up." He waited for Shelby's eyes to focus.

"Is the boy still…the Indian boy…is he…?"

"They tell me dis bullet you had in your shoulder is for him." His mustache moved and Shelby thought it signaled a faint smile. "Now I know it is true. The boy has it not so good. The lead was near his spine. Perhaps he will walk again. Perhaps not. It falls into God's hands now."

"You took the pellet out?"

"I use the new sleeping liquid," he said, nodding. "Not enough for you, but you were already unconscious. And—this death everywhere—the boy is not to blame."

"Where is he?"

"Just in the next room." The physician gestured and then appeared distracted by his own palms. "All in God's hands," he said again.

An unusual concentration of doctors practiced in and near San Antonio, Shelby learned, ever since German immigration began spilling out onto the escarpment not far west of the capital. With many able to convince Indians they encountered that they were not the same people as the English speakers, several German communities had established trust and trade. But as far as Dr. Weidemen knew, the child was the only Comanche treated after the Council House slaughter. The dozen chiefs inside the meeting hall had been killed outright, and twice that many were mortally wounded in the street or chased down by patrols and vigilantes.

"Who knows if dis is what was the plan all along?" The doctor put his hand up to his lip. "Or outrage about the poor woman they brought in, only one hostage and so pitiful. Maybe that drives the anger. From a soldier telling, it was twelve warriors inside suddenly raising their hatchets, but a preacher holding a Bible says the men in uniform drew rifles first to kill." The doctor looked off to the room where the boy lay in critical condition. "We will never know—only that we haf too much death—always—too much killing."

When Shelby was able to walk, he took some comfort that it had been his right shoulder injured—he was thinking once more about being able to grab a saddle horn with his left hand, put his left foot in the stirrup. Now, both his knee and shoulder on the right side were of less use than before, but he could move his other limbs well enough. He swore to himself he would eventually get on his horse and ride. Hugh McLeod stopped by to see his progress firsthand, and both men knew there could be no casual discussion of the disaster.

"We're heading back to Austin in the morning," the general said, having spoken no more than a word to Shelby in a long while. "It's already been a fortnight, days longer than we thought we'd be, but we had two men ride post to let President Lamar know…what transpired."

"The Eberly House ?"

"I'll stop by myself. I'm sure the captain's wife is worried."

"And short on help."

"Angelina's boy and stepson appear old enough to fill your shoes," McLeod said. He stood without speaking, and both men appeared sworn to avoid recriminations. Such slaughter elicited only solemnity from men of character, soldier or civilian. "Looks like you and Dr. Weidemen have become friends. You should stay for a few months, help him a while… heal properly yourself before you think of taking the road back." McLeod shifted position, his earlier thigh wound likely troubling him. But when he raised his head, he was looking toward the room where the boy still drifted in and out of consciousness. Someone had surely apprised the general how Whitmire came to receive his gunshot wound. "If the child never remembers what happened, he'll be lucky," McLeod said.

"He was just playing with the other boys." The lump in Shelby's throat made it hard for him to go on. "What came to my mind, before the hellfire started, was how Thomas Weeks used to enjoy a rare morning for play on the Natchez strand…He and I would…"

"I wouldn't have taken a bullet for the boy in there."

The two men had first met over three years ago. The revolution was like that, bringing total strangers together, in a closeness that brothers seldom felt. But Whitmire studied McLeod, and both men sensed they were at a crossroads.

"You wouldn't have caught this bullet," Shelby Whitmire said, ready to end the conversation, "and I wouldn't be wearing that uniform, I suppose."

Fall 1840, Austin, Texas

16   Lost and Found

By early September, Shelby Whitmire had grown attached to the boy they all called "Yoo-rah." It was the one word the child had said over and over as Dr. Weideman and his wife tended to him. The handyman from Austin had heard the same expression come from a dazed attacker down in the creek bed, and he thought it was probably Comanche for *thank you* rather than the child's name. But it looked to be a miracle the boy had not been paralyzed. Youruh could walk by the middle of summer. And by fall, he appeared at ease with the name his caretakers had given him, and eager to help in small tasks at the surgeon's office.

San Antonio after the March disaster, though, was not a place where a Comanche any age could move about the streets freely. When Shelby began grooming Sawdust and readying himself for the ride back to Austin, it was decided that Indian boy would go with him. There was no telling where any of his surviving relatives might be, if others waiting outside the Council House that fateful day had been family. The grandfather whose bad tooth had been pulled was killed as he tried to reach the wounded child. All the bodies had been moved to the edge of town and buried well before the youngster regained awareness and health.

"Ya, ees goot he cannot speak the questions in English," Dr. Weideman said. "But he is maybe only six. With children this age, lost memories help da healings. Perhaps he will always have that day forgotten."

It was certain that the cruel loss of so many elders had dispersed the nomadic Indians deep into west Texas for the time being. Shelby and the physician decided that Austin's citizenry would be less jittery about repercussions. With political wrangling foremost in the minds of residents there, it seemed possible that one small Comanche could be brought inconspicuously into the capital of Texas.

Shelby and the boy slipped into town with less commotion than he might have predicted. When he stepped from a side entrance into Angelina's dining hall, the woman was overcome with emotion.

"I little realized how much you cheered our family when Jacob was out on a far-off duty," she said after hugging him and hiding her eyes in the edge of her shawl. "Then word comes back that a surgeon is working to take a lead ball from your shoulder and…"

"There were dozens worse off."

"Just when you were regaining strength in your knee," she said, stopping herself to take full notice of the brown-skinned child positioned behind Shelby. The boy had smiled shyly when she wrapped her arm around the man, but under scrutiny his expression became solemn and alert again. "Shelby, I don't know if—"

"I thought Youruh and I could make ourselves comfortable in the stable for a while. It may be some of the Tonkawa by the river have a better place. For now, the room where I was staying may be a bit too formal for his comfort."

Angelina Eberly was trying to take in all that her handyman implied, but she appeared grateful she would not have to explain to anyone why an Indian child lodged inside her hotel. She had guests, right or wrong, that might prefer to shelter in a tent alongside Bullock's pigsty.

"Samson only takes up one corner. I can get Alex to help you string up blankets and make the space amenable. But I don't want you taking on any tasks for a good long while, Mr. Shelby Whitmire of Natchez. I've almost lost you twice now, and the third threat to your survival might not end as mercifully!" She took one more glance at the boy, who now only gazed at the floor. "Since you left, there's been a shift away from goodwill in this town. Lord knows when these hurt feelings are going to mend."

It was after dinner and too early for supper, so no guests loitered. The child sat behind the counter where Delilah warily set a plate of peppered beans before him. Angelina began telling Shelby how the Count de Saligny's second visit had torn the town into spiteful opposition. He had purchased a beautiful young Caribbean consort in New Orleans. "A delicate thing with hair going on blond, a tiny waist," Angelina said, shaking her head. "And by the time the count's coaches made it four days through the blistering July sun, the pretty slave girl was pale enough to pass for white." Not a one of us in this republic, in possession of domestics or not, could abide what he did bringing her here. Anyone could see she was too delicate for our outpost and climate. It was terrible to see the little thing dragged into Bullock's lobby, all but dead."

"Did the Harper women come over, like before, to see how their use of French might help?"

"The only talking needed was with the undertaker." Something crossed Angelina's expression, like an understanding that Shelby would ask soon enough about how Dr. Robertson's immediate neighbors were faring. "I've seen Miss Harper's Yarico walk on her own down this way since then. So much has changed."

"The doctor's assistant, then… Miss Adeline, she's hasn't suffered from the heat or…"

"She's suffering from what ails everybody else, that's what I'm trying to tell you." Angelina looked over at Delilah, who nodded that she was doing all right in getting the boy to accept their cooking. "With everybody vexed at the count, he was in a rush to move his entire parade right next door to us in the big cabin that went vacant. Now there's only a handful of folks still friendly with de Saligny's people, and near everyone else cursing the count's footprints. Bullock won't let me have coffee in his dining hall with the Linder woman anymore."

"How can it be the fault of Adeline's aunt that the courtesan died?"

"Well, I'm leaving out one detail that makes matters fester. The count, according to Richard Bullock, didn't pay up his bill for the month he spent in a sickbed over there. That stagecoach trip damn near killed them all," Angelina said bitterly. "I surely am proud you had sense not to travel home until September, though it's still hot enough to wither anyone not toughened by the revolution." She stopped herself from that train of thought. "Say, you'll never guess who briefly boarded right here at Eberly House rather than dine under the same roof as Mirabeau Lamar—Representative Sam Houston of Nacogdoches! If he'd uttered one snide word about my cooking, I'd have pinned him to the hearth with my soup ladle. He should suffer hellfire a good while for his order to set San Felipe ablaze!" She shook her head. "Listen to me, no better than the others in this tinderbox town."

To Shelby Whitmire it appeared there was enough heat left over and enough grudges to go around that the entire city had been transformed in character during the months he'd spent recuperating in San Antonio. Gossip flew: about how much the count owed Bullock; whether Bullock had double charged for doctor care; which white people besides the

Harpers and the Presbyterian Reverend Haynie had attended the black courtesan's funeral at the northeast edge of town; about how often the count's secretary threatened to slay pigs that wandered into his herb garden at the West Pecan cabin; about the speed with which de Saligny might be recalled to France for apparently failing in his diplomatic assignment; about how soon Bullock might find rifle shot to be a more satisfying remedy for the insult of an unpaid bill.

One day, Shelby happened upon Yarico walking toward the count's compound, and he paused to ask if she'd let Miss Adeline know he was recovered and glad to be back with the Eberlys. But the social chasm only grew between anyone with French connections and all associates of the Bullocks—including Angelina, who consulted with and helped the hotel owners when peak occupancy called for it. The older woman Margaret Linder and her niece Adeline Harper discontinued their strolls toward the French compound, which would have required their first passing by the Bullock Hotel. As a courier for seamstress work that the Macon women often took on, Yarico traveled the short distance discreetly.

"I don't bear a one of those women any ill will," Angelina said, hushing a dinner guest later in the week. "And I don't know what part of Africa their Yarico came from—her original people—but I wouldn't doubt she had a regal ancestor."

"That's all I was going to say, Mrs. Eberly—that her fancy work is superior, so it's too bad the Harper ladies are known as well for their French—too bad they're now at cross purposes with so many folks."

"No one in this town bears the Harpers ill will. Miss Adeline has done a medical stitch or made a poultice for just about every man in this town." Shelby was glad to hear Angelina speak up, because his head had begun to pound. Now he and the innkeeper were both looking out to the street where Yarico had just passed by. "If that man staggering doesn't learn not to relieve himself in public view…"

"That sandy-haired vagrant?" The guest turned in her chair and shook her head. "I once saw him shaking his fist at the Harpers while they sat on their porch—like he had any connection to this infernal dispute."

When Shelby readied Angelina's rig one morning at sunrise, Youruh was standing at his side with a hopeful expression easy enough to read— whatever errand his protector had in mind, he wanted to go along. The boy wore a western hat shrunken from rain, but still big enough that it flattened out his ears over his glistening black braids. His bright, wide-set eyes eased the man's mind about the excursion's purpose—getting the boy acquainted with the Tonkawa settlement on the outskirts of town. Shelby felt, too, that the child's company would make him feel more natural about looking for an opportunity to say hello to the marginalized Macon women.

The man could not believe his luck when he took the rig to the corner of Pecan and Congress and saw Miss Adeline coming out of Dr. Robertson's office with a patient, a youth about Alex's age, on crutches. She was turning, carrying an extinguished lantern, and perhaps about to return to the women's side of the dogtrot. The avenue remained clear of other wagons, as well as pigs, and Shelby took the Eberlys' rig across the way. Whatever troubles the ladies suffered from their friendship with some of the Frenchman's staff, he couldn't find anything but an easy cheerfulness in her greeting.

"Who's your partner this morning?"

"This is Youruh," he said, putting his hand on the boy's shoulder. "We both had to stay under Dr. Weideman's care in San Antonio for a good while." Shelby staunched the impulse to add that the first infant he delivered had also been named *Thanks*. Adeline just nodded soberly and then glanced across the street toward Bullock's, shaking her head.

"That German sleeping potion might be what's needed in Austin these days," she said. "Maybe the capital of Texas would next wake up to its right senses." Shelby smiled, but with Youruh by his side, he refrained from bringing up how the liquid had eased a tooth extraction for the child's grandfather.

"We're headed down to the Tonkawa outpost. A boy needs to see some people his own age…" He let his sentence trail off, but he had the sense Adeline Harper knew he meant *the same color*, as well.

"Not long before Santa Anna took the Alamo," she said, "we were guided toward safety by a Tonkawa man. I don't know what my aunt and Yarico and I would have suffered without him." When Shelby touched the brim of his hat, the young woman drew up her cloak before settling the lantern again in her grip. He and Youruh watched until she opened the door latch and slipped inside. Shelby wanted to reach the Indian encampment in full daylight, but he preferred to move on down Congress toward the Colorado before wagons and observant pedestrians clogged the thoroughfare.

Congress Avenue was now entirely lined with log structures for the next two blocks, though the closer one got to the river, the more tents and temporary shelters cropped up. Not far down Congress from the newspaper office, an undertaker was now established with both cedar and pine boxes on display. Shelby knew his way to the path leading west along the riverbank, because he went frequently to a clearing at the outskirts of the settlement to trade for fish that the Tonkawa were superior at catching. Their freshwater catch had become a favorite at the Eberlys' dining table. The Indians with a reputation for peaceful trading had been encouraged to settle in at the edge of Austin, with the understanding that they provided some buffer to the white population from the incursions of hostile groups. Out on the edge of the Tonkawa camp was a mixture of people more comfortable with enterprise of any kind than kinship groups. In a broad lean-to, an extended family of Lipan Apache made themselves available to scout for hunting parties that set out from Austin. The wife of one Tonkawa man was a Caddo who had traveled with him down the Camino Real from the Nacogdoches area.

Another man, recognized by his tattoos as a member of the main settlement, preferred nevertheless to reside in a buffalo hide hut on the edge of the enclave, where he was willing to guide people of any color to one point upriver where the opposite bank curved close in. With braided ropes spanning the current and a sturdy lashed-log raft, he provided safe crossing, two or three at a time, for travelers who recoiled at the cost of the grander ferry downstream.

"Are you here for whisker fish?" the ferryman asked Shelby, who eased the rig to a stop and nodded.

"Yes, we'll want some before we go back to town." He had seen the Tonkawa man guiding the ferry before. "We thought there would be crossings this morning. The boy and I just wanted to watch, if you don't mind."

"Comanche?" the man wondered aloud. "He will know how to take his own horse across a river when he is a man." The ferry driver and the child were studying one another, and Shelby felt Youruh's hand drift onto his own as he clasped the reins. "Do you know tattoos?" the Tonkawa asked the boy. If only his arms had been decorated by patterned ink, both Shelby and his ward might have conversed without staring, but the man's face was also marked with delicate streaks of darkest maroon or black.

"My nephews this morning are catching fish. White ladies do not cook this one. Let your Comanche friend watch how we surprise the fish." Shelby nodded, memories of his Natchez neighbors suddenly flooding back. "I am Walk Far," the man said after Shelby secured the rig to a cottonwood.

"Shelby Whitmire." The Tonkawa man extended his hand, showing his ease with the town's ways. "This is Youruh."

"I have heard the word spoken—a good name." Shelby saw how quickly Youruh lost his shyness and followed the ferryman to riverbank grass, where two brown youngsters were wading in the river shallows. The child moved with ease in the natural setting. And as fearsome as the tattoos made this Tonkawa's appearance, his manner exuded good will.

"A sad one—you do not need to tell the story, how you come to be this boy's friend," Walk Far said to Shelby, who had found a place on the slope in view of the raft and within earshot of the children. "The sky is not big enough to swallow so much sadness." He studied Shelby a moment longer before judging two hunters approaching on horseback to be his first ferry customers of the day. "You know which woman trades whisker fish. On another day, you and the little Comanche will come back. Before the birds lose their homes for winter, he and I can give you a better name." When the ferry runner made an odd sound after turning away, Shelby realized the Indian was laughing. "For a white man," he said, "you found a good name to call the boy."

In the next weeks, Shelby Whitmire knew it was right to let Youruh stay for longer stretches with the Tonkawa on the edge of their settlement. Eventually, it was the Eberlys' handyman who visited the youngster once a week, sometimes more often. He missed the child's company, and kept telling himself that his sense of loss was irrational. He reminded himself how much better his knee and shoulder felt after sleeping on a real bed in his old room inside the inn.

Meanwhile, the town was caught up in a battle between hope and nostalgia. Every conversation appeared rooted in an observation about the camaraderie lost since the first inaugurations in Austin. The count with the unpaid bill, however, was said to be planning a grand French house on a hill east of town, and there was hope that his distance would cool the feud. Residents might regain their usual hospitality.

If Shelby thought de Saligny's plans would ease the strain on the Harpers and make conversations with them more frequent, a day in November put a halt to his hopeful mood. Angelina's husband had been off on a scouting mission on the southern range to assess the presence of hostiles there—either from across the Rio Grande or from nomads out on the plateau. Jacob had never returned. News of the captain's death came almost a fortnight after the accident. There were few details, something about loose rocks and being thrown from his horse. Eberly House descended into mourning, and Shelby found himself immersed in care for family members where sympathy was accepted.

It was hard for anyone to console Angelina Eberly, who once again found herself needing to take charge, to bear a tragedy without letting her support of the living slip. She comforted Alex and her stepson by assigning them a man's duties. She accepted less of Shelby's help, it seemed to him, instead of more.

"Your knee and arm are mending so well," she said to him one morning over coffee. She turned the conversation away from herself. "You should embrace another adventure before Sawdust gets so old he balks at a long ride. And before you let that San Antonio disaster taint your appetite for seeing something new." Her husband had been riding a spirited new mount.

"I don't think I ever had an appetite for such adventure. What many feel about seeing the other side of the mountain," Shelby admitted, "I'm not so sure I ever shared."

Mrs. McIntyre was visiting again from Refugio. The Natchez man drank his coffee faster when it was only these widows at the dining table with him. There were already two men in town, though, both with the surname Jones, calling on the attractive lady from the republic's Irish colony.

"Rebecca, I've told you before that Shelby came to Texas in search of a young friend, one of those poor boys who joined up with Fannin."

"In these parts it's selfish to mourn a husband too long," the Widow McIntyre said. "I have to remind myself of that. You have to think of all the other wives, sisters, and daughters, though it sounds as if your friend was too young for marriage and fatherhood."

"He was just a Mississippi boy, really," Shelby said. He didn't particularly want to talk about Thomas Weeks, but hoped to steer the topic away from lost husbands. "I suppose my mind will be put at ease, to learn his fate and…" Both Angelina and Shelby were caught off guard by the visitor's change in expression. She had reached into a beaded pouch at her waist to pull out an eyelet handkerchief. The two watching her gave the lady a chance to compose herself.

"Mississippi? A Mississippi lad?" She excused herself as she dabbed at her eyes and nose. "I have a friend in Refugio, a Mrs. Molloy, who was left inside the sanctuary with other stranded families, after our men held off Urrea's attack, but they ran out of ammunition and…"

She went on to tell Shelby that two wounded men in William Ward's battalion had been left in the church there as the other volunteers slipped out into the night in the direction of Victoria. Mrs. Molloy had told her that another soldier died just as the Georgia Battalion made its escape. One still alive was a Mississippi youth, wounded and left in her care. When Mexican forces overran the church the next morning, the townspeople were herded off to another building in town, and plans to claim the injured boy as her son fell through. Because of his delirious mutterings, he came under suspicion, and his wound then gave him away. He had either died in the sanctuary or been dragged away and shot with a handful of other captives.

After so many months, years now, of assuming his friend's demise, Shelby still found it difficult to question the woman further.

"Did your friend mention the color of his hair? Did your friend say there were others in the company? Maybe it was another volunteer that came from Mississippi?"

"He was but a young lad, that's all I remember. Ward's men were rags and bones, every last one. Mrs. Molloy said that the night they slipped out the church toward Victoria, they moved already as quiet and solemn as ghosts…" The three at the table sat without speaking for the next minute, and Shelby went against his instincts by breaking the silence.

"If I see his name on a marker one day…a muster roll listing him as killed…Thomas Greenleaf Weeks…"

Greenleaf was also the widow's maiden name, and she began to ask Shelby about the family Thomas was born into in Natchez, who the mother's family was and where in Mississippi the grandfather, Mrs. Ann's father, might be living. If it pained Mrs. McIntyre to think that another of her relatives, besides her first husband Captain Ira Westover, might have been slaughtered with Fannin's army at Goliad or Refugio, it pained Shelby in a different way to find himself talking about Ann Weeks.

"Dr. Robertson's assistant," he went on, "said some of the Georgia boys, several from Macon, would surely have tried to place my friend among relatives of a Weeks family in her hometown. Hard to say who's kin."

"Of course. More than one Mr. Jones right here in a single day…" The visiting lady smiled, but there was a tremor in her voice. "It's all sad enough, as a new calendar unfolds—the terrible recollections before we commemorate San Jacinto…yet to think another man lost might have been family." Shelby couldn't abide causing her fresh tears, so he was more than relieved when her favored suitor—an Oliver Jones—entered the inn and sat down, placing a hand kindly on her wrist.

Later in the week, Angelina found an opportunity to call Shelby aside out on her porch. She was a striking dark-haired woman, he and any man would have agreed, but Shelby had noticed something else about her when she was on her own. When she took on all responsibility, the appealing woman gained a complete self-possession that changed her tone of voice and her stance. He had seen the difference when she ladled beans outside Brazoria and warned an impatient customer. After the death of Captain Jacob Eberly, she acquired that same regal command. He was prepared when he drew closer to her for a confidence or consultation he should not take lightly.

"Shelby Whitmire, I'm going to tell you and no other soul…"

"Anything—it will not go any further."

"Of that I am sure." They stood looking across to Bullock's pigpens and listening for any foot traffic coming from the direction of the hotel or the count's lodgings. "Even when you were a boy, when you said you'd keep Texas a secret, I knew you would. I was sure my Jonathan and I wouldn't be followed here because of anything you ever told."

"I never did."

"Of course not. Well, what I'm telling you now is…that I'm done with marrying. With my luck, it ends in tragedy for one thing."

"It hasn't been very long…that the captain's been buried."

"That's true," Angelina said. "But here's Rebecca McIntyre…her first husband cut down at Goliad, then her second drowned only a short time after vows." She was making a sound as she shook her head, and Shelby realized he'd be useless if she were going to cry for the first time since Natchez. "I'd wager she'll be Mrs. Jones—one suitor or the other—before the next full moon. And that's how my friend knows herself best…as some good man's wife." When she laughed, Shelby felt a wave of relief. "My best role in life may be matchmaker. At least my reputation is leaning that way. But here's what I'm saying only to you. I never will marry again. I don't care how handsome a man might look astride a horse or how he minds music on a dance floor. I won't agree to matrimony again."

"You manage so much on your own, Angelina."

"It takes too much out of me, after I soften, to dredge back up the single-minded person I have to be to take hold of the reins again. And you know what else, Shelby?" A half grown pig broke out of the Bullock pen and trotted toward them. "You know what else? When I finally get full power in my brain and my shoulders again?"

"I've seen it," he agreed already. "I know what you're going to say." She looked directly at him and nodded, as if to indicate that was why she was speaking her mind to him.

"I feel like myself when I'm on my own. It's only when I have the whole weight of survival and happiness, every burden resting on my own shoulders and every blessed joy coming direct from my own efforts that…" She made a gesture that sent the pig running. "I feel like myself."

"My life was in peril that day you left the Natchez shore," Shelby remembered. "Down on the boat dock, if you had judged me to be loose-lipped about your destination…" They both smiled at the recollection but Angelina turned to him, maybe to take him aback in a different way.

"What about you Shelby Whitmire? Do you have half an idea what makes you feel like yourself, what makes you happy?"

He felt the blood rush to his cheeks, and he wished John Holliday would stroll around the corner of Bullock's and up their end of Pecan.

"I've missed the boy some in the last month," he stammered. "I must have some natural flair for fatherhood…from the affection missing in my own papa's home, I suppose. My friend Thomas saw some of that in me, though I was only a few years older."

"Alex and Mag and the captain's children were drawn to you from the start. You're right about that. But are you also like the captain was, Shelby? Or your friend General McLeod? Are you more content out on a mission than at home with the next domestic chore to attend to?"

"It's pretty clear I'm more fond of the hearth," he said. "You wouldn't have hired me on with your family if you hadn't seen that."

"I hired Mr. Whitmire from what I remembered of him back on the Mississippi. You kept my secret, but don't forget I kept yours pretty well myself."

"Oh," Shelby balked. "I wish your friend Mrs. McIntyre hadn't questioned me about my hometown. I really didn't want to…"

"I knew you didn't want to bring up Ann Weeks," Angelina said. "But what I'm talking about—and it's not my matchmaking reputation I'm trying to burnish…"

"It was McLeod who convinced me to ride as far as San Antonio." Shelby dreaded the leaps this muscular woman could take in conversation. "He passed word to me, saying I'd lend some credence to the peaceful purpose of the mission."

"It was my question, I know, about your preference for wandering or domesticity, but I could have sworn to the answer already."

"It's true I might not have made the journey, without Dr. Robertson's need to know about inducing sleep for surgery. All that medical practice I fell into along the way in life, gone rusty now except for my own healing—where that arrow went clean into my knee…and then my shoulder…" He was losing the thread, but Angelina studied him with piercing eyes, as she had that day on the Natchez shore. "Weideman was busy enough, so I had to doctor myself plenty."

"You wouldn't have come to care for that boy, if you hadn't gone," Angelina said quietly, "and looking after Youruh—that's the happiest I've ever seen you." Shelby Whitmire had no more will to resist her line of inquiry.

"I might have changed my mind about going, at the last minute, but then Miss Harper talked with such zeal about the new potion the surgeon was using…"

"Well," the innkeeper said. She had a smile, but it was not the kind she exchanged with the McIntyre lady about which Mr. Jones would prove the most attentive admirer. "Now, we'll hold a new secret for one another."

"I don't know."

"You'd rather take another arrow and another bullet," she said gently, "than find out you've set your heart in a losing direction…for the second time." Just then Mag came out onto the porch to ask if Delilah could open a packet of cinnamon sticks. From around the corner of the larger hotel, two drunks began to stagger. "Mission or hearth, dear Shelby Whitmire, I don't pretend to know how happiness is written for anyone but myself. But I will testify to the care you took finding that Indian boy a happier home. And I'll pledge to a whole congregation that you've made a lifelong friend of me. But if you turn vagabond," Angelina went on, gesturing at the two men wandering the opposite side of the street, "I'll jump out onto any shore and throttle you back to your senses."

1841 Austin, Texas

17   Friends in Absentia

By the new year, citizens of Austin had begun calling the feud between hotel owner Richard Bullock and the French dignitary Alphonse de Saligny "The Pig War." Sensible residents were appalled that the conflict could be taken so lightly and that the term *war* could be used so loosely. *Had nothing been learned from the dreadful sacrifices made in the revolution?* Even Mary Bullock could be caught musing, when her husband was out of earshot, that she would sell her china and pay the bill herself if it would bring peace back to the community and a greater appreciation of the cheerful songs she played on her piano. But others had dug in with their prejudices and threats. Shelby was relieved that many in the count's staff, people the Harper women had befriended, spent days up on the hill where the great house was being constructed.

Some servants quarters were crudely erected off the edge of the property, a kitchen separate from the main house was already functional, and workmen had begun putting in vegetable gardens on the east side. Adeline Harper, whose medical expertise fell from demand as Dr. Robertson traveled away to Bastrop less often, helped Yarico hem linens and curtains that would be used eventually in the French compound. The aunt, Shelby learned from Angelina, had suffered a seizure. When the other Harper women weren't busy with seamstress work, they took on every chore connected with the older woman's care.

One mild day at the start of February, after Shelby had fished a creek off the Colorado with Youruh, he rode up Congress, thinking he should have gone ahead and promised the boy use of Sawdust for the duration of an upcoming trip to Santa Fe. Holliday had passed him a note from McLeod, inviting him to ride along in one of the medic wagons. But the man still healing from two wounds the year before had not yet committed to the expedition. He couldn't decide which course would make him seem more pitiful in his own eyes, trekking such a long way for the childish satisfaction of seeing snow or staying put for the unreasonable hope of winning a young woman's affection.

Shelby glanced toward the Harpers' cabin as he approached Pecan. The window was cranked open, a sign that the women were making full use of a lapse in the winter chill. He was filled with images of the boy dashing about the riverbanks, and he thought he could just stop and mention the miracle surgery Dr. Weidemen had performed. He thought the aunt might be cheered by the opportunity to sit a while on the porch and hear about the child's remarkable recovery.

For weeks, Shelby had imagined a casual conversation with Adeline Harper in which he might bring up the Santa Fe expedition that President Lamar planned for spring. After enlisting with McLeod's growing battalion, John Holliday exuded the demeanor of a dutiful captain again. They were to head for New Mexico by March. Shelby convinced himself that a visit to Miss Harper's cabin might give him the chance to tell her how many civilians were going along on the peaceful trip—newspaper journalists, geologists, tanners, medics, and wheelwrights. He had pictured Adeline springing up from the bench on the dogtrot porch, her face alight as it had been when she spoke of the German doctor, to tell Shelby Whitmire she could not allow him to head out on such a strenuous journey. As one medic to another, she would remind him that such an excursion could impede the final healing of knee and shoulder. He had imagined, against his own voice of logic, that she might declare she could not tolerate another season far from him. Had Apokta been fishing with him and the boy that morning, his Natchez friend would have put it this way—"It is time to speak a man's mind."

Often quelling Shelby's urge, though, was an image of the Brazoria youth Zeke Moreland, now deceased. He would never erase from his memory the boy's look of surprise about an arrow lodged in his chest. He could not forget that the callow soldier had mentioned an aching fondness for his schoolteacher back home, or that Adeline's aunt had prattled on about the love letter her niece still kept. With so many single men residing in Austin, Shelby had heard more than one suggest why it was the doctor's assistant resisted any gentleman's flirtations. Most said she was obliged to care for the sickly aunt, but some assessed her to be one of those rare female bookworms sworn to spinsterhood. Shelby had held his tongue. Since he knew what it was to harbor ill-fated love, he thought it most likely that the cheerful young Macon woman pined at times for love she had left behind in Brazoria.

But he had eased the injured soldier down from his horse. He had helplessly watched the boy die. It was possible, Shelby told himself as he hitched his horse loosely in front of the doctor's porch, that the Harpers had already mourned Private Moreland. When he stepped over to the women's side of the dogtrot, he saw the thin curtain billowing gently in the breeze. No, he thought, he did not need to ask today about people in Brazoria whom they might all have known. He only wanted to tell Miss Adeline what a marvel it was to see Youruh bounding from the edge of the creek up the bank even faster than the Tonkawa boys. He would tell her he had only stopped to testify about the long-term impact of the surgeon's sleeping potion.

He knocked at the women's door. When there was no answer, his heart fell. The open window had encouraged him, but now he supposed the ladies were up at the French Legation. They could have thrown open the window on the street side for an airing, with assurance that no one in direct view of Bullock's would risk mischievous entry. His second knock brought no answer. He was ashamed about the impulse that came to him next, as he stepped away from the door. Instead of going down the breezeway in the direction where Sawdust was hitched, he turned and put his face briefly up to the inviting window where the curtain moved softly. It was a childlike action, and he only did it on the certainty that no one was home.

He peered for just a moment as the muslin billowed, but there was no doubt in his mind that the person inside—besides the napping aunt—and sitting at a small table near the hearth… reading a book…was Yarico. After turning a page, she let her gaze move to the window and Shelby touched the brim of his hat, feeling no less embarrassed than he had years ago passing a female foundations shop in Natchez. When he glanced back at the Harper cabin, from across the street near Bullock's, he could see Yarico standing just inside the doorway and looking his way, possibly with a stricken expression, but most assuredly not smiling.

Two weeks later, just when residents of Austin felt that the ongoing feud between de Saligny and Bullock might cool, the hotel owner delivered physical blows to the count's clerk and people held their breath to see if the man would survive. The worst elements in town began to threaten similar harm to anyone with French affiliation, and Shelby was horrified to hear from Angelina that the slender Harper woman and her family had been threatened before. Close to March, on one of the last wintry evenings in the Texas capital, Shelby stepped out from the Eberlys' stable to see Miss Adeline coming their way up Pecan just before dusk.

The mansion on the hill east of town was nearly complete in its construction, but the count still resided comfortably at his log compound in town. Shelby eased farther out from the enclosure where he'd been mending a rein. He didn't think a low conversation could be overheard at the inn, and he wanted to start off by letting her know that Yarico's literacy would be a well-kept secret. But Miss Harper appeared so absorbed in her own thoughts that she was oblivious to any pig or person occupying the same street. Her brow was knitted with worry and her lips moved as if breathing were punishment. She passed by the Eberly House on her way to the count's residence without a glance in his direction. In less than a quarter hour, Shelby had stood in the stable doorway and watched her return, like a wraith ordering the darkness to recede and let her pass. It was days before Shelby drew up enough courage to ask Angelina if any further hardship from the feud had troubled the Harpers.

"I know. Delilah and I saw her walk by, too. We felt then something dreadful had happened, but it's not a result of the pig war, as far as we know," Angelina confided. "It's been some time since I've chatted with the girl's aunt, who appears well into her dotage. So much hostility between the Frenchman and Bullock—it was no good for my business to appear too sympathetic with the count. All the Harper women were right friendly with the De Saligny staff. And that Yarico, speaking their language so easily."

"She'd go by at least once a day to visit or sew with the count's people." Delilah made this point with a tone of admiration, yet she shook her head in disbelief.

"We thought something might have troubled Yarico." Angelina said, nodding. "I don't expect you ever noticed—she was a beautiful woman, especially when she smiled."

Shelby Whitmire had noticed, and some concern had registered the previous year in Austin, where there were as many as ten men for each female. He, too, had seen her walking by herself the short distance down Pecan to the Frenchman's home. Though he respected the servant's self-confidence, he had no trust in some ruffians who drifted in and out of town.

Now, he felt a wave of regret that he'd kept to himself for the last several days. Since hearing the news passed on from Mrs. Molloy about Thomas, he'd grown more troubled about the packet of Weeks letters in his possession. He had spent more time watching Youruh and the spirited Tonkawa boys catch fish, reminding himself not to bite too hard on guilt over the keepsakes—or about spying a book in the hands of a black woman. He'd begun wondering if fresh scenery, like snow in Santa Fe, could bury his ill-advised affection for Dr. Robertson's assistant.

"Yarico? Something happened to her?"

"What exactly…we don't know," Angelina sighed. "But she can't be found. I think the Harper girl has aged years since there being no word. You were down at the Indian settlement again when she stopped here to ask if we'd heard whispers of any kind. Was that the day before yesterday?"

"That woman was not the kind of domestic to run off from her people," Delilah said, nodding and then shaking her head. She struggled to say more, and Angelina reached out to pat her hand. "No sir, there was something bad happened, because anyone on God's earth could see how devoted she was to Miss Adeline. Of course, the girl once had her own mama, but whatever put her first mother in heaven, anybody could see how Miss Yarico took up the purpose with equal love."

Both Shelby and Angelina looked at Delilah to see if she aimed to speak further. Ordinarily—except about inn-keeping matters with Angelina—she was as spare with public comment as the wooden figure outside the tobacco shop.

In the first days of March, a gloom grew more intense than in other years. Who could wish any of those lost at the Alamo or Goliad to see how Texas fellowship now fared? Shelby turned over in his mind the Refugio woman's account of Thomas. The end his friend met included some uplifting elements.

He went into God's arms there, my dear Mr. Whitmire. Angelina's hotel guest had declared. *A Mexican bayonet likely ended his agony, but he was in a house of God, and my friend Mrs. Molloy was fretting over him in his last moments. He wasn't alone.*

The articles and letters Shelby still carried in his saddlebag, entrusted to him by Thomas himself, and first bundled by Mrs. Ann, might best be laid gently upon the outdoor fire at Bullock's. He had long believed Thomas to have eavesdropped on details of his father's dubious past. During that late night conversation between Ann Weeks and the woman then known as Angelina Peyton, he had likely overheard from the upper railing.

Shelby imagined flames consuming those letters from New Yorker Levi Weeks to Thomas, but his reluctance to destroy his friend's artifacts was visceral. The inlay box had been given away, but the letters still made his saddlebag fair use as a pillow, as Hugh McLeod had advised. The Mississippi man decided one thing—that the upcoming expedition, even though danger was inherent in any crossing of Comanche territory—would offer him a landscape wide enough to stretch out longings, old and new, and allow them to thin. He would use the opportunity to prove himself a better friend to McLeod, who was a fair-minded leader. Shelby wanted to cultivate gratitude for a fate much kinder than many had met.

If he were to end up seeing snow for the first time, he thought, the experience might lend him some peace for the remainder of his life. Should Santa Fe mountains prove as beautiful as many claimed, Shelby imagined himself staying until next year, letting nature and strangers look upon him without guessing the sorrow he'd known as a motherless Natchez boy. He felt a serene lightheartedness when he handed the reins of Sawdust to Youruh.

"I couldn't leave him with anyone but you. I know you'll look after my saddle, too. I won't fault you for the worn look of the tassels. One's all but torn off." The boy didn't duck when Shelby touched his shoulder and hair. "You're already Sawdust's friend. He'll remember me, no matter when I return. Both of you will."

Others in the expedition might be going along for the physical challenge or monetary reward, but in the days before meeting the medic wagon on its way north of town, Shelby realized it was nothing less than spiritual revival he sought. Who wouldn't be feeling uplifted to escape the petty feud still consuming Austin?

On the morning of departure, he positioned under the wagon seat a handsome travel satchel that Angelina and Delilah had fussed over and helped him pack, but he couldn't keep himself from looking where Reverend Burke's reading room remained only a charred smudge on the opposite corner.

"The Sunday School Man would have reminded me to embrace the joy of pilgrimage," he told Captain Holliday. His officer friend had ridden in to accompany several wagons out to McLeod's bivouac by Brushy Creek.

"You might better scoot the bag out where you can rest your right leg on it. Easier on your knee." Holliday looked different sober, and Shelby thought the expedition had already provided some redemptive powers.

Once more, he looked in the direction of the Burke ruins. He didn't speak a word, though, about the striking girl who had stood up from her Macon paper there, how her face had seemed to be the brightest light shining in the newly opened room.

Lately, Shelby was forgiving himself for stealing a look into the Harper cabin, for beholding Yarico engrossed in a book. He told himself his observation could not have been the incident prompting her absence. Slave literacy was not clearly forbidden in the new republic, and though proof was best kept private, the lack of discretion had been his. No, Yarico would not have stolen away for fear of reprisal from Shelby Whitmire. The other two had said the servant was relieved about his recovery, so her regard for him had long been warm. Still, he was at a loss as to how he could provide any solace to Adeline Harper. Years after last seeing his friend Thomas, he himself was still knitting the threads of grief and remembrance. How could any minor acquaintance comfort the young woman in a state of anguish about her missing companion?

1841-1842, the expedition to Santa Fe

18   The Kind Face of Death

Halfway up the coast from Veracruz to Galveston, the *Rosa Alvina* tilted as it pitched upon the gulf's huge swells before rocking steeply back the other way. Its continuous dislodging from balance made the healthy passengers ill. But most of the transports and some of the crew were already struggling against yellow fever passed along from the Mexican town of departure. There would be deaths, bodies thrown overboard, before the Texas island came into view.

"Mc Leod's men," Shelby heard a man on deck say, "…any poor bastard from the Santa Fe capture will die first."

"And two coming out of prison at Perote already knew battle with the small pox."

The discussion came to a stop, and just inside the sick quarters Shelby turned with the rolling of the ship. He was remembering two soldiers and one journalist dragged out from their cells at Castle Perote, their inert bodies so diminished that a single youth with a bandana over his face handled the extractions one at a time.

"Do you know the distance from there to Santa Fe?" Shelby thought it was the first mate asking. "Along the way, I am sure they were praying to meet death. Nearly two thousand miles in the winter months…on foot."

"And now the yellow fever."

"The black vomit on a rocking ship is cruel. But not so cruel as that march from Santa Fe in winter."

We were cursed from the start. Shelby imagined his own voice joining the discussion. *We were delayed three weeks at the outset, because of McLeod's old wound. It flared up and he had to be escorted all the way to doctors at the same island we're headed for.*

"Some will live," the first mate said. "The hospital in Galveston is better than most in Matamoros. I myself have been there twice. The priests are in charge. Their physicians care for anyone in need. Some will live to tell stories."

"General McLeod does not appear to have the fever, but the arrow point in his thigh is a curse all its own."

"Tell me, *por favor,* how do you march two thousand miles with an arrowhead deep inside your leg?"

Just as you would stagger that distance with a mangled knee and shoulder, Shelby imagined saying. He felt the tears welling in his eyes, but he knew there was no one to rebuke him for an unmanly reaction. If he deserved mockery, then so did poor Captain Holliday lying on a blanket just a few feet away. Sweat or drool trickled from the corner of the officer's mouth. The enclosed space, with only three portals that let in humid air, was filled with frail men groaning and crying and vomiting. At least no chastisement went with this suffering.

The guard who took my spyglass laughed before he whipped me. Then I fought off tears when they stripped us of our clothes in the San Miguel plaza, Shelby admitted to himself. *Long before the town near Santa Fe, hunger had made us weak.*

Other perils and losses before their capture he had faced with the same stoicism the others showed—soldiers and civilians alike—even a near mutiny during the expedition's delay over McLeod's leadership. Many complained that the president favored him as general for being suitor to a Lamar cousin. Then, only three days after the delayed start, one soldier committed suicide. How could that not haunt the others? It was a bad beginning, with only worse to come.

Expedition members had eaten heartily for a fortnight out from their Brushy Creek departure, but it was soon clear that supplies would never last across the West Texas desert. Another halt for resupplying allowed hostile Comanche to hack away at McLeod's caravan. They scalped and lanced a private sent foraging, then let him stagger back into camp. A dozen horses disappeared during another night. Then, expedition scouts met ambush and murder near the end of the first month out. And worse yet was an error that proved nearly fatal for all. Thinking of it now made Shelby only close and open his eyes. He was too weak to curse. A battalion guide had declared with certainty that a butte in northern Texas was the signpost for turning directly west. Two hundred military men and another hundred adventurers at first felt a surge of optimism at spotting their mark. They interpreted the turn as a straight and short line to Santa Fe.

But there are scores of such land formations, we realized later. It was not the right butte. Where we cut in only led to a winding route along the top of a brutal river canyon.

"Even today," the first mate out on the deck was saying, "General McLeod will not admit it was a mission to conquer New Mexico."

"If he still wishes to court the president's niece, he is wise to deny it."

McLeod took care of us on the march into Mexico, as best he could! Whatever his faults, he looked after his battalion! When a tear trickled down Shelby's cheek, he remembered the day Adeline had come to check on his damaged knee. The eyes of any man could water after prolonged suffering. A survivor of the Santa Fe Expedition deserved every scrap of happiness he might find, he thought. *Damn every uniform to kingdom come! So what if McLeod's orders were to take Santa Fe by force if necessary? Any mortal living through these last twelve months of hell deserves his shreds of joy! Here's my toast to McLeod and Rebecca Lamar, if the man wishes to wed! Damn everything…*

Shelby was imagining speech, but he had propped himself up on one arm without admitting the balance it would require. The precarious tilt of the ship made him retch on the wooden planks beside his ruined blanket. Inside his head, the voice stopped. He peered down in the darkened room to see if the puddle looked black like the vomit of his friend John Holliday. No, it was only the clear liquid ejected from an empty stomach. He fell back flat again and let his head roll from side to side, a habit that had helped him to rest and finally to sleep in the Perote prison.

Calmed from his imagined defense of Hugh McLeod, Shelby nevertheless latched onto one fact affronting his own common sense in the last twelve months—the expedition had started off without a single printed map of the stretch between the interior of Texas and the New Mexican town of Santa Fe! He winced again, recalling how he had almost let himself weep when stripped of his clothes. Poor McLeod, though, had kept his composure. Even earlier, when it was clear that one of his own men, the scout Captain Lewis, had betrayed the position of the weakened battalion, McLeod displayed no emotion. The general had coldly faced the smug traitor, who sat upon his horse while arresting officers sent out from San Miguel shackled the wandering Texans.

I need my strength, Shelby told himself. He could see that John Holliday's homecoming was in doubt. As contagious as yellow fever was, the Mississippi man would protest any order to throw victims overboard before they had expired. He needed to rest so that he could stand and defend his comrades if necessary. He knew very well he would not have survived so far had it not been for the efforts of McLeod and this officer. At first, encouragement had come from the captain.

Before the treachery by Lewis and the arrests, Holliday had ridden back along the ranks forging desperately in the direction of Santa Fe.

"How're the leg and arm holding up, Whitmire?"

"Both still attached to my body." Shelby had been about to ask his medic partner whether there was enough laudanum, now that they were nearing their destination, that he might take a dose to recover his stamina. But he had changed his mind. He'd had a nagging dread, heightened when pain shot regularly through his knee and when his shoulder throbbed above the old bullet wound. Even then he had a premonition that worse was in store for them all. But he never imagined how some pains could make a man long for death.

"I don't like McLeod's proposal to split the expedition into two," Holliday had confided, "one half going on without being able to communicate with the bivouac." Shelby had nodded as he made a grim connection.

"Like when Ward's men took off from Goliad?"

"That's what I mean." In the rocking sick bay, Shelby looked over at the man who had a weakness for the bottle when he was not in uniform. He thought the captain deserved forgiveness for his one bad habit. If he died soon, he would slip into eternity sober. The Goliad survivor had gone on talking. "No one at La Bahia guessed our future. Men were cursing Fannin—some were—for his indecision, but who could blame him? We didn't know what was happening to the companies at Refugio. We just kept waiting and waiting for news of the Georgia men. Turned out those few days we stayed put were giving Urrea time to move in closer and follow us out toward the creek at Coleto."

"I heard most of Ward's men ended up at Goliad by Palm Sunday."

"They were there—and worse off than most of us who'd remained under Fannin. They'd spent days lost in the desert prairie. But others went out for water…never seen again."

In the stifling sick ward on the *Rosa Alvina,* Shelby Whitmire tried to purse his lips to lick where they were cracked and dry. He had taken a sip of water earlier in the morning, so he would not have complained had he been able to speak. One of the crew just outside on the deck was gone to check a captain's order. The sails had to be kept taught and catch the wind precisely so that the ship would keep tacking northerly and not be blown out to sea. Now the first mate returned and the two continued their assessment of the expedition survivors.

"McLeod's men all together don't eat as much a solitary ship rat." Shelby heard pity in the man's laugh. "We may not need to purchase so many supplies for the return trip."

"Do you see how the general's coat hangs loose? But McLeod maintains his good humor, does he not? I have heard him say he would recommend the march from Santa Fe to Perote for any future bridegroom too fat for his formal coat."

"What could they have eaten from El Paso del Norte to Durango?"

"I think there are only four lizards that call the wasteland home."

I tried to eat a rodent abandoned by a buzzard, Shelby thought. I could not keep it down any better than the grass Holliday and I tried on another day. We butted our guard's horse away from a greenish mound and stuffed the bitter strands into our mouths.

"There are some angels of mercy living in the villages along the way."

"More than one of McLeod's men will say it was poor villagers that came to a tiny plaza, offering tortillas and beans to the prisoners…"

"And ill-fitting clothes," the first mate said. "Only McLeod has his own coat from before. Perhaps the others tried to eat their better shirts—"

"The rest had been stripped of all their own clothes, *Señor,* you remember?"

"Of course. You are right. Still, I do not understand what they ate or drank for the first six weeks."

Crickets, cactus—spilled grains of uncooked rice on a fortunate day, Shelby imagined informing them. *And have you ever seen a thirsty man put his face to the ground, trying to bite off a mouthful of mud? Have you ever seen a man, his hands in chains, try to hold his fingers together and make a cup so that he could drink his own urine?*

"God's punishment will be harsh for any mortals who have been so cruel to one another."

"It is not for us to say, but…" the first mate started off. His voice fell to a hoarse whisper. There was a lull in the coughing around him and Shelby was able to hear how he finished his thought. "I would have kept the miserable prisoners in Santa Fe for the winter. Where would they have gone, if we had let them escape?"

I will tell you where one prisoner went after the man with a mouthful of mud lay beaten near a rock. Another prisoner, one with a loose shackle, staggered faster than we thought any of us could go. He skipped across where the guards had made a fire and reached a pistol lying on a brightly striped blanket. He had it in his hands and was able to cock it before John Holliday lunged in his chains. The man was inching the weapon toward his own head.

The Texas captain had put an elbow to the private's ribcage and the weapon flew away into the dirt. Shelby recalled how even the stunned guards could only watch as Holliday leaned over to scold the desperate man.

"You want to die? You want to fly away from torture? You have so many troubles, too many for your feet to listen to your brain even one more day! Too tired to keep going?" He growled the next words. "The men shot down in the San Antonio River would have taken on our plight! Tell those bones at Goliad about your god-awful troubles!"

The shackled captain had kicked at the dirt, and one of the guards came up behind him with a compassion that startled everyone. The Mexican soldier had put a hand on John Holliday's arm to keep him from striking the demented prisoner.

"I don't close my eyes in sleep without seeing those Goliad bones! Tell the poor boys who ran until they were gut shot or split in two from the back! Go on and tell them about the hardships of a long, long walk!"

Just a few feet from where Shelby Whitmire now lay, Captain Holliday gagged and moaned. Since a day out from Veracruz, he had only mumbled incoherently. But in the interminable months since their capture—almost a year—the man from Natchez heard the Goliad survivor shout repeatedly in his sleep *All those bones at La Bahia! Tell your woes to Goliad's forgotten!*

Shelby's dizziness was subsiding. He wanted to turn his thoughts away from shackled skeletons, staggering and stumbling at gunpoint. And he did not want Holliday's words to prompt a clear imagining of Fannin's last horror. Imprisonment could teach a man to concentrate instead on any cheerful experience. Sometimes he could recall a moment as simple as Thomas scooting over in the Weeks cart behind Apokta. He could sometimes imagine how Angelina often gently put her hand on Delilah's arm after a long day. Sometimes, he could reconstruct the evening when Adeline Harper sat in a reading room absorbed in a Macon newspaper.

But often when Shelby awoke from fitful sleep—had he cried out?— he'd dreamt of Fleur biting down on the cuff of a moccasin. The occasion frequently presiding over Shelby's consciousness was the birth of Apokta's first grandchild, the smell of sweat and blood, and the high-pitched wail of the wriggling infant. Playing next in Shelby's memory would be the scene in McLeod's headquarters, the night several soldiers stood awestruck, after Shelby's touch had altered the birth outcome for a desperate woman already mother to three. Then, he would revisit the recent and most unlikely incident.

Only halfway through the nightmare march to Perote, guards overseeing the other contingent of prisoners caught up. One evening, the expedition leader intervened calmly on Shelby Whitmire's behalf. At first Shelby didn't recognize the Texas general because of the pounds he'd shed. McLeod had approached astride a donkey. Then the guards let him help Shelby up and walk alongside for the distance back to the other encampment. A concubine traveling with a Mexican officer stayed mostly out of sight in their cook wagon, but since not long after the Rio Grande, it was clear to all that a child was on the way.

"In the last two villages, midwives were sent in, but the woman is not so near her time. She's just so little," McLeod informed Whitmire. "If we're lucky, she won't be due for several weeks. The officer appears to care about her. He was relieved when I told him of your… doctoring specialty." His wits dulled by the traumatic march, Shelby could speak no word of thanks. He had only blinked. "The cook wagon will mean some respite for your swollen feet."

Apokta's daughter talked to me after her child was safely born, Shelby remembered. *And at Fort Jessup, the woman nursing her infant kept whispering "Yes, doctor. Yes, doctor."* Out in the Mexican desert, where death reached out its hand to more than two hundred desperate prisoners, the little concubine had reached up to touch Shelby's hand when he dabbed at her forehead between pains. She was a wispy thing, and the medic helping her was not at all sure she could push a baby into this world.

The dark girl should still have been enjoying her own childhood, he had thought to himself. Like Youruh, she ought to be running on a riverbank to catch fish. Instead, she had reached for Shelby's palm. She'd placed his fingers on her throat. Her eyes were wide, and when she closed them he saw that her lashes were long and beautiful. She pressed his fingers against her throat. The tiny woman preferred quick death to agony with the same outcome.

But the birth had concluded miraculously. And when Shelby laid the squirming newborn next to the new mother, she was smiling. She had squeezed his arm again and smiled with him. *At the moment of new life,* he thought, *one touch is a testament. What did it matter if the first words a child heard were Spanish or English? What could it matter to a suckling infant if political borders were settled or in dispute?* He could not explain to himself why such questions often prodded his recollection of the slave stockades beyond Natchez outskirts. *Of course, the pair chained separately, and shipped to who knew where, would keep on loving one another!*

At Castle Perote, south from Mexico City, there was even less food and water for the prisoners on many days. But at least the nightmare march had halted—no more trudging on broken and bleeding feet. And when the prisoners were at last granted release, close to a year from the expedition's ill-fated start, the Texans trekked as stiffly as unearthed mummies to nearby Veracruz. Fresh clothes some were given flapped loosely in the gulf breeze. So near starvation, most asked only for water once aboard the transport ship. Then the yellow fever took hold. And now, the *Rosa Alvina* was rocking its way up the coast of Texas.

When Shelby Whitmire opened his eyes, he was startled to find Holliday looking calmly right at him from where he lay. At first, the Natchez man feared it was the frozen gaze of death, but the captain's lips moved and it became clear that the stricken soldier was trying to speak.

"I'm…no Catholic," Holliday whispered. Shelby was ready to nod and console his friend, no matter how senseless his ramblings might become. "But…my confession…"

"We're not far from Galveston now. You're past the worst."

"No, listen to my worst—I want you to hear it…" His lips trembled as he shook his head. "Right after Goliad…I left a man, a brother from La Bahia…I ran off and left him to die."

"I saw you save a man's life more than once," Shelby countered softly.

"After he went to find food…I heard Spanish… From the creek where I was hidden, I thought Mexican guards were coming." The captain's eyes closed for a moment and Shelby waited to see if he would take in another gulp of air. "Those infernal piles, those bones were nearby," Holliday went on. "My partner tried to spare me the truth. But I'd seen the bloody stumps even before he found me. I knew from the stink…I couldn't abide a return to Goliad."

"No one would have."

"Earlier…I smelled the damn place. I knew we were lost in a circle." The man's whispering trailed off and his head fell limp again. Shelby thought the captain was gone, until his eyes fluttered open.

"Can you sip some water? Can I move a blanket under your head?"

"I left John T. Spillers…when he went off for food," the ill man stammered. "He was trying to save us both…but I left him to be caught again."

"Let me get you some water."

"God forgive me. I deserted John Spillers…to save my own skin." This time Holliday's head kept steady, but so did his eyes in their open stare. His gaze froze in an expression of concern and finality. He did not look capable of cruelty, Shelby wanted to tell him. He had seen the captain expend all his own strength to help other prisoners find some of their own.

"God forgives you," Shelby spoke to the form lying still now, "and John Spillers, too."

The prisoner that General McLeod called Whitmire had no strength to protest how Captain John Holliday was carried unwrapped from the sick room to the railing of the ship. He was helpless to stop his own tears when he heard the sailors grunt while managing the body. Inside the sick bay, he let his head rock from side to side when the unwieldy refuse hit below with a dull splash. He dreamt for days that he himself was the next ghastly lump discarded from the *Rosa Alvina*. And when he awakened groggily in the crowded hospital, he quickly succumbed to hallucinations that he, too, was under water, that every movement around him was a sinking corpse. Every word spoken near his cot sounded like the gloating recriminations of the devil himself.

A fortnight after being tended to by Galveston priests, as much as by the island's overworked physicians, Shelby identified a voice one morning as that of a well-known friend.

"You've been on the brink of…final departure," Hugh McLeod said to him. "I wouldn't be telling you this if you didn't look more fit for this world than I've seen you for days."

"Months," Shelby whispered. For a long time after the debacle at San Antonio's courthouse, the two had depended on an intermediary for communication. The estrangement might have grown permanent except for their recent, shared trauma. Like an apparition one day, McLeod had ridden into the other prisoner camp where Shelby was guarded. He'd pointed out the Natchez man as a *medico* who could deliver babies. Talk between the two men would never again diminish in honesty or warmth.

"We've been gone well over a year," the general went on. "And from the celebrations some of the townspeople are giving on our account, you'd think we'd bargained our way back from the underworld." He grimaced as he shifted in a ladder-back chair. Shelby was seeing a fairly clear single image, he realized, instead of the blurry doubles tormenting him lately.

"Your leg is bothering you, it looks like."

"The aggravation will be what vanquishes me in the end," he laughed. "But now I'm certain you are coming back to life—already worrying over someone else."

"How long since we made shore?"

"Starting on the third week now." Hugh McLeod opened his mouth and then chewed his lip in indecision. "I've been in a hurry to get back to Austin as soon as possible, but the priests have control of the infirmary and they've made me promise to stay put until Sunday. If there's any dispute about first use of a quinine shipment, they want me in command. And a preacher will make the rounds with communion for Protestants..." He scanned the room, where several patients clung tentatively to life.

"You would have gone back to Austin without...some of us?" Shelby turned his head toward a dozen other cots.

"Most of you boys need lots more rest. I don't know why my recovery has taken hold so speedily." He reached down and tugged at his belt in embarrassment. "My breeches are already snug at the waist again." His expression conveyed gratitude, and pity for the condition of so many others. "I'll take a schooner to Velasco and get a steamship to take me a ways up the Brazos. I can't tarry in Galveston while President Lamar is still uninformed about what became of us—the details—and where blame can be laid for our losses. What builds in me like a fever is a need to ride out where we made that blasted turn west."

"They took us in chains without any aggressive move on our part."

"Don't try to talk, Whitmire," the general said. "Not a shot fired on the part of Texas," he agreed, "and I don't doubt that's been construed as a blight on our military reputation."

"You proved your fortitude. I know I couldn't abide all that political talk."

"Well, we've shared our differences about duty before, when it's defined by wearing a uniform." McLeod chewed his lip again in an odd way that had Shelby wondering what other topic he felt less obliged to bring to light.

"It looks like I'm going to live, but I don't reckon I'll be fit for stagecoach or riding for a while yet."

"I'll let folks in Austin know that you're among the sure survivors." The expedition leader was quiet for a moment, as if waiting to see which individuals the recovering man might require him to inform. "The whole Eberly House will have a fit of relief when I tell them."

"Save the story about delivering yet another baby, will you?"

"Those details are yours to tell."

"What is it?" Shelby didn't think he had ever given away to McLeod his private thoughts about Adeline Harper, but he could have sworn the general was stepping around the topic as Angelina Eberly sometimes did.

"Did I tell you who the postmaster is here? Mosely Baker, a captain who was with Houston at San Jacinto, and before that in San Felipe. Mrs. Eberly blames one of the two for the torching of her inn there."

"Is it something in a letter you got? Is everyone in Austin faring well enough?" Hugh McLeod's eyes were grave, but he thumped the patient's arm reassuringly.

"There's no such thing as purely good news in these times," he said. "Baker was in possession of the French house for a spell, after a school there went on decline. Doc Robertson is looking at the property now, he says, but it's not about the Georgia girl."

"Just tell me the god-awful feud ended."

"It has. The count's gone for good," McLeod said softly. "But…so is…Mrs. Eberly's boy Alex." Shelby had to close his eyes and let his head rock as his friend told him about two other Austin men who had squared off in front of Bullock's hotel. It was only days after Angelina herself fired cannon shot in the direction of thieves leaving town with the republic's records. "Houston's gambit, they say," He stopped short of political recriminations. "The whole town was already heaved up. In a new fray, one hothead was fatally shot, as well as young Peyton, who'd only stepped forward as a bystander to forestall bloodshed. He'd been taking on a man's duty in the last year or so."

"Can you get me passage on that schooner?" Shelby blurted out. "I should go with you to Austin. It's a cruel loss no mother should bear, but Angelina…"

"It makes my other news easier to tell," McLeod said. "I don't dare call it a loss." He looked as if he might lose his appetite to speak. "Mr. Baker has some letters accumulating there at the postal shelves with no return address. He finally opened one or two. They're from Knoxville, near where the Harper women call home." He stopped for a moment to see how the recovering man would take mention of that name. "A ragged man used to ride in every January to collect a single piece of mail. But for the last three years no one has come—no ragged man. The letters arrive but the name on the envelopes is just fiction, Baker figures."

"You learned some news about Macon?"

"He implored me to read one letter. Said I could judge whether the bundle should be saved or discarded after all this time." In his weakened condition, Shelby was only half listening. He was trying not to imagine Alex with the same look of surprise he'd seen on the mortally wounded private in Nacogdoches. "It was a humble letter about vegetables and church, except to say that the whole town of Knoxville would be at the wedding of…Joanna Troutman."

Shelby blinked. His mind raced as Hugh McLeod went on to say he thought he'd better pay attention to handiwork of the almighty. He wished the sweet Knoxville woman well. She would be happy to stay near her parents and siblings. But there was yet another news story bubbling in Galveston circles from ships passing in and out of the bay. A vessel had sunk off the coast of Savannah recently and many were drowned. The difference in this story, though, was that a tall woman had jumped into the water not only to save herself but to help ashore as many other victims as her strength and deft swimming would allow. Rumor had it that the heroic female was a niece of outgoing President Lamar himself!

"Your Rebecca?"

"Providence. That's the other reason I need to get to Austin speedily," McLeod confessed. "After talking with Lamar—and after riding out to view that miserable western turn—I have much to do. If I don't see the correct, godforsaken butte, while looking at a map this time, I'll never forgive myself. I'll never sleep soundly, or be a damn bit of good to any woman. But next, I'll need to find fair land for constructing a house, maybe here on the island."

"And then, you'll make a trip to Savannah, I imagine."

"To see if Rebecca will have me." Both men ceased their talk and took a moment to assess the possibility of being refused. "I never told you about having coffee one morning in Austin," McLeod went on warily, "with the young Harper woman. It was when you and I weren't speaking much." Shelby eyes grew wide and a pounding picked up in his ears. "She had mistaken me for another soldier as I was ready to mount one day at the hotel."

"She thought you might be Private Moreland?"

"His name never came up," McLeod told Shelby. "It was a man from Macon she was hoping to see. A neighbor, not a sweetheart. But her tears did make me think…" The general stopped for a moment and smiled at his friend. "I've known for a long time it's not gallant or fair to court two women at a time, much less three. But there's no doubt about the Harper woman's appeal. When I heard her talk about the Macon man, considerably her senior, it occurred to me she might not be opposed on principal…to a man whose hair has started to gray."

As a child, Shelby believed his stepmother's scolding had stripped the color from his father's hair. He could only smile weakly at his own change in appearance. So much news suddenly drained him of all energy. The pendulum swing from grief over Alex to optimism about Adeline left him as weak as he'd felt the day he was carried ashore. He knew he had no strength to join Hugh McLeod on the journey to Austin. By the time he gained sufficient stamina, the newly re-elected President Sam Houston might already have relocated the Texas capital back to the coast—if not to Galveston itself, farther inland to a new town bearing the hero's name.

"You'll let Angelina…and the Harper women know…that I'm all right, that I'm gaining strength?"

"Oh Lord, I meant to tell you as soon as I walked in, but so many reports from the postmaster came to me first, and my own plans and…"

"I can't withstand much more, Hugh, I'm—"

"I saw someone—back near the priests' quarters—someone I never expected to lay eyes on here. Adeline Harper and her aunt kept a house servant close, if I remember. I didn't recognize her at first. Her dress is plain, but it's not the usual coarse gray."

"Yarico?"

"I don't know her name, but she looked right at me when I nodded. The man she was with took her arm and they disappeared into a back room."

"A man took her arm and forced her away?"

"Calm down, friend."

"She'd gone missing. Miss Harper was inconsolable!"

"It's a dark man with her, Whitmire. The priest says the two are husband and wife. I didn't ask further since it wasn't my business," he said, trying to read the emotions of the recovering patient. "It's just that I'm in a rush now to take the next ship to Velasco, and I thought you'd want to know."

"Her name is Yarico."

"Brother Beaulieu can't get away since he's tending to invalids in need of quinine, but he said something about their awaiting an escort to head up the Mississippi."

"Up the Mississippi," Shelby repeated, before drifting off into fitful sleep.

1842 Galveston and points along the Mississippi and Ohio rivers

19   Poor in Spirit

For the next weeks, Shelby Whitmire did little more than lie and turn as Hugh McLeod had last found him in Galveston's convalescent hospital. One day he would feel a small surge of energy, but then his strength would fall as if through a sieve. He grew aware that each week brought a new roster of volunteers making the rounds with soup, cool rags, and prayers. Only once when Brother Beaulieu passed by his cot did Shelby consider reaching for the priest's loose sleeve to pull him closer and whisper: *The female servant you harbor went missing from her home in Austin over a year ago. The head of her household, Adeline Harper, needs to know that the slave Yarico is stranded here in Galveston and looking for passage north to the free states.*

It was true that slavery grated against the deepest beliefs of many Catholic officials, but few were willing to openly flout harsh runaway laws. If only he had the strength to journey overland to Austin. Shelby felt he could meet with Miss Harper and judge her current understanding of the fugitive's whereabouts. But the convalescent believed any inquiry he might make of Galveston authorities would result in the immediate apprehension of Yarico and public charges against some clergy. He recalled how Mrs. Elizabeth Greenfield, neighbor of the Weeks family, was known only as a kindly eccentric years ago in Natchez. Twenty-five years later, however, her ire against slavery would be characterized as treason in many states. No wonder she had moved with the gifted little singer to a sympathetic home in the North.

Even the next month, when Shelby Whitmire felt well enough to walk from the infirmary to a veranda and then a short distance to sand and lapping waves, he had to wrench his thoughts from the Yarico issue and concentrate on making steady steps. The original wounds to his knee and shoulder had left him with an uneven gait. Certainly, the forced march from Santa Fe further hobbled him. He walked greater distances with a crutch he'd crafted, and shoreline roads in the town's saloon district reminded him of his childhood.

He observed a muscular guard manhandle two drunks out beyond yellow swinging doors. On the stoop of one establishment, a woman with pale hair secured garish feathers behind her ears. Shelby tried to shake rough memories. Only once, not long after his twelfth birthday, had a Natchez saloon girl succeeded in luring him into her private room. She might have been just a few years older, but he had been mesmerized by her hair—the color of corn husks—and eyes as blue as an August sky. He couldn't have paid her if she had demanded money, but she had only hugged him afterward. She'd wept quietly before telling him he could come back whenever he wanted.

From then on, the boy doing chores for the Weeks house committed himself to a faster pace as errands took him by the bawdy house. He had only wished fervently that Mrs. Ann would never guess who else had beguiled him and where he had spent an awkward hour.

Now, as a recovering man in Galveston, Shelby smiled ruefully at his shifting follies, and he nearly convinced himself that there was no need to get overwrought about the status of Miss Harper's servant. Perhaps Hugh McLeod mistakenly identified the domestic. He thought it very likely that the general had never observed her except from a distance. If her clothing struck McLeod as changed, maybe the woman he'd seen in the priest's protection was a different individual altogether. Even if he had been correct, and Yarico had indeed nodded in recognition before disappearing, that encounter had occurred almost a month ago.

In the weeks of his convalescence, Shelby reasoned that Adeline's servant and the man Brother Beaulieu said was her husband had likely moved on toward New Orleans. Shelby told himself that the pair could already be up the Mississippi and beyond Natchez by now. He himself saw no evidence of the fugitive slave. In another fortnight, he would be well enough to travel by ship and coach back up to Austin—a town all but deserted since relocation of the capital to Houston. If Dr. Robertson kept an option of settling in at the old French Legation, Miss Harper would probably still be in the Colorado River town. Upon his return there, he could honestly tell the young woman that he had only heard of a single sighting, that a priest claimed Yarico and a companion were aiming to travel north.

But one morning, when he was most convinced there was no longer a dilemma forcing him to act, Shelby witnessed the woman on the arm of a lean, dark-skinned man. Brother Beaulieu was directing the couple to a secluded hospital anteroom. Shelby tried not to stare after them, and he half expected Adeline Harper to come walking into the foyer next. The two carried travel bags, and the familiar individual's bonnet was a deep blue, like the man's vest—not the dull brown of house servants or field workers, as McLeod had mentioned. They were not dressed to attract attention, but Shelby could sense the priest's caution in having them step away from the main hallway. Even in Galveston, where several freemen toiled at the docks for their own keep, none looked as refined as this pair.

"May I speak with the two you escorted to a side room?" Shelby found himself asking the church official.

"They are under my care here."

"I only want to ask if they have a message…for anyone…where she's from." Shelby looked toward the doorway where the pair had been taken, and the priest appeared to be assessing his interest. "She and her people doctored me Austin when I needed mending."

"She tended you some here, too, at night when you were first brought in."

"Yarico did?"

"She and her husband helped in the evenings. She asked that we take special care of you, my son." Shelby's use of the woman's name put the clergyman at ease. "Yes. Go on in. Later this afternoon, I hope to escort them to a ship. I meant to travel with them as far as New Orleans. I would have purchased more quinine…but there are too many still in our sick wards. Mr. and Mrs. Giroux say they dare not wait any longer for their journey to Cincinnati. Talk to her now, before their ship pulls anchor."

In the small waiting room, Shelby and the couple took part in an encounter that was strained at first. The man named Bernard rose when Shelby entered, and then gently touched Yarico's shoulder to keep her seated. The husband introduced himself and extended his hand, though he looked all but certain the white man would decline the courtesy. Out of public view, though, their greeting unfolded as if they'd all been waiting together for Walk Far's ferry.

His wife's demeanor suggested both confidence and sadness. The two had been wed in Bastrop under Reverend Haynie's officiating, Bernard told him. It was not until the husband better understood Shelby's acquaintance with the Harper household that Yarico did more talking.

"Miss Adeline has forgiven me for my sudden disappearance." She spoke calmly, without quite looking directly into the eyes of the expedition survivor.

"I never saw Miss Harper…so distraught, as when she doubted your wellbeing." If the two were still on the run, Shelby realized, they could do no other than to claim they had been given permission to travel and that all was sitting well with the mistress.

"I would have sent a message sooner, had I known of her Aunt Margaret's passing."

"Her aunt died?" Yarico nodded and she took a moment to untie her bonnet, which she set in her lap. Bernard, a man Shelby now recognized as footman for Count de Saligny, put his arm around her shoulder as she leaned forward. The woman's brow knitted in emotion, and a less beautiful woman would have lost some appeal by showing deep concern.

"After the burning of Gonzalez, Mrs. Linder was never the same. If talk ever turned to her lost nephew, her mind would wander off."

"So, Adeline had family in Gonzalez?"

"Miss Maggie's nephew went on to the Alamo, we suspect, but…" Bernard looked as if he had heard this painful story before.

"We have many reasons, you see, to seek passage north, *Monsieur* Whitmire," he said. "After the Alamo, such a terrible exodus, my wife can describe—but you and I cannot imagine so many running. In another country, she can perhaps forget. This I believe." Both men allowed a silence to expand, while Yarico covered her eyes.

"Margaret Linder wasn't Adeline's aunt by anything except fondness," she suddenly confided in Shelby. "No blood or legal relative, no more than I was a slave in the Harper house, according to papers Adeline's mother left me." She began to reach in a handbag that crossed over her shoulder, and Shelby realized she was ready to produce documents whenever the issue might be forced on their journey. She had probably practiced handling the pages without close inspection, should the ruse of illiteracy need perpetrating.

"Then Adeline is alone in Austin? Is she still there, across from Dr. Robertson's office?"

"When he settled more in Austin, he had need of his full dogtrot. He bought them another little cabin along Pecan the opposite way from Eberly House," Yarico said. "Miss Margaret was there with her for a time." She was smiling about something, but the thought had made her eyes fill with tears again.

"It is not by herself she is living now," Bernard said tentatively. Suddenly Shelby looked down at his own feet, still prone to swelling. Standing awkwardly, he took out his stopwatch to judge how much time had elapsed since he first started his morning stroll. He didn't know if he could bear learning the new last name of a recently married Miss Harper.

"We are leaving Adelphine…we're…leaving our baby girl in Adeline's care," the woman stammered. "We don't know how safe the trip north will be, much less where we can settle."

"Her *chère maman* could not put the child in danger." Yarico was overcome and after Bernard gave her a little hug, he gestured toward the door, where Shelby followed. "Brother Beaulieu will see us safely to our ship—this much he can promise." Then he lowered his voice to a whisper. "Adelphine is as pretty as her name, so like her mother. But her eyes are green, and in her hair are gold rays like the sun. There are dangers in this world, *monsieur*, for such a girl." The fellow with glistening black skin waited to read Shelby's expression. He was not the natural father of the child. "Not every man in Austin lives with honor. Not every man there was like you and your General McLeod."

"Adeline has care of…Yarico's little girl." Shelby could only manage repeating that fact, but a surge of anger made him recall more than one unattached male in Austin's streets who was dastardly enough to press himself on a defenseless servant.

"Letters already come from New Orleans to the hospital here. Other priests there will help us. A steamboat will be arranged. My wife and I, we will go on to Louisville, perhaps Cincinnati." Brother Beaulieu, a rosary in one hand, was coming back down the hall with some documents of his own. "When we make a home—safe for a small child—we will find a way to bring north our Adelphine."

Shelby Whitmire spent the rest of the afternoon in a whirl of reflection. He knew very well that the story of this traveling pair, told later in the week on hotel verandas and over the dining tables at inns, would put the Perote survivor in the role of dupe. Most Galveston residents might now caution Shelby how a slave bent on escape would use the slyest trickery. Freedom papers could be cleverly forged for a price. The well-spoken Bernard might have made off with some of the count's fortune, for all anyone knew. Methodists and Presbyterians wary of the priesthood might fault the Catholic clergy for being taken in too easily, as well. And as for the claim of a child left with the owner, that could be entirely false or only half true. Perhaps the infant slave was left as some compensation to the mistress in Austin for loss of an adult servant.

The recovering man imagined an unfolding indictment of his own action. He admitted to himself a sense of relief when Brother Beaulieu escorted Bernard and Yarico to the nondescript schooner just after an afternoon squall broke out. Porches and fishing docks emptied of bystanders during the downpour, and Shelby watched the priest take the lead with a small black umbrella held high. The couple leaning against one another followed under a larger canopy.

What the expedition survivor did two hours later, he could explain simply enough to himself. Even if parts of the story Yarico and Bernard traveled by were untrue—though he'd detected no hint of duplicity— one feature of their circumstance he could testify to. The two were in love. He too had known such affection. He himself had suffered the unrequited kind, first as only a child and a young man can. Who was he, Shelby Whitmire, to take a course that might send a shackled Yarico in one direction and her soft-spoken lover to a different auction block?

The Natchez man had been on a tortuous march through hell in the last year. He did not wish to walk through the fires of repentance for an eternity. He would escort Mr. and Mrs. Giroux up the Mississippi to their desired destination. If he returned to Austin to find Miss Adeline Harper offended that he'd enabled their escape, he might wait some months for her understanding. He would tell her honestly what he had done. If she declared she could never forgive him, he would think about a second attempt to see Santa Fe covered in snow. He didn't think much could injure him more than a cold turn in Adeline's disposition toward him. But a forced separation of Yarico from Bernard would dim his spirit more.

He would take off on foot to Santa Fe, if the worst unfolded. Apokta had told him years ago that most Indians will leave a crazy man at peace. If Adeline spurned him for helping Yarico and Bernard, he would begin walking north and then west toward the impossible desert. He would concede that his life was reduced to a perilous circle. He would invite the snow to fall on his own mind and soul.

Once aboard the small ship taking regular junkets from Galveston and New Orleans, Shelby Whitmire suffered less from dramatic sensations.

A familiar, dull queasiness took hold of him as the vessel departed and blew farther into the gulf waters. Brother Beaulieu had advised him to keep his distance from the escorted couple, as a less sympathetic handler would do. The husband and wife also had been reminded to maintain silence and detachment for their own security. With all passengers of color kept entirely below the airy decks and Shelby compelled to lean at a railing whenever he could, the travelers had no problem avoiding attention for the three days it took to reach the Louisiana port.

The survivor of Perote might have thought he'd find New Orleans an uplifting change, but a stronger wave of nausea hit Shelby when passengers from Galveston disembarked. The magnitude of activity made him feel his legs might give out. Shelby had not considered what burden he might cause companions, how his weak knee and shoulder might bring extra toil to the pair with him. He had endured the cruel march from Santa Fe without much weight in clothing, certainly with nothing to carry.

But the necessity of being helped by Mr. and Mrs. Giroux worked in everyone's favor. There was no dubious assignment of roles in the public eye. Familiar with the port city, Yarico and Bernard quietly directed Shelby from behind and managed the travel bags for all three. Still considerably lame, he simply walked ahead as best he could. He was grateful for the second-hand shirt and jacket Brother Beaulieu had given him. The woman with the blue bonnet kept her head respectfully down, and her male companion looked to have his duties understood.

After a short coach drive, with Shelby riding inside and the married couple sitting on an open platform at the rear, they settled into a tiny inn where a padre that Brother Beaulieu knew lent his private guest rooms to the trio. He had already made special arrangements with the captain of a small steamer—the *Petit Soleil.* In a few days, ample quinine would arrive for Galveston. On his return trip, Shelby could shepherd medical supplies back to Texas.

Obliged to stay at the inn until next daylight, he realized that—for the first time in nearly seven years—he was journeying along the same paths Thomas Weeks had taken. Though Shelby had never been enticed down the Mississippi as a youth, he would soon be traveling upstream. Even now he was at a quaint lodge near the New Orleans docks where Thomas might well have earned modest keep. As he and the couple waited for a coach in the morning, Shelby thought of the exhilaration his friend must have experienced at the outset. Bernard and Yarico were stirred by their own memories of the city.

"Not so many avenues from here, it was a hotel favored by Monsieur de Saligny. He was not the villain too many in Austin believed. My freedom from the indenture of *mon père* is but one proof."

"We would be wise, I've been thinking," Yarico searched for a way to express her worry, "to keep our statements simple until we set our feet in the streets of Cincinnati."

"But of course," her husband smiled. "You are wise, always."

"Press my arm if I burst into French."

"Your fondest thoughts pour out in two languages. But this we make our secret."

"I keep looking for a kind concierge we all depended on, and for a portrait artist we came to know," she said. On the way to the docks, they passed a desolate courtyard and the charred remains of a Spanish building. She murmured something about mistaking the location of a small inn where the Harper women once stayed.

"In seven years, every corner is a new world." It was Bernard speaking, but Shelby nodded, too. He reminded himself it was 1842. Recently, the "count" had been recalled to France. The people Yarico knew had likely long ago ceased strolling a nearby avenue. Thomas Weeks would nevermore stride around any corner. Bernard had spoken, but all three shared the sobering perspective. Shelby read more in the woman's expression. She was surely wondering how long she would be separated from the little daughter left behind.

On the second evening of their journey upriver, a clump of black people not chained in the hold of the packet steamer *Petit Soleil* were allowed to stand near a back railing to get some fresh air. Among them were a cobbler and his wife, a liveryman and his brother—all freemen hoping to reach Louisville. They gripped the wooden bar to keep their balance. Yarico and Bernard clung discreetly to each other at the edge of the group. The boat carried oranges and lemons and molasses from the port, and only a handful of white travelers, but Shelby moved toward the shadowy figures. He had been watching the shoreline and enjoying his first water travel without seasickness. The couple from Texas steadied themselves on the railing as their escort drew close enough to talk.

"It appears much like the Alabama River by moonlight," Yarico said. "So much shrinks to sameness in the dark." Her voice was as mellifluous as the sounds of nature on the riverbank, her diction educated. Shelby imagined this woman and Adeline reading to one another at a Macon hearth. His throat ached with appreciation.

"On the shore where I grew up," he managed to say, "there were few stretches of anything as smooth as this. The wagon wheels and piano tunes went on all night long. Shouting and gunshots at all hours."

"Adeline and I…and her mother, we never gave much thought to moving from a little piece of land we called Sweet Pine. Even after Miss Delphine died, days went by like a peaceful dream. The Ocmulgee River ran alongside our town, but I expect it never crossed our minds what river travel might be like."

"Like gliding on a cloud, this ship takes the river, *non?*" The gulf schooner to New Orleans had met waves unusually placid for sea travel. "From home in the Antilles, my knowledge of great sail ships gives me no love for a saltwater voyage," Bernard admitted, "but I forget you suffered on the passage from Veracruz, *Monsieur* Whitmire."

"The ones who suffered most are at the bottom of the ocean."

The expedition survivor was sorry he'd let their short conversation end on such a somber note. He judged it good for Yarico to think about her happier days in Macon, rather than dwell on the child left for a time in Austin. The dark and fragrant pines inland from the riverbank spoke to any observer of peace.

Shelby slept well in a cramped berth, but he before dawn he sought the deck and stood again near the boat's paddle wheel. The primary engine quieted at night while shipmates with lanterns and poles struggled to maintain upstream progress. Soon the Natchez native heard early workers stoking fires below in the boiler room, and he knew that the vessel would soon charge upriver. He was filled with equal parts apprehension and joy at the thought of seeing Natchez again, and he felt disinclined to make conversation with Mr. and Mrs. Giroux or anyone else gathering to see the sky lighten. As the *Petit Soleil* navigated a dramatic turn in the river, Shelby pictured himself as a boy—hanging off a pier up ahead, waiting to see what new passengers the Mississippi would bring.

Another traveler arriving early at the railing carried a small candle covered by a glass. The trader, wrapped in raccoon fur, spotted something on the shore. On an impulse, the fellow held his light out over the edge of the ship, but of course the riverbank was no more illuminated, and the glow only accentuated the man's anxious expression. Something had changed suddenly about the landscape after the little steamship's last wide turn. For a short bend in the river, the boat faced east and a glow on the horizon brightened the forest silhouette. A shocking outline elicited a gasp and then silence from those on deck. Shelby could see that taller pines had been snapped waist-high from the ground. What might have toppled so wide a swath of trees, he strained to imagine. Possibly a terrible battle had erupted. Maybe cannons like the two McLeod brought downriver for Texas had misfired a thousand times.

An eerie hush fell over the waterway as other vessels navigated past the devastation. As the Mississippi turned again, Shelby felt a leaden weight in his stomach. Could Natchez, not far upstream, have changed so much in his seven-year absence? *Under-the-hill* had thrived in its rough, chaotic ways, just as the serene part of town where the Weeks family lived seemed never to change in character. He steadied himself on the wooden rail as the paddle began turning in earnest. A shipmate who'd been managing a pole overnight drew alongside to suck on his pipe.

"I saw a mean waterspout off the coast in Pensacola," the man said, "back when I was a lad working the crawfish rigs. Never had seen what a land cyclone can do."

"A cyclone came up this far?"

"Tornado is what they'd call it in Nebraska territory."

"…funnel storm…"

"A helluva tornado."

"When was this?"

"You must not be from around here." The steamboat worker studied him. A handful of passengers eased in their direction to hear. "No one from these parts could forget 1840."

"I've been…away."

"Folks were sitting down to supper. The rain had been a-fallin' steady, but then there came a roar like a passel of locomotives There was nothing most people could do by the time they heard the grinding sound. Trees being whittled to splinters and sawdust, and…"

"Did it stay downriver here? Or…" Shelby was afraid to ask.

"Most damage was done up in Natchez. If you think the shore looks bad now, just wait another quarter hour."

A deep murmur spread among those listening. The *Petit Soleil* was scheduled to spend two nights at the town for unloading and stocking up on engine wood before continuing to Vicksburg.

"Three years ago, that under-the-hill part was almost erased," the pole man went on. "Plenty flattened in the pretty streets up on the bluff, too."

For the next fifteen minutes, Shelby braced himself for witnessing what had become of his boyhood home. He'd intended to stay at Mr. Todd's hotel if there was room. So many of the fancier steamships were luxurious floating hotels, and he thought that shoreline inns might be pleased for any customer—and willing to house servants in an outlying building. Yarico and Bernard had joined a handful of domestics on the far side of the paddle, but their alarmed demeanor told Shelby that they, too, had seen the shoreline.

A dark fear gripped the Mississippi native. He tried to shake off the possibility that Ann Weeks Harris had perished in a violent act of nature, that all traces of her vibrant existence had been obliterated. From upriver, he had often viewed the approaching turn through a spyglass. The same bend now was like nothing he'd seen before, its shoreline shredded and washed away. Dozens of structures on stilts had disappeared altogether. New beachfront domiciles and trade buildings appeared hastily erected, as if the folly in constructing anything more glorious was painfully ingrained.

Passengers clung to one another as the *Petit Soleil* docked. Lumber fragments, strewn randomly, contrasted with the coordinated movements of workers at the port so crucial to the great trail east. Survivors of the tornado had gathered their wits. Though their homes had been lost, they'd scraped a living after the destruction.

"You can keep your pallets on board the next night or two for a dollar," the packet captain told him. "They won't get in our way, but the deck and hold need scrubbing first, after our stock unloads." Shelby knew he meant two chains linking human cargo below, as well as the crates of fruit stored topside. He had noticed with some disgust that pens on the strand to hold slaves in transit had been among the first refortified. "We won't be going on to Vicksburg until two mornings hence." The captain cleared his throat before continuing. "There's still decent lodging on yonder bluff, but there's a charge for the cart ride up. Or we can let you and your servants lodge on the rear deck. The edibles won't be more than tolerable. "

Both Yarico and Bernard declined Shelby's suggestion that they walk along into town with him, if only to stretch their legs. They felt comfortable enough with the honest captain, and the husband assured *Monsieur* Whitmire that walking topside would invigorate them well enough.

Someone from the upper part of Natchez might have described the town's lost attributes before stepping onto the landing plank. Shelby, however, shared no such parting observations with the couple. He wasn't sure he had the heart to venture up the hill and see how Mrs. Ann had fared, but he would learn first whether the tornado had spared his former cabinet shop. A rising dread came with his need to know how Apokta and his family had managed.

Like weeds appearing after land has been scraped, rough enterprises had sprung up in the last three years. Along the water's edge stretched makeshift docks. A lapboard cabin larger than a single domicile appeared to be the first place travelers risked spending nights ashore. Back from the riverbank, gambling shanties stood with no heed to where paths made corners previously. Passing a saloon where ladies let their arms hang loosely over railings, he kept his attention on the thoroughfare, just as he'd done as a boy. He wondered, though, if among them was the one who'd acquainted him once with passion. The collection of strangers and haphazard structures streamed by as in a blurry dream.

A bearded man carrying a whiskey barrel looked familiar, but the fellow was cursing and it was hard to distinguish his features. Past the area that had been Silver Street was a new sign with the same name, but all the buildings were recent, crude construction. When Shelby rounded a corner near the bluff, he was astounded. There on stilts stood the cabin that had belonged to his parents, though the stairway up to the shop door looked hammered together by inexperienced carpenters using green wood.

Shelby took the steps gingerly. His bad leg now throbbed from inactivity on the cramped deck. Knowing that property abandoned long enough belonged to whoever moved in, he did not approach the door as an owner would. But his heart pounded with the hope that Apokta or some of his family had made use of the building. Any survivors would know the Creek father had done woodworking alongside Shelby.

When a white woman allowed the door to open slightly, the Natchez native stood speechless. At first he thought he had never seen her before. Her hair, once blond, had darkened to the hue of driftwood. The luster was gone from her blue eyes, and only slowly did Shelby realize he was talking to the lonely girl who'd enticed him once into a saloon. He took off his hat and apologized if he had disturbed her.

"No customer been here in months, if that's what you mean." She looked over her shoulder and laughed weakly. "I can wash up, if you—" Then her eyes grew round. "It's you! They said you was never comin' back!"

"I'm not…I haven't…I'm just going upriver and thought I should stop by to see…"

"What Jesus threw down on all our sins?" Others might have said it mockingly, but there was a note of true sorrow in her voice.

"I didn't know anything about the cyclone…the tornado," Shelby admitted. "No one deserves this much ruin."

"Fair and polite. That's how you always struck me, but the graying hair…You never fell in with the ones who shook their fingers and predicted hellfire." She nodded, seeming to remember him better now.

"I only wanted to—"

"Come on in and let me heat up some coffee. I do recollect how to greet a visitor."

Shelby did not want to recall the time this woman had compromised him, but he stepped inside. His emotions swirled since coming along the banks of fallen trees. He felt sure, though, that she would know something about Apokta. Glancing in the direction of the old neighboring cabins on his way up, Shelby had seen only rubble. He fought off an odd queasiness. Inside the former Whitmire home, he found a stool by the wall where tools used to hang. The window there was latched, but cool air seeped in and he gulped a deeper breath.

In this Natchez cabin now occupied by a woman of the streets, secrets lurked—no less intense than the secrets Mrs. Ann and Angelina had whispered to each other long ago in the Weeks house. A doorway beyond where a small coffee pot now came to a boil was the room where his father and stepmother used to scream at one another until worse violence erupted. It was the same room where both finally succumbed to fever. Before Shelby now, where two sawhorses used to stand, was a cot likely used by this female and her customers. He worked to recall where it was Apokta used to set down boards after first cuttings.

"How did this cabin…stay in one piece?"

"The Bible quoters have their explanations." She was smiling. "Don't worry. Them that claim the cabin's owner must have been a saint, they weren't made any wiser."

"I didn't see anything else on shore that looked intact," he said, looking away from her.

"The slave shanties on the southern edge didn't need much rebuilding—they always looked thrown together by the devil."

"How did anybody—how did you survive?"

"The fellow who was on top of me suffered the roof coming down." He thought she'd made the jest many times before, but in Shelby's company she didn't laugh. Surely everyone close to the Natchez catastrophe had pondered the slim difference between survival and annihilation. After the Santa Fe ordeal, Shelby could detach himself from no one's suffering. His leg and shoulder would always be vulnerable, but not as fragile as his emotional hinges were now. Nausea washed over him again.

"I knew this visit would be hard, even if I stayed only a short while," he started. "I knew even a brief stopover would fill me with—"

"I know who you're going to ask about." She looked at him tenderly, and Shelby felt ashamed that he'd seldom even glanced her way in the years after their encounter. On his regular walks from Todd's inn to the cart incline, he had passed by brothels countless times without looking in their direction.

"With everything that was swept away, I can't bring myself to ask."

"Your lady friend is doing right well," she reassured him. Shelby felt cool and hot at the same time, and it seemed impossible that this stranger was talking to him about his friend's mother.

"My lady—"

"Most everyone down here knew about you leaving the Natchez shore. Some said you followed her boy that went off to the Texas wars—the two of you was hardly a breath apart as young'uns. But I knew it was melancholy over the widow taking another husband."

"Mrs. Ezekial Harris."

"Well," she said cautiously, "he didn't live long enough for me to remember his name."

"What?"

"If the Weeks house hadn't been so well built—everyone talking about what still stood and what disappeared in the whirlwind—her first husband's name wouldn't come to mind either."

"What happened to Mr. Harris?" Blood pounded in his ears.

"They say the couple had near three years together. It wasn't but nine months after the man died of heart failure, she bore him a child." She paused, as if not sure whether more conjecture was appropriate. "He wouldn't be the only man I knew to give up the ghost in the middle of …"

"She had another child?"

"A little boy. They're all doing right well, I can promise you—her and her children, and all her sisters, but I'd place money you'll want to go on up the hill and see for yourself."

"I saw the incline was washed away."

"You have to go around the edge of the bluff these days, but the cart ride on the other side is steep like it always was—as if I have any reason to go up."

"Who could have predicted which structure would survive?"

"Like this place." She laughed a little, before picking up her cup with surprising delicacy. "I don't know if you'll be wanting your cabin back. If so, whether you'd be agreeable to letting that side room, or…"

"No, I—I don't plan to stay—it wasn't at all my thinking…" Shelby felt a little comfort in imagining Mrs. Ann back at the original Weeks house. It was a different question nagging. "But you say the cart path has moved—does that mean Apokta and his family have rebuilt on around the bluff, too?" The woman looked at him in such a strange way that at first Shelby thought he'd overestimated her memories of him. Just because he felt himself inseparable from the Indian family, maybe their long partnership had not been so obvious to other inhabitants, especially those preoccupied with their own endeavors. "There was a large family of Creeks," he began again. "Apokta always wears a sash. He's tall, and he used to handle the cart when I was a boy, and then when his own son came to an age…"

"I remember him," the woman said. "His wife brought me a poultice once when my fever wouldn't break. Never said a word, but the wet rags seemed to ease me right away."

"You remember?" Her tone of finality chilled him.

"They're still movin' savages through here, you know, up to the Oklahoma territory. But it's not like when the great swarm of Cherokee was forced on the march."

"Is Apokta gone? Was it the tornado? Or before, because of…"

"Well before the monster storm…they loaded 'em all up from around here. The whole bunch of 'em that used to live around the corner from your shop here… It was that cart driver and his boy and several women with babies, all they could round up—I remember his name. I remember his face that day."

"Loaded them up?"

"The papers had the story about the ship sinking. It was in the news all around here." She waited for Shelby to say one word or make a sound before going on, but he didn't look as if he breathed. He looked as if a black funnel were snapping trees before his eyes. "There was a whole steamship full of Indians—maybe two hundred—just barely moved off from the shore. It was only one boiler that exploded they said, but it was enough to sink everything in ten minutes if that."

"…Apokta…"

"None could swim or even had a chance with it going down so fast."

Shelby Whitmire sat down on the cot. He tried to remember the day the two had worked on a cabinet, the day Tail Feather had come to the door to call his father home, when it had really been Thomas wanting to talk privately. It was Apokta who had consoled him and advised him about Ann Weeks—the friend who had given him a horse and saddle with tassels and a blessing for safe journey to Fort Jessup in Louisiana.

Then, Shelby lay down stiffly on the thin mattress and commanded his memory to replay times when his stepmother took to thrashing him with the hearth poker, when he would have to cover his head with his arms and hands. He worked hard to remember that easier pain, though the time of thrashings was gone forever, like everything else about his early life, all gone, all washed away.

When he blinked after a long lapse of consciousness, he could tell he had not moved from the position he'd taken the day before. A child no more than four and a toddler stared at him from several feet away.

"Mama be right back," the blond boy said. "Are you dead?" Shelby made a sound in his throat, and the smaller child began to whimper. "Mama said not to touch you."

Shelby tried to find a mental place again, where he had been before losing consciousness. He wanted to remember childhood beatings instead of the other thing, the old news about Apokta's family. He could only bring to mind a sinking steamship and the cries of people, his friends who could not swim.

"Mama be right back."

"Are you all right, sir?" More than an hour later, it was Mrs. Giroux asking him. She had come off the steamship by herself, since a black individual attending one white person was a common sight. The two women maneuvered him into a sitting position. Yarico wiped his forehead with a clean rag and carefully helped him back into his coat. "We need to move on back to the ship, if that's all right." This time she looked directly into his eyes, checking to see how much of his surroundings he understood. Shelby nodded. "If I'm gone more than thirty minutes, Bernard will come striding this way on his own. We don't want that, do we?" Shelby shook his head. "If you're steady on your feet, I'll just come along behind, so we don't cause a stir. It's not but early light yet, so we'd best move on now, Mr. Whitmire." She and the Natchez woman helped him stand up. "You've had a terrible shock." She looked at Shelby as if she were afraid to voice her next thought. "If you aim to stay here, if you have people to see, Bernard and I can help look after you a week or two. It's the least we can do…if you aim to stay a spell in Natchez."

The thought of being waylaid in Natchez gave Shelby the jolt he needed to navigate the cabin steps and make unsteady progress toward the shore where the *Petit Soleil* was docked. When they boarded, Shelby sank onto a sturdy crate. He was perspiring even though it was chilly, and Bernard whispered that he was glad the ship's owner had gone on shore for a meal at one of the rebuilt taverns.

There was some commotion the next morning when a family of nine disputed their fare with the captain. He had thought there would only be six, but the parents were saying their youngest offspring were too small for full fare. The debate continued even as the craft released its moorings and the engine fired up. A couple miles upstream, the owner noticed Shelby Whitmire's state, his vacant stare and his perspiring despite the cold. He put his handkerchief over his mouth and hissed to the couple that their master might be coming down with a fever. When he began to mutter about depositing the white man and his two slaves on the wharf at Vicksburg, Yarico explained the shock he'd suffered.

"He's lost some family, sir. The tornado was bad enough news." The captain studied Shelby as if he were working to regain his friendly demeanor.

"I forget those from other parts learn of it like it was yesterday."

"And what happened before that…" she went on. "He was neighbor to some of the Indians who went down, lost in the river." At this the captain's eyes grew as glassy as Shelby's.

"My brother-in-law was shipmaster. His whole family was with him when the engine blew." He appeared to comprehend his passenger's diminished state of mind. "For a month afterward, my own children barely ate." He paused to check the healthy sound of engines propelling the *Petit Soleil* safely upstream. "But you two attend to your gentleman and let me know if he gets bloody vomit or anything the like."

By Vicksburg, Mr. and Mrs. Giroux had succeeded in getting Shelby to take some nourishment and the captain nodded reassuringly. A dock official strode aboard to make sure there were no "miscreants harboring runaway slaves," but the two attendants openly assisting the weaker white man did not arouse suspicion.

"Mr. Shelby Whitmire of Galveston Texas, and his two domestics— one docile male, one obedient female," the captain told the wharf inspector. "The fellow has business as far as Cincinnati as I recall. He was left somewhat weakened by the Santa Fe Expedition."

"That disaster!"

"Keep your voice down," the captain said. "Mere mention of it addles the poor man." He had taken on more protectiveness after learning that the steamship tragedy was a personal sorrow to the Texan. "I hope these three can rest safely here a day or two, seeing as this is my turnaround."

"But will he weather the turmoil he's likely to encounter upstream?" the official wondered. "Arkansas can give close scrutiny to anyone taking a string of blacks northerly, but it's Missouri these days where tussles foment. Who can abide those crazed abolitionists?"

"Can you vouch for a safe ship taking the Ohio River on through Louisville and as far as Cincinnati?" The official spat before answering.

"All I can swear to that far north is that the so-called free states will be the ruin of the entire country!"

At an Arkansas dock two days later, the less sympathetic captain of a larger steamship accepted some coins from a "Deputy Wilcox." The port official was allowed to board and scrutinize domestics. When Yarico looked about to reach for her freedom papers, Shelby quietly touched her wrist to stop her. With most documents suspected of forgery, the three were safer to carry on as they appeared—loyal servants tending to a frail master whose business required northerly travel.

A Missouri port the next day did little to give the woman and her husband a sense that they were closer to hospitable territory. In this half-free and half-slave state, the wharves were supposedly neutral for the time it took a ship to let some passengers off and others to board. Recovering some strength, Shelby walked Yarico and Bernard out to the railing that faced open water where they could take in the breeze and relative calm on the deck. When a shot rang out from the shore, he rushed to the dock side only to see a dark-skinned human shape, lying still. The shackled man had attempted to flee. He could not have expected to get far, but he'd likely prayed for the embrace of abolitionists. Shaken, the Natchez man took as reality that from this spot on up the Ohio River, fortune might indeed turn the other way. Americans might very well counter a slave owner's claim of possession.

As the steamboat continued upriver, the three travelers from Texas developed a routine, where Shelby and the couple would walk in the open just at dusk and take several tours around the ship's first deck until cabin doors began opening to torchlight on the upper level. Then the three would retire to their small suite where a curtain made two compartments reasonably private during the night. Only Shelby would emerge during the day, since he was able to bring enough food from the canteen to keep the pair comfortable. Again at sunset, the three would walk, with Yarico and then Bernard coming behind Shelby single file. Appearing in this arrangement, the trio was ignored.

Passengers beheld much more interesting sights on the river—flatboats carrying more pigs or chickens than people, luxury steamships like floating coronations, rowboats of townspeople heading out for an island picnic, furtive boaters irritated that a larger ship might startle fish away from their lines. Once, Shelby saw a watery log onto which a man clung, but who waved as if he were delighted with free means of transportation. After a tense stopover at Louisville, which proved Kentucky to be as agitated over the slavery issue as Missouri, the Texans shed some apprehension. Shelby was grateful that his companions' welfare consumed his attention. With Apokta's family past help forever, the task of shepherding Mr. and Mrs. Giroux lifted him slowly from despair.

"There's been notable work done by abolitionists up this way," he said one last evening in their partitioned berth. "A neighbor when I was a child moved up north, just precisely so she could join their cause."

"Not much seems ever to change in the South. Or even as far up this way as Louisville," Yarico said solemnly. The day before they had all watched the wharf dumbfounded as two business partners—born free or at liberty after manumission—drove a covered wagon from the dock into the busy streets of that city. Though the wagon bed was mostly obscured, chained slaves could be seen huddled against one another. None of the three watching could articulate their shock. Drawing closer to Cincinnati the next day, they found words more easily.

"Most of Texas seemed somewhat better than…what we've seen on this river trip," Shelby observed.

"Too many die too easily even getting there." It was rare to hear contempt in Yarico's voice. "Those enslaved who don't survive transport see their toil come to an end, but their dreams too. A dozen people in irons went sliding from a river raft once. All I could do was watch," she said. And they all remembered how Count de Saligny's purchase of a mulatto consort ended.

"My wife and I spoke for the first time," Bernard went on, "at the funeral of the New Orleans slave who lived only to reach the hotel of *Monsieur* Bullock." Shelby felt himself among friends and inclined to speak his mind.

"It's true the horror at Natchez could have unfolded just as easily in Texas—two hundred Creek Indians forced onto a doomed ship." A hush fell again inside the steamship cabin.

But upon arriving in Cincinnati, they learned that freemen and their families still faced a range of troubles there. The desk clerk at an off-street hotel advised them to maintain their discreet demeanor. The poorer white citizenry, he explained, were generally opposed to abolition because of the competition that would give them for much-needed work. There had been such dangerous riots two years previously that as many as half the city's black population fled to Canada or moved one direction or another out of the city. Quite a few had meandered back, but as wealthier Cincinnati residents relocated to houses east of 6th

Street in downtown, hostility in the old sectors brewed up again. The poorer parts of the city, with Irish or German neighborhoods, continued to lean toward violent protest. When Shelby asked the helpful clerk what he knew about the atmosphere in Philadelphia toward liberated slaves—since that was the direction Mrs. Greenfield had headed with the girl singer—the man only shook his head.

"I heard one official say that the 'City of Brotherly Love' was seething with the worst hatred for colored folks that he'd ever witnessed."

"At least here in Cincinnati, part of this town allows for enterprise among our people. They trade with each other and stay self-sufficient," Bernard said to his wife. "They defend themselves as they find necessary."

"Texas was safer than these parts in only *some* ways." Yarico emitted a guttural sound that made the men turn to her. "Maybe no riots," she said in a strained voice, "but it was no safe place for a person of color to set foot on the streets without a white owner's protection."

"Or a strong husband as an escort," Bernard said, putting his arm around her shoulder.

"We can't keep running away until Jesus comes down from heaven to set the world aright." She paused to regain her composure. "We'll find a spot safe enough here in Cincinnati. Besides, we don't want to travel any farther, for fear it will make it difficult for Adeline to bring Adelphine next year…or the next."

"Maybe Miss Harper will let me make that trip, too," Shelby said thoughtfully. "A single woman and a child might face real danger traveling alone."

"*Monsieur* Whitmire," Bernard spoke up. "We are in your debt for your help along this trip, and I hope we can be friends always." Shelby had thought he might stay to make sure the two were settled, but it was his own loneliness he had been dreading, his own solitary trip downstream. Outside their hotel, they could look toward the busy intersection and see people of African descent conversing and trading openly along the thoroughfare. Two men shook hands and began to laugh. One lady held a parasol, and she patted the head of another woman's pigtailed child.

"It looks as if you can prosper here…" It was true that white residents kept shops on the other side of the street, though no hostility appeared to subdue business and personal exchanges.

"A man I met this morning tells me there is peace on most days for our side of town. The city wishes for prosperity. We can live in Cincinnati."

So, Monsieur Giroux has already made acquaintances, Shelby thought. *He would make anybody a very good friend.*

"I don't doubt you'll get a foothold." Shelby wanted to ride with them deeper into the safe Cincinnati district, but he saw he would have to let the couple go on their own. He sensed that Bernard needed to take charge and have a final handshake. A porter brought the bags of all three out onto the boardwalk, and the parting suddenly felt final.

Shelby fought the inclination to give Yarico a brotherly embrace, since such signs of affection would have shocked people on either side of town. She must have read his mind, and she made a little curtsey, saying, "You get on home safely now, you hear Mr. Whitmire? There are people in Texas who will shed tears of relief to find that you are still among the living." As a plain carriage approached to take the pair on, she turned aside. "This reminds me so of a departure in New Orleans—of darling Adeline." When she and Bernard were situated, she leaned to say, "Some would be happy to throw their arms around you for all your kindness."

The solitary man took his hat off and assured the couple that he would let Adeline Harper know of their safe arrival. He had the address of the postal office near the hotel, a safe place in Cincinnati for exchanging news. The next steamship going downriver was scheduled to pause at the shore within an hour, and Shelby bid the two *adieu* before turning to collect his own bag.

How lonely he felt as the open rig wheeled the Texas couple around the corner and out of sight. When he spotted the bench where he would rest his legs while waiting for his own coach, the image of Private Moreland flashed before him again, the soldier's last expression of disbelief. But the next face Shelby imagined was Apokta's as his family was marched to the docks. And then he wondered if Angelina Eberly had been at the inn with Delilah when someone ran in with the terrible news about Alex? Or did she herself witness the street tragedy and get escorted to a rough bench like the one Shelby approached? How terribly far away his home now felt—not Natchez, Mississippi, which he hoped he would pass by while sound asleep one night soon. It was a curious jolt after all these years to realize his heart and hopes had taken root in a fading Texas town called Austin.

1843 Austin, Texas and Goliad

20   Voices Near and in the Wind

On his third morning in the stable at Eberly House, Shelby Whitmire awoke disoriented again. He could not remember if he was still in the prison at Perote or in a Galveston hospital or on the spare cot in his father's cabin. His legs and shoulder had improved during the return trip from Cincinnati, but he still couldn't trust his mind very well. The abandoned inn was empty except for the first floor room that had been his, where the bed was still made with a simple striped blanket and a tin cup rested on a side table that Youruh had helped him craft. He'd found a note folded under the cup.

Gone to the coast—likely Indianola. No lodgers here. Thankful to hear you lived through the expedition. I hardly recognized McLeod—so lean!

We missed you most when Alex was laid to rest. Mag and Delilah send their love. Come see us,

Angelina

Upon reading Mrs. Eberly's note the first time, Shelby felt so alone that he bolted from the starkly empty interior to the adjoining livery. Signs of life were absent there as well, except for a rake, which he used to mound up loose straw into a pallet. He made himself walk several times from the Eberly buildings to the main crossroads of town, where the Bullock Hotel was under new ownership and the sitting log now looked no more inviting than a large piece of debris on the Natchez shore. Resting on the hotel steps was a ragged fellow, Hiram, who did errands for the man running the place now.

"Everyone still calls it *Bullock's*. Him and his missus left town and right quick Mr. Bullock died—that was nigh a year ago."

"It looks like Doc Robertson still has his sign out," Shelby observed. He felt numb to more tragic news but he pushed away the worst possibility. He'd trained his eyes on the cabin window where he'd once spied Yarico engrossed in her reading.

"Keeps his sign hung as some insurance no one ransacks him. He's been out of town for a fortnight, though, if you're lookin' for someone to doctor that leg." They both squinted at the knee for a moment.

"No, there's no help for it." Then Shelby gazed across the way again at the dogtrot half the Harper women had rented from the physician. "Do you recall if his lady assistant stayed here in Austin?"

"Never found occasion to say howdy, though I seen the little thing followed by a mixed child sometime early last spring. It musta been her. She was brought into conversation back then when the few wives in town questioned who was left to school their children."

"She's fond of books…" Shelby's saddlebag now bulged with two bundles of personal letters. The post manager in Galveston wasn't sure why McLeod had declined to take the Georgia envelopes on up to the Harpers. Shelby wondered if his friend had guessed he'd need a concrete reason to seek out the Macon woman.

"Truth be told, I ain't seen much in the way of females for months." When the hotel worker laughed, it was clear his teeth were mostly absent, too. "When I say everyone calls this place *Bullock's*, that would be me and the new inn-keep. He rents blankets for almost nothing."

"I'll just bed down in the Eberly stable while I'm in town."

"Used to be the archives was kept in her safe…after that time Houston's boys tried to carry them off." Hiram stood up to stretch his legs. "Now, all the Texas papers stay under lock over at the old government fort. There's three cutthroats paid to keep watch."

"I heard Mrs. Eberly fired a cannon at thieves making a getaway."

"A wasteful ruckus over a stack of writing, if you ask me. But the guards there now are too rough for anyone's hotel, is what I'm sayin'. If you think again about where to sleep, you'd have your pick of rooms."

Shelby limped back to the stable and napped until noon. He awoke wondering why he'd let the rig driver take him up Congress from the riverbank in the first place. Anyone could deduce from the deserted intersection that Austin had fallen from stature. It would have been more productive to venture west of the squat steamer docked on the Colorado, to seek the boy keeping Sawdust and to find supplies more easily. But he dreaded learning that the enclave of friendly Indians had been overrun by Comanche. He could not put into words his worse fear, that an ignorant posse had decimated the settlement.

He could admit only to himself why his new bundle of letters kindled such sense of purpose. The envelopes were addressed from a town very few miles west of Adeline Harper's childhood home. Not long after Shelby's return from his trip north, the Galveston postmaster handed him the bundle, and both had shrugged.

"They're yours to deliver wherever you think best, Mr. Whitmire." The sender's name on all but one envelope was *John T. Spillers*, the man Captain Holliday thought he'd abandoned to certain recapture. Yet, clearly, Spillers had lived and found his way home. Shelby knew that dark and agonizing fate was real all too often, but so apparently were flickering miracles. The envelopes had been a small spark after his long convalescence.

In the next few days, he let himself venture a short way down Pecan in the direction of the steep ravine and creek, where pecans lay plentiful. When he counted out half the shelled nuts and swapped them for coarse bread and a jug of spring water, Hiram was standing in for the proprietor at Bullock's. Shelby thought he would revive enough to explore the cross-street east toward the count's hill and fancy house, but he could stomach the search no more than three doors past what had been Burke's Reading Room. If he were to sink in despair on the stoop of a desolate structure over that way, he might not be found until his bones bleached in the sun. He tried to remember why he hadn't stayed put in Austin while it thrived, why he hadn't just knocked gently on the door of Dr. Robertson's assistant and offered Adeline what help he could.

The absurdity struck him. He'd lacked the courage to speak with her about the missing servant, to confess that Yarico had looked up from her book and caught him at their window. Shelby thought he might go mad from laughing if the choice were now given to him—either speak in honesty with the gentle brown-haired girl, Adeline Harper, or walk half naked in winter from the bleak hills of New Mexico to a prison two thousand miles south.

On the straw pallet in the stable, Shelby Whitmire tossed and turned until it was close to dusk and time to reach for the lantern. Only minutes after the flame settled down into a steady glow, drowsiness returned. He sought sleep as escape, a habit he and his fellow prisoners clung to during the expedition ordeal. When he detected the soft thud of hooves, he was unsure how long ago he'd set a match to the lantern wick. Someone approached on horseback from the ravine end of Pecan, and Shelby judged that he had no time to slip powder into his rifle if it were a hostile Comanche scout. Instead, he grabbed the rake handle and went limp on the pile of straw so as to appear sound asleep. His heart pounded when he recognized the sounds of a person sliding off a horse, and it crossed his mind that there were worse places to get murdered than in Angelina's stable, in the last structure he would have told anyone he'd called home.

"Tassel Man." It was the name that Walk Far had given Shelby eventually, but the voice inside the stable was not as deep as the ferryman's. He judged the speaker to be a stranger, but no one hostile. When Shelby opened his eyes, he did not recognize the bare-chested Indian, only slightly more man than boy. "You came back. I saw your light."

"…Youruh?"

"I ride in to get *Two Mothers*," he said, "…Miss Adeline. Come with me. Father Walk Far needs a doctor. We must hurry."

The next hour unfolded as the kind of oddly comforting dream Shelby seldom had, where some abiding assurance underlies tense, eerie events. Youruh helped Shelby up on his horse. Both boy and animal trotted eastward up Pecan to where shadows enveloped cabins and shacks on either side of the avenue. In only one structure did a covered windowpane shimmer from light within. The boy handed Shelby the reins and ran to the covered stoop, leaving the weak visitor astride Sawdust. A woman came almost immediately to the doorway, and the man on the horse could see her pulling a cloak around her shoulders. The Comanche youth raced back to stop Shelby from trying to dismount.

"There is no time," he said. "She must wake the little one. No time to hitch horses to her wagon. She and Bright Hair will ride their big horse."

"You should—"

"I can run. Will you take hold of her supply satchel?" It was Youruh asking, but the arms reaching up on the other side of Sawdust belonged to Adeline Harper. She lifted up to Shelby a wide leather case that women of more robust stature might have been unable to hoist.

"Let me give you this before I wake Adelphine."

"Miss Harper," Shelby heard himself say. When he took the medical bag, she touched his boot at the ankle. She had pulled the hood of her cape up over her hair, already let down for the night. Another woman might have appeared vulnerable at dusk, her head tilted up and her hair undone. But Adeline looked right at him with eyes brave enough to rejoice.

"You are here. You're alive."

"I brought some letters to town that you might want." She had already turned to go wake the child, and Youruh was rushing on to her stable to saddle a Harper horse. Shelby knew it wasn't the right moment to bring up envelopes from Knoxville, but he felt another wave of appreciation for his friend Hugh, how his prescient gift—a second letter bundle—had allowed him to speak at all upon seeing Adeline Harper again. Otherwise, he might only have gone slack-jawed like one of Bullock's log-sitters.

Shelby Whitmire had a vague sense that he should have been in the lead as the group went down Congress Avenue toward the river. The woman riding ahead of him was barely into her twenties, and the sleepy child clinging to her from behind was too young to leave alone. A long shawl wrapped around the girl and Adeline's middle, keeping the two secure. The Comanche boy ran well ahead of their horse, sometimes on into the deep shadows as the medical team passed an abandoned cabin and then again into a dull circle of light as they rushed by an inhabited shack. Shelby lagged behind, keeping Sawdust at a slower trot.

One boarded-up storefront took him aback. The count's staff had bought and sold needlework there. Had he even looked at Austin's main street when the rig brought him up a few days earlier? He didn't recall the next squat building either, where headstones and engraving styles were displayed. Feeling not so far from needing a cemetery plot himself, he hoped his strength would hold long enough to see the emergency through. He had heard Youruh tell Adeline about his *grandfather's* fever and shaking. As they neared the riverbank, the man riding Sawdust tried to clear his mind about what to do if there was dark vomit by the time they made the settlement—aim his rifle at the other two and the tiny girl, order them to keep their distance? A rising dread sliced through weeks of indecision and despondency.

"Youruh!" Something in Shelby's voice made the youth stop and wait for the second horse. "It was right how you came for Miss Adeline. But it could be something easy for the child to catch, something dangerous. Keep the girl with you. Let Miss Harper and me take a look at Walk Far." Gripping the saddle horn, Shelby slid to the ground with the satchel. He shook off the old pain that jabbed at his knee. The slight woman in charge of the other horse had already untied the knit shawl at her waist and was motioning to the boy.

"He's right," she said to him. "Take her." The little girl slipped down onto the boy's back and put her arms around his neck as if she had traveled that way before. Her unusual hair, earthy curls tinged with gold, sprang down to her shoulders in contrast to the youth's black braids. "You all come along with Sawdust. Mr. Whitmire and I will go see how your grandfather is." Adeline's eyes grew wide and solemn as she nodded at Shelby.

"Are there coals? Can you get a fire going?" he asked Youruh. He still couldn't believe how tall the boy had grown in two years. Fear flickered in the youth's eyes, but he only nodded, masking his concern.

"I'll make Bright Hair a place by the fire." He shifted her weight so that she could wrap her arms tighter around his neck. "If there is catch on my river line, after you take the fever from Father Walk Far, we'll grease the fish pan."

Only one lean-to nearby was still enlivened by a lantern's glow. The oilcloth teepee alongside had to be the boy's. Others in the enclave appeared to have trickled away many months ago. Just beyond the fire trench, where the two young people were headed, Shelby walked alongside the Harper horse. Adeline had drawn her knees up high on the animal's flank, and the man shook off reticence, steadying himself by holding onto the empty stirrup.

"I should be carrying that satchel," she said.

"I've got my balance. We're almost there."

"I never came down here before." The regret in her words made Shelby dare to look up in the fading light. He couldn't see the green in her eyes, the way he had in candlelight at Burke's place. But he overcame the sudden urge to speak, to say how much he admired her expressive brow. "Youruh brought in a friend with a broken wrist about a year ago," Adeline went on, "and then the next day he and Walk Far rode back up Pecan from the creek."

"I used to come here two or three times a week."

"They told me," she said. "They missed you." The Harper horse was just outside Walk Far's riverbank dwelling, and Shelby looked up at her again, thinking how many times he had watched a bend in the Mississippi and never spied anything as heart-stopping. "They brought me and Adelphine shawls and fish and pecans. I taught Youruh to read, but I never…"

"You can't go in there now," Shelby said to her gently, "until I see it's not yellow fever or anything as deadly." She turned in the saddle to look back where Yarico's little girl sat near a growing fire. "She'll be lost if anything happens to you."

Adeline had set her teeth on her lower lip, he could see now, but she was nodding, and when she leaned to bring her skirt and leg from the other side of the horse, Shelby set down the satchel. Trembling at the thought of helping her, he let her alight by her own method.

"One terrible night in the spring of '36," she said, "it was Walk Far who watched over my aunt and me, and Yarico." She was torn in her concern, but then she smiled faintly. "McLeod said you'd likely accompany her and Bernard up the Mississippi."

"They are safe," was all Shelby managed to say. He felt he was losing his power of speech. Adeline appeared so slight in stature now that her feet were on the ground. Her shoulders were close enough that he could have lifted his good arm to console her as a friend would. "You'd best show me what's in the medical bag," he said.

The first two days that Shelby looked after Walk Far, the younger man kept wondering if Youruh knew how a Tonkawa elder might wish his body to be prepared for the afterlife. For one part of an hour, the ill man would shiver so violently that four blankets and layers of deer hide could not at first arrest his chills. Then, rapidly, he would appear to be suffocating from sweat that trickled from his wide forehead to his tattooed cheeks. Even when Adeline's underskirt was soaked in river water and tenderly draped over the patient, the heat at his temples subsided only somewhat. It was during one of the sweating spells, when Shelby had tried to let some early autumn air circulate and cool the skin of their suffering friend, that daylight shone on the rash winding up Walk Far's side.

"With this red rash, nothing like smallpox, and how he shakes his head if you try to give him water…"

"Scarlet fever very likely," Adeline said. "I'll stir some salt into dark tea. Tell him to let it reach the back of his throat and then spit. Later, we'll bury the jar."

"He's not shaking as much as when we first came, but he has a blank stare that scares me, even when I'm talking to him."

"Scarlet fever can take the hearing, and sight, too." They were just outside the buffalo hide door of Walk Far's hut, and she looked off where the boy and Adelphine were gathering dry reeds for kindling. "I'm worried you'll come down sick, too." For the first time, she averted her eyes.

"They said I might have fought off the yellow fever, or else only suffered a very mild bout. I've kept my bandana over my mouth," Shelby told her. "The German doctor you sent me to watch in San Antonio followed practices I never forgot."

"If I hadn't wished you on that journey, your arm would still have its strength."

"We wouldn't have Youruh's company." In a moment, she turned back to Shelby, and he was ashamed that he'd recently thought of her as barely past girlhood. Her eyes were so serious and wise.

"When I realize how hard it will be to take Adelphine up north… maybe next year… I don't ever consider how she came to be—only how selfishly I'll miss her."

"You might need company coming back downriver—if you'll be heading on home to Texas."

With Shelby showing no signs of the affliction a week later, Adeline Harper let herself hug both children in celebration of Walk Far's recovery. Youruh beamed alongside Tassel Man. Insisting that the two females curl up in his tent each night, he had slept by the fire and kept watch over the coals. Now he remembered to tell both medics about a family his adopted grandfather had ferried the week before, how their children had showed no appetite for days.

"They were moving west part way to San Antonio" he went on soberly. "If they made it to German town, they will have medicine." Shelby thought the youth should know the worst.

"Walk Far will live a long time, it looks like…but he can't hear a thing right now, or speak yet. It could be both are gone for good."

"Are his eyes working?" Youruh's grave expression relaxed when Shelby nodded.

"He studies me, maybe trying to understand how my hair can have more silver than his." The expedition disaster had accelerated his early graying. "And I've caught him looking at the doorway, too—looking for you."

They stayed at the riverbank for another handful of days. Youruh was the only one who could get Walk Far to eat, but they agreed that a vacant cabin on Pecan, next to the Harper home, would be better shelter for the recovering man. Adeline explained that a family from Bavaria had lived next door when her Aunt Maggie was still alive. They'd had daughters whom she tutored, and it would be uplifting to have the well-constructed domicile inhabited again.

One Sunday afternoon in late January, Shelby looked from the window in the men's cabin and smiled to see the Tonkawa elder sitting watch near their stoop. Youruh and Adelphine crossed Pecan to a shanty the two families were using as a chicken coop. A friend from Bastrop, Tabitha Ellinger, had ridden in with one of her sons before the first frost and brought Adeline five hens and a rooster. There were eggs regularly and a few chicks were already half grown. On Tabitha's assurance about maintaining numbers, the two Austin families had enjoyed a roast chicken on Christmas. Having lunged for rice grains on the excruciating march, Shelby felt he'd forever look at a spoonful of scrambled egg as a feast.

During Mrs. Ellinger's stay, the two women reminisced about several seasons the Harpers spent in the pines east of Austin. The Bastrop woman merrily recalled Adeline's mending of wounds with needle and thread—"Lord, the first time you stitched men up it was after a swarm of savages attacked near town! If I remember, it was the afternoon of your thirteenth birthday!" Her speech raced so fast that even Shelby had difficulty comprehending. But he appreciated how the younger woman took both of Tabitha's hands and asked her if she could slow her telling.

"Walk Far is just getting where he reads lips if the words don't fly by too fast," she said. "And if you turn just a little, too, he can keep up with the story." Mrs. Ellinger's cheeks flushed since she had forgotten how many others were listening.

"Adeline and her family acquainted us long ago with your name, Mr. Walk Far. According to their account, they would have been tracked down by Santa Anna himself or else gone lost on the prairie to starve, if not for your ferrying and help."

"We don't mean to tell about the Indian attack, Miss Harper, without saying we understand your friends to be capable of no such atrocity." The son who had come with her spoke with conviction, and he nodded to everyone gathered in the larger cabin, but Shelby noticed that the young man's gaze fell often on Adeline. He had been one of her older students when the Macon women first drifted to the forest area after the revolution. As Tabitha's son excused himself to check in at Bullock's, Shelby Whitmire felt his own face grow hot with relief. When the Bastrop woman and her son boarded their carriage the next morning, though, Shelby denied himself any twinge of envy as Adeline gave each friend an affectionate peck.

"You all come visit us in the pines next spring, Addy. You'll have just turned twenty!" Mrs. Ellinger laughed. "My grandbaby will probably be walking by then."

"My mother will prove how doting she is. Have you grandchildren yet, Mr. Whitmire?" The Natchez man had only shaken his head as the rig rolled easterly. He'd once hoped his graying sideburns made Mrs. Weeks think of him as older. But in the empty Austin avenue, he no longer cared to be older or younger or anywhere else than where he was at that moment. Adeline had come to stand by him and to slip her wrist through the crook of his arm as they both waved.

A Sunday evening ritual was born on that date, a time for reading aloud before the men retired to their cabin. After a passage from the New Testament, Adeline often spoke a half chapter of *Robinson Crusoe* from a copy that had survived Burke's fire. Then Youruh or Shelby would work through a Longfellow stanza, while the little girl held a picture book. But most anticipated was Adeline's final reading, sometimes just one page from the next envelope in the Galveston bundle. It was impossible to determine who took greatest joy in the letters from Knoxville.

The plainly worded news from John T. Spillers made Adeline Harper's voice take on a deeper register, as if she struggled to keep emotion from robbing her of steadiness. Noted in most letters were the business successes of a young battalion survivor—maybe the only Macon volunteer to make it back. "Sam Hardaway," one paragraph started, "was much like a son to me in those cruel months at Goliad when home seemed as far away as the North Star." Adeline had brought the tip of her apron sash to her eyes, remarking simply that the sentence was one of the writer's longest. Shelby wanted to move his chair closer to hers or say something comforting to Yarico's little girl, whose lips had pursed in concern before the reader regained her voice.

"I used to run up a hill when I was a child, before dawn on many mornings. The neighbor's land would be edged with first light, and I could often see the North Star."

The Troutman family was frequently mentioned, and Spillers shared news about the family Joanna and her husband had started. When Adeline read such passages Shelby swallowed and nodded on behalf of Hugh McLeod. First love should not be forgotten, he told himself, even by someone born to lead soldiers into battle. It was that evening near February when Adeline realized she was coming to the end of the envelope parcel. The Knoxville letters had been claimed the first years after the revolution—by whom, no one at the coast seemed to recall. Then, however, the annual mailings arrived and sat uncollected, and the fastidious Galveston postmaster carefully placed the most recent letters at the bottom.

"There's one more in the same hand we've come to know as our John T. Spillers. But the last one looks different." Usually Adeline read aloud as she came upon each page herself, but she was so absorbed in the first letter's contents that she forgot to speak while the others watched her intently. Her lips moved, though, and Walk Far—perhaps grasping the gravity of a sentence—put his hand on Youruh's arm to indicate it might be time for the men to bid goodnight. Shelby, too, felt it best to offer her some immediate privacy. "No, stay," she said. "I'll get my composure in a moment. It's something we all need to hear, but I feel sure providence meant this letter for Mr. Whitmire's hands."

"A letter for Tassel Man?" Adelphine was trying to understand the interruption in reading. When her "*tante*" went back to the first page, the girl's frown disappeared.

A message had slowly been passed on to him, Mr. Spillers explained, through the bank in Macon where people knew the Lamars. That family had heard from General McLeod about the Knoxville letters mailed to "a ghost in Galveston." Still, the Goliad survivor wanted to write one more time. Still, he wished to address the absent *F. D. Bahia.* The content was nothing about happenings in Georgia. It put words to a piece of the Texas Revolution that only he knew and remembered. Grieving the loss of one particular American volunteer, he wished to write out the factual occurrence. She began to read aloud:

On Goliad's dark day, I was helped away from the slaughter by a Mexican soldier and his young son. Left alone to make my way, I came across a wounded Kentucky man who'd been with Captain Duval. He was wrapped in creek vines. I thought him dead at first. He was weak. I didn't learn his name until our third day together—John Holliday. We feared starvation, so at next sunrise I went to scavenge food, but without clear attention to where he waited for me. Later, I searched for him a long while. But I grew fearful of circling back to Goliad, and I finally struck out again without him. I trust God gave him peace in his final hours, as I don't doubt he was recaptured or lost to expire in the prairie. John Holliday stays in my prayers.

Shelby had rarely brought up the expedition, but whenever he broached the subject Adeline put down her mending or paused with a medical book to let him speak. She learned from him of Captain Holliday's suffering and burial at sea. They had both remarked about the Kentucky soldier's likely preference for such a death, as opposed to a fatal knife fight or fall after too much drinking at Bullock's. Some days later, after they'd taken Adeline's cart north of Austin streets to show Walk Far where Aunt Maggie now had a headstone, Shelby had recounted the captain's dying, words.

"Margaret Linder might never have met me and Yarico, if she hadn't been in flight from terrible circumstances." Adeline had gone on to say how often there seems to be some kind hand nudging destinies despite cruel times. Shelby had spoken up gently about Holliday, and now with the last Spillers letter read, the adults in the cabin sat watching Youruh spin a top for Yarico's little girl.

"Mr. Spillers and Captain Holliday proved themselves to be thoughtful men," Adeline said. "Some people come slowly to their concern for others. So very few are born with a tender heart that they never lose."

The final letter from the Knoxville man was so powerful that the two cabins on Pecan Street suspended reading the next week. Extra sugar was stored at the hotel, and Hiram offered Adeline a half pound in exchange for eggs and a hen. She also bargained for use of the hotel oven, and when she removed a pecan crumb cake late that afternoon no one complained that the next reading would be postponed.

On the back of the remaining envelope, the last name Spillers was in the rounded script of a youngster still perfecting cursive. But the first name was neither John the father nor his namesake. With its awkwardly drawn *W*, the name was William, and the following Sunday Adeline grew anxious as she pried off the wax seal. She feared the envelope held tragic news about the Spillers family. But after perusing the single page to herself, she sat shaking her head for a while. Neither grown man could tell how close she was to tears, but Youruh put his fingers to his lips to let Adelphine know the top would not be spun until after *"tante"* found her voice.

Dear Mr. Bahia,

First I sent a letter about this to Natchez in Mississippi. My papa has no more writing to put down. He says young people need to see how far their words go.

That envelope came back to me. It was gone almost one year. The post says no Shelby Whitmire lives at Natchez anymore. They think he is in Texas. My father says Galveston is a good place for my new letter.

Papa never did write about one time near Goliad. But I heard him tell my brother Johnny and Mr. Hardaway.

Did you know a boy soldier at Goliad named Thomas Weeks?

He was shot and they had to leave him at a church called Refugio. Thomas spoke last words to my papa. He told about his friend Shelby Whitmire. His friend was like a father for him. He said Mr. Whitmire was a blessing.

Letters are even slower in Texas. Please give this to Shelby Whitmire if you ever meet him. Tell him Thomas Weeks went there to make him proud.

I also tell the wind this story so it goes as far as need be.

Yours truly,

William Spillers

P.S. I have a big family. They call me Will.

While Adeline read, Shelby was slowly rising from his bench at the table. When she finished, she folded the page and put it back in its envelope. She walked over to the man who had been such a good friend—like a father—and she put the letter in Shelby's coat pocket. When he rested his arm along her shoulder, she leaned against him.

"We will go and light our own lantern," Youruh said to Walk Far. The Tonkawa, who spoke little after losing his hearing, nodded. He touched Shelby's elbow as they went to the cabin door.

"Tassel Man," he said hoarsely. "Long ago your home was very far from here."

"Belle-mere." It was the tiny girl. Tears, other than her own, worried her, and she thought her guardian's distress was about coming to the end of letters. As Shelby and Adeline comforted each other, the child went

to a box near the young woman's bed. She knew its contents, and she reached up with a leather folder of drawings.

"My *maman*," she said, finally getting the reader's attention.

"Yes, this picture has your mother in it, our portrait with beautiful Yarico."

"And look. Another letter."

"Oh, we don't need to read that one," Adeline said. "It's only the envelope I'm so fond of." Shelby had let his arm slip to his side, as if he braced for an inevitable blow. Sensing his disquiet, she said, "What I remember is my aunt accepting it from a boy—he was an older student in Brazoria." She patted Adelphine's curls. "I remember how hopeful Maggie and Yarico and I were as our wagon left town. We felt we were only days away from finding Gonzales and a new home."

"Your aunt spoke once about a love letter you kept." He watched Adeline tug the yellowed envelope from the girl's fingers.

"When she passed it to me, I made a firm statement—to my *Two Mothers*, as Walk Far would say—against courtship foolishness."

"First love should be remembered," Shelby mumured. "Do you ever wonder…about the boy?"

"No more than I do about what became of Mr. Bullock's wife Mary. Far less than I do about the family from Bavaria who used to live in your cabin, or a lady back in Macon who bought me blue silk." Yarico's daughter looked from one adult in the cabin to the other, as they both seemed to be weighing their words. Shelby made sure his pocket flap was down.

"I'll keep this close."

"Mine needs a simple burial," Adeline said. "I should have taken it with me when we went out to look for Alex Peyton's grave and stand by Maggie's headstone."

"Maybe you and Adelphine will come along, if I set out to Goliad one day. All those papers I never handed to Thomas, the whole bundle should be laid to rest near La Bahia."

"We'll all go, if Walk Far wishes, when the rivers ease up in late spring."

The rivers of Texas did not ease up until June. In the meantime, the two families only talked from time to time of taking their wagons down to Goliad and then coming back by way of Bastrop, to see Tabitha

Ellinger again. Such an excursion would take almost a month. But it was fortunate they had not ventured in the direction of the coast earlier, because the next letter delivered to the hands of Adeline Harper was from Cincinnati. Yarico had written after the new year that she and Bernard now possessed the second floor of a shop where their tailoring and millinery work was in demand. They had a safe home for their little daughter and wished fervently that a trip back up to Ohio with her would not prove too taxing.

Out on the steps of their cabin, Walk Far was showing Youruh a knot he didn't know, and the two were chuckling at the attempts Adelphine made with a length of yarn. There would be travelers at the ferry crossing soon, and the subject of their moving back to the banks of the Colorado had been gently brought up. But both families knew the import of the letter from Cincinnati, and they all adjusted their expectations for the next weeks.

"I wonder if Copano is an adequate departure point to New Orleans, like Velasco." Adeline spoke to them all from a rocking chair on the Harpers' porch. "I can testify that the terrain is remarkably flat from near Goliad to the coast south of Brazoria." Shelby finished scraping dung from one shoe. He began contemplating safe lodging ahead as well as landscape.

"It might prove a much more pleasant port than Galveston."

"Would you like to go see a big ship, Adelphine?"

"A boat?"

"Yes, would you like to travel a long time, and then see your *maman…* and your papa?"

"*Mais oui, tante!*" The child raced with her strand of yarn out into Pecan Street and skipped to the music in her head. Youruh laughed, but then he turned as solemn as the others, who were trying not to envision days without Bright Hair's company.

"We can go as far as Goliad," Walk Far finally said to the boy.

"Yes, closer to the coast, they will not encounter hostiles."

"I walked many times under that sky. We will go see the yesterday stars. Then back to work the ferry." So many sentences together put a strain on the Tonkawa's voice, and silence stretched out after he spoke.

Shelby nodded and looked at the shoe scrapings. When Adeline came to sit on the step next to him, he couldn't help thinking about the porch in Nacogdoches where he had been busy with the same chore before a young soldier took up conversation.

"I'm very happy to go along, Miss Adeline. An escort makes travel much safer. And you don't want to come back down the Mississippi all alone."

"That's what I've been thinking," she said. They were watching the little girl who had paused in play to throw her head back and let the sun warm her face. "After all this while, you should just call me *Addy*."

"After leaving Yarico and Bernard in Ohio, I felt so alone coming downriver, passing Natchez especially…" Shelby had thought many times that he already knew what it felt like to have an arrow lodged where he breathed. He made himself go on. "I could have drowned from loneliness, if I hadn't kept thinking about coming back here—back here where you are."

"That's what I've been thinking," she said again, putting her hand over his. "And it seems to me that at Goliad or Copano, maybe in New Orleans…one clergyman or another will surely help witness and record all this tenderness."

A fortnight later, two small wagons from Austin were camped on the outskirts of Goliad. They had been invited to stay inside the fort's gray walls, where the parade grounds were expansive and there was a well. But the five travelers declined, preferring to watch the sun come up over the banks of the San Antonio River. They stayed three days in the blooming fields, where paint brush blossoms faded into patches of primrose, and bluebonnets were finishing their show. Besides making flower wreaths, Adelphine and Youruh had spent the sunlit hours searching for the smoothest river pebbles, and then for occasional bones that the two medics could identify as clearly human. When a young priest walked out to their encampment on the last afternoon, Shelby had already dug a simple trough not far from a live oak.

The Weeks family papers were set down onto the exposed soil, and then Adeline set the Brazoria envelope alongside. The adults were gratified that both young people took such care arranging the bone fragments they had found. The pale, delicate pieces rested close together without touching. Walk Far had folded his arms across his chest, and Shelby looked as if he held Adeline up, until she slipped from his embrace to bend down and lay a blue silk handkerchief over the remains. Loose dirt was swept back over the opening, and then the children tenderly placed stones to mark the spot. Even the padre, who'd been asked to come out and say a few words, commented pleasantly first about the compelling flowers, before he grew collected enough to speak a dedication. Only Youruh fixed his eyes away, down at the riverbank, maybe to steel himself about the next morning when his two medic friends and Adelphine would head out on their own to the port.

"So many times," the priest began, "we have no words for either the pain we bear or the love we feel. We ask a blessing on those who have spoken and written their last words. May those who perished near these riverbeds know they are not forgotten." The little girl suddenly crouched down to adjust how some petals lay. "With God's mercy, may every troubled soul find a way home. May enduring love comfort and lift all those assembled here."

Epilogue: Austin, Texas 1866

Shelby knew his wife would have cautioned him against saddling a single horse, but she had already taken their smaller rig up to the French Legation to accept the Robertsons' offer about hosting visitors. There were more arrangements to make if the whole Whitmire family hoped to be in Bastrop the following week to greet Yarico and Bernard as they began their visit. The horse was no taller than Sawdust had been, but Shelby felt the speckled mare was less sympathetic to his awkward mounting.

"No trotting," he pleaded with the animal as they approached Congress Avenue. In just one year since the end of the war, the town and the crossroads had gone from pitifully inert to bustling again.

"In-telli-Gen-cer! In-telli-Gen-cer!

"I'll take one!" Shelby hollered to the newspaper boy just outside the hotel. He felt fortunate that copies were still available. Bullock's old place appeared packed with lodgers.

"Does Mrs. Whitmire know you're riding out that-a-way?"

"Mornin', Isaiah. I'm just going down the hill to the encampment. I'm looking for Francis."

"They're gonna make your son a general if he spends any more time with those soldiers. Unless the Yankees still can't abide the rise of a rebel."

"He can make the case that his father only served as a medic. Mrs. Whitmire and I ended up tending to all sides."

He was thinking *all ages*, too, though many older soldiers they treated in Galveston's infirmary had also called for their mothers. The younger Whitmore boy was not even old enough to muster, but Shelby felt the youth handing him an issue of *The Southern Intelligencer* was best engaged in simple and short conversations.

"What other newspapers have you got there?"

"Just a couple called *Philadelphia Inquirer*—but they're nowheres new."

"I'll take one issue. We're expecting company." Shelby was sorry he'd let that slip.

"If we had company a-comin', my mama wouldn't hardly allow me time to work for the paper. She'd have me mixing starch for dipping the curtains and—"

"Well, Mrs. Whitmire requested me to find Francis. I'd better go try to fetch him."

Shelby angled his horse past two stagecoaches, a lumber wagon, a dozen pedestrians and as many pigs in order to reach the west side of Pecan. Even though he believed everything that mattered in life had slowly worked out to his favor, he usually avoided the length of street so connected to his lonelier days.

Eberly House was now a boarding establishment. It was Angelina Eberly's grandson running her coastal property in Indianola. First Mag had died and, just before the war, Angelina herself. He would let Adeline break such news to Yarico. Having sat in on reminiscing between his wife and Tabitha, Shelby reminded himself to brace for shifting emotions. They would all be careful about how much sorrowful news they recounted, since the visit was meant to cheer Bernard into the hopefulness he used to exude. The months he'd spent shackled on the Confederate side with other emancipation activists had left Yarico's husband more mute than Walk Far.

Shelby felt some of his own self-assurance ebb as he drew closer to the edge of the creek embankment. His shoulder and knee ached, and he wondered if Isaiah would have taken a quarter to go down into the ravine on foot and call for Francis. As chilling as it was to recall how an arrow once pierced his knee, he thought he'd suffer more if he soon fell off his horse and rolled to the bottom of the ravine near encamped soldiers. If he broke his neck, he didn't think he'd merit a plot next to Hugh McLeod's headstone in the state cemetery. No less respect came to that Southern officer for having succumbed at last to an imbedded arrowhead.

A swath of blue shirts and coats marked an expanse of level ground beyond the creek below. It was still a shock to see so many Union uniforms in Texas. An odd thought made the hair on Shelby's neck rise—how if everything had worked out in Aaron Burr's favor ages ago, an army wearing neither blue nor gray might be readying on the rise for a surprise attack. In both directions, the majestic limbs of live oaks sprawled out from wide trunks, but the aging father ordered himself to concentrate on how his horse edged down the slope. Once safely past the steepest embankment, Shelby squinted to see if the commanders' tents were still pitched some distance off where they had been before the recent autumn rains. He'd long ago forgone bitterness over the loss of an excellent spyglass.

"Doc Whitmire!" a private called out. Friendlier than some Union men were to townspeople, the soldier was one that he and Adeline recently treated at a convalescent facility established near Congress. A late enlistee, he'd broken both feet when a cavalryman's horse fell on him. His story would not have stood out for being a case of broken bones followed by malaria, but this youth had ventured all the way from Canada. The Whitmires wished their own three children were more inclined to keep roots in Austin. "Over here!" The young man handled a black skillet over open flames. "We're heating some leftover biscuits, sir. You want one?" As Shelby drew closer, the private lowered his voice. "There could be card dealing in the tent where your boy is at, but I think he just likes listening while the stories swap."

"Francis will skip meals for a week to hear battle bragging."

"He's over in the tent where all the jackets are hanging on rifles."

"A good use of rifles in any weather."

When he reached the drying uniforms, Shelby shifted in his saddle. He stretched and hoped he wouldn't have to dismount. But the fourteen-year-old who looked uncannily like him emerged a moment later from the noisy tent.

"I heard your voice out here."

"You heard Private Gowen calling out my name, I expect." He couldn't help smiling back at the irrepressible boy. "Your mother is going to need some help in the next few days."

"How come Thomas doesn't have to quit what he's doing? He's not even two years older than I am."

"I can't see anyone winning an argument that poker is more important than an apprenticeship." Here was the son that should have been named *Thomas*, he thought. Like Shelby's childhood friend, this boy could shift talk speedily from a losing opinion. After the youth mounted, the two ceased conversation until they had nudged their horses back up the steep slope.

"Custer's men say the colonel is due a promotion. He was outside this morning, taking in the sun while his officers shaved. He doesn't have much use for the scissors and blade himself, so he was giving the other men a hard time about getting their faces scraped."

"Custer's an eccentric—takes pride in standing out, I suppose. But he's done a good job getting peace to take hold."

"It could have been Bobby Lee in charge back there. That's what Mama said, if Sam Houston had talked him into sticking with the Union. How long was Lee in Texas laying down the law to renegades at the Rio Grande?"

"Some months before the war broke out, I think. Anyway, we're all going to keep to conversation about weddings and babies and such, while Yarico and her husband visit." As they reached the western end of Pecan, Shelby could see that his son's attention had already drifted.

"When do you think my own mustache will come in?"

"It won't ever be as pretty as Custer's, if you take after me."

"His men say they accept signatures on their muster roll for as young as fifteen, if they have at least one parent to witness." Shelby knew full well that Francis wouldn't get permission from either, and he unfolded the Philadelphia front page as their horses ambled.

"Here's the name of a lady doctor right here. I know Yarico will take an interest in whether your sister Maggie applies to medical school." The youth laughed hard enough that his horse began to trot.

"After last legislature, she's all but in love with that San Antone lawyer!" Shelby couldn't be sure whether the boy was quoting his mother or guessing, so he decided to let that topic rest for the time being.

"Well, she can still apply her skills if she chooses schooling closer to home."

"When can I do whatever I choose to do, Papa? I am your youngest, but I'm no child."

They were passing the Eberly place, and the familiar cluster of buildings made Shelby wonder how much might have been altered, over time, if so many bends in the river had been different. He told himself that Angelina might have been happy to have Youruh and Adelphine stay a while in the discreet lodging addition that had once been a stable. But he admitted relief that the striking couple would be coming in soon from near Castroville by a less known, safer route. The new parents would enjoy tranquility at the former French Legation, where the doctor and his wife had already restructured some of the servant quarters into guest cottages. No, the reunion of the original Harper women and their families was better off taking place on the eastern hill removed from town. It wasn't too many autumns earlier that vigilantes had driven a neighboring white farmer and his black wife all the way to the Mexican border.

"You should feel free to consider all your choices," Shelby said at last. "When you turn sixteen, you'll be near done at academy, and you can choose any direction that makes you happy. Even if it's signing up with Custer the next time he comes through."

Francis looked to have brightened at his father's last comment, but after crossing Congress, Shelby fixated on the Philadelphia front page again. Suddenly, he stopped his horse to look at a column more closely. They were only a few blocks from the Whitmires' cabin arrangement.

"What is it, Papa?"

"Your mother and Yarico will be gratified to read this. But I wish my friend Angelina were still alive."

"What is it?"

"A child singer Mrs. Eberly and I heard back when I was a boy in Natchez. This will cheer Bernard, too, because the little black girl moved to the north and grew up free—Elizabeth Greenfield."

"Is she coming here to sing?"

"Not likely. The article says she's on a ship to England, after an invitation from Queen Victoria."

"Someone else finding a parcel of adventure in life," Francis said glumly. Shelby Whitmire let his horse follow after his son's. He had let the reins loosen, so that he could read the short article again, and he was reminding himself to take the newspaper with him when he went up to French Hill later to see how he could help Adeline. Her expression would be a bright light.

The boy turned around as they neared the Whitmire porch. "I'm going to hold you to that promise about joining Custer's battalion. Could be the next gold rush is up in Montana. They're heading out soon, but when he comes back in another year or so, I just might be the first one to muster with him by then."

"In the meantime…" Shelby murmured. He hummed a melody that began coming back to him. He was half reading, half recalling one cheerful day in his own childhood. "In the meantime," he nodded, "we can be grateful for…*all good gifts around us.*"

Afterword

When our family arrived in Houston in the fall of 1959, I thought I already knew everything that was important about Texas history— no one much *on our side* walked away from the Alamo. I could belt out the refrain to television's *Davy Crockett* anthem. What else could be of interest?

Though I clearly remember taking Grandpa Hunt, from Georgia, to see the Goliad Monument, I was more struck by his expression than by the names of ancestors carved into stone there. In the next half century, however, I replayed that homage visit. In recent years, I have imagined again and again what it might have been like for the Georgia Battalion on their 1,000 mile journey to Texas from Macon, as well as their short march outside Goliad's walls to execution.

In *How Far Tomorrow*, I felt so indebted to and in awe of my ancestors that I needed fictional names to free my writing hand. Our ancestral uncle Francis M. Hunt became Francis Gideon, his cousin Joseph Stovall became Joseph Tidwell, and Thomas G. Weeks became Malacai Mulholland. Thinking I had finished my research on the Texas Revolution, I kept looking only casually for more information about Thomas Weeks. The Weeks surname has a place among our early Georgia people, so I wove this character into my first novel as another cousin.

Then, I found one Goliad survivor's written account mentioning "a Mississippi lad" as the first to fall at Refugio. Next, I verified that unfortunate young man as Private Weeks, a native of Natchez, Mississippi, and possibly with no connection at all to my Macon ancestors. I felt sure, though, that Francis Hunt and Joseph Stovall would have greeted him warmly with the hope of discovering family ties.

As I worked to get a true read on this Natchez youth, my research inspired an entirely new narrative featuring the events of 1836. Thomas' life story prompted me to investigate his father Levi's murder trial years earlier in New York, as well as the topographical and social division in Natchez itself on-the-hill and under-the-hill, a schism that might have produced more than one lonely child. Later, while reading a biography of Austin heroine Angelina Peyton Eberly, I latched onto the fact that she and her husband went down the Mississippi in their rush to Texas, paralleling the circumstances of better known figures such as Sam

Houston, Jim Bowie, William Travis, and David Crockett, who each left one distressing situation or another to write fresh pages in Mexico's territory.

At the same time, I was learning through living relatives of a unique family group in the Knoxville, Georgia, area near Macon. Many descendants of battalion survivor John T. Spillers have remained close to their ancestral hearth. They've also maintained an appreciation of the role the presidio at Goliad played in the Texas fight for independence. I was further drawn into the Spillers story because his middle name Turner also appears in the oldest branches of the Hunt family tree.

It is impossible to know which recollections of that short, terrible war John T. Spillers ever shared with his family. Records show he was among more than a dozen captives culled from battalion ranks in Victoria to toil at shipbuilding. As is true of most other men under Fannin, what he suffered in the last days of March, 1836, or on the journey home can only be supposed. No one will ever know with what difficulty he subdued memories in order to live on happily, but there can be little doubt that thoughts of the three hundred and forty who perished at Goliad stayed with him for all his days.

There are so many ways to approach historical fiction that I can testify only to my own intention and practice from the outset. If woven into likely circumstance, characters born in my imagination certainly seem alive to me as a story unfolds. As for historical individuals, I always feel bound to place them accurately as I research events and backdrop. I try to portray non-fiction figures, the famous and the overlooked, with fitting dialogue and disposition. Some readers have asked me which characters inhabiting this story lived true, flesh and blood lives. The less widely known include:

Thomas G. Weeks *Ann Weeks *Levi Weeks *Angelina Peyton Eberly *Jonathan Peyton *Delilah and Samson (with the Peytons) *Elizabeth Greenfield (elder and her ward, the singer) *Hugh McLeod *Joanna Troutman *Colonel Troutman *John T. Spillers *Matilda & Martha Spillers *John, Will, Eliza Spillers *Sam Hardaway *Francis M. Hunt *Joseph Stovall *William Ward *Juan Seguin *Captain John Holliday *James P. Trezevant *Ezekial Harris *Captain Bonnell *Captain Jacob Eberly *The Widow McIntyre (Westover) *Chief Bowles *Cynthia Ann Parker *Alphonse de Saligny *James Burke (Sunday School Man) *Richard and Mary Bullock *Dr. Joseph W. Robertson *Celia Allen and Dolly *Alex and Mag Peyton *Mosely Baker

Acknowledgments in *How Far Tomorrow* express my gratitude to archivists who gather and edit histories in print and online so that the rest of us can enlighten ourselves. I certainly still owe very much to these dedicated researchers. Following this commentary is a partial list of print and online sources that informed my story as I wrote. Always, I owe thanks to family, especially my parents, for raising children to be curious about and appreciative of ancestors. I hope Francis Hunt and Joseph Stovall are at peace about my finally slipping their real names into a scene or two of this sequel.

There is even more upon finishing a second book that I owe my mother Josephine Hunt Mills. My first Texas Revolution novel took me many months of concentrated research and writing, during which she and I conferred and shared amazement every day about history I had come across. *Those Bones at Goliad*, however, was completed after a significantly longer gestation. It begins in a year well before the opening of my first novel, though its epilogue is set decades after. I confess here that I took on almost more than I could finish. Had it not been for my mother's encouragement and gentle prompting in the four years since *How Far Tomorrow* was released, I might have shelved the second effort. I am grateful, too, to aunts and uncles who expressed enthusiasm about a sequel. I owe them, other family members, and friends many thanks for their interest in the Georgia Battalion and in my writing.

I want to express appreciation again for my publisher Plain View Press and its founder, the late Susan Bright. I am certainly grateful to Pam Knight of this press for staying independent and open to unusual projects and for her willingness to carry the torch "onward."

Having paid special homage in my first book to battalion volunteers who never came home, and in my sequel to some of the fortunate survivors, I find myself intrigued now by those very few whose Texas service did not end with the Goliad executions. Recently, I happened upon a website generated by descendants of another soldier in the Second Company. In corresponding with the two cousins who research for and maintain the site, The Georgia Battalion Project, I am learning about their ancestor James Peter Trezevant. Their pages make me want to understand all I can about soldiers who escaped capture near Victoria and made their way to Sam Houston's growing army. How could I possibly leave the revolution era without telling the story of such survivors and their contribution at San Jacinto? Already, I am envisioning one thread of a third Texas Revolution novel.

Let me end with a comment about the opening chapter of both novels, since they each incorporate scenes and dialogue reminding the reader that slavery was taken for granted in the South at that time. Truly, what compelled me to write in the first place was a sense of wonder about the lost uncle who left his comfortable Macon lifestyle to be part of an 1836 fight for independence. I feel I've embraced that ancestor and the spirit of his fellow volunteers. Just the word "volunteer," of course, conveys freedom of movement and action. Surely no less disturbing than the image of slaves laboring to erect our nation's White House is the image forty years later of the Georgia Battalion's compelling, hand-made banner "Liberty or Death" as it passed near plantation fields and human cargo on auction along the docks.

While Adeline Harper emerges as the protagonist of *How Far Tomorrow* and Shelby Whitmire lands that role by the last section of *Those Bones at Goliad*, it is Yarico's love and determination to claim freedom that buoy me in both novels. Her dignity and courage will share the spotlight in a third book as well. Two lines from Thomas Grey's "Elegy Written in a Country Churchyard" come to mind again at the close of my second Texas Revolution story—

> *Perhaps in this forgotten spot is laid*
> *Some heart once pregnant with celestial fire.*

Sources

Books and Periodicals

Barker, Nancy Nichols (translated and edited). *The French Legation in Texas, Volume 1: Recognition, Rupture, and Reconciliation.* Austin: Texas State Historical Association 1971.

Bradle, William R. *Goliad, the Other Alamo.* Gretna, Louisiana: Pelican Publishing Company, 2007.

Brands, H. W. *Lone Star Nation.* New York: Random House, 2005.

Crawford, Ann Fears, and Crystal Sasse Ragsdale. *Texas Women: Frontier to Future.* Austin, Texas: State House Press, 1998.

Elrod, Frary. *Historical Notes on Jackson County, Georgia.* Jefferson, GA: Frary Elrod, 1967.

Fehrenbach, T.R. *Lone Star: A History of Texas and the Texans.* New York: MacMillan Publishing Co., Inc., 1968.

Kerr, Jeffrey. *The Republic of Austin,* Austin: Waterloo Press, 2010.

King, C. Richard. *The Lady Cannoneer.* Burnet, TX: Eakin Press, 1981.

Lamar, Howard R. *Texas Crossings: The Lone Star State and the American Far West, 1836—1986.* Austin: The University of Texas Press, 1991.

Mills, Betty J. *Calico Chronicle: Texas Women and Their Fashions, 1830-1910.* Lubbock, Texas: Texas Tech Press, 1985.

Monroe County Historical Society. *Monroe County, Georgia: A History.* Forsyth, GA: Monroe County Historical Society, Inc., 1979.

Moore, Stephen L. *Savage Frontier: Volume 1, 1835-1837.* Denton, TX: University of North Texas Press, 2002.

Roell, Craig H. *Remember Goliad! A History of La Bahia.* Austin: Texas State Historical Association, 1994.

Scarborough, Jewel Davis. "The Georgia Battalion in the Texas Revolution: A Critical Study." *The Southwestern Historical Quarterly,* Vol. 63, No.4 (Apr., 1960). Austin: Texas State Historical Association, pp.511-532.

Spellman, Paul N. *Forgotten Texas Leader: Hugh McLeod and the Texan Santa Fe Expedition*. College Station, TX: Texas A&M University Press, 1999.

White, Rev. George, M.A. *Historical Collectibles of Georgia*. New York: Pudney & Russell, Publishers, 1854. (Reprinted in Danielsville, Georgia: Heritage Papers, 1968.)

Online Sources

Davenport, Harbert. Notes from an Unfinished Study of Fannin and His Men, 1936. H. David Maxey, Editor. Web. 2011-2014.

http://tsaonline.207.200.58.4/supsites/fannin/hd_abou_htm/

Handbook of Texas Online. Web. 2011-2014.

http://www.tsha.utexas.edu/handbook/online/articles/

Historical Society of the New York Courts. People v. Weeks. Web. 2011-2012.

http://nycourts.gov

Index to Military Rolls of the Republic of Texas 1835-1845. Web. 2011-2014.

http://tshaonline.org/supsites/military

Lively, Garland. Colonel James Walker Fannin's Regiment at Goliad. Web. 2011-2012.

http://militaryhistoryonline.com

Macon Telegraph Archive (Georgia Historical newspapers: Macon Telegraph). Web. 2011-2015.

http://www.galileo.usg.edu

Presidio La Bahia. Web. 2011-2015.

http://presidiolabahia.org/

Report of the trial of Levi Weeks: Library of Congress. Web.. 2011-2012.

http://www.loc.gov.

Sons of Dewitt Colony. Web. 2011-2014.

http://tamu.edu/ccbn/dewitt/dewitt.htm

Trezevant, Robert(webmaster) and Richard Allen (primary researcher). The Georgia Battalion Project. Web. 2015.

http://georgiabattalionproject.com

About the Author

Judith Austin Mills moved to Texas from up north when she was ten. The absence of distinct seasons and the spare, sprawling landscape in her adopted state may have been what taught her to look closely for signs of change. Her writing, both fiction and poetry, portrays awakenings. Since 2010, the complex shifts brought on by the Texas Revolution have fascinated her.

In 1989 at the University of Texas, the author earned her M.A. in English with a concentration in creative writing. Stories from her collection *Lost Autumn Blues* have appeared in literary journals. One piece from her poetry book *Accidental Joy* received a Pushcart nomination in 2015. The novel *Tripping Home* won the Writers' League of Texas mainstream manuscript competition in 2001.

Judith Austin Mills still teaches occasionally as an adjunct associate professor of English for Austin Community College, and she takes on French students when the opportunity arises. She has been teaching and writing in Austin for over thirty-five years.

She is more and more convinced that hopeful change springs from a careful look at history.

Websites: judithaustinmills.wordpress.com and jaustinmills.info.